THE
LEGACY
of
the ROSE

Kasey Michaels

POCKET BOOKS

New York   London   Toronto   Sydney   Tokyo   Singapore

This book is a work of fiction. Names, characters, places and
incidents are either products of the author's imagination or are
used fictitiously. Any resemblance to actual events or locales or
persons, living or dead, is entirely coincidental.

An *Original* Publication of POCKET BOOKS

POCKET BOOKS, a division of Simon & Schuster Inc.
1230 Avenue of the Americas, New York, NY 10020

Copyright © 1992 by Kathryn Seidick

ISBN: 0-671-73180-7

First Pocket Books printing July 1992

10 9 8 7 6 5 4 3 2

POCKET and colophon are registered
trademarks of Simon & Schuster Inc.

Printed in the U.S.A.

To Gail Link, who said I should do it;
To Maryanne Colas, who made sure I could do it;
To Anne Csencsits, who listened;
To Holly Stitts, who blushed while proofreading;
To Susan Geissinger, who said "Wow!" as she read;
To Rita Clay Estrada, who cried at just the right place;
And to Joan Hohl, for the generous gifts of her insights,
her ear and, at times, her shoulder.
No one ever had better friends.

And to my editor/teacher, Claire Zion,
who took a chance
and let me out of my box.

Long is the way
And hard, that out of hell leads up to light.

John Milton, *Paradise Lost*

PART ONE

PARADISE LOST

1812

At certain revolutions all the damn'd
Are brought: and feel by turns the bitter change
Of fierce extremes, extremes by change more fierce.

John Milton, *Paradise Lost*

CHAPTER 1

Now came still evening on, and twilight gray
Had in her sober livery all things clad.

John Milton, *Paradise Lost*

*H*e landed on the Sussex coast, as had Julius Caesar, the Saxons, and William the Conquerer before him. Back from the war just two weeks before Christmas, and feeling far from a conquering hero, he was nevertheless sure of his welcome.

The bitter wind blowing in from the Channel cut through his worn greatcoat as he levered himself into the cracked leather saddle of the rented mount, and he cursed beneath his breath as the wound in his thigh gave him hell at being so rudely jarred. The gray December day had turned to grayer dusk, and the horse bowed its head under a renewed onslaught of swirling snow as he spurred it out of the inn yard.

A more prudent traveler would have waited for morning before concluding his journey, content to wait out the storm at the local inn, sipping spiced punch and pinching the fleshy bottom of the comely barmaid. But Lucien Kingsley Tremaine, who had spent the better part of two years

fighting his Royal Highness's battles, and the worst part of a month trying to get back to England, wasn't about to let a little pain, or a little snow, delay that longed-for welcome.

He was going home.

Home to the mother who had appeared to be uncommonly apprehensive as he prepared to leave, clinging to her only child until the last possible moment, begging him to reconsider casting in his lot with Wellington. Were it possible to go back in time, to change the past, Lucien knew he would still have chosen to fight for his country. To do anything else would have been unthinkable, unworthy of the proud, unblemished name of Tremaine.

But he would have been less jovial, more compassionate in his leave-taking, for his mother's fears had been well founded. Only women, who gave birth, who buried sons, knew the idiocy of treating war as an adventure. War convened a bitter school for little boys, for callow youths dreaming of glory, with the only lesson learned that of how to kill other women's sons. He was lucky to be coming home at all.

Home.

Home to his father, who had gently drawn his wife away and into his own arms that last morning, begging her to be brave. Lucien had refused to acknowledge the glimmer of tears in that proud man's eyes, only offering his hand and a smile, some silly platitude dribbling from his lips as his horse, sensing his master's mood, stamped his hooves, also impatient to be away.

The first thing he would do after he greeted his mother would be to take his father in his arms and tell the man how much he loved him, not caring that they had never before indulged in such obvious shows of affection. The boy in Lucien had indeed believed such displays demeaning, but now the man in him needed that healing embrace more than he needed air to breathe.

Home—to Melanie.

His darling Melanie. More than his mother, more than his father, Melanie called him home. Holding each other,

whispering promises, loving passionately, their private fare-
wells had not ended until the coming of the dawn. He had
felt his only moment of unease as he left her in Bath, and he
bitterly regretted not having wed her before taking up his
commission. But it hadn't proved possible. His commission, applied for before he met Melanie, had come through
suddenly, leaving him only time enough to kiss Melanie
good-bye and pay a flying visit home to his parents before
taking ship.

But all Lucien's dreams for his future with Melanie had
been seared into his heart, his mind, his soul, as he lay in
that filthy hut in Spain, sword drawn, swearing to skewer
anyone who tried to preserve his life by slicing off his leg.

He had won that battle, had come back to his love still in
one piece. But he had paid a heavy price, a toll exacted by
fever and infection, so that whatever traces of the carefree
young gentleman from Sussex that hadn't been destroyed by
two years of first-hand observation of man's inhumanity to
man had been snuffed out forever in that godforsaken hut
just outside Albuera.

Lucien could not be aware of it, but his dark good looks
had taken on a new leanness, the deeply tanned skin drawn
tautly over his high cheekbones. Narrow lines now ran along
either side of his thin, aristocratic nose and down past his
tightly compressed lips; lines of pain that deepened and lost
their hard edges whenever he smiled.

Lucien smiled now, as the high hedgerows gave him
temporary shelter from the keening wind. He listened to the
faint crinkling of the carpet of leaves that lay beneath the icy
puddles as his mount plodded its way slowly along the stony
track. How he loved this countryside, in all its faces, even
the winter that came suddenly to the Sussex coast, so that
the frost slipped quietly over the slopes of the downs,
surprising the rose hips that still garlanded the hedgerows,
and freezing the hawthorn berries that grew on the thorn
shrubs.

For, even with the weather at its worst, he knew spring
would come again, the sun picking its way through the trees

to dance on bubbling streams and warm the early primroses and violets just rousing from their winter naps. And periwinkle—there would be soft carpets of periwinkle everywhere, vying to outdo the brilliant blue of Melanie's eyes.

Melanie. As always, no matter where his thoughts took him, all roads led back to Melanie. They'd be married in the spring, Lucien decided arbitrarily, just as the earth stretched itself awake, and he would spend the rest of his days with her, loving her, cherishing her, never again leaving her side.

The snow was abruptly replaced by an icy, driving rain as he left the hedgerows behind and turned his mount into a familiar sloping meadow. The soggy turf muffled the sound of the horse's hooves as Lucien sought to shorten his ride by heading for the narrow lane that passed beside the family cemetery, the most direct route home. His greatcoat soaked through, he fought to see through the darkness to the spot on the horizon where home would first be visible.

His wound throbbed without mercy, a distraction he refused to acknowledge, the pain a part of him for so long that he had almost accepted it.

At last he could discern the ghostly pale white stuccoed outline of Tremaine Court rising above the trees, its high, steep roof sprinkled with chimneys, dormers, and small, fanciful turrets. Drawing on his depleted reserves of strength, Lucien spurred his mount into a fast trot. His eyes never left the sight in front of him, tears freely mingling with the rain on his face as thoughts of his mother's joy at seeing him made him oblivious to all but the need to keep moving . . . riding . . . reaching out for *home*.

Light blazed through the dozen or so tall, narrow windows cut into the thick front wall of Tremaine Court, streaming onto the divided gravel avenues leading out beyond the forecourt, lighting his way while casting weird shadows on the statuary that stood like silent sentinels amid the large circle of shrubbery near the enormous paneled oak entrance.

Lucien wearily slid from the saddle, his knees buckling for a moment as his boots made contact with the slippery stones. He let his mount's reins hang, knowing the rented horse was too broken in spirit to wander. Then, laughing at the useless vanity of it, he lifted his sodden hat to push a hand through his overlong black hair in an attempt to improve his appearance.

After sparing a moment to glory in the sight of his childhood home—assuring himself it had not dared to change in his absence—Lucien mounted the wide steps and lifted the heavy brass ring, listening as his knock echoed through the cavernous foyer within. He stood straight, tall, even as every muscle in his body cried out in protest, craving nothing more than to collapse against the solid oak. And then, finally, the door opened.

"Yes?"

Lucien blinked twice, nonplussed, looking at the tall, unknown young woman of about twenty who had opened the door. She had never figured in his dreams of this longed-for moment.

"Who are you?" he asked at last, not at all tempted to be in charity with the strange female who dared not to know him. "Where's Hawkins?" He had planned for so long, had known just how he would handle this homecoming. He would enlist the butler in his plan. Hawkins would bring his mother to him first, and then his father, dragging out the welcome, prolonging the sweet joy of it. Who was this servant girl, this unsmiling chit who had ruined all his plans, who so stupidly did not recognize him, who presumed to look at him as if he didn't belong?

"My name is Kate," the girl answered shortly, her matter-of-fact tone telling him she was oblivious to his frustration. Her unblinking gaze inspected him from head to foot. "Kate Harvey. You're dripping."

This declaration came just as a droplet of cold rainwater slipped from the brim of his hat to splash onto his nose, as if proving her point. Lucien believed she could have opened the door to see him standing there afire, and just as calmly

pronounced, "You're blazing." He thought he would have laughed out loud, if the very sight of her hadn't been so disconcerting.

Kate reached out to steady him, then seemed to think better of it and withdrew her hand. "Are you lost?"

Lucien shook his head. "I was, but I'm not now."

She didn't react. She merely stood there, her curiously remote gray eyes looking through him as if he was nothing, less than nothing. Her calm yet arrogant scrutiny annoyed him. No. Annoyed wasn't the proper word. It bothered him. There was a difference. "All right, then. I'll ask again. Where's Hawkins?"

"I'm sorry, sir, I don't know any Hawkins, and Beasley must have his nose tucked in a bottle again, which explains why it fell to me to answer your knock. Are you sure you are where you think you are? This is Tremaine Court."

"And here I am, believing I'm in Westminster Abbey. That explains the lack of a choir, doesn't it?" Lucien drawled, suddenly weary of this conversation, while at the same time unwittingly leery of this strange girl dressed in servant garb who spoke unaccented English and held her chin a fraction higher than did the queen. Damn her for stepping, unwanted, into his homecoming. He banished his unexpected reaction to her presence with a shake of his head, and deliberately concentrated on the matter at hand.

Without Hawkins to perhaps give the game away, his plan to surprise his parents had an even greater chance of success. There was no need to abandon it now. He'd merely amend it. "I'm, um, yes—I'm here to see Mr.—no, *Mrs.* Tremaine. I believe I'd rather not be announced, thank you. Just tell her Father Christmas has come a little early this year. Do you think you can handle that?"

"*Mrs.* Tremaine. Of course you are. I should have known. I doubt it will be too taxing to relay your message, Your Highness," Kate answered. If anything, her tone had become more uncompromising.

Lucien nodded, giving up the contest of wills that he

seemed to have joined without his consent. He had better things to do at the moment than bandy insults with the girl, no matter how intrigued he might be by the contradictions she presented.

Raising his own chin, he stepped over the threshold to stand dripping rainwater onto the sparkling black-and-white tiles of the foyer. He removed his greatcoat, throwing it in Kate's general direction, revealing the cheap suit of clothes that had replaced his ragged uniform. "Tell Mrs. Tremaine I'll await her in the morning room. No, not the morning room. It had better be the music room. It's closer."

Once he'd reached the warmth of the music room and its glowing fireplace, he picked up the soft blue wool shawl that lay across the rear of one of the chairs and draped it around his freezing shoulders. His senses were suddenly alert. The shawl held the familiar, gut-clenching scent of Melanie's perfume. He knew he could be three days dead and that heady, evocative scent would still hold the power to rouse him.

Could he be so lucky? His mother had promised to invite Melanie for a long visit at Tremaine Court, so that she could get to know her "future daughter." Was it possible his beloved was still in residence? It would be just like Mother to insist Melanie make her home with them until his return. His mind eased, for he had worried so about Melanie's welfare, cursing the inefficiency of war that had limited his mail to letters written on the run to both Melanie and his parents.

"Ahem!" This deliberate clearing of a female throat caused him to turn. "Mrs. Tremaine will be with you directly." Kate had stopped just inside the doorway to make her announcement, as if unwilling to come nearer, and then withdrew.

"Thank you *ever* so much, Miss Harvey," Lucien drawled to her departing back. "Not exactly slaying the fatted calf, is she?" he asked facetiously of the figurines on the mantelpiece as he leaned against it. He looked around the room,

frowning as he realized the furnishings had been changed, before the slight rustling of silken skirts captured his attention.

The woman who entered the music room in a graceful glide brought spring with her from the sunshine yellow of her tumbling curls, to the bright periwinkle blue of her huge eyes, to the soft, warm blush of youth on her skin, and the fragile violet hue of her low-cut gown. She brought warmth and rebirth as her gifts to the weary man who stood transfixed at the sight of her.

His prayers had all been answered!

Her voice was as he remembered it, soft and rather high pitched, the innocent voice of a young girl. Her words, however, spoken even before she'd taken a look at him, were not childlike. "That ignorant chit told me you behave as if you belong here, but I assure you—"

"Melanie!"

"How dare you address me informally—" And then she saw him, and stood stock still, as if frozen into place. "Good God! *Lucien?*"

"Yes, my darling girl. Wet, tired, and a full two stone less of me than there was when last you saw me, but I'm home!"

The blue shawl slipping from his shoulders, Lucien took three faltering steps toward her, his arms outstretched so that she could fling herself into them and her healing embrace would banish all the wounds two years of war had carved into his soul.

Yet Melanie made no move to approach him, to touch him, to hold him. He wasn't disappointed. She was a sensitive young woman, easily overset. Clearly the shock of his altered appearance had proved too much for her. It was left to him to make his way across the room and gather her close, his body trembling with need and exhaustion.

"Lucien—darling? Can it really be you? Edmund believed you dead!" Her voice was thin, tremulous, almost disbelieving. "You—you look so different—so changed. Stop that! Oh, my poor love, you're so very wet and—and

you *smell*. Let me go, do, else you'll ruin my new gown. Um, darling, does Edmund know you're back?"

She felt so soft, yet there was still something unyielding about her, a strange reluctance. It wasn't just her torrent of contradictory, tumbling words that told him, but her refusal to put her arms around him, to hold him, to welcome him. Melanie's flowery scent teasing him, Lucien stepped back a pace, blinking rapidly as he tried to make some sense of her unexpected reaction.

"Father? No, he doesn't know, not yet. I asked for Mother, but that servant girl sent you instead, not that I'm sorry. Don't tell her what a favor she has done me, for I am convinced such news would ruin her day. But enough of that. I would have asked for you first, had I known you were here. Forget your gown, Melanie, and let me hold you. I'll buy you a dozen new gowns for your trousseau. Five dozen! It's been two long years."

He attempted to pull her into his arms once more. "God, Melanie, you'll never know how much I've missed you!"

She pushed herself free of his embrace, looking toward the doorway. Her whisper held a note of panic. "Lucien, much as I would like you to, you mustn't. We mustn't. Not here, darling. Things aren't what you think. Everything's different now."

Lucien smiled, but there was no humor reflected in his eyes as he stared down at her, his quick temper aroused. Had his worst fears come true? "Yes, darling, I agree. You didn't used to be so concerned with your gown when I held you in my arms. Two years is a long time for a beautiful woman to wait for her betrothed, isn't it? Is that it? Have I been gone too long? Have you found someone else, someone who wouldn't desert you to fight for king and country?"

Melanie backed toward the doorway, tears clouding her periwinkle eyes, shaking her head so that the golden ringlets danced around her bare shoulders. "You haven't lost me, darling. I love you. I swear it! I've *always* loved you. But, yes, you did go away. You *left* me! I needed help—

desperately—but you had gone, leaving me nowhere else to turn. I had to do it, Lucien, I had to take certain steps, had to protect—"

He watched, unable to comprehend, as tears streamed down her beautiful face.

"Oh, you won't understand! You were always so noble, weren't you? We'd have shared no more than a few chaste kisses until our wedding night if I hadn't—let me summon Edmund." She turned and took three quick steps toward the foyer before whirling to face him once more. *"Please,* Lucien, I beg you, I have to summon Edmund. Then, later, we will talk—privately. I love you, Lucien. You must remember that I love you! I will make you understand everything—I promise!"

She disappeared into the foyer, a small, exotic bird nervously fluttering out of sight. "Edmund! Edmund! You must come at once! Lucien is back!"

Lucien's jaw clenched as he longed to scream his contradiction into the empty room. He wasn't "back." He was home. Damn it! He was home!

But he struggled for and found some semblance of control, to stand quietly, no longer warmed by the fire, his trembling body feeling every mile of his journey as fever and fatigue combined to send the familiar yet unfamiliar room spinning out of control.

Had he really believed nothing would change in the years he'd been gone? Much as he might have wished he could have sealed Melanie, his parents, even this house, in a pretty box and tied it shut so that it would await him unaltered upon his return, he knew such things were impossible. His longing to have his arrival unfold the way it had in his dreams had been no more than childish nonsense. He couldn't blame Melanie, or his parents, or even that impertinent servant girl for not knowing the lines of the script he had fashioned in his head.

That didn't mean, however, that it didn't hurt.

But he had to control himself. This wasn't the time for

splitting hairs. Melanie loved him. He would forgive her little dalliance, the minor indiscretion with some local swain she may have indulged in to help her through the long, lonely months. She was here, wasn't she, with his parents? Surely she had committed no terrible sin or else his parents would have banished her from Tremaine Court. Wasn't it just like Melanie to overreact? Silly, darling girl. Did she really think he would cut up stiff over a harmless flirtation? Besides, soon he would be well again, whole again, and they would be married. Everything would soon be the way it should be.

He raised his eyes as he heard the sound of approaching footsteps, his smile wide, his right hand closed in a tight fist. Everything would be just fine, he had already absolved Melanie in his heart—but God help the man who had dared to try luring her from him. He was a forgiving man, but he saw no reason for that charity to extend to Melanie's opportunistic swain. There was such a thing as honor, after all.

"Father!" he cried out, catching his first glimpse of the man who had taught him all he knew about honesty, honor, and justice.

Edmund Tremaine, looking immeasurably older and more frail than Lucien remembered, stopped just inside the doorway to the music room, his hands hanging at his sides rather than held out in welcome. Lucien had not really expected his father—always a proud man, a man who did not easily display his feelings—to fall weeping onto his neck. But couldn't the man at least smile? Couldn't he say *something*?

Melanie appeared, to hover behind Edmund like a glorious crystal butterfly, her periwinkle eyes wide as she watched Lucien from the doorway.

A log broke in the fireplace and Melanie uttered a small squeak at the resultant fountain of sparks that showered onto the hearth, the only sound to be heard in the music room for several long seconds. Lucien looked from his

father to his fiancée, his heart beginning to pound, his battle-sharpened senses at last piercing his confusion and fatigue and telling him that something was wrong. Something was very, very wrong. "Father?"

"So," Edmund said at last, his tone dull, devoid of affection. "Melanie was right. You're back. I can't say you look much like a conquering hero. The least you could have done was clean up your dirt before presenting yourself."

Lucien shook his head in disbelief—and sudden, blind fright. "Clean up my dirt? I know you've never been one for waxing poetic, but is that all you can find to say after two years?" Lucien's voice was low, trembling. His world began to narrow, grayness creeping into the room like a killing fog, until it blocked out everything but the sight of his father standing before him as cold and unyielding as any of the statues in the forecourt.

"No, Lucien. That's not all, unfortunately, for both of us. Let's get this distasteful business over as quickly as possible, shall we? Even if you deigned to write to us only rarely in your absence, we've seen your name mentioned in published dispatches several times, until a few months ago. And up to this moment I had held out the hope that your silence and your penchant for foolhardiness had meant the end of you—saving us this distasteful encounter."

Lucien closed his eyes, shutting out the sight of his father, desperately trying to blot out the man's words as well. "I'm having a nightmare," he said through clenched teeth, his exhausted body beginning to sway. "This isn't happening. I'm still in that damned hut, and the fleas are making a banquet of me, so that I must either hide in dreams or go mad. Packer blew out his brains, you know. He preferred it, rather than to let himself be eaten alive, bite by burning bite. Yes, that's it. This is no more than another nightmare." He opened his eyes to glare at the vision of his father. "But where's Mother? Why isn't she in this nightmare with us?"

"Try to be a man about this, Lucien." Edmund Tremaine raised his chin slightly, staring across the room at his wife's

son, his face devoid of expression. "And any nightmare is mine, discovering just who you are—and who you aren't. Melanie, darling, this must be distressing to you. Please leave us."

Lucien's head snapped up, his body as well as his senses once more at attention. "What a queer sort of nightmare this is. 'Darling?' That's an odd way to address your son's fiancée, isn't it, Father?" As nightmares went, this one was the worst he could remember. He felt a very real shiver, as icy as Spanish steel, caress his spine. "And answer my question! Where's Mother? Damn you, where is my mother!"

Edmund's reply was deadly cold, as cold and unyielding as the grave. "Pamela—your mother—died approximately six weeks after you left for the Peninsula. It wasn't the sort of news one puts in a letter to a man in the middle of a war, even if there had been any real hope it would be delivered. In any case, I saw no urgency, as you couldn't be here for the funeral."

Lucien staggered, as if dealt a physical blow. *"No!"* he cried, clapping his hands to his ears, refusing to hear more. "Stop it! This isn't happening! I don't believe that! I *refuse* to believe that! This is all a nightmare, some twisted torture of my mind! Damn it, *I'm home!* Why can't I wake up?"

But Edmund continued to speak, spitting out the damning words like bitter seeds, while Lucien helplessly continued to hear. "If only it were a dream, but it's all too true. Pamela died—"

"Oh, no," Lucien groaned, slipping to his knees as he looked to his father for salvation and found nothing but the man's unrelenting dispassion staring back at him. "Oh, God—no."

"Edmund," Melanie cried in a pleading voice, laying a hand on his arm. "Don't you think—"

Edmund pushed her away so that she stood once more near the doorway, her cheeks streaming with tears, her expression more fearful than sympathetic. He spoke quick-

ly, as if to have it all said as soon as possible. "Your mother died, leaving me to deal with the knowledge that she had played me false." Each word drove Lucien closer to the floor, as if he were seeking shelter from a hail of French bullets. "Leaving me to deal with the bastard son she had foisted on me three and twenty years ago. It would have been better for all of us if you had died as well, for it disgusts me just to look at you. Melanie is my wife now. We have a son—my *only* son. You're no longer welcome at Tremaine Court, Lucien. I'll have Beasley call for your horse. We want you gone."

His mother—dead? *No!* His beloved Melanie—wed to his own father? Impossible. *Impossible!*

"Father, no . . . please . . . please, no. This is insane. It can't be true. I won't let it be true. Melanie?"

But no one answered. No one helped him. He was completely and utterly alone. Both his father and Melanie had quit the room, leaving him to cower, wounded and defenseless, in the shards of his shattered dreams. He bowed his head, praying for merciful oblivion.

"Mr. Tremaine has ordered a fresh horse brought round front, as yours is worthless for more travel tonight."

Lucien looked up to see the girl called Kate Harvey standing in the doorway, staring down at him with her curiously blank eyes. His own dark eyes flashed with sudden, blind hate. She was the one. She had been the start of it all, the beginning of his nightmare. "You! What are you doing in my nightmare, damn you? Get out! *Get out!*"

The last of his strength ebbed away, leaving behind only exhaustion and unremitting pain. He slumped completely to the floor, his head buried in his arms, his knees drawn up against his chest—a terrified, trembling child, afraid of the demons of the dark.

"Mother? Mother? . . . I'm home. . . ."

Lucien saw Kate's expressionless gray eyes, even with his own eyes shut tightly against all that he did not wish to see, all that his tortured mind refused to face. Those damnable eyes intruded harshly behind his tightly shut lids, swimming

and swirling until they dissolved into a smothering gray fog that mercifully turned to darkest black.

Kate paused on the broad landing to peer out the large window overlooking the forecourt, the twin avenues, and the always-unlatched gate that opened onto the rest of the world. Icy rain lashed against the panes, so that she had to squint to see past her own reflection and pick out the faint outline of the marble statues she had come to think of as her only friends here at Tremaine Court.

Had she been in residence for only a year? It seemed longer. It seemed forever. Such a cheerless house, full of schemes, secrets, and unremitting hatred. And sorrow. There seemed to be an entire universe of sorrow hidden behind the eyes of each of its inhabitants, save one. The changing of the seasons seemed not to alter the environment inside these walls, not the warmth of summer nor the fair breezes of spring and fall. No. Inside these walls it was always winter, dull, gray, and endlessly dreary. And cold.

Like her own life. She pulled a face at her reflection in an attempt to banish her foul mood, then paused to look more closely at what she saw. The sight did little to improve her disposition. Too tall, too thin, her body was all but obscured by the dull brown wool gown that more than made up for its lack of style by way of the sheer mass of its shapeless material covering her from chin to ankles.

Her long hair, ruthlessly scraped into a tight bun at the back of her head, seemed to disappear into the darkness, so that she appeared almost bald. That ludicrous thought brought a thin smile to her face. Too tall, too thin, *and* bald. So totally bland as to be nearly invisible. Surely that should be enough to make Melanie Tremaine happy, although it did not appear that much of anything served to cheer the woman. No, that wasn't fair. There was one thing that made Melanie happy, but it wasn't best to dwell on such matters.

But she hadn't been invisible to the man who had come to the door earlier either, throwing the household into a short-lived tumult. He had seen her, seen straight through

her, and then cursed her, condemned her as if she were the source of all his troubles. The arrogance of the fellow! It radiated from him even as he lay crumpled on the floor, bleating like a sheep as he called for his mother, called for salvation.

Salvation? Here, at Tremaine Court? Kate smiled without mirth. If he had applied to her she could have told him. He'd find no salvation here. Damnation was more like it.

CHAPTER 2

Christmas Eve found the small family assembled in the Tremaine Court drawing room before dinner to exchange presents. The yule log crackled in the fireplace and holly garlanded the walls, making the large room appear bright and festive, while aromas so delicious the kitchens couldn't contain them filled the air with the smells of the season.

Young Edmund Tremaine lay propped between his parents on a striped satin settee, his chubby legs kicking at his skirts, contentedly chewing on one ear of his new pink cloth rabbit as Melanie, dressed in a deep red velvet gown of startling décolletage, tore the wrappings from a present to discover the diamond earrings and bracelet that were her gifts from her husband.

"Oh, Edmund," she exclaimed, slipping the bright stones in her ears, "they're a perfect match for this necklace you gave me when Noddy was born. How very clever of you not to have buried them with Pamela, darling, and so economical as well. Do you think we could possibly remove to

London for the season so that I can show everyone what a wonderfully generous husband I have?"

Edmund refused to be baited by her words and carefully put aside his own present, only thinking how apt their gifts were: diamonds for the beautiful, vibrant wife, and a lap desk for the gray-haired old man she had married. The foolish old man she'd married. But she seemed reasonably happy with him, at least for the moment. He had long since found his life easier to bear when Melanie was happy with him.

"I thought we had already discussed this, my dear," he replied wearily, "and in some detail. We'll see, that's all I can say. He might decide to remove to London when he can travel."

Melanie moved across the room to admire her new earrings in the elegantly designed William Jones mirror Edmund had given Pamela Tremaine on the tenth anniversary of their marriage. Pamela had cried when it was hung, proclaiming it the perfect reflection of their love. The mirror was the only legacy of Pamela's that remained in the entire drawing room. Each room of Tremaine Court contained one piece of furniture, or one painting, or one delicate vase, one memory of Pamela for him to see, left there as if by plan.

Edmund winced, averting his eyes from the reflection of Melanie captured in Pamela's mirror.

"*He* might decide to remove to London? Oh, pooh. I fail to see why it should matter to you where Lucien goes— especially when I consider that you've dearly wished him underground these past two years. You did say that, darling. I heard you."

"Melanie, please—"

" 'Melanie, please,' " she parroted in her innocent, childish voice, smiling into the mirror, seeing her husband's reaction as his face was reflected in the glass. "Lucien has been in this house for a fortnight and neither of us has seen him. Why should you worry about meeting him in a city the

size of London? Or is it something else? Oh, dear—are you jealous, darling? Perhaps even afraid I would use Pamela's son to make a cuckold of you, as she did with his father— not that I wouldn't have reason. After all, dearest Edmund, who knows more than I about the sad state of your pathetic manhood?"

"Melanie!"

"Oh my, aren't these pretty? I was right. They match this necklace perfectly." She skipped back to the settee to stand before her husband, leaning forward so that her firm white breasts were exposed, gifting him with a glimpse of her rosy pink nipples. "There, darling, how do I look?"

"You know how you look, Melanie. My opinion isn't necessary." Edmund swallowed hard, longing to reach out and strangle her—or bury his head between those soft, enticing mounds. God! He was despicable. Did he crave human touch so desperately? Why else did the memory of Melanie's lovemaking linger?

Melanie retreated to a nearby chair and sat down. "Now you're cross, aren't you, darling? Oh, don't pout at me as if I'm being naughty. I heard you tell Lucien you wished he had died. I was shocked speechless! And where is that girl? Noddy's beginning to fret. Honestly, that chit is worthless. She knows Noddy is to be presented for a half hour only. It's an absolute marvel I haven't sent her packing long since, and I will the moment Noddy is weaned."

"I'm not pouting, Melanie, but I retain enough conscience to regret having wished an innocent man dead. It's Pamela's sin I despised, that I still despise. Lucien is as much a victim of her deceit as you and I. And it's her bastard's removal from Tremaine Court I desire, not his death. I know that now."

Edmund picked up his son, cradling Noddy gently against his chest, and offered the teething child a knuckle to gnaw on to ease his aching gums. He leaned down to kiss the soft blond curls, marveling at the depth of his love for this small scrap of humanity. What would he have done without this

child, this marvelous gift, his second chance at immortality after the first had been so ruthlessly snatched away by Pamela's confession?

"Allow Noddy to stay a while longer, Melanie. He's over a year old and doesn't need his nurse every moment. The boy has already cut six teeth, a fact you would know if you spent any time in the nursery. I'm surprised Kate hasn't complained by now that our young man has chewed off her nipples."

"Really, Edmund, that's disgusting!" Melanie rose from the chair to stand in front of her husband, looking down at him accusingly. "And you dare berate me for my frankness? Must you be so crude—and so familiar with the servants? You know I dislike such speech. In fact, I find the whole business of feeding a baby distasteful, as if women were no more than cows—with their offspring noisily tugging on their teats. Now I'm going to ring for Kate before Noddy drools all over your waistcoat. Beasley will be announcing dinner at any moment."

Edmund watched as his wife gracefully glided over to the bell rope, wondering yet again how he had come to be married to Lucien's fiancée.

Everything had happened so quickly: his discovery of Lucien's true parentage, Pamela's accident, his marriage to Melanie in a wild attempt to revenge himself on both his late wife and her bastard son in one decisive stroke. He had paid for his haste, for he and Melanie did not suit. But he had also been blessed, in the person of young Edmund Tremaine. The child allowed him to forget the pain.

Almost.

But now Lucien had come back. Lucien, who still bore the Tremaine name, even if he didn't carry a drop of Tremaine blood. Lucien, whom he had loved and raised, believing the boy had been the true child of his loins. His very existence bore damning evidence of Pamela's lies, her betrayal. Edmund had longed for the day he could think of Lucien and not wish him dead, as if only that death had the power to rid his mind of the dark knowledge that his first marriage, his

love, the majority of his life, had all been a charade, a sham, a cruel trick that had left him broken, beaten, bereft of trust.

Lucien.

For the past two interminable weeks the boy had lain far removed from the family chambers in a small bedroom in the north wing, hovering somewhere between life and death, a violent fever and physical exhaustion keeping his mind shrouded in shadow. Moina had more than once openly despaired of her patient's life. But at last Lucien showed signs of being on the mend, Moina telling Edmund just that evening that he had regained consciousness for a few minutes earlier in the day.

Edmund refused to credit his elation at this hopeful news to anything other than his anxiety to have Pamela's son out of his house. But he could not put a halt to his compulsive daily trips to Lucien's bedside, although he had sworn Moina to secrecy about his visits. He did not want to give Melanie any more power over him than she already had, for he did not judge himself so senile as not to know that his was no longer the final word in the Tremaine household.

How and when he had been usurped he was not certain, but he knew it had happened within days of Pamela's death, when he had been locked in his chambers, overcome with grief and anger. And wounded pride. He'd had time to admit that, at least to himself.

What would he have done if Melanie hadn't been visiting Tremaine Court? Melanie—whom he had previously seen only as the sweet, beautiful, orphaned creature who was to marry his beloved son—had revealed a sterner side of her character during those first dark days.

She had taken charge, dismissing all the servants, and told him after the fact that she had thoughtfully tried to remove all memories of his unfaithful wife. Hawkins, who had adored Pamela, had been the first to be sent packing, and once the longtime Tremaine butler had gone Edmund found it impossible to muster sufficient outrage to put a halt to the purge.

Only Moina, who had been a power unto herself at

Tremaine Court since coming to the estate with Pamela, whose childhood nurse she had been, had refused to budge. Curiously, Melanie had not fought the woman, who was now his second wife's personal servant. Edmund avoided Moina whenever possible. For it was true. The woman was a constant reminder of Pamela, not of her life, but of her death. Of his irreclaimable loss. Of all his losses.

Next to go had been Pamela's possessions and favorite bits and pieces of decoration, all banished to the attics, so that within a few months of his marriage to Melanie, Tremaine Court bore his new wife's stamp everywhere he looked.

Everything was gone, except for a single item in each room. His new wife, he had decided, was a master at torture.

All sorts of torture.

Edmund watched as Melanie poured herself another glass of wine. The liquid splashed into the crystal and she lifted her fingers, one after the other, to slowly lick the gleaming, clinging droplets from her skin with the tip of her talented tongue. Her eyes, wide and innocent, watched him the entire time. And then she smiled.

Entire worlds of torture.

His own fingers tingled against his will as he remembered the touch of that silken tongue against his own skin, and the exquisite form hidden beneath her blood red gown.

How deceptively malleable she had felt beneath his hands when she had crept into his chamber to comfort him the night of Pamela's funeral, offering him a goblet of mulled wine to ease his pain.

How gently she had held him as he cried.

How sweetly she had fumbled, attempting to kiss away his pain.

How willingly she had spread herself for him as he knelt beside the bed, allowing him to explore and taste every soft curve, each dark, hidden valley of her young body as a passion he had never felt before invaded his senses.

He could taste her yet.

Later, he had even suckled at her perfect breasts, whim-

pering like an infant, and she had cradled him, telling him that this was right, this was meant to be. They had both been betrayed, one by the mother, the other by the son. All they had left was each other.

It was only right that they should find solace in each other's arms.

Melanie had been all he could think of, all he could ever want or need. His only real memory of those next few months was the taste of her, the smell of her, the wet, hot heat of her.

Yet he hadn't been invited back into her bed after Noddy's birth, not that it mattered any more, for she had destroyed his manhood with her taunts, her blatant ridicule of his performance, his weak tears. She used her perfect body now only to torment him, to offer him glimpses of what he could not possess.

His beautiful young wife wouldn't even suckle the child born of their short union.

Edmund shifted Noddy to his lap as the child began to squirm within his father's fierce embrace. He remembered how Pamela had nursed Lucien, the two of them lying side by side in bed so that he could watch the babe, his little fists kneading at her breast as he greedily took his fill. And then, with the baby sleeping contentedly, mothers' milk still pearling on his lips, Pamela would shift closer and offer Edmund that same sweet sustenance.

"God's death!" he muttered beneath his breath. "It's true, what the poets say; there is no fool like an old fool. Pamela's gone, Lucien is all but dead to me, and my young wife openly despises me. But I do have Noddy. Thank God, at least I have Noddy."

"Edmund. Edmund! For goodness' sake, you're woolgathering again, and talking to yourself into the bargain. I vow, I begin to think I must have Moina mix up a restorative tonic for you if ever I should hope to keep your attention above a few minutes. Kate has been standing here forever, waiting for you to hand Noddy to her."

"Forgive me, my dear," Edmund said, reluctantly giving

the child over to his nurse. "My wife is correct, my mind was somewhere else. Kate, I think Noddy could do with a bit of something on his gums. He has all but chewed my knuckle down to the bone."

Kate, lifting young Edmund Tremaine high into her arms, nodded, saying, "Moina gave me something just this evening, sir, as Master Edmund has been woefully out of sorts most of the day."

Melanie, always quick to sense an opening, attacked. "Then why on earth did you allow him out of the nursery, you incompetent slut? What if he's not teething, what if he's sickening for something? You are totally irresponsible. This child is Mr. Tremaine's *only* heir."

Her voice rose shrilly. "I know you have no real regard for human life, seeing that you have just to stretch yourself out once more in the gutter to put another brat in your belly. I, however, am delicately made, and may never bear another—"

Edmund winced as Kate stared at him levelly, her clear gray eyes blank, her face devoid of emotion, proving to him that she was purposely hiding her feelings. "Melanie, for the love of God," he began.

"Don't bother, sir," Kate said. "When she lies, I'll correct her, but for now she speaks the truth. Or at least as much of the truth as her sort is capable of comprehending. But I am not stupid, and I value my situation here too much to jeopardize it by neglecting my charge. Master Edmund is quite safe with me, I promise."

"My sort! *My sort!* Edmund! Did you hear what that ungrateful slut said about me?" Melanie's cheeks were flushed deepest red as she watched her son being carried out in the servant's arms. "How dare you allow her to talk about me that way? And after the way we took her in when she couldn't pay her charges at the Fox and Crown. Well, she'll be gone in the morning, I can promise you. No, better yet—I'll turn her off tonight. Let her slink back to the vermin-infested cribs she came from. Moina will tend to Noddy."

"Have you forgotten that it is Christmas Eve? Besides, my dear, Moina is well past caring for an infant. Kate stays. She stays, madam, or else *you* will take charge of our son. Have I made myself clear?" Edmund intoned sternly as he stood, his disgust of his wife's crude ravings momentarily lending a measure of stiffness to his backbone, reminding him of the man he once was. But that heady feeling wouldn't last. It never did. Already he could feel it fading, leaving him even more tired than usual. "Look, darling. Here's Beasley come to fetch us to our Christmas feast. Please, won't you avail yourself of my arm as we go in to dinner?"

Lucien thrashed about wildly beneath the covers, sweating profusely, his right arm raised as if wielding a sword, his dark eyes wide, taking in the carnage that appeared all around him as the nightmare gripped him tightly in its thrall. His voice, hoarse from shouting, and terrible in its agony, filled the small room.

"Here they come again, the filthy bastards. To me, men, to me! We'll show them what we're made of. Garth, stay close at my back. On your left. That ends him! Master killers, that's what we are. Let them come!"

This was a fight to the death, and he and Garth were the only officers left alive after three days of pitched battle. He had already seen Hasbrook go down, his legs cut from under him by some dirty Frenchman's saber. Young O'Connor had died only that morning, a ball in his chest, his life's blood gurgling crimson in his mouth as he gripped Lucien's forearms, fiercely struggling to hold onto life, his eyes eloquent with fright.

There was blood in Lucien's eyes now, the blood of the man he had just skewered through the throat. He watched as the Frenchman clawed at his neck after the sword had been removed, vainly trying to scream. Lucien raised his foot and pushed the man away, turning to face another attacker. His arms ached from killing, his boots slipped in the gore that made the rocks beneath his feet slick and dangerous. But

still they came. He would no sooner kill one man than two more would take his place. There was no end to them.

This was not the romantic's vision of war, no glorious fight for Mother England. No banners waved, no trumpets blared, no voices were raised in patriotic song. Here, on this barren mountainside, there was no right—no wrong.

There was only living. Or dying.

"God's death! There must be a hundred or more this time! Look to your right, Garth, at the crest of that hill. Are they ours? Thank God! Men, take heart! This day will be ours!"

All you did was hang on, hang on until it was over, until you killed enough of them that they ran away, unwilling to let you kill them all. Then you were free to wage war on the hunger, the cold, the vermin, and the aching, never-ending loneliness. Until they came back and the killing began all over again.

"Oh, God! Oh, sweet Jesus, my leg! Garth! I'm hit! I'm hit!"

The pain rapidly became unbearable—hot, and deep in the bone. His thigh burned as if on fire, while the rest of his body had grown cold, so cold. But all of it remained remote, distant, as if he had stepped out of his body, only watching the agony from a distance.

From somewhere above his head Garth talked to him, his voice unnaturally loud. "Lucien! Lucien, old friend, hear me. You're going to be just fine. I've paid these sluts well. They'll tend you until you're on the mend. Crimmons is here too, and Packer. They're not too badly off, and they'll help you, but there's nothing else for it. I have to go on with the men. God, Lucien, don't you die on me. Do you hear me, you black bastard? Don't you dare die on me!"

Bastard. Bastard. Why didn't you just die? It disgusts me just to look at you.

"Garth! You know! How did you hear? It's not true! Don't leave me, Garth. Don't leave me here! How did we fare? Oh, Lord, it hurts. It hurts so badly. Are there many dead?"

Dead . . . dead . . . dead. Your mother's dead. She played me false. You disgust me. Bastard!

"Mother? Mother, I'm home. I told you I'd be home. Come kiss me, Mother. It hurts so badly. Kiss the pain away. I'm home. I kept my promise. Mother? Garth, have you met my mother? Oh, Mother, I kept my promise. Why didn't you? Mother!"

Cannon fire! There were cannon in the distance, keeping him from sleep. Was he to be allowed no peace? He was tired, so tired. Who was touching his leg?

"No! Keep away! Damn you, keep away. Crimmons, my sword! They're trying to take my leg. Sweet Jesus, don't let them cut off my leg. Stay back, you bastards! I go home in one piece or I don't go home! Stay back or I'll kill you all! Dirty bastards!"

Bastard . . . Melanie is my wife now. We want you gone . . . we want you gone . . . gone . . . gone. . . .

"Melanie! I won't let them touch me, my darling, I swear it. I'll come to you a whole man. Crimmons, don't let me sleep. If I sleep they'll cut me into little pieces. Don't let me sleep. Melanie!"

You haven't lost me, darling. I love you. I swear it! I've always loved you. We'll talk later. Let me call Edmund. He'll explain everything.

"No! Don't go. Melanie, come back to me. Did you see her, Garth? Isn't she beautiful? And she loves me! She's my darling, my only darling. Everything is all right! Crimmons, some water. I need water. Mother? I'm home."

Edmund stood beside the bed, his arms wrapped tightly about himself so that he wouldn't reach out to Pamela's son. "I thought you told me he was better today, Moina, but he's worse. At least he used to lie quietly. Now he's hurling himself about like a man demented. Christmas Eve or nay, I think we should get the doctor. Or a priest. The boy's dying."

"Young Master Lucien's not for dying," the old woman said in her deep, raspy voice, not looking up from her

knitting as she sat in a rocker in a darkened corner of the small room tucked beneath the eaves. "Don't you go hanging your wishes on that. This boy's for living, not that he's going to like it much."

"When I want your opinion, Moina, I shall ask for it. Just tend your patient." Edmund turned to leave, refusing to argue further with the woman. He had to get back downstairs soon or Melanie might come looking for him. Such a proud man. Such a strong man. Ruled by women. No wonder Moina and Melanie looked at him in disgust. He was disgusting. Pitiful, yet not pitiable; even self-pity was denied him.

The servant rose creakily to her feet, her stooped figure so thin and brittle that it looked as if a whisper of wind would blow her down. "I doesn't need you to tell me my business. I birthed this boy, breech and all, and I tended his dear mama when she died. I'll be getting him well, iffen you like it or nay. Mayhap he'll kill you then. Wouldn't that be a treat!"

Edmund bolted from the room, Moina's dry, cackling laughter cutting off abruptly as he slammed the door behind him. He leaned against the wall, taking deep breaths of the cold air in the darkened hallway, fighting the stabbing pain in his head. He looked dumbly at his hands, trying to form the numb fingers into fists, but it took several moments for his muscles to respond to his commands.

You're an old man, Tremaine, his body seemed to mock him. An old, weak, stupid, unhappy man.

CHAPTER 3

So absolute she seems
And in herself complete . . .

John Milton, *Paradise Lost*

Katharine Marie Elizabeth d'Harnancourt ignored her reflection in the ancient, clouded mirror as she smoothed the ivory-backed brushes through her hair. The badly tarnished chased-silver edges of the brushes glinted dully in the candlelight as her hands moved, rhythmically stroking, the soft bristles soothing her scalp after yet another endless day of having her waist-length hair cruelly tied up beneath her starched cap.

Another year had passed. A few hours from now, at midnight, the New Year of 1813 would begin. She smiled as she remembered other years, happier years, innocent years colored by high hopes for the future.

She had left it all behind her, her family, her legacy, her innocent youth—even her future—turning her back in disdain on all she had known. But she had clung to this one happy memory—the feel of these brushes as her maid Amy had lovingly tended her hair.

"Never let nobody cut it, Missy Kate," Amy had implored time and again. "It'd be a sin. It surely would."

31

A sin.

Kate allowed her eyes to meet those of her reflection. "Poor, loyal Amy, turned away without a reference for trying to protect me, for coming to me and offering comfort, ministering to me with these same brushes." She winced, one of the brushes catching on a knot that had worked its way into her hair. "I never cut my hair, Amy. But, dear Lord, how I have sinned. Bless me, sweet Jesus, for I have sinned. I have told the truth, the worst sin of all, and now I am forever damned."

She pulled a lock of hair across her upper lip to form a mustache, made a comic face into the mirror, and laughed out loud.

Just as quickly, she sobered. "Oh dear, I believe I really should care more than I do."

Replacing the brushes on the scarred tabletop, Kate rose, her midnight black hair falling around her, hiding her nakedness. She had washed again that night, scrubbing herself from head to foot in the lukewarm water she had carried up three flights from the kitchens, thoroughly saturating her apron in the process.

Maintaining more than a rudimentary regimen of cleanliness posed certain difficulties without access to a bathing tub like the one Melanie Tremaine kept behind a screen in her dressing room, a bathing tub much resembling the one that had stood in the corner of her own bedchamber at The Willows. So pretty it had been, with its painted decorations of flowers and birds. Kate longed for only two comforts from her past: Amy's ministrations, and her bathing tub. Who used the tub now? Did her bedchamber still exist, the furniture and clothing neatly arranged, awaiting her return, or had the room been stripped of all evidence of her, the tub now serving the swine at one of the tenant farms?

She shrugged into the coarse white nightgown that she had rolled up that morning and stuffed beneath the thin pillow on her narrow cot. The hem of the gown barely reached her ankles, as she stood at least half a foot taller than the Tremaine servant who had worn it last. Taller, and

definitely thinner, for the gown gaped widely at the neck, reducing her slim body to a shapeless, sexless shadow beneath the tentlike expanse of cloth.

Kate hoped the man down the hall would be quiet. What a pitiable creature. Three weeks earlier, when he had collapsed in the music room, his last words before losing consciousness had seemed to condemn her, which proved his delirium, as she had done nothing more than open the door for him. She had thought him dead, but Moina, who had a disturbing habit of slipping unnoticed into a room, had appeared with two footmen in tow, ordering the man to be taken to the servants' quarters at once.

She had been able to forget the man's presence for nearly two weeks, what with Noddy's general crankiness and Edmund Tremaine's frequent requests that she attend him in his study, to read to him till all hours of the night. Yet, for the past seven, nearly interminable nights, the unknown man had shattered her rest with his ravings and heart-stopping screams, the first and worst of them keeping her awake until nearly dawn on Christmas Eve.

It seemed odd that the Tremaines would open their house, or even a single room of their servants' quarters, to an injured soldier back from the war. Still, it did not concern her. She hadn't even bothered to learn the man's identity. Kate, as wet nurse, knew herself to be one of those isolated servants who were neither fish nor fowl, accepted or confided in by neither the lowly nor the high.

Not that she minded her isolation. Katharine d'Harnancourt sought out no one, needed no one, wanted no one.

Although she told herself she didn't desire companionship, she had lately begun talking to herself, if only to hear a human voice in the darkness. "I don't know who Garth is," she said now, "any more than I know the identity of my screaming neighbor who persists in calling out his name, but I most cheerfully wish them both on the other side of the moon. Between Noddy's sore gums, Edmund's demands, and that man's bloodcurdling shouts I have about reached

the end of my patience. He can either get well or die as is his pleasure. I only wish he would do it quietly."

Kate didn't believe herself to be cruel. But she had learned long ago that life was easier if she simply refused to feel. She slid beneath the thin blanket, shivering as she braided her hair into a single long plait, then blew out the stubby candle end she had stolen from the drawing room.

She turned her back on the small room and the last hours of 1812 and quickly fell into a deep, untroubled sleep, her conscience at rest, her own time of nightmares past.

Six days into the New Year Melanie Tremaine paced the plush carpet in her pink-and-white bedchamber, wringing her small hands in frustration. She was naked except for the sheer white nightgown that flowed around her, a scant bow to propriety through which her dusky nipples and the triangle of golden down at the apex of her thighs were clearly visible. She was beautiful and she knew it. She was also hungry. Very hungry.

She stopped in front of one of the windows, lifting her hands to cup the underside of her breasts, her thumbs teasing at her nipples, sending anticipatory tinglings winging from their taut tips like small, exotic birds, to nest low inside her eager belly. "God's death, Moina, it has been nearly a month. He must be recovered enough by now. When can I go to him? I need him so much I ache with it!"

The servant's cackling laugh came to her from the far corner of the room. "What makes you think he'll want you? You're his stepmama now, remember?"

The lovely birds of passion fluttered their wings and flew away, leaving her empty. Melanie's hands fell to her sides and she pouted, suddenly crestfallen. "But that wasn't my fault, Moina! I know I can make Lucien understand, if only I can be alone with him. Oh, to be alone! Edmund tags at my heels like a puppy, or a gaoler. Do you think he suspects anything? He has become strangely stubborn these last weeks. What am I going to do?"

Moina gave one last stir to the dark liquid she had been

preparing at a small table, then tapped the silver spoon against the side of the heavy crystal goblet, announcing its readiness.

"You can just forget Master Lucien for now, dearie, that's what you can do. It's too soon. You'd kill him sure. Why don't you go to that old man and tell him what-all you done to my babies? Then he can clasp Master Lucien close and toss you out. That'd be a real treat."

Her eyes narrowed with spite, Melanie stormed across the room to snatch up the goblet. "Nasty old woman! You'd love for Edmund to know, wouldn't you? But then I would have to tell him your part in this charade we've been playing out ever since, wouldn't I? Don't try to gammon me with this talk about your 'babies,' for I won't believe it! Yes, Moina, I'd have to tell him what you did to assure yourself a home. Then you'd have to leave your beloved Tremaine Court, to wither and die beneath the hedgerows." Melanie leaned forward until she was nose to nose with the old woman, and then she smiled in real pleasure. "Wouldn't *that* be a treat, you bitch?"

Straightening, she held the goblet up to the light coming through the windows. Her former belligerence vanished, to be replaced by hope, and the memory of other days, other potions. "Are you sure this is the potion Melly wants? She's so tied up in knots, she needs release."

"Have I failed her yet?" Moina answered as she began slowly lowering her thin, bent frame into a chair, her gaze steady and unblinking as she watched her young mistress.

"Failed me, Moina? I'm not with Lucien. Does that answer your question?" Melanie walked over to the bed to carefully place the goblet on a nearby table while she stripped off the filmy negligee and climbed the small stepping stool onto the high, wide tester bed.

"This had better work, old woman," she said, the earlier hardness back in her voice as her hunger increased, "or I'll twist off your nose. I live for the day I know your recipes, but I won't wait forever."

So saying, she leaned over to grasp the goblet with both

hands, draining its contents to the dregs. She looked at Moina, the woman's bent, withered frame disgusting her. How she loathed physical imperfection. "Bring me Melly's pet, and then get out. I'm sickened by the sight of you."

"It'll work," Moina murmured quietly, but not so quietly that her mistress didn't hear. "It'll work. Mayhap even better than you want."

Melanie decided to allow this small insubordination, for she had more important things on her mind, more pressing business to attend to. Melly's business. After all, both Moina and Melanie knew who was really in charge here, who called the tune while everyone else danced.

Moina reached into the small cabinet beside her and withdrew a long, smooth wooden cylinder bearing an ornately carved silver handle. As Melanie watched, the servant dipped its rounded tip into a container of sweet oils before carrying it to her mistress.

"Oh! How lovely." The potion had found its way into her bloodstream and Melanie's hunger increased with each heartbeat. She writhed about on the bed, her hands pinching and tugging on her firm, pink nipples, all the exotic birds of passion coming home to roost.

Moina's words barely penetrated her fog of pleasure. "That's the way of it, dearie. This one works real fast, but it lasts ever so long. Feel it. Feel it grow."

Melanie answered in her lilting, childish voice, the sound sweetly impure to her own ears, her tongue curiously swollen, making it difficult to form the words. "Oh, Moina, yes! This is wonderful, wonderful. Sweet Moina, you take such good care of Melly. Melly loves you, Moina, I swear it. She'd never send you away. Oh, this is *so good!*"

"The bitch in heat," the servant crooned, her voice coming to Melanie as if from a long distance as she traveled deeper and deeper into the private territory of her sensual paradise. "A man could put his two great fists in you now and all but bite those fine titties right off, and still you'd be begging him for more. Melly wants her pet real bad now, don't she? She wants it fast the first time. She wants it hard."

"Oh, what a pretty picture you've conjured, sweet Moina. Yes, yes, give it to her. Oh, I can't even see it! You put it in Melly, Moina, put it in her now. God, she's on fire! What have you done to her? This is the worst, the best. Hurry, Moina, hurry!"

Melanie flung her legs wide apart, raising her hips high off the coverlet, her body contorted in lust, her blond hair already streaked with sweat. Where had Moina gone? Damn the woman! Hadn't she heard her? "Put it in Melly!"

"You need Moina now, don't you?"

Melanie stilled as she felt the servant's hot breath close beside her ear and listened intently as the woman whispered to her.

"Moina can ease the burning. Moina can ease your troubles, too. Hark to me, you pretty little white-haired bitch. You have to be careful. You have to stay away from my Master Lucien. You have to bide your time. You have to let Edmund stew a while longer. He has to pay, missy, remember that? Remember our bargain? Melly's potions for your time. He has to pay! Only then can you have it all."

Melanie's eyes stretched wide, her pupils deep black holes rimmed with brightest blue. Her heart pounded so hard and fast she could hear it screaming in her ears, urging her on. Her head pressed back into the pillows, her neck arched sharply, her throat grew tight with need. Anything. She'd agree to anything. Promise anything.

When she spoke her teeth were clenched, her lips drawn back over her gums in a feral grimace. "Yes, yes. You're right, Moina. We can wait. As long as Melly has this. As long as you give us this. *Lucien!* Oh, we feel it, Moina. We feel it! Lucien, yes! Do that, darling, do that! Oh, God, Moina, I'm going to die. God damn you, woman! Put it in me! Help me, help me!"

Melanie watched in agonized fascination as Moina—her gnarled, veined hands showing obscenely dark against the silver handle, lifted the cylinder, turning it this way and that—admiring the way the slick oils glistened in the lamplight.

"Damn you, Moina! *Now!*"

The servant dropped the cylinder on the bed and turned to leave the room. "Help yourself. There's still things I won't do."

"Damn you, Moina! *Damn you!*" Melanie scrambled to her knees, her lovely blond hair falling around her face, her gasped curses blistering the air. She grabbed up the cylinder with both hands and plunged it home.

Kate sat on the window seat in the Tremaine Court nursery, her legs tucked under her as she leaned her forehead against the cold glass pane, watching the early January snowstorm. She was tired, so very tired. It had been one thing to be asked to share her nights with an invalid this past week in order to spell Moina, sleeping fitfully in an uncomfortable chair while keeping one ear open, lest her patient should require attention.

It was another thing entirely to spend those nights desperately trying to hold the man down while he cursed and screamed and did his best to reopen his wound. She hadn't known an injured man could be so strong.

Kate knew her patient's name now, thanks to Moina. Indeed, from the other servants she had finally learned as much of the Lucien Tremaine story as was commonly known—which probably amounted to more than the injured man knew himself, considering how he kept calling for his "darling Melanie."

It was an impossible situation and she wanted no part of it. Yet, against her wishes, her heart went out to both Lucien and Edmund Tremaine.

But that didn't mean Lucien hadn't begun to rattle her nerves. "Between caring for Noddy and that man's ravings I've—"

"Here you are, hiding from honest work again. I should have known. Your precious Mr. Tremaine should see you now, shouldn't he, *Miss Harvey?*"

Kate winced, not because she had been caught resting in

the middle of the day, but because Melanie Tremaine's voice, when raised in anger, became irritatingly shrill. Slowly, and without embarrassment, Kate lowered her legs and stood to face her mistress, her face devoid of expression. "Are you lost, madam? This is the nursery."

"Impertinent slut," Melanie hammered out, fussing with her skirts, the insult seemingly issued more from habit than actual anger. "I know where I am. I have just come from my son's room. Why has he been left alone?"

Kate had once had a gown in just that shade of blue, although it certainly wasn't in that style. Hers had actually sported a bodice, and not just a minimal bow to decency. Her lips tight, she answered, "Noddy is napping soundly, madam. I will hear him if he stirs."

Melanie stood, hands on hips, one small, slippered foot beating a tattoo against the carpet. "Yes, well, I'll be the judge of that, won't I? You didn't hear *me*, after all. I don't understand why my husband insists upon championing you. He must fancy himself as a savior of fallen women. Don't think I've been deceived by your put-on airs and fine speech, or the way you read to him out of those dusty books he seems to love so much. You've got the stamp of the gutter all over you."

Kate squared her shoulders. "Mr. Tremaine has been most kind to me. But I am not an object of charity. I earn my keep."

She knew she had made a mistake the moment she'd opened her mouth. When would she ever learn? She was Kate Harvey now. Kate Harvey, fallen woman. Kate Harvey, Master Edmund's wet nurse, given employment as if she were a cow or a goat, in order to give sustenance to the young heir. Pride had no place at Tremaine Court. Certainly not d'Harnancourt pride.

Melanie's periwinkle blue eyes narrowed dangerously. "Yes, you do, don't you? How could I forget that you have graciously agreed to extend your *duties* by helping with the late Mrs. Tremaine's bastard?" she gibed, her soft red lips

contorted in a sneer. "Tell me, as your duties with Noddy at times include keeping him clean—do you bathe your patient as well?"

Kate felt herself blushing as she remembered what had happened just last night, when Lucien had fought her as she tried to force some broth between his lips. His arm had swung out wildly, spilling the contents of the bowl all over himself and the bedcovers. With no one around to help her, she had been forced to strip him, wash him down, and maneuver his body into another nightshirt.

It had been difficult for her, in many ways.

Lucien had been muttering in his delirium, going on and on about his "darling." At one point, as she had leaned over the bed, trying to force the nightshirt over his head, he had opened his eyes, staring up at her sightlessly. His hands had come up suddenly, pulling her down on top of his naked body as he ground his mouth against hers endlessly, his hands intimately roaming over her body, releasing her only when she dug her knee into his groin.

She had spent the remainder of the night curled up in the chair, hating him, a hand to her lips as she relived demon memories she had thought long buried.

"I have, on occasion, been asked to tend to his needs," Kate said at last, knowing Melanie waited for her answer. She lowered her head, sighing. "Mrs. Tremaine, I really don't think this is—"

"Shut up, slut!" Melanie stormed closer, looking up into Kate's face, her breasts heaving to the point that they put an almost unbearable strain on the blue fabric of her gown. "No one has asked you to think. You are here to obey my orders. I want to hear about this bathing. I want to know what it is you do for Lucien. Tell me! Do you lift the sheet to wash him, exposing his defenseless body to your lascivious eyes? Yes, yes, of course you do. And you love it, don't you? Even a slut like you would know that this is no ordinary man. How do you begin, Miss Harvey? Do you lave his muscular chest . . . your tingling fingers warm and slippery

with soap as you draw circles on his firm stomach . . . as you slide those same fingers down, to lift and mold his proud, hard—"

Moina spoke from the doorway. "Miss Melanie."

Kate—bile rising in her throat, panic having kept her rooted to the spot even as every instinct cried out that she should run as far and as fast as she could, taking her away from the sight of Melanie Tremaine's bright eyes and wet mouth—stumbled back onto the windowseat as the other woman whirled about at the sharp sound of her name.

"Miss Melanie!" the voice called again. "What are you doing up here?"

"Moina, I didn't hear you come in," Melanie chirped, her smile childlike as she put her arm around the maid's thin, stooped shoulders. "Goodness, but you startled me. I was just speaking with Kate here, inquiring as to her care of my dearest Noddy. A mother cannot be too careful, can she?"

Kate sneaked a look at the maid from beneath her lashes. Moina's ugly face was unreadable. "Missy Melanie," she said dully, "I fetched that draught you been wanting. It's downstairs, in your rooms. You'd best come with me now."

Melanie's small nose pinched with her sharp intake of breath, rather, Kate thought, like a hound that has just caught the scent of its quarry. The pink tip of Melanie's tongue darted out to moisten her lips. "The one I've been asking for, Moina? The same one as last week? It does ease my headache so. Oh, darling Moina. Of course I shall come with you. How terrible of me to force you to climb the stairs to find me."

Kate carefully kept her eyes blank when Moina peered back at her as she led her mistress from the room. Everyone thought Melanie controlled Edmund Tremaine, controlled Tremaine Court. Kate knew differently, but she kept that knowledge to herself.

It did not come easily to her, subduing her normally strong, at times even arrogant, personality, but Kate knew she must. She was young, penniless, and incapable of

changing either her situation or that of the inhabitants of Tremaine Court.

She could only protect Noddy the best she could, in gratitude to his father, who had taken her in when she was in need, and out of love for the child, the only person to have touched her heart in a very long time.

CHAPTER 4

And in the lowest deep a lower deep,
Still threat'ning to devour me, opens wide,
To which the hell I suffer seems a heaven.

John Milton, *Paradise Lost*

*T*he moonlit gardens were wrapped in winter, almost as cold as Pamela's skin had felt when he had found her lying on the downs. Edmund kept walking, trying to keep warm, his favorite hound at his side.

He hadn't been back to the sickroom in the last few days, ever since Moina had told him that the periods of delirium had abated and her patient had finally begun to regain his senses, although he still slept most of the time. He wanted to go to Lucien, explain what had happened while the boy had been on the Peninsula, if only to ease his own conscience, for Lucien was being punished without knowing the reason.

But a confrontation would come soon enough without his seeking Lucien out, for if he knew nothing else, Edmund knew his "son." Once he could leave his bed, Lucien wouldn't rest until he had heard it all.

Huddling deeper into the collar of his greatcoat, Edmund slowly picked his way down the curving bricked path, remembering Pamela's delight in her garden.

Pamela. His darling wife. His life.

Lucien. His beloved son. His bid for immortality.

His whole life had been a lie, a terrible, unbearable lie.

Why hadn't Pamela lied? If she had, they'd all be together today, rejoicing at Lucien's safe return from Spain. He could have lived with her lies.

He just couldn't seem to live with her truths.

Pamela had insisted upon admitting to everything once he had confronted her with the packet of letters—almost seemed to be glad of his discovery—even to producing a miniature of Christophe Saville that had utterly proved Lucien to be the Frenchman's son. But she loved her husband, Pamela had sworn to him on her knees, tears streaming down her face as Edmund had slapped her clinging hands away before slamming out of the house, to scream out his rage and hurt in this same garden.

By the time he had gotten himself back under control Pamela had run from the house, just as a sudden storm had swirled in from the Channel, bringing wind and driving rain to the downs.

And by the time he had found his wife the damp had invaded her lungs. She had died three days later, despite Moina's dedicated nursing.

"Oh, God," he groaned, staggering over to sit down on a cold stone bench, the hound at his feet. "Why, Pamela? Why?"

He dropped his head into his hands, his mind prodding him, beating at him with its memories. Was that when his grief had turned to hate? Had he felt cheated twice over, first by the destruction Pamela's truths had wrought, and then by her death, that had cruelly snatched away any chance of salvaging anything good from the ruins of their marriage?

Could that be why he had wished Lucien dead as well, so that he could be free to wallow in his misery and not feel tempted to begin again?

And then there had been Melanie. Beautiful, shallow, selfish Melanie. She too had been betrayed, she had pointed out, betrothed to a penniless bastard, stripped of her future.

What could she, an orphan sent to Tremaine Court by her adoring fiancé, do to rescue herself?

Edmund shook his head as his mind spun backwards in time once more, to the first night Melanie had offered him her comfort. What a calculating bitch she had been, he now knew, cold-bloodedly prostituting herself for the security of Tremaine Court.

"The bleeding pity of it is that it worked," he said aloud, reaching down to scratch behind the hound's ears. "She traded the bastard for the fool, my friend," he told the dog, "and her body for a certain fortune."

The hound whimpered, pushing his head against Edmund's leg, as if impatient to get back to the warmth of the hearth rug in the study.

Edmund stood, and began walking back along the path. "Yet if there had been no Noddy, if I had thrown her out when I finally came to my senses, I still could never have gotten Lucien to believe his darling Melanie to be anything less than the angel she allowed him to see," he explained to his uncaring audience. "But I was blind, blinded by my grief, my hate, my despair, my pride. And by my own inexcusable lust.

"Even now, now that I know I must tell him what happened, I may not be able to make Lucien look at Melanie as more than a victim. But Melanie is my punishment, not Lucien's. He may have lost his mother, his inheritance, his name, but some good has come from this mess. At least I have saved Pamela's son from Melanie. Dear God, let him mend quickly, so that he leaves this place."

Edmund stopped walking to look up at the north wing and saw the faint light of a candle casting moving shadows on the windowpanes. He watched the light disappear, to reappear in the next window, and then the next. He had believed everyone else at Tremaine Court to have been asleep for hours.

Then, suddenly, he knew. Without question, he knew. The candle could be carried by no one else. It had to be Melanie.

He had nearly waited too long!

Edmund began to run, determined to stop her, then dropped to his knees on the ice-cold stones, his heart pounding, his body suddenly too weak to stand, the hound whimpering, using its teeth to tug on Edmund's greatcoat, urging him to rise.

Edmund thought his head would explode, the pain hot and burning, even as his legs tingled and went numb, leaving him powerless.

He sprawled on the stones, resting his shoulder against the hound's flank, watching as the candlelight disappeared near the end of the corridor. "I can't. God help me, I can't! I must play the coward to the end. Poor Lucien! He's the child of my heart, Pamela's child. How could I ever have believed my love for either of them had died?"

A few minutes later, the numbness easing, he struggled to his feet, and wearily, guiltily, made his way back to the house.

"How did I become so weak? Now it will be Melanie who will tell him what he wants to know, twisting the facts to better serve herself. But Lucien is no fool. He'll listen well. Dear God, give me the strength to play my part, and please let him listen well."

Kate slipped the blanket from her bed and flung it around her shoulders in preparation of spending another uncomfortable night in the chair beside Lucien Tremaine's bed.

He had been quiet for the past few nights, peaceful, and unheeding of her as he slept, even as he had been unaware of her during those times when she'd been forced to hold him down as fever and delirium had locked him in their violent grip. But Moina had told her he was coherent whenever he awoke during the daylight hours, a development that seemed both to please and bother the old servant, who had gone so far as to admit to Kate that she wished the man out of the house.

Tonight, Moina had also informed her, would be the last

Kate would be asked to spend at his bedside. She was grateful for the news, and not only because she would then be allowed back in her own bed. She knew herself to be in danger of becoming too attached to her patient—a man who had yet to acknowledge her presence at his bedside.

Lucien Tremaine was as helpless as Noddy in his own way, and his vulnerability tore at her heart—the heart she had supposed dead to emotion. What she did not want now was more involvement with the people of Tremaine Court.

She would have departed the estate long since if it weren't for Noddy.

"And Edmund," Kate admitted to herself sourly. "He has helped me retain at least a shred of my dignity, much as I despise his weakness. And now the bastard Tremaine, with his ravings about his dead mother and his 'darling Melanie,' has forced me to pity him as well."

She sniffed derisively. "I truly believe the weak of this world are in reality the strongest of us all. Their cloying dependence makes them all powerful, and has us bending to their needs while delaying our own." She cocked her head toward the door. "Now, what in blazes is that?"

There had come a slight scraping sound outside, as if someone had tried her doorknob, and Kate stiffened for a moment in remembered fear, even though she knew she had turned the lock. That had been the only requirement she had insisted upon when she first came to Tremaine Court: a lock on her bedroom door and the only key in her keeping. Edmund Tremaine had possessed the good grace not to question the reason behind the demand.

Now, waiting only until she heard the shuffling sound of slippered feet moving away, Kate unlocked the door and stepped halfway into the hall.

"Hello, hello," she whispered under her breath. "What have we here? Could it be Mrs. Holier-than-thou Tremaine skulking down the hallway by the light of one small candle, wearing naught but a negligee and a bucket of scent? Where are we off to this time, dearie? That strapping young

footman ran from here weeks ago to escape you before he died an old man at two and twenty. Have you selected your next victim so soon?"

Kate quickly stepped back into the doorway as her mistress stopped before the third door on the left, then turned to check the hallway as if to be sure she hadn't been followed. When Kate dared to peek around the doorjamb, it was to see the filmy hem of Melanie Tremaine's gown disappearing into the room where the injured Lucien Tremaine lay sleeping.

Kate felt her facial muscles set themselves into their now familiar, unreactive lines. "That bitch would copulate with a corpse if nothing else was at hand."

She continued to watch for a few more minutes, wondering if Lucien would throw her out, but the door to the room remained shut.

"Ah, well," she said, locking her door once more, feeling vaguely disappointed, "as I don't hear him ordering her out, it would seem the gentleman has decided to entertain his visitor. If he pulls her down onto his bed she won't complain. So much for pity, my dear, gullible Katharine. Water will seek its own level, even dirty water."

She spread her blanket once more on the cot, and then slipped between the covers, fighting a sudden, unexplained sadness as she allowed her chronic exhaustion to turn her bones to water. "What do I care? It makes no difference to me if they play the beast with two backs all the night long."

Kate deliberately turned her head to the wall, roughly pulling the blanket up over her head. "Just so they keep their hallelujahs to a minimum."

He was dreaming. Again. He seemed always to be dreaming—dark, awful dreams. He dreamed of the war, of Garth, of those first terrible weeks after he had been shot.

But there were other dreams, dreams in which he was running, always running, without any hope of ever getting closer to home. Those were the worst dreams. He had tried to explain those dreams to Moina, but without success. She

had only forced more medicine between his lips, sending him back to those dreams with not a single answer to arm him, so that he had resigned himself to recovering his strength before he tried again.

He thought he could feel a cool hand touch his brow, then move lower, gently easing open the buttons of his nightshirt. If this was another dream it was of a different sort—a lovely dream. He didn't ever want to wake up. "Melanie?" he rasped, his throat tight, prepared for yet another disappointment.

"Yes, darling Lucien, it's your Melanie. I've been waiting forever for you to be well enough to see me. They kept me away, you know, else I would have been beside you night and day, nursing you. Welcome home, my darling."

He could feel his heart begin to pound painfully in his chest. Was it only a dream? Could he take the chance? Could he open his eyes, only to see some ravaged, flea-bitten senorita hovering over him, forcing him to swallow more of her swill? No. Not a senorita. Now his dreams were not of the Peninsula, but of Tremaine Court. He would see those strange gray eyes, those unknown, haunting, unreadable gray eyes. The eyes of the interloper. He was confused, so terribly confused. . . .

"Darling? Open your eyes. Don't you want to see me? Moina said you were so much better today."

Moina? Yes. Yes, he remembered now. This couldn't be a dream. He was definitely home. Wasn't he? A tremor ran through his body. He had to try, he had to know. His jaws clenched, his hands drew into tight fists. Slowly, a silent prayer on his lips, Lucien opened his eyes—and felt his heart stop. "Oh, God. Oh, sweet Jesus—*Melanie!*"

"Yes, darling, yes. It's your Melanie. Welcome home, my love." Melanie's lips were soft, warm against his, and Lucien drew her down to him, savoring her sweetness as her full breasts pressed against his bare chest. Her mouth was as he remembered, hot, avid, seeking, promising.

Their first long, stirring kiss over, he held her tightly against himself, taking great gulps of air into his lungs.

"Thank God . . . thank God. Melanie! I was so afraid. I thought—no! It was a nightmare. Just another damnable nightmare. Ah, my darling, I've had such bad dreams. There's so much I can't remember. How long have I been home?"

"Shhh, darling, there's no need to talk about such distressing things now. Let me get rid of this silly gown so I can welcome you home properly."

Welcome him home. Yes, that's what had been missing. His welcome. He had been so weary. He must have swooned the moment he slipped from his horse.

Withdrawing from the bed, Melanie quickly disrobed, and Lucien marveled at the sight of her small, perfect body and the way it seemed to glow golden in the candlelight as she slid beneath the coverlet. "There, isn't that better? It's as if you've never been gone. Oh, how I've missed you, darling. You lie still now, and Melly will take care of you. It has been so long. *Mmm,* you're so nice. I cease to be a lady when I'm with you, darling. How is it you can make Melly want to do such terrible, wicked things?"

Lucien didn't speak, couldn't speak. His limbs tautened as her tiny hands roved his body beneath the coverlet, her fluttering fingers lifting the hem of his nightshirt to draw light, erotic circles on his lower stomach. Her wet mouth sought and found his manhood, her tongue, teeth, and lips working frantically, as if to devour him.

It was no good. He had waited for this, longed for this, fought and clawed his way back from the very edge of hell for this, but it was no good. Reluctantly pulling Melanie back up to him, he held her tightly against his chest, his breathing shallow, his body bathed in perspiration.

"Melanie, my darling, I'm so ashamed. You're wonderful, everything I've ever hoped for, everything a man could ever dream. I want to, I really want to, but—"

He watched, entranced, as she used her tongue to draw a moist circle around the sensitive skin just inside her opened mouth while she held him tightly and ground her pelvis

against him. She seemed not to hear him, as if she were lost in the throes of her own passion.

"Don't apologize, my silly darling. Let me help you. No one loves Melly quite the way you do." She giggled, her laughter sounding more hysterical than amused. "Most especially not that stick Edmund. He's so old, darling, and his skin's all soft and wrinkled. Not like you. You're so strong, so hard, so eager. Ah, see? You did miss your Melly. I feel it now. Your manhood is beginning to strain against my belly."

She rose to her knees, reaching down between his legs. "Here, darling. Just let me help you."

Lucien continued to watch as she maneuvered herself above him, ready to mount him as she would a stallion she wished to take out for a gallop. He wanted her, really wanted her, yet something held him back, something beyond his weakened physical condition.

His weary mind slowly sorted through Melanie's ramblings, searching for a reason for his reluctance.

Suddenly he raised himself up and captured her head between his hands, rolling over to press her hard against the bed beneath them. "Edmund? *My father?* Then it wasn't a dream? It's true? Dear God, it's *true?* Answer me, Melanie! *Answer me!"*

Melanie shook her head free and reached up to lick at his bottom lip. He remained frozen, unable to push her away. "Shhh, darling. Of course it's true. Don't tell me you don't remember? Edmund was so embarrassingly dramatic about it all. Besides, darling, what does it matter—now that your Melly is with you again?"

Her voice remained light, almost carefree, as she answered, so that it took him several moments to separate her happy tone from her soul-destroying words.

Lucien closed his eyes, fighting his returning memory, struggling with the horror of it, trying to understand. "I don't believe it. There has to be some sort of mistake. There has to be!"

"So much silly talk, darling, when there is no reason for words." She wriggled suggestively beneath him, wrapping her legs tightly about his waist. "Oh, darling, feel how open your Melly is for you," she breathed, her little-girl voice husky with need, "how ready, how eager. Help me, darling. Come inside now. Nothing else matters."

But something else did matter. He remembered now. He remembered it all. Still Lucien didn't react, totally unaware that he was having this conversation, nearly naked, lying atop his own stepmother, his manhood pressing hard against the door to her womb as she ground her hips against him.

He couldn't understand it. He couldn't understand any of it.

His nightmares had all merged, to become one nightmarish reality. Somehow, some way, his entire world had been shattered.

His mother was dead.

He had been branded a bastard by his own father.

Melanie had married his father. No—not his father. Melanie had married Edmund—and given him a son!

Reality came crashing into his mind at last, with ten times the force of any nightmare he had suffered.

Yet Melanie's hands and mouth persisted in their attempt to pull him down even deeper. Her hot, wet cavern sought hungrily to suck him in, to envelop him in the cloying vortex of some terrible thrall she called love.

This was madness; this was the most vile form of insanity.

He might as well fornicate on his mother's grave, in Edmund's bed.

He roughly pushed Melanie away and fell back onto the mattress, his chest heaving, his facial muscles frozen with shock, staring blindly at the weird shadows the flickering candle threw against the ceiling.

"Now you're angry," Melanie said, pouting, so that he nearly laughed out loud at this latest lunacy. Lucien would have laughed, if he hadn't felt so close to tears. "Don't be

angry, darling." As she spoke, she leaned over to press teasing kisses against his throat and chest.

"I'm not angry. Just give me a moment, Melanie. Just lie here, and talk to me." He grabbed her hand as it tried to stray onto his stomach, gripping it tightly as he lay there, his every sense alert, listening intently for her next words. There was more to hear; he was sure of it.

"That's it, darling, you relax while I explain everything. It's not as bad as it seems. You'll see."

The tip of her tongue came out again, to lave one stiffened male nipple, so that he nearly convulsed with revulsion. "Umm, you taste so good, darling. Tell me, what else was I to do? Edmund cut you off without a penny. I couldn't stay here unchaperoned once Pamela was dead, even if Edmund had allowed it, worrying you might die too, leaving me nothing. Yet Edmund wanted me, I could see he wanted me. And I wanted—*needed*—money desperately. So I did something brilliant! I married him. For you, darling—for *us.*"

"For us?" Lucien had to remember to breathe.

"Yes, my silly darling. Surely you can understand that? Even Moina understands what I did, what I had to do. You see, there is this terrible woman—"

"Moina? Moina knows?" No wonder his old nurse hadn't wanted to answer his questions. She was in on this mad scheme, a part of it. Anger at her betrayal forced bitter bile up into his throat.

"Yes, of course, Moina. Such a good woman. She volunteered to be my personal maid and has been so very helpful to me. But enough of this. You must listen to me. Darling, you know I love only you. I've always loved you. Nothing has to change; we can still be together. Edmund is sick; he can't live much longer. I am mother to the only heir, and he is within my control. I've seen Edmund's will. The fool has named me for half his fortune, believing I'll come to love him someday. As if I would! But you must see it—it's all so simple! We can have it *all,* darling. Noddy's share and mine. We'll just have to be careful. Then all our problems will be solved."

She struggled to free her hand. "Please, Lucien, no more talk. I can't stand any more. Love Melly, darling, love her now."

Lucien couldn't hear any more, think any more.

He could only react.

He pushed his stepmother away, leaned over the side of the bed, and retched.

Melanie, at last appearing to have roused from her sexual fog to realize she had committed some fatal error, seemed to panic, scratching at Lucien's face as he roughly lifted her naked body up and over his shoulder.

He carried her down the long, winding corridors, down the stairway leading to the second floor, along the corridor leading to the master bedchamber.

He kicked open the door to see Edmund Tremaine sitting, staring into the fire—as if waiting for him. He remembered how Edmund had handled Lucien's childhood misbehavior, never cuffing him or even raising his voice. No, Edmund had chosen to remain quiet, waiting for Lucien's conscience to bring him, cowed and repentant, to his side. The method had never failed to make its point, until now.

Lucien's anguish and anger doubled, and redoubled yet again.

"Here!" he declared, spilling Melanie's flailing form onto the hearth rug at Edmund's feet.

When Edmund failed to react Lucien grabbed at Melanie's legs, half lifting her by one ankle and pushing her naked buttocks up toward her husband's face. "Look! Look, damn you!" he yelled. "See what I woke to find crawling into my bed to welcome me home. Look how wet she is, how ready to rut! And you knew she had gone to me! I can see it in your face. You knew, and you've been sitting here, waiting like a spider in its web, waiting for what would happen next. Did you think I'd welcome her? She says she loves me! Isn't that wonderful? My *stepmother* loves me!"

He took a deep, shuddering breath, shaking his head in lingering confusion as he added quietly, "No, not my stepmother. Never my stepmother."

"Put her down, Lucien." Edmund's voice was low, and very tired.

"*God damn you!*" Lucien released Melanie's ankle with a disgusted sweep of his arm, still glaring at Edmund. "You *wanted* this to happen. Well, now it has. I remember you as a proud man, the proudest man I'd ever met. How very proud you must feel at this moment. The bastard's destruction is complete."

Edmund rose, stripping off his dressing gown and tossing it toward Melanie, who was trying to cover herself with her hands as she sobbed hysterically. There was no more talk of love to be heard from her now that her husband was present, only a tearful disclosure that Lucien had tried to rape her.

Glaring at the man he had once believed to be his father, the man he loved more than life itself, Lucien listened as Edmund said quietly, "This scene wasn't necessary. Yes, I know where she had gone, and why. And now you know for yourself what sort of female my beautiful young wife—the mother of my son—really is."

What did Edmund mean? This entire scene had been meant as a lesson? And what was he to have learned? Lucien spread his hands, palms up. He stood in front of Edmund, weakened by his illness but still powerfully built, unaware that his youth and good looks cast the older man very much into the shadows. "Why? In God's name, *why?* Why couldn't you have come to me yourself? Why did you allow yourself to be subjected to this humiliation?"

Edmund raised his chin, his spine ramrod straight. "You've been gone for more than two years, and things have changed. I have not made my own choices for some time, Lucien. I'll assume you're feeling vindicated now, having brought my wife to me, warm from your bed. All I can say is that I suggest you savor that feeling as you leave this place."

Lucien stared at Edmund for a long moment, ashamed and angry and utterly lost. He could feel the warmth of the blood that ran down his thigh and onto his calf, visible beyond the hem of his nightshirt. His wound had reopened, but he didn't care. He held out his hands. "Father—"

Edmund recoiled, as if afraid of him. "I'm not your father! Christophe Saville is your father, damn his soul. Go to *him* if it's fatherly comfort you seek. I have but one son, and he is in the nursery. For her sins, at least Melanie has given me Noddy."

Edmund turned his back and bent to assist his wife to her feet.

Melanie threw herself into Edmund's arms. Tears ran freely down her alabastar cheeks; her eyes were drenched with moisture as she looked into her husband's face. For all her nakedness she resembled a small, innocent child whose parent had just unjustly punished her.

"He did, he truly tried to rape me. Edmund, you do believe me, darling, don't you? I don't love him, I love you. You know I love you, don't you? I just went to see if he was all right. Moina said he was asking for me . . . but when I entered his room he was waiting for me. He pulled me down onto the bed . . . and he . . . and he . . . *oh, Edmund!"*

"Yes, I know, my dear, I know," Edmund said, his voice a dull monotone as he looked over his shoulder, and straight into Lucien's disillusioned eyes. "You will oblige me by leaving at first light."

"No, sir," Lucien said, already limping out of the room. "I will oblige myself by leaving now. I'll stay at the Fox and Crown until I've visited Mother's grave."

He stopped, turning back to add, "Kindly tie up your slut until I've quit the neighborhood. She's as moral as a barnyard cat, and I don't want to wake again to find her rubbing her sex against me."

Melanie fought to tear herself out of her husband's arms, screeching wildly, her fingers bent into claws. "Bastard! Filthy, ungrateful bastard! I'll make you taste hell for that!"

Lucien looked at Edmund and Melanie, standing together in his mother's room, and his features hardened. He wanted, needed, to have the last word, the final, parting shot. "There's really no need for you to exert yourself— *darling,"* he intoned coldly. "Any such action on your part could only be seen as redundant."

CHAPTER 5

Tears, such as angels weep, burst forth.

John Milton, *Paradise Lost*

*T*he grave was headed by a simple granite cross, no more or less elaborate than any of the other markers in the ancient family cemetery that had existed since the original estate had been laid out several centuries earlier. It was just newer, making it possible to still trace the faint outline of the coffin where the sod had been replaced.

Lucien still remembered his weekly visits to the small cemetery with his mother. She had always insisted upon tending the graves herself, placing fresh flowers before the three dozen or so headstones each week, and then holding her young son's hand as they bowed their heads in prayer. Moina had condemned the procedure as a stupid waste of time, had said that dead was dead, and the only thing sillier than putting posies on the graves was thinking that such a gesture made any difference.

Lucien had tended to agree with Moina, seeing that the flowers were always quite dead within a week, and no one was there to see or smell them anyway, but he'd never

confided this to his mother, who had seemed to find some sort of peace in the ritual.

Nevertheless, when he was twelve and his favorite spaniel, Hero, died, Lucien had slunk out to the graveyard at midnight, sobbing as if his heart would break, dragging Hero behind him in a large sack, to bury his friend and say a prayer over her. But he had never laid flowers on the small, unmarked grave.

He had discovered compromise.

Now Lucien took a long, shuddering breath and slipped painfully to his knees in the icy mud, propping the handful of holly sprigs, the berries as red as blood, against the base of the stone. He raised his right hand to trace the sign of the cross on his head and chest before rustily reciting one of the prayers learned many years ago at his mother's side.

Then he looked once more at the chiseled inscription that ran across the width of the crosspiece.

PAMELA KINGSLEY TREMAINE

1770–1810

BELOVED MOTHER OF LUCIEN

There was no mention of Edmund Tremaine, Beloved Husband of the deceased.

Damn the man!

Had Edmund thought to summon a priest before his wife died? Had there even been time? Lucien knew not even the slightest details of his mother's death. He only knew the lies that must have caused that death.

Had a priest prayed over his mother's body before it was left to become food for the worms? Lucien raised his eyes to look across the valley at the cross-tipped spire of the small Catholic church, knowing there hadn't been a priest in residence for years. How his mother had hated being away from Mass for all save one Sunday a month, away from the Sacraments. Had Edmund let her die unshriven, unforgiven?

"My mother was a saint," Lucien ground out through

clenched teeth, raising his eyes to the cloud-filled heavens. "She had no sin on her soul. She couldn't." He collapsed onto his haunches, his chin lowered onto his chest as the cold wind slapped the collar of his greatcoat against his cheek. "She couldn't. Oh, dear God. Please say she couldn't."

And then, for the first time since he had come home—and, he swore, for the last time—Lucien Kingsley Tremaine cried.

"If I live to be one hundred I shall never forget this pain." Kate walked quickly, as if she could outrun the chilling wind that cruelly beat at her as she left the shelter of the trees and entered a stretch of open countryside. "As if childbirth weren't enough, God has to make us do Eve's penance again when there's no further need for our milk. My breasts feel as if they're about to explode. Damn that Tremaine bitch!"

Kate had been barred from the nursery for three days, away from Noddy, who had sobbed and clawed at her each time he saw her, trying in vain to get at the engorged nipples that were hidden behind the yards of tight binding Moina had strapped around her in an effort to dry up her milk. There was to be no gradual weaning, which would have made it easier for both nurse and child.

And both child and nurse were paying the price. For three days, and three long nights, Kate had walked the floor, wondering which would kill her first, the pain in her breasts or her thirst, as Moina had limited her to one cup of water a day, saying it would help to dry up the milk that was her sole reason for being kept on at Tremaine Court.

At last, unable to stay within the walls of her small room, Kate had thrown her worn cape over her shoulders and run from the house, away from Noddy's cries.

The time had come for the child to be weaned, Moina had assured her, but Kate would be damned if she understood why the child should be denied the one thing in his life that gave him ease. Except for his father. Even in the midst of her

anger, she acknowledged that Edmund Tremaine dearly loved his son.

As did Kate. When she had first come to Tremaine Court she had seen Noddy as a convenience, a way to use her disgrace to earn her daily bread until she had recovered enough from the birth of her own child to seek other employment. There had even seemed to be a sort of quixotic justice in it at the time.

She hadn't counted on feeling anything for young Master Edmund Tremaine. She had mourned the loss of her own child, but childbirth had somehow opened her to maternal longings she hadn't known she possessed. Within a few minutes of Noddy's first ravenous tuggings at her nipple, his small, fair head cradled in her arms, Kate had fallen deeply, wondrously in love for the first time in her life.

That was a pain Moina's bindings and advice could not ease.

Edmund had already assured her she could stay on as a nursery maid to assist Mary, the maid who slept in Noddy's room and tended to his less endearing bodily needs. Kate didn't believe him. She had seen the look in Melanie Tremaine's eyes when she had decreed Noddy be weaned immediately—the same morning Kate had awakened to learn that Lucien Tremaine had departed the house sometime during the night.

Melanie Tremaine hated her, for reasons Kate had never bothered to examine, as she hadn't been sufficiently interested in the workings of Melanie's mind. That had been a mistake. She had left it too late to try ingratiating herself into the woman's good graces.

The beautiful mistress of Tremaine Court had already taken the first step in making Kate superfluous. One way or another, Kate felt sure she would be out on the road within the week.

Edmund Tremaine was a spineless creature, and Kate would rather depend on the moon falling into the Channel than to pin her future at Tremaine Court on the man. Not that it had always been that way. Although she had never

been accepted by the other servants, she did take her meals in the same small dining room, and she had heard the stories. The servants may have been new to the Court, but they were old to the neighborhood, having grown up in the nearby villages.

Edmund had once been a strong yet fair man, and a good and generous employer. But all that had changed when Lucien went off to war and Edmund's first wife died, and he had outraged the community by wedding his absent son's fiancée scarcely before his first wife was underground. Noddy had been born almost eight months to the day later, a fact that the maids giggled over, although Kate had heard it said that the Tremaines had not shared a bedchamber since the birth.

"If he did deign to go to her chamber, odds are he wouldn't find her in residence," Kate said into the wind, "or, if he did, I doubt she would be alone. But even the maids don't dare hint at such things out loud. It's left to me to say them, out here, where no one can hear. Not that her whoring about does me much good, for now that she has gotten her husband an heir, she seems to have learned how to have her little frolics without having to pay the piper. Ah well, Kate, it matters not. As your papa said a lifetime ago, you have made your bed. Now you shall just have to continue to lie down on it."

The heavens rapidly turned white as thick clouds rolled in from the southwest, and the wind grew sharper, colder, hinting of snow. Kate decided to abandon the path and cut across the frozen fields to Tremaine Court. Her plan had worked, but only to a point. Her feet were icy cold, her nose sore and running, but her breasts still burned hot with pain. She had not exchanged one pain for another; she had only given herself a choice as to which hurt worse. Head down, grumbling under her breath, she moved off into the wind, aiming for the relative warmth of her room, the wind howling around her ears as the first snowflakes swirled out of the sky.

By the time she reached the small cemetery she found

herself grateful for the high walls that she usually shunned, stopping to rest against the cold stone, out of the worst of the storm. She stayed there for a few minutes, trying to catch her breath, before a movement somewhere ahead of her alerted her to the fact that she was no longer alone.

Pushing herself against the wall, trying to blend in with the shadows, she watched the man as he plodded slowly toward her from the cemetery gate.

She recognized her patient, Lucien Tremaine. She was surprised to see him, having thought he was far away by now.

He looked old, as old as time, his cheap black greatcoat molded against his tall, rail-thin body by the changing winds as he limped along, one foot dragging badly, as if it lacked the strength to step out on its own. His face showed white as the swirling snow, his lips drawn into a thin grimace of pain.

Kate didn't fear him; if he dared to attack her it wouldn't even be a fair fight. She was young, strong, and healthy. She had learned how to protect herself and knew herself to be no longer at the mercy of the stronger sex. Her hands stayed in her pockets, but she made no move to grasp the knife that lay cold and comforting against her knuckles.

She could see that he had no interest in her. He probably didn't even know she stood there. He appeared locked in his own personal hell, away from the rest of the world, suffering tortures unknown to her.

As he came abreast of her he stopped for a moment and raised his gaze to her face, looking deeply into her eyes without acknowledging her.

Involuntarily, she flinched.

Without knowing why, she reached out a hand to him as he moved past, his steps a little more plodding than before, and then she slipped to her knees in the frozen slush, her hands to her mouth.

She had seen his eyes dark with hurt, with disbelief, as he lay slumped on the music room floor. She had seen his eyes wild with pain, with fear, as he fought his private demons in

that small room in the north wing. But only once before had
she seen eyes that looked as his did now.

They were the same eyes that had looked back at her from
her mirror the day she had decided to leave The Willows,
eyes as darkly blank and unfeeling as the bottom of a newly
dug grave.

Melanie paced her bedchamber in a vile mood—a dangerous mood—full of pent-up fury that had so far found no
outlet. How dare Lucien treat her this way! Didn't he
understand? They could have had it all—Tremaine Court,
the money, their love. What did her marriage to Edmund
mean? Nothing! Less than nothing! It had been a necessary
expedience, nothing more. It didn't really *mean* anything.
Not now, not with Lucien back from the war. Not now,
while she still needed more money than Edmund allowed
her. Lucien was to be her salvation!

Never had Melanie known a man who excited her as
Lucien did. She loved him, loved him madly. Not Moina's
potions, not the most wondrously endowed member of the
household staff, not even her own inspired ministrations,
could make her feel the way she did in his arms.

Why had he pushed her away when she had gone to him?
What had he been trying to ask her, that her answer had
turned him into a madman? Melanie had been so caught up
in her own wants, her own needs, that she hadn't really
listened to him. Or to what she herself had said. She had
been on edge, hungry, and oblivious. His questions had all
been ancient history to her—like Pamela, dead, and moldering in the ground. Hadn't he understood that she, his
darling Melanie, was still very much alive, and on fire with
need?

Why couldn't he understand? Lucien had been so far
away, unable to help her, and Edmund had been there, close
at hand, hers for the taking. She had a responsibility to think
of herself first, hadn't she? Besides, the real fault lay with
that weepy bitch Pamela for giving her the idea in the first

place. She had been very clever, seizing her opportunities where she could. Lucien should be proud of her.

Perhaps it had been a mistake to visit his room, and she had truly hated him for the way he had humiliated her in front of Edmund, the way he had treated her as if she were no better than some low-born slut like Kate Harvey. She could have killed him at that moment.

She could have killed him, if she didn't love him. But she did love him, had always loved him, from the first day they'd met. Lucien Tremaine had appeared in the assembly rooms in Bath—in Melanie's life—at precisely the right moment, his gentle wooing so far removed from what she had grown to expect that she knew at once that she had found perfection. He had cherished her. Yes, that was the word. *Cherish.*

And he had inflamed her senses, satisfied her, as no man had been able to do, not before or since. Was she to live forever on Moina's potions? No! She had to go to him, explain everything. Surely then he would understand.

"You called for me? What is it? It's your time of the month. You know I won't give you any now. It's too dangerous—and I'm not done with you yet."

"What?" Melanie wasn't attending, still deep in her own thoughts. "When will you learn not to sneak up on me, you miserable old harridan? I sent for you hours ago. How dare you keep me waiting?"

Moina came further into the room, to perch herself on the edge of one of the chairs near the fireplace, arranging her rusty black skirts around her like a duchess presiding over an elegant gathering. Melanie sneered in disdain at the ludicrousness of any such comparison.

"I've been packing up Master Lucien's old things from the attics to send to the Fox and Crown," Moina said, "not that they won't hang on him like sacks. Poor dear boy, he never should have gone. He had to go away for a space, to think, but it's still too soon. I blames you for that, missy. Remember that. We had a bargain, you and me. I warned you to bide your time."

Melanie sat in front of her dressing table to peer into the mirror at the faint lines between her brows, and then purposely relaxed her features. She was young, only three and twenty, although, to the world, she had not yet passed her nineteenth birthday. She had at least a dozen years of unblemished beauty ahead of her if she was careful. Her beauty had always been her major asset, her single unbeatable weapon, and she valued it more than the diamonds that hung around her neck.

Melanie touched a fingertip to the corner of her mouth, smoothing a small dimple that could harbor a frown line if she were not careful. "I cannot tell you, old woman, how I shall lose sleep fretting over your anger. Are you sure Lucien is at the Fox and Crown? He hasn't removed to London?"

Moina's dry cackle of laughter ended in a cough. "He could be sipping tea with the king of Spain for all the good it'll do you. Master Lucien wouldn't touch you right now with a dirty stick. A smart woman would be asking me for something to slip into her husband's toddy, if it's bedwarming she'd be after. Edmund Tremaine drooling after his slut wife again, wheezing and groaning as he humps his wrinkled whorepipe up and down in your pasty white body. Now wouldn't that be a treat?"

"Don't be vulgar. Edmund disgusts me. We have an unspoken arrangement, he and I. I stay away from Noddy and he turns his head at my little—indiscretions."

Melanie rose from the velvet stool and walked across the room, to glare down at the old woman. "But now Lucien is here, Moina, and all bets are off. I want Lucien back. I *need* him back! Tell me what I have to do."

The servant returned her mistress's look for a long moment, then smiled. "Very well. You'll have to bide your time a mite, missy, like I said before. I warned you, remember? You all but ruined it for yourself, playing your hand too soon. My baby's hurting now, grieving for his poor mama and his lost love. You always knew it would take time. Let him be."

"How long, Moina? How long must I wait? Will I be able to see him?"

The old woman slowly rose from the chair and headed for the door. "Edmund won't go to London, nor let you go traipsing off without him. You'll have to get Lucien back here. Six months, I expect, maybe more. You shouldn't have crawled into his bed. I warned you to play the innocent. You were supposed to tell him the wedding was all Edmund's doing, but you wanted him to think you were so smart, didn't you, and you did it all just for him. Now you must wait. Maybe even a year, I'm thinking. Any sooner and he'll spit in your face, missy. Give him time to start missing the tricks you do with that fine body."

"A year!" Melanie forgot about the lines between her brows as her features reassembled themselves in an expression of horror. She was devastated, and her full lower lip began to wobble. "I can't wait that long, Moina. *I can't!*"

"Like I said, missy. I can mix up a little something for Edmund for you, if that's your problem. And there's that new lad down at the stables I saw you eyeing. Hung like a stallion, ain't he?"

"Damn your potions! And damn you!" Melanie exploded, crying in earnest now as she picked up a vase and threw it against the door so that it shattered just inches away from Moina's departing back. "It wasn't supposed to be this way. You promised me Lucien would be mine! *You promised me!*"

Melanie collapsed onto the carpet, her full skirts fanning out around her knees, and buried her face in her hands, sure her heart was about to break. "She doesn't understand. *Nobody* understands. I love Lucien. I love him. . . ."

Lucien was tired. So very tired. Locked in his room at the Fox and Crown, away from the prying eyes of the innkeeper who had known him since he'd been in short coats, he lay on his uncomfortable bed, an arm thrown across his eyes, his breathing labored and shallow. He had never felt this weary, not even after two days of forced march with nothing more

in his stomach than some maggoty horsemeat and a swallow of ditch water.

Strangely, he didn't want to die. Not that he hadn't thought about death, even welcomed its promise of eternal nothingness, an end to thinking, to suffering, to remembering.

But then they would have won. Edmund. Melanie. Even Moina. He couldn't let them win. He wouldn't allow them to bury their guilt. He'd live, if only to taunt them with his life, a constant reminder of Pamela Tremaine, the woman they had destroyed with their self-serving lies.

His mother had been their victim, Lucien was convinced of that, although he hadn't been able to sort through the random bits and pieces of information he had learned in order to come to any real conclusions as to exactly what had happened to destroy his happy home, his hopes for the future, his adored mother.

Most of the blame lay with his "father," Lucien was sure of it. Edmund had coveted Melanie, had wanted her, had lusted after her beauty, her perfect young body. But Pamela had stood in his way. Pamela and Lucien.

Edmund had destroyed Pamela and somehow temporarily turned Melanie against the man she had promised to love forever. Melanie had always been so sweet, so giving. And she had loved Lucien, he was sure she had.

He hadn't recognized that woman who had crawled into his bed that last night. What had Edmund done to turn such an innocent child into that ugly, grasping monster?

Lucien dragged himself from the bed to sit at the table, trying once more to eat some of the dinner the barmaid had brought to his room earlier. He needed his health back if he hoped to recover the ability to think clearly.

The stringy beef resisted his feeble attempts with the knife, his hands still lacking any real strength, and he picked up a large slice to pull at it with his teeth, eating like an animal, for sustenance, uncaring of the flavor.

He was still struggling to understand. The innkeeper, when questioned, had expressed his sympathy and ex-

plained how Lucien's mother had somehow become lost in a storm and died soon after being rescued.

The innkeeper, the entire neighborhood, might have considered her death a tragic accident, but Lucien believed differently. To Lucien, Edmund was a murderer. Of all the lies Edmund could have told, did he have to say that his wife had played him false? Pamela had been so gentle, so much the lady, and so terribly religious. It must have destroyed her to be forced to listen to the wild, malicious, totally baseless accusations that had doubtless been the cause of her flight, her death.

But Edmund's had been a brilliant ploy, Lucien acknowledged silently, that one lie serving to rid himself of both of the obstacles in his path. Not that the man seemed happy with the prize his treachery had brought him.

He acted as if he hated Melanie. As if they hated each other.

Lucien threw the uneaten portion of meat down on the pewter plate, deciding to drink his dinner, seeking the oblivion the wine promised. "I'll kill him slowly. I've seen how the Spanish kill, drawing out the moment of death with exquisite, unbearable pain, killing by inches. And then I'll have my turn with Melanie. I'll listen to her, try to understand. And then perhaps I'll kill her as well."

There came a knock on the door, startling him. "Go away! I've already told you I don't want to see anyone, damn it."

The knocking came again, intruding on his solitude, his jumbled thoughts. "Mr. Tremaine, please, open the door. It's Kate, a maid from Tremaine Court, remember? Moina sent me with some medicines, and a few of your belongings. She gave me a message as well, but I'm not about to stand out here and shout it through the door at you for all the world and his wife to hear."

"Moina?" Lucien's pulses leaped and he staggered across the room to unlock the door. Hah! Already they had begun to come crawling back to him.

Lucien's anxiety to hear Moina's message did not render

him completely unaware of the female who walked into his room, a large portmanteau dragging at her arms. He recognized her immediately as the tall, blank-faced young woman from that first terrible night. He could see that she was as young as he had thought then, little more than a girl, and almost beautiful—her hair midnight dark, her skin smooth and white. Only her eyes, strangely elongated and a curious light gray, looked old—old and totally uninterested in the world around her.

Yes, he remembered her eyes most. And liked them least.

She bothered him, and he took refuge in gruffness. "I don't know you, girl. Why would Moina choose to send you? Where's Nora, or Betsy, or even Hawkins? Tell me your name again."

He watched as Kate looked down at her burden, then across to him before shrugging, as if to say "he'd never be able to lift it," and dumped the large portmanteau onto the table with enough force to set his plate and fork clattering.

"I've already told you my name, Mr. Tremaine. It's Kate. Kate Harvey. I'm nurse to—that is, I'm a maid at the Court. I don't know any Nora, or Betsy, or even any Hawkins. They must have been before my time. Have you found Garth yet? You were calling for him loud enough for him to hear you in hell."

Her arrogance angered him, as did her cold, imperious beauty. "Impudent chit! Give me your message and get out. I've just sat down to dinner."

Kate looked at the plate, and the ragged piece of beef that lay half on, half off it. "Yes," she said dispassionately, "I can see that. It looks utterly delectable."

Then, as he stood there, disbelieving her forwardness, she picked up the knife and fork and began slicing the meat into bite-size pieces. "I saw you at the cemetery yesterday. Moina says you were probably visiting your mother's grave for the first time. I'm sorry if I intruded. I was out for a walk and stopped by the wall to get out of the storm."

Something about her tone, the calm way she went about

her mundane chore as if he were a child in need of assistance, grabbed his attention anew. Perhaps, he realized, she was the single sane person in all this madness. Sane, but an enigma. She didn't *fit*. Yes, that was it. Kate Harvey didn't fit at Tremaine Court, certainly not as a maid—not at any level. So why was she there? "Did you know my mother?" he asked, sitting down and beginning to eat.

She shook her head as she began unpacking the portmanteau, and he recognized clothing he hadn't seen in over two years as she laid it in the small chest of drawers. "I came here about a year ago from The Will—that is, I'm from a small village near Wimbledon. I only know the current Mrs. Tremaine. One's enough, thank you. There you go, all done. The shirts are a little musty, but they'll do. Oh yes, I almost forgot to give you the message. Moina would have come herself, but she hasn't left Tremaine Court in years. Perhaps she's afraid Mrs. Tremaine will lock the gates behind her."

She repeated the old servant's message quickly, as if wanting it over with as soon as possible. "Moina said you are to go away for a while, to lick your wounds, and she'll be waiting when you come back. She says she understands why you're angry with her, and she's sorry for that, but you're not ready just yet to hear all she has to tell you."

Kate averted her head as she ended. "She also said to say you're the living spit of your father—and that she should know. Lastly, there's a rather sizable packet here, in with your things. I believe it's from a London solicitor. Mr. Tremaine? I—I am sorry."

The fork had stopped halfway en route to his mouth. Lucien couldn't breathe. He stared at Kate without seeing her, his last hope gone, his worst fear realized. His father could be a lying lecher, lusting after a younger, more beautiful woman. His fiancée might have somehow turned into an immoral, greedy bitch. He could take care of that, and revenge was sweet.

But his mother had been a whore. His beautiful, saintly mother had been nothing but a cheating whore, foisting her

bastard son on her unknowing husband, then having the unmitigated gall to pass herself off as a good, holy woman.

Even worse, she was beyond reach of his vengeance.

There was nothing left. Nothing to love, nothing to believe in. There wasn't even anything left to hate. It was gone. It was all gone.

Kate laid the packet on the table and bent to look at Lucien, her hand on his shoulder. "Mr. Tremaine? Are you all right? Maybe you'd better lie down."

Lucien looked pointedly at Kate's comforting hand, then up into her face, hovering so close to his. His voice was low, threatening. "Why? Why are you always here? You and those damn gray eyes. Do you enjoy witnessing my defeats?" He pushed her hand away. "Get out."

She straightened immediately, her chin raised in defiance. "Of course. Certainly. Kate, get out. Just get yourself back to Tremaine Court, you've served your purpose. Why aren't I surprised? You Tremaines are such a cheery bunch. You could give your stepmother lessons in bad manners. Well, good evening to you, sir!"

"Damn you, woman. *Get out of here.*"

Once Kate had gone he reached out to examine the contents of the packet, the heavy embossed paper crackling as he read the terms of his inheritance from his natural father, as he read about the fortune that was now his, and stared at the deed to the mansion in London that had been purchased in his name. He held the small ruby ring to the light to read the initials scratched into its underside: *C.S.*

Only then did he pick up the small, gilt-edged miniature that had fallen out of the packet onto the table. Only then did he look at the painting of a man wearing clothing a quarter century out of date—a man wearing his own face.

And only then did he open the second, smaller envelope and draw out an aged, yellow paper covered in a thin, spidery hand, a letter Christophe Saville had written to Pamela Tremaine, begging her for news of their son.

He read the letter all the way through—twice. Then he

held the paper over one of the candles, watching as it burst into flame and then crumbled into a small pile of ashes in the middle of his dinner plate.

He continued to sit at the table, until the candles guttered in their holders, until the room disintegrated into absolute blackness, staring into the deep nothingness as his red-rimmed eyes smoldered like dying coals.

During the cheerless hours that presaged the dawn, the man who had once been Lucien Tremaine died, without another living soul about to mourn his passing . . . and another man—a dark, lonely, friendless man—was born.

Edmund winced visibly as Moina stood before him, smiling her toothless grin, the weight that had settled in his chest taking on a new heaviness. "He's gone, isn't he? It's done."

Moina heard her blood singing in her ears as she saw how much older he had become almost overnight, the lines of his suffering showing harshly on his face. "Yes, he's gone. He left the Fox and Crown at first light, hating you, that white-haired bitch, all of us. You got just what you thinks you wanted, for now. But it ain't done. Oh, no. He'll be back, my baby will. He'll pick his own time, his own way. We none of us ain't seen the last of Lucien Tremaine. I can wait. Can you?"

Moina left Edmund's chamber, her step lighter than it had been in years, to seek out her mistress.

Melanie looked up blankly as the servant entered the darkened bedchamber, her wits dulled with the wine she had been drinking to ease the pain of the strange headache that had kept her locked in her chambers for nearly a week, ever since the morning after Lucien had so callously rejected her love.

Moina smiled pleasantly, and Melanie's eyes began to tear. "He's gone, isn't he? My darling Lucien is on his way to London, without a word to me."

Moina stared at her mistress impassively. The headache she had prudently concocted for the woman had served its

purpose. She went over to the small cabinet to prepare a restorative potion. "Like I told your loving husband, he took himself off at first light. But don't you fret overmuch. You just keep on doing what I tell you, and he'll be back."

She turned away from the cabinet, deciding against the healing potion for another day, adding beneath her breath, "He'll come when I'm ready to put an end to it, missy—and not before."

A week after Lucien Tremaine's departure for London Katharine d'Harnancourt, known to the people of Tremaine Court as Kate Harvey, stood rigidly erect in front of the granite stone, refusing to look at it, then dropped a small bouquet of flowers onto the winter-dead grass and rapidly walked away, calling herself seven kinds of a fool for thinking she was capable of even this small, tender gesture. She preferred her emotions buried, like the dead Pamela Tremaine. She didn't want to care.

Her place at Tremaine Court assured now that Edmund had suffered a debilitating episode that had left him bedridden, Kate had charge of the man as well as the child, feeding him and reading to him in order to help pass the hours.

Melanie had been painfully vocal in her objection to the arrangement but, to the surprise of everyone save Kate, it had been Moina who had settled the matter. She didn't ask how the old woman had managed to win the argument. It was enough that she could stay with Noddy, and she felt she owed Edmund her loyalty, as he had taken her in. Besides, she had nowhere else to go.

What did surprise Kate was Melanie's continued occupancy of Tremaine Court now that spring would soon be here. With Edmund safely abed, there could be nothing keeping his young wife from a season in London. London, where Lucien Tremaine had gone. Yet Melanie stayed, cooling her heels, ignoring her husband, and moving the new stable hand into the dressing room next to her bedchamber.

Kate paused at the open gate that had been cut into the

stone wall, turning back for one last look at Pamela Tremaine's grave, her lips tightening, knowing she had begun a ritual today that she might come to regret.

"I really shouldn't feel sorry for you," she said as she hesitated, wrapping her cloak tightly about herself to keep away the wind, reluctant to begin picking her way back across the muddy meadow that led to Tremaine Court. "You're dead, you're out of it. It's the rest of us. It's just the rest of us . . ."

INTERLUDE

1813

∾

My sentence is for open war.

John Milton, *Paradise Lost*

12 March 1813

Dear Mr. Tremaine,

Although our acquaintance has been of a brief and not remarkably pleasant nature, I have presumed upon Moina, (who, as always, knows everything of note), for your current location in order to make you aware of a situation now existing at Tremaine Court.

Since your departure from the Fox and Crown, approximately 15 January, Edmund Tremaine's health and disposition have both undergone decided turns for the worst. He has little appetite and for the most part has taken to his bed, suffering the effects of a debilitating malady that defies the doctor and Moina as well, although she has prescribed a tonic that seems to do no harm.

As to Mr. Tremaine's mental state, it is with sadness and apprehension that I inform you his condition borders on the melancholy, his soul racked by the unfortunate circumstances of your abrupt departure and whatever breach has developed between you. It is my considered opinion that his chances for recovery most particularly depend upon your return.

I await your timely response and arrival.

Yours most truly,
Kate Harvey
Tremaine Court
Sussex

My dear Miss Harvey,

How you wound me! How could you have termed our brief association unpleasant, when I remember the interlude with such fondness? Indeed, I had to flee Sussex entirely to thwart my baser instincts (there are many base things about me, I fear), so that I could not be tempted to take advantage of your sweet beauty. You are a fiery redhead, are you not? Rather small of stature? Large green eyes? You see, I have not forgotten.

As to your belief that Edmund Tremaine's recovery depends upon my return to Sussex, may I say that you have cheered me no end with this information. Alas, as the Season is about to get underway and I find myself with many pressing engagements as well as a most important series of appointments with my tailor, I find it impossible to tear myself away from Mayfair to act the savior at this time. Perhaps after the king's birthday in June, if Edmund still lingers?

Yr. most obedient servant,
Lucien Kingsley Tremaine
Portman Square
London

Mr. Tremaine,

Reluctant as I am to open myself to your faint wit for a second time, I find myself obliged to inform you that my employer, Edmund Tremaine, due to frailness of spirit and an increasing numbness affecting his lower limbs, is now reduced to the confinements of his bed and, on his good days, a Bath chair.

Mrs. Tremaine, fractious at her own confinement at the Court, has not, I fear, been the comfort she might be to her husband in his infirmity while, Noddy (in the eyes of the world, your half-brother, Mr. Tremaine!), has become the innocent victim of the understandably dour atmosphere of a household dragged down by illness.

As a consequence of several long conversations with Edmund, (which, I am convinced, would only cause you pain were I to catalogue them for you), each passing day increases my conviction that you and you alone, Mr. Tremaine, hold the key that will unlock the door to Edmund's future, to the future of all the inhabitants of Tremaine Court.

If you cannot forgive the painful personal revelations of the past, perhaps you might take into account the considerable blessings of your own pleasant childhood and grant little Noddy some small solace in his. I fear for the boy, and for the father. With the hope you will find it in your heart to have pity, I remain,

Respectfully,
Kate Harvey
Tremaine Court
Sussex

Dear Miss Harvey,

   Mr. Lucien Tremaine has charged me with the mission of conveying to you his most profound regrets at being unable to join your house party at this time. Although he confesses that your description of the pleasures to be found among the company intrigue him, he will be in Scotland for the next few months with a select group of friends.

   Mr. Tremaine suggests you engage a traveling company of players to enliven your gathering in his absence.

   Also, being forwarded under separate cover is a three-volume set of Miss Mary Wollstonecraft's writings, A Vindication of the Rights of Women, *which Mr. Tremaine is assured you will find tame reading. Hoping that this communication is of assistance, I remain,*

Yr. obedient servant,
James Riley, Esquire
Solicitor to Lucien Tremaine
St. Albans Street,
London

Mr. Tremaine,

Thank you for your thoughtful gift of Miss Wollstonecraft's books. I have read her work carefully, committing several passages to memory. Vindication. An interesting word, yes? Such a small step is needed to travel from vindication to revenge—*a sword that cuts both ways with equal intensity.*

I trust your sojourn in Scotland proved a success. I only wish Mr. Riley had given me your direction. I might have joined you, as I've long harbored the notion of hunting down a baboon.

Our party has been sadly flat without you, but we have managed to muddle through another few months in your absence.

I have passed the time teaching Noddy his half-brother's name, and he looks forward to meeting you. He wished to know if you had played with the toys in the nursery and might therefore miss them now that you are gone, but I assured him you seem most happily involved in riding your hobbyhorse in London.

Edmund's condition remains stable, and may even have improved. I offer you this information as a yuletide present, with hopes that this particular gift may continue to give you pleasure for another thirty years.

> *Joyeux nöel,*
> *Kate Harvey*
> *Tremaine Court*
> *Sussex*

23 February 1814

Miss Harvey,
You cease to amuse, darling. Kindly do not dip your poisonous pen in ink again unless he is dying.

L.K.T.

PART TWO

LIMBO

1814

<hr>

His form had yet not lost
All her original brightness, nor appeared
Less than Archangel ruin'd, and th' excess
Of glory obscur'd.

> John Milton, *Paradise Lost*

CHAPTER 6

*When night
Darkens the streets, then wander forth the sons
Of Belial, flown with insolence and wine.*

John Milton, *Paradise Lost*

See that ring he's sporting? That's no ruby stuck in its center, you know."

The man's voice lowered conspiratorially as he continued to point toward Lucien Tremaine, who was just then coming down the dance with Viscount Hartley's youngest, a vacant-faced chit whose major assets were at the moment all but peeking out above her low-cut gown. "I heard the truth at White's. It's really a petrified heart. He carved it from a living dove during a black mass."

"Good God! Really!" Garth Stafford exclaimed in shocked accents, raking the man with his eyes to take in the man's dangerously high shirt points and puce waistcoat—and his sad lack of a chin. "We all have our suspicions, of course, but how daring of you to say so out loud. I commend your bravery."

"Wh—what do you mean?"

Garth pushed himself away from the pillar he had been lounging against, carefully looking right and left as if to be

sure no one else in the crowded ballroom could overhear his next words.

"I mean, old man, what if Tremaine heard you? Why, his revenge would be both swift and terrible! Perhaps next time we see him he'll even be wearing a much larger 'ruby'—on a chain around his waist. Oh, leaving so soon? That might be wise, as you are looking a trifle pale."

Garth smiled in amusement as the man scurried away, but his humor faded as he turned to watch his friend Lucien.

No, not his friend. Not really. Garth sighed, correcting himself silently, again questioning why he bothered to beat his head against the stone wall of Lucien's indifference. Lucien hadn't been Garth's friend—hadn't been anyone's friend—since those last terrible days on the Peninsula.

Garth didn't know this man. He wasn't sure he even liked him.

For Garth Stafford had conspired with a younger Lucien at school as they secreted a small bag of ripe manure beneath the proctor's bed. He had laughed with that Lucien as they had chased a noisy, fat sow through a muddy Spanish barnyard, having elected themselves a committee of two intent on supplementing the meager diets of their men on the eve of a battle. He had sung bawdy ditties with him as they shared a bottle in a damp cave, fought back to back with him in bloody fights on and off the battlefield, and held him as Lucien sobbed inconsolably over the broken body of a small Spanish child mown down by a runaway cannon.

Where had that Lucien Tremaine gone?

There had been changes in the man since Garth had been forced to leave him lying gravely injured in a small hut high in the mountains, changes in Lucien's appearance and demeanor that had become disturbingly evident to Garth in the scant week he had been back in the London social scene.

These changes began with Lucien's appearance.

Lucien's tall frame was outfitted in what Garth had already learned was now his friend's usual impeccable, controlled black and white, the precise styling showing his

long, supple muscles to advantage as he faultlessly executed the intricate steps of the dance. Maturity had lent a new strength to Lucien's physical makeup, his once faintly gangling body now a finely tuned instrument. His skin was tanned from long hours spent in the saddle; his well-groomed, thick ebony hair was arranged in a simple style.

And, as Garth's now absent companion of a few moments earlier had pointed out, Lucien's jewelry was limited to the single gold ring on the last finger of his left hand, the large ruby in its center throbbing blood red in the candlelight.

But the changes in Lucien were more than physical, or even sartorial. Those changes kept Garth alert, wary, and watchful of his old friend. There existed an icy aloofness about Lucien now, an invisible, impenetrable barrier the man had thrown up that kept even Garth firmly outside of all but the most superficial aspects of his friend's life.

To Garth's knowledge (and he had been discreetly asking questions about Lucien every day since his return to London), his friend had not fought a duel, not shown any tendency toward violence in the year he had been moving about in society. No one Garth had spoken to said a single word against him. Perhaps no one dared. For although Lucien's sense of humor remained very much in evidence, that wit had clearly turned cynical, and he had somehow gained a reputation for ruthlessness.

And then there were the rumors.

These fanciful stories were whispered to Garth out of the corners of male mouths or gushed at him by giggling misses. They hinted at everything from debauchery, to perversion, to devil worship—anything the *ton* could offer to explain the menacing, dark, almost sexual thrill they felt climbing their spines as Lucien Tremaine sauntered into their midst, his eyelids drooping lazily over midnight black eyes, his slight half smile mocking them all.

Yet, unbelievably and, Garth felt certain, much to Lucien's private amusement, the man remained welcome everywhere.

The very first evening Garth had ventured out he had discovered his old friend at Lady Hereford's ball. This alone surprised him, for Lucien had never been one for the hustle and bustle of London society. As Lucien had explained to him at great length years earlier, he much preferred the "real" life, that of an English country gentleman.

After a jovial greeting, complete with backslaps and calls for a bottle, Garth had asked Lucien about Melanie—the paragon, the adored fiancée he had been forced to hear about every night around the campfire—already looking about the ballroom for the young woman.

It had been an innocent question, but Lucien's dark eyes had flashed hot for a moment before becoming shuttered, unreadable, as he drawled, "Why, surely you don't expect me to limit myself to a single female? After all, darling, consider the waste."

Darling. The term hadn't been employed as an affectation. It most certainly hadn't been meant as a term of affection, not to Garth's discerning ear. No, it had been a warning, Lucien's way of proclaiming, "That's close enough, you will oblige me by advancing no farther."

Garth had quickly learned that Lucien appeared to use the word off-handedly, scattering the drawled endearment through his speech with the delicacy of rose petals drifting onto finest velvet. He found it amusing that there actually existed in their small, insular world persons (for the most part, female) unintelligent enough to hear the word and believe they had been flattered.

The majority, however, seemed to know differently. For Lucien's was a darkness of excessive light, as he employed his brilliant, brittle facade of bored sophistication smoothly, smiling even as his eyes penetrated to a man's most vulnerable core, so that he felt stripped naked, sure that Lucien could read his innermost secrets, expose his most profound fears, and lay bare his very soul for a leisurely inspection.

Garth, too, knew differently, and he had not ceased to mourn the fact that Lucien hadn't exempted him from the

veiled insult. How he hated it when Lucien felt impelled to use the term with him. He'd rather the man called him a son of a bitch—even called him out—anything would be better than that so subtle, so deflating, *darling*.

Yes, Lucien was handsome, urbane, sinfully wealthy, and cuttingly witty. He was also hard, emotionless, and very, very mysterious. Women fell at his feet, each sure she was the one who held the key to his heart—while men, knowing he had none, fawned over him, ridiculous in their fear of putting a step wrong.

To Garth, after a week spent observing the man, the answer to Lucien's behavior had become painfully obvious. Lucien Tremaine just didn't give a damn. About anything. About anyone. Including himself. Especially himself.

All that remained was the question: Why? Edmund and Pamela Tremaine had never made themselves a part of London society, so that Garth's discreet questions among the *ton* about Lucien's parents had found no immediate answers.

Perhaps it was time he traveled to Sussex.

As the dance ended Lucien signaled to Garth that he planned to adjourn to the gaming room. The gesture could not be construed as an invitation, but merely a politeness on Lucien's part. Garth hesitated, then followed after Lucien, silently cursing himself for continuing to punish himself this way. The man neither needed nor even particularly wanted his company.

"But then you always were a stubborn bastard," he reminded himself quietly as he slipped into an empty chair next to Lucien and reached for the cards, knowing neither of them would rise from the table before dawn.

"Good evening, Mr. Stafford, sir." The tall, gray-haired man who opened the door of the Portman Square mansion a few days later surveyed Garth with faded blue eyes.

"And a very good evening to you, Hawkins," Garth replied cheerfully, shrugging out of his cloak as he deliber-

ately stepped past the man and into the large black-and-white tiled foyer. "He's in?" He allowed the butler to take his hat and gloves.

"The master is in the drawing room. If you would be so kind as to wait here, sir, I shall inform him of your arrival."

"That won't be necessary, Hawkins, thank you," he said quickly, already brushing past the butler. "I'll announce myself. And please, relax. I promise you, dear man—I'm not armed." Hawkins had proved fiercely protective of his employer, a fact that amused Garth, for never did there exist a man more unlikely of requiring protection than Lucien Tremaine.

Lucien stood alone in the drawing room, one elegantly shod foot braced against an andiron, his forearm leaning on the Italian marble mantelpiece as he stared at the folded letter in his hand, its wax seal clearly broken.

Unwilling to play the role of eavesdropper, Garth coughed, alerting Lucien to his presence.

"Well, hello there, my friend," Lucien said, his movements unhurried as he turned away from the fireplace and slipped the letter into his jacket pocket. His dark eyes were free of expression even as his quick smile indicated his pleasure. "Please forgive me. I didn't hear Hawkins announce your arrival. Or, from that satisfied smile you're sporting, may I assume you have succeeded in locking the dear fellow in a closet?"

"I wouldn't be so daring. I'm sorry if I've interrupted you." He inclined his head toward Lucien's jacket, his intention at the moment no more than idle curiosity. "Something important?"

"Nonsense." Lucien easily dismissed Garth's allusion to the letter. "I am one of the idle rich, if you'll recall. We make it a point scarcely ever to do anything of importance. Entirely too fatiguing, you understand. Tell me, Garth, would it be wrong of me to assume we are promised somewhere or other this evening? I seem to have forgotten, although I notice that I am dressed to go out. Perhaps I

should consider having Hawkins pin notes to my sleeve. What do you think?"

"I advise against it. Such an action would quite ruin the line of your coat."

Garth moved to the side table and poured himself a drink, wishing he could know what his friend had been thinking as he stared at that letter, for Lucien Tremaine never forgot anything.

"Tonight holds nothing extraordinary for us, Lucien, I'm afraid—only the usual boring round, and the Season not yet officially to begin for another fortnight. The theater, a few private parties, ending at one of your favorite gaming hells, I imagine, unless you've been banned from them all. You have the devil's own luck with the cards, friend. I hear Orton's all to pieces after his play with you the other night. The man's an ass, but a harmless enough sort for all that. Did you have to trounce him quite so thoroughly?"

Lucien took the drink Garth handed him and leaned against one arm of the settee, crossing one leg over the other. Since Garth had not been blessed with the ability to read his friend's mind, he had quickly learned to understand the language of the man's body. Lucien crossed his legs as he had once crossed swords with the enemy, the action a sure signal to his friend that he had unwittingly crossed the line and become too personal.

If Lucien's posture didn't convince him, the man's next words did. "You'd rather then, darling, that I played for straws?"

Garth decided to push on, ignoring the veiled insult, hoping to discern some small indication of the way Lucien's mind worked. "He was at Watier's last night, Alvanley said, mumbling something about putting an end to it all. Such an occurrence might not bother you, my friend, but it could be damned distressing to the ladies if Orton were to be discovered tomorrow morning, dangling from some Bond Street lamppost."

Lucien's expression didn't change, except possibly to look

even more bored with the subject of his latest gambling partner. "I shouldn't do this, dear Garth, I know, for it might spoil you, but I shall explain myself this one time. Orton's a man grown, so that I foolishly credited him with knowing what he was about when he sat down to play."

"That's true enough," Garth admitted, nodding.

"Yes, I know, though it pains me to point out the obvious. Also," Lucien rose, adding softly, "I would spare him my pity were I you, as he possessed wit enough to discover a less personally painful way to settle his debt. I had his sister in here today without invitation, wringing her hands and begging for pity, even going so far as to rend the bodice of her gown to the waist and plead with me to take her soft, ripe body as payment. Poor Hawkins nearly suffered an apoplexy. Have you ever seen the delectable Susanna Orton in the buff, my friend?"

Garth leaned wearily against the sturdy side table. He watched Lucien's face intently as the man finished his wine and dabbed at the corners of his mouth with a fine linen handkerchief, wishing he didn't feel it necessary to ask his next question. He knew Lucien to be punishing him for his impertinence, and as he somehow believed he might deserve it, he responded just as he felt certain his friend wished him to do.

"She didn't! The chit actually stripped off her clothes in front of you and offered herself up for ravishment? Good God, man, what did you do?"

Lucien turned to him, smiling as he adjusted his Mechlin lace-trimmed cuffs and smoothed down the sleeves of his coat, prolonging the moment until Garth ached to punch him. "Perhaps I should say I barred the door against the swooning Hawkins, threw her to the carpet on her rosy rump, and then proceeded to have my wicked way with her numerous times, in sundry, ah, *educational* ways, before throwing her out—still, of course, intent on collecting payment in full from her brother? Is that lascivious enough for you, Garth?"

The smile disappeared, to be replaced by a most comical

frown. "But, alas, I cannot claim any such acts even to titillate you, my friend. In the end, I felt myself compelled to let Orton off, on the condition he and dearest Susanna quit the metropolis for the remainder of the Season. But I must beg you not to tell a soul. After all, think of the damage it might do to my reputation."

Closing his eyes for a moment in relief, Garth pushed himself away from the side table. It could have been worse; it could have been much worse. He silently damned Orton for a spineless fool. He likewise damned the histrionic Susanna who, following the lead of so many other females, from the pinnacle of society to the most hardened *fille de joie,* had probably believed herself half in love with Lucien.

"Please forgive me my questions, and my moment of doubt. You were exceptionally kind to her, Lucien."

Lucien eyed him owlishly through a gold quizzing glass that had been suspended around his neck from a black riband. "You really think so, darling? Not to beggar the question, but which do we term the greater insult? To deflower the child, or to resist what I am sure she considered to be her fetal—oh, dear, I must rephrase that, mustn't I?—I mean, her *fatal* charms? I had to cudgel my brains for some time before acting, you know, as either way I might have injured her irreparably."

The quizzing glass fell, to lie once more against his pristine white waistcoat. "Shall we go?"

"The girl was innocent," Garth pointed out as he followed Lucien into the foyer. "You had no choice."

"No female is innocent," came Lucien's offhand reply. "As it happened, Susanna slapped my face for my pains, highly indignant I had refused her. Only when I condescended to give her a small sample of what she believed she had been asking for did she flee."

Lucien allowed the butler to lay a many-caped greatcoat around his shoulders, condescending to tie it himself before accepting his hat and gloves. "Now say your good-night to the so loyal Hawkins, and promise him with all your heart that you will take exemplary care of me until I am once

more returned safely to his bosom. He worries so, you know, poor man."

Garth laughed and shook his head as he retrieved his own cloak, hat, and gloves from the impassive butler. "Lucien, you're heartless."

"Not heartless, darling," Lucien corrected, already stepping into Stafford's carriage. "No, as I was thinking earlier —just as you came in, as it happens—I really believe it to be something other than heartlessness that compels me. Something hereditary, perhaps? Yes, that may be it. Garth, are you coming? We wouldn't wish to be more than fashionably late for the theater."

Dawn had begun creeping into London before the carriage drew up once more in Portman Square, and Garth knew himself to be more than two parts drunk. He watched with bleary eyes as Lucien disdained the offered steps and leapt down gracefully onto the flagway, looking as well groomed and as sober as he had done when the evening began.

"How do you do it, friend? We've drunk and played ourselves damned near through the night, and you still look as fine as fivepence. Perhaps it's true, then, and you have made a bargain with the devil."

Lucien's black eyes twinkled as he turned to bow to his companion. "Did you ever doubt it? After all, why travel to the depths of hell if you cannot benefit from the experience?" he asked, saluting. Then he turned to call out to the driver, "Take your master home, my good man, but do so carefully, if you please. The poor fellow's in pain."

"Wretch," Garth muttered, settling back against the soft leather cushions as the carriage prepared to move off, feeling rather pleased with himself, for Lucien had been an entertaining companion—almost as pleasant as his memories of the Lucien he had been with in Spain. Garth believed he might even have initiated a small breach of the man's sturdy brick wall of studied indifference. Turning himself about, he shot one last look toward his friend—just in time

to see four dark-clothed men emerge from the shadows and run at him.

"Lucien! Behind you!" Garth shouted, instantly sobering as lessons hard learned on the Peninsula sprang to the fore. Flinging the carriage door open, he jumped lightly to the street, already reaching for the slim knife he always carried when abroad at night.

His warning had come just in time, as he saw Lucien wheel about, his body in a defensive crouch, his greatcoat flung back over his shoulders, exposing the white satin lining. The blade of his own stiletto glinted dully in the half light.

The first attacker couldn't halt the forward progress of his body, already committed to the act of sinking his weapon in his victim's unsuspecting back, so that he very accommodatingly impaled his thin chest on Lucien's blade.

Unfortunately, Garth saw, the force of the dying man's impact caused Lucien to stagger, temporarily losing his balance and giving the three remaining men the opening they needed. Only Garth's fierce yell kept them immobile for the heartbeat in time it took for Lucien to rid himself of his encumbrance and leap onto the third step of the portico, above his attackers. Garth spared a second to marvel at the dashing figure Lucien cut as he tossed his hat to the flagstones, his greatcoat swirling about his knees. Lucien Tremaine was a worthy adversary.

The ragged trio seemed similarly impressed. They looked quickly to Garth, now close behind them in the gutter, and then back to Lucien, who stood, his feet slightly apart, expertly tossing the blood-wet stiletto from one hand to the other, his cold, menacing smile wordlessly taunting them, urging them to try their hand with him.

"What say you, my friend?" Lucien questioned, his voice calm, as if he were requesting Garth's opinion on the merits of horses lined up for a race. "You want the one to my left? His ears may require a bit of a bob, merely for aesthetic purposes, you understand."

The attackers once more looked over their shoulders to

see the man who stood behind them, their eyes all but popping from their heads. Trust Lucien Tremaine to find the sport in the thing. Garth smiled as he used his blade to point to the man in the middle.

"Ah, Lucien, have you not noticed the nose on this sorry soul? Surely he only needs half as much to smell his cabbage. I think I shall do my Christian duty and rid him of the rest. You may have the ears, thank you anyway."

"Always the fastidious one, my friend," Lucien acknowledged with a slight inclination of his head. "But I think we forget something."

"Too true. And what of the third, Lucien?" Garth asked, his blood singing as two would-be assassins, their hands raised protectively to their heads, began slowly to sidle toward the alleyway. He let them go, somehow sure Lucien wished him to do so, and concentrated on keeping the last of the men from following.

Lucien's smile slipped fractionally as he descended the flagway, his full attention clearly taken by the third man. "That depends. If he tells me what I want to know, I may not geld him." He took a step forward, now close enough that he, like Garth, could smell the thug's fear. "My goodness, Garth, take a peek at that face. Look hard—peering past the dirt. He resembles a wren, doesn't he? So tell me, please. Are you going to sing for me, little bird?"

Garth, confused, remained silent. Hadn't this been a robbery attempt? Had he drunk so much that he had missed something, some pertinent clue that had alerted Lucien that there were motives deeper than simple theft behind this attack? Of course! Orton must have decided he liked London more than he did the countryside and hired himself some killers. But, again, as he had by sending his sister in his stead, he had underestimated his man. It would take more than four clearly inept inmates of the bowels of Piccadilly to do in Lucien Tremaine.

The remaining villain began to shake as Garth lifted him off the ground by the scruff of his neck, the nasty-looking cudgel he had been holding dropping into the gutter. "Oi

don't know nothin'," he appealed to Garth. "Jacky 'ired us and yer kilt 'im. Let me go, guv'nor. 'E's loony, this gentry cove is, and 'e says 'e's gonna snaffle me ballocks. Let me go, guv'nor, please—turn me loose."

Lucien's stiletto lightly pressed against the man's filthy crotch. "You're not singing, little wren," he pointed out, his jaw hard. "You're bawling like a babe in arms, and my patience wears thin. Surely the estimable Jacky told you who hired him to put a period to my existence. Just give me a name, little wren, and I'll let you fly away."

"Oi told yer! Oi don't know! Jacky told us it were sum'one 'e seen when 'e loped off ter see his mum awhile back, that's all. Fer Gawd's sake, sir, let me loose! Aw, Jeezus, Oi gone and pissed m'self now! Please, sir!"

Garth eased his grip a fraction, assured the man was now too frightened to run, and looked at his friend. Lucien's face was as dark as a thundercloud, his mouth compressed into a thin white line. Lucien could kill this man and not even blink, Garth felt sure of it.

He gave the man a small shake. "And where does Jacky's soon-to-be bereaved mama reside? Tell us, and you may yet live to catch the pox. Hurry, man, as I fear my friend Mr. Tremaine grows weary, and the knife might slip of its own accord."

"In Sussex! Jacky's mum lives somewheres in Sussex!"

Lucien's face became impassive as he withdrew the knife. "Let him go, Garth. As it is, Hawkins will have the maids scrubbing Jacky's claret from the steps for a fortnight," he said softly, turning his back.

The terrified man bolted for the alleyway, forgotten, as Garth moved to follow his friend. "Sussex, Lucien? If the fellow had said St. James Street, I would have understood it. But Sussex? I've attempted to control my curiosity, but perhaps it's time we had a small talk about what happened when you returned home from the Peninsula?"

"And perhaps not, darling," Lucien returned, not bothering to look back at his friend as he mounted the steps to the mansion. Hawkins, holding an evil-looking pistol, held open

the door to allow his master to pass inside. "Thank you for your assistance, my friend. I shan't forget it. Truly."

He hesitated at the top step. "But wait. Something tugs at the corner of my mind. Ah, I remember now. I believe I was remiss earlier this evening, Garth. You do recall that my mind was much of a muddle. Have I told you that as of tomorrow I shall find myself out of town for a space? No? That explains it. Forgive me that lapse of manners. Yes, sadly, I must bid you good-bye now, as well as good night. Such a pity, as we have only just met again."

He looked round, casting a glance toward the alleyway. "There is nothing more to fear here, Garth. Your coachman will bear you safely home."

"You'll be going to Sussex?" Garth already knew the answer, but it was all he could think to say. Any offer to accompany his friend into the countryside would be brushed aside, if not totally ignored.

"To Sussex? Yes, I should think so. Or to hell, dear Garth," Lucien replied quietly, stepping across the threshold, "as I have already visited both, and fail to recollect the difference."

CHAPTER 7

Thus with the year
Seasons return; but not to me returns
Day, or the sweet approach of ev'n or morn,
Or sight of vernal bloom, or summer's rose,
Or flocks, or herds, or human face divine;
But cloud instead, and ever-during dark surrounds me.

John Milton, *Paradise Lost*

*O*nly a thin line marks the division between love and hate, or so Lucien had read, the emotions explained as being no more than two sides of a single coin, or two views of the same face; but then nothing the world has to offer is so complex that fools could not reduce it to a toothless maxim, a meaningless string of words to be nodded over, clucked about, neatly catalogued, and then dismissed.

Lucien knew himself to be both a victim of love and a guardian of hate, his life for the past year and more a fragile construction of conflicting emotions that had alternately soothed and battered him, until he had molded himself into an enigma not even he fully understood.

He had grown to enjoy his time in London, as much as he retained the ability to enjoy anything, and although he could not be unaware of the whispers, he refused to take pleasure in his considerable reputation. To the *ton* he might be the clever, mysterious, unapproachable, possibly even danger-ous Lucien Tremaine, but he recognized the figure society

99

fawned over to be nothing more than a reflection of the disillusionment he had suffered upon his return from the war.

He had no real friends, save Hawkins, who knew everything, and possibly Garth, who knew nothing. But Lucien did not consider himself unfortunate. True friendship demanded a measure of intimacy, a capacity for caring, and Lucien had moved beyond the ability to produce either. He had arrived at a place where he depended upon and truly cared for nothing and no one. Not even himself. Especially himself.

Yet Lucien could not shake the niggling fear that, locked somewhere beneath his purposely cool exterior, carefully shuttered away behind his dark, unreadable eyes and cynical smile, cowered a tormented, whimpering child.

It was, he acknowledged regretfully, that child who pulled the curricle to a halt at the crest of the grassy hill to look down at Tremaine Court nestled in the small valley below.

How he hated this place. How he loved it.

The Court resembled a French château more than an English country house, a resemblance Lucien had taken for granted before his return from the war but now saw as the epitome of irony.

The time-stained facade still showed a dusty gray in the thin morning daylight. The front walls would turn nearly white in the early evening, when the setting sun cast long shadows from the tree-lined avenue to the wrought-iron railings and stone columns that delineated the forecourt.

Lucien knew well the history of Tremaine Court.

Edmund Tremaine's great-grandfather, Hollis, only son of a successful coal merchant from Leeds, had prudently gathered up his industrious sire's fortune and transported it, and himself, to Sussex, as far away from the smell of the shop as possible. Tremaine Court had been called Kingsley Manor at that time, the estate having passed from one generation to the next from the time of its construction in the sixteen hundreds. Centuries of Catholicism and its attendant poverty had resulted in near penury for the

Kingsleys and, as luck would have it, a providential purchase for Hollis Tremaine. The Kingsleys had been forced to be content with a small cottage on the edge of their former estate.

Hollis had almost immediately embarked upon an orgy of building, thoroughly renovating the interior of the house so that the main rooms were relocated from the first to the ground floor, while at the same time planting the long avenue of beech trees, creating the enclosed forecourt, and adding a large, building-long terrace to the rear of the four-story house. The multi-leveled terrace had extended to include two small, delicate domed pavilions at either end of it, each containing private sitting rooms and ground-floor exits that led directly into the gardens.

Hollis's purchase had also included the surrounding farms. His dedication to the land and each passing year had removed the Tremaines further from the taint of coal and closer to respectability. But it had taken Edmund Tremaine's marriage to Pamela Kingsley, last in the line and only child of her widowed father, to return a pure-blooded Kingsley, and Catholicism, to Tremaine Court.

Pamela had also brought with her a refining influence bred into the Kingsley bones over the centuries but seldom before coupled with funds sufficient for their full expression. Soon the rooms of Tremaine Court had taken on a beauty and gentility that had endeared her to husband, son, and servants.

The extensive rose gardens had proved her most ardent passion, so that Edmund had ordered the construction of a greenhouse expressly for his wife's use. Lucien smiled now, remembering his mother's flustered apologies as one long-ago day she had raced up the stairs to change for dinner, her fine dark hair all but escaping its pins, her lovely face streaked with dirt, her apron soiled, and her fingers stained from repotting a new variety of rose that had just arrived from South America.

"Time just seems to fly away from me when I am with my flowers, dearest Edmund," she had murmured breathlessly

as she entered the dining room to find her family already seated, her husband rising to kiss her cheek as he held out her chair. "Lucien, my pet, do sit up straight," she had admonished kindly. "You are all of nine now, and must learn to behave as a gentleman should. And what are you laughing about?"

"It's your hair, Mama," he had replied, loving her so much his heart ached with it. "Is that some new decoration?"

"Oh, dear me, not again!"

Pamela's hands had flown to her hair but Edmund's were there before hers, carefully extracting the small, wilting rose petals that had somehow found a home in the artless tangles, holding them in front of her face so that they could all enjoy the joke.

Try as he might, Lucien failed to share his mother's passion for digging in the dirt. He had nevertheless grown to manhood with a deep love for nature, and to enter a room without being met by the welcoming fragrance of freshly cut flowers had become an anathema to him.

Now, rising slightly from his seat, Lucien could see the greenhouse from his vantage point, the hundreds of glass panes either dulled by dirt or, here and there, missing altogether. His lips tightened into a thin line, a very real pain invading his chest.

Clearly Melanie did not share his mother's love of flowers.

His sight of the ruined greenhouse stripped all nostalgia-induced myopia from Lucien's eyes and centered his attention on the woefully neglected condition of the remainder of Tremaine Court.

Grasses bordering the wrought-iron enclosure of the forecourt had been left to grow unchecked by the taming influence of a scythe, and the long, branched stretch of gravel drive appeared scarred and rutted, with tall, seed-heavy weeds strewn everywhere like scattered soldiers taking cover in the midst of cannon fire.

The tall chimneys could not have been properly tended since he had left for the war, and one smaller chimney

appeared to be entirely useless, a large, intricately constructed stork's nest securely capping it.

Yews planted on either side of the front entrance, and always scrupulously maintained, had been allowed to grow wild, uneven branches spiking out in every direction, the trees now looming higher than the massive oak doors.

The uneven rows of seemingly carelessly placed, deep-set windows, their panes usually throwing off brilliant starbursts of reflected sunshine, looked somehow darkened, as if all the light bathing the outside of the house could not warm them to their usual welcoming glow.

He saw a patch of damp extending down from the turret that bordered the north wing, the facade stained nearly past redemption, small, uneven patches of it chewed away, giving the impression that some great creature had been gnawing on it.

A house the size of Tremaine Court required nearly constant care, as Edmund himself had told Lucien numberless times. Lucien remembered his lessons well, although Edmund would seem to have forgotten them.

This sad, crippled building little resembled the nurturing home of his youth or the reassuring vision that had sustained him through two long years of war. While on the Peninsula Lucien had worried that Tremaine Court might be altered in his absence. But this disheartening reality had proved even worse than his fears. From steeply pitched slate roofs to the missing stone on the wide circular front steps, the house projected an air of defeat, neglect, and dishonor.

It was impossible, here on this isolated hill, for Lucien to maintain a grip upon his harshly disciplined emotions. Anger such as he had not allowed himself to experience in well over a year shuddered through his body, his hands twisting into fists around the reins.

Tremaine Court had not merely changed.

It had died.

"God damn him!" he shouted to the skies, so that a family of sparrows, drowsing in a nearby tree, took flight. "God damn him to the foulest regions of hell!"

If Edmund Tremaine were to appear in front of Lucien at that moment he would kill the man without compunction, without sorrow, without guilt. He fought a fierce internal battle to conquer the urge to spring his horses, drive pell-mell into the forecourt, and leap from the curricle to confront the man who had wrought this destruction.

Lucien looked out across the meadow behind Tremaine Court, to the small enclosed cemetery he had last visited in the hope of discovering some sort of rational explanation for the nightmare of disillusionment he had stumbled into upon his return from the war. Slowly, he felt his anger drain away, leaving only a faint sadness. Tremaine Court had long since ceased to be his concern, whether it were to become the premier estate in the kingdom or be swallowed up whole beneath the land it stood on.

With a flick of the reins, he turned the curricle in the direction of the small path that led to the cemetery gate.

Later there would be time and enough to deal with Edmund. For now, he had to make his final peace with the woman who had given him life, who had gifted him with her comforting love, and who had died while he could not be there with her, leaving him behind to deal with the legacy of her one damning deceit.

Katharine d'Harnancourt looked up from the pages of the book she had been reading to see that the sun had climbed beyond the rooftops of Tremaine Court, signaling that the time had come for her to return to her patient. She closed the book, reluctant to leave, and glanced toward Pamela Tremaine's headstone.

"I must be going now, Pamela," she said easily, rising from the small stone bench as she pulled a thin knitted shawl over her shoulders. She had been coming to the small enclosed cemetery for more than a year, forever, having found that talking to a dead woman, although an odd practice, made her feel less foolish than conversing with herself.

Over two years she had been at Tremaine Court, the first

spent as wet nurse to Noddy, and the remainder serving as companion to the master of the house. They had not been happy years, but they had not been entirely unhappy either. Kate considered them rather as a sort of limbo, some indefinite plane partway between heaven and hell, and mercifully distant from the purgatory she had suffered through after fleeing The Willows.

But Kate, with her strong mind and the resiliency of youth, had rediscovered much of her thirst for life while existing in that limbo. She had begun to chafe at her self-imposed confinement, fighting the nagging conviction that she had been cheated out of something very important, that the world held more for Katharine Marie Elizabeth d'Harnancourt than her troubled past or her current monotonous existence.

Soon she would reach her twenty-first birthday, and her life would be her own. No more would she have to hide at Tremaine Court, fearing discovery and a return to her father's house, or the asylum he had threatened to put her in if she did not repent of her accusation. Soon she could go where she wished, when she wished, be her own mistress.

Not that she would ever even dream of returning to The Willows. Her life there seemed so far away, so long ago, that she had nearly succeeded in blocking the memories of her home from her consciousness.

Except in summer, which brought with it remembrances of lazy days spent painting watercolors as she sat in the dainty gazebo where, years before, her dearest mother had sung to her and concocted silly stories they would both giggle over until it came time for Kate's governess to call her to supper in the elaborately furnished schoolroom at the very top of the mellowed pink brick house.

Except in the autumn, when the piercing sound of blaring horns and barking hounds called back recollections of her carefree gallops, her favorite mount Pâquerette beneath her as, together, they flew across the endless expanse of newly harvested fields, the stallion's giant hooves kicking up huge clumps of fragrant earth and sweet, crushed wheat.

Except in the wintertime, when the new-fallen snow caused her to recall being bundled to the chin in softest furs as she snuggled close beside her father in the brick-red sleigh, the shiny, round bells attached to the horse's harness jingling merrily as, guided by the light of the full moon, they returned home from visiting her cousin Roger's house on Christmas Eve.

Except in spring, once her most beloved season of all. Now, seeing the budding flowers and the unfurling of fragile, light green leaves called her back to the horror of those last terrible weeks spent in her bedchamber, to which she had been banished in disgrace, to be locked out of sight of decent, God-fearing people until such time as she agreed to admit her sin.

So many years. Yet, on days like these, days when the nearby meadow had blossomed into a carpet of wild flowers, and the delicate fragrance of apple and cherry blossoms permeated the breeze, glorious sunlit days that found the banks of the nearby stream crowded with early primroses and sweet violets, her memories of The Willows were as close as yesterday, and as painful.

If she were somehow to be given rule of the world, Kate Harvey would outlaw spring.

She bent to pick up the book, not her book, as she had precious few possessions, but one she had borrowed from Edmund's extensive library. It was one she instinctively knew he would never ask her to read to him, if, indeed, he were ever to recover the power of speech. Ill for over a year, gradually losing nearly all mobility in his legs, so that his useless muscles had dictated that he venture no farther than the Bath chair Kate employed to push him about the neglected gardens, Edmund's latest episode had robbed him entirely of the power of verbal communication.

During the day Kate ministered to the master of the house, feeding him, reading to him, sneaking Noddy into the heavily draped ground-floor chamber for fleeting visits whenever Melanie could be counted on to be occupied with one of her lovers. Late at night, lying in her narrow bed in

the small room adjoining his, Kate could hear Edmund's pathetic, whimpering cries as he suffered through the long, sleepless hours until dawn.

They shared an intolerable existence, made palatable only by the strange affection and intimacy that had grown between them, and their unspoken determination to keep Noddy safely out of Melanie's path.

Edmund and Kate also shared one damning secret, one daring plan whose success hinged entirely upon Melanie's continued ignorance of her precarious position as mistress of Tremaine Court. Were Melanie to hear of this plan while her husband still lived, Kate would be banished immediately, leaving the crippled, helpless Edmund entirely at his wife's sadly limited mercies.

Hence Kate's continued outward attitude of servility, her apparent indifference to what went on around her, and her willingness to subjugate her renewed interest in living. She must do nothing to arouse Melanie's attention.

But each passing day threatened their plan, as Melanie's behavior had become increasingly bizarre, her tantrums more terrifyingly violent, her excesses more blatant, going so far as to even approach Kate with the abhorrent suggestion that, as the servant seemed unaffected by men, perhaps she, Melanie, might offer her an afternoon's diversion.

Only the appearance of Moina, whose presence seemed alternately to anger and soothe Melanie, had saved Kate from stepping out of her subservient role to slap her mistress's innocently beautiful face. Melanie's allusions to strange, perverted acts, however, had caused Kate to fear not only for her own safety, but Noddy's as well.

There was nothing else for it—Melanie must be routed from Tremaine Court. Kate already knew the method of that removal; she had only to gain the power to implement it.

Unpleasant as the conclusion might be, a week earlier Kate had concluded the time might have come for Edmund —tragically locked inside a useless body, and woefully unhappy—to die. Yet she felt convinced that Edmund

doggedly clung to life, hoping against hope that Lucien would return to Tremaine Court one last time, to forgive Edmund, to understand why Edmund had done what he'd done, and to pledge his assistance to Kate. Only then would Edmund allow himself the healing peace of death.

Having listened to Edmund's story many times over the course of this past year, Kate no longer believed Lucien Kingsley Tremaine would ever return to Sussex of his own volition, except perhaps to burn Tremaine Court to the ground. And, of course, there had been the letters, an exercise in futility that still served to embarrass and anger her each time she thought of Lucien's replies to her entreaties.

Still, she had done what she had done, and nothing could change it. Lucien Tremaine had requested that she not write again unless Edmund was dying, and she had taken him at his word. Edmund was dying. Or at least he should be allowed to die. If there was a difference, and if there was any sin connected to that difference, she would gladly take it on her soul.

"I've pinned all our hopes on your son, Pamela," she said now, giving one last glance toward the headstone before turning for the gate, only to stop abruptly, her head snapping back as she looked up into the coldly mocking dark eyes of Lucien Kingsley Tremaine.

"God bless the wench," she heard him drawl smoothly, as if addressing the world at large, smiling as he spoke. "She speaks to the dead, eliminating the possibility of rebuttal. Is she mad, or is she brilliant?"

Kate's shoulders slumped in dismay. Wordlessly, she took in the many-caped driving coat left open and slung carelessly back over one shoulder to reveal impeccably tailored traveling clothes, the white-cuffed top boots, the curly-brimmed beaver set at a jaunty angle atop the stylishly cropped head. This couldn't be Lucien Tremaine, this elegantly clad, immeasurably assured, magnificently handsome, well-set-up, useless social parasite who looked as out of place in Sussex as would she if she and her faded

kerseymere gown were suddenly to be transported to the heart of fashionable Mayfair.

This Lucien Tremaine, this pretentious dandy, could be of no more help to her than a spurless peacock in a cockfight.

Where had the tortured boy gone, the badly battered victim of another's crime, the injured youth to whom her heart had gone out despite her determination to remain aloof? Where was the anguished creature who had lashed out at her when, she now knew, the message she had relayed to him at the Fox and Crown had proclaimed him the bastard son of a betraying wife?

Kate watched as Lucien, still smiling, lifted his left hand to touch the foaming white cravat at the base of his throat, the blood red ruby ring on his last finger capturing her attention. She remembered that ring, had seen Moina stuff it and a painted miniature into the packet she had delivered to him at the inn.

Did he wear it as a reminder, meant to keep his hate alive? Perhaps she had judged him too soon. Her eyes narrowed thoughtfully, Kate looked once more at Pamela Tremaine's son, concentrating on the man within the polished exterior.

He seemed so much bigger now than he had a year ago, not just in height, but in consequence, his wide-shouldered, leanly muscular body emanating power and intimidation, even as his finely chiseled, suntanned features exuded a brooding sexuality that caused her breath to catch low in her throat.

She had seen a fashionable London dandy because he had wished her to see him in that light. Had he made a conscious decision to disguise himself before the world, presenting himself as less than he was, as if he had a private agenda— or a secret to protect?

Kate, who had seen him at the nadir of his existence, witnessed firsthand the destruction of his hopes, his dreams, could guess at the reason for his scrupulously constructed facade, could sense some of the bone-deep hurt and crushing disillusionment that might lie hidden behind the enigma of this sardonic dandy.

Yet she could not at this moment discern any suffering young man cowering behind that facade, his body weakened by years of war and months of pain, his defenses down, his emotions vulnerable. Even upon close inspection, nothing of the youth became visible, and his smile did not quite reach his cold, dark eyes.

Once she had pitied him. Once her heart had gone out to him. But not now. If Kate felt sympathy for anyone at this instance, she felt it for herself, for she at last concluded that the carefully fashioned London gentleman who stood before her was a dangerous, dangerous man.

Had her last curt communication summoned a rescuer, or merely introduced another spider into the web?

Lucien spoke again, his deep, sensuous voice sending a shiver skipping down her spine. "Still the same taciturn Miss Harvey, I see, for all your newly acquired eccentricity. It is you, Miss Harvey, isn't it? The *servant*, Miss Kate Harvey? You must understand, I quite pride myself on never forgetting a scowl."

Knowing it best to begin as she planned to go on, Kate drew herself up and answered tightly, "And it is you, Mr. Tremaine, isn't it? The *bastard*, Mr. Lucien Tremaine? You see, I am likewise reasonably proud of my memory. You received my letter?"

She watched his left eyebrow, a finely drawn ebony wing, lift fractionally before he brushed past her, to stand beside Pamela Tremaine's grave. His back to her, he said, "Your letter, yes—along with another, rather more direct invitation, delivered at the tip of a knife." He swung around to face her, the supple material of his driving coat swirling about his knees. "But then, you wouldn't know anything about that, would you?"

CHAPTER 8

*L*ucien didn't remember her as beautiful. He remembered her youth and the promise of beauty, but the realization far surpassed his idle expectations. Her long, unbound hair was richly dark and lustrous, her features definitely patrician and finely crafted, while her tall, slim body was achingly ripe, even behind that dreadful shroud of a gown.

He knew he shouldn't have been surprised, as he had only vague memories of her at all, most of them centering on her strange, vacant light gray eyes. For more than a year he had faced those uncaring eyes in his nightmares, mocking him, looking straight through him, silently calling him down, down, deeper and deeper into a bottomless pit of despair and hopelessness.

Yet now, looking at her as her clear forehead wrinkled in an uncomprehending frown, Lucien felt other memories stirring, soothing memories, yet equally unsettling: a hazy recollection of whispered words of comfort in the night, the touch of a caring hand cool against his fevered brow, the feel of a woman's body, soft and pliant beneath his desperately

seeking hands, the healing pressure of female lips pressed against his before being hastily drawn away.

Could it be possible? Could he truly equate this rigid young beauty with the memory of such sweet, unselfish care? How could he compare the beauty before him with the author of those cutting letters?

"You spoke of a knife. Someone tried to kill you, Mr. Tremaine? How perfectly dreadful. To think that someone might wish you dead! I imagine you've been able to narrow the suspects to under one hundred?"

Lucien smiled in real appreciation of her wit, easily subduing his momentary discomfort, his fleeting, unaccustomed feelings of vulnerability. Had he really ever thought her eyes to be blank? On the contrary. They sparkled with intelligence and humor—and anger directed against him.

"You don't like me, do you, Miss Harvey? I can't think why, for I am convinced I have never done you any harm. In fact, I have always believed myself to be a wonderful fellow."

Kate gave a toss of her head, exposing her long, slim white throat to Lucien's admiration. "Of course you are, Mr. Tremaine. Your mention of a knife came purely as a conversational ploy. Pity."

"A pity, you say?" Lucien advanced on her, not stopping until he stood only a few inches away. His eyes concentrated on her full, red mouth. What would she do if he dared to steal a kiss? "A pity that I would descend to such an obvious attempt to gain your attention, Miss Harvey?"

She stood her ground, unflinching, so that Lucien found himself admiring her courage. Lesser persons would have— indeed, had—mumbled excuses and fled beneath his intense scrutiny. Didn't she feel the tension that had risen between them, a tension that had nothing to do with their conversation?

"A pity that your attacker so obviously failed in his mission, Mr. Tremaine," she answered, adding, "Much as I am enjoying this little chat, I'm afraid I am needed back at the house. It is time for Edmund's medication. Besides, I

must hurry to see that Cook slays the fatted calf in honor of the prodigal's return. We'll meet again, I am sure, at which time you may wish to discuss the contents of my latest letter."

"Edmund? How wonderfully familiar that sounds. You have been busy in my absence, haven't you, darling?" Lucien remarked, bowing most elegantly before stepping aside to allow her access to the opened gate, refusing to be baited into discussing the very real possibility of Edmund's death. "When you return to the house would you please inform the housekeeper that my man Hawkins will arrive shortly with my luggage and my mount, Caliban. I'd appreciate rooms prepared for us. And yes, Miss Harvey, I accept your thanks for responding so swiftly to your letter begging my appearance at Tremaine Court."

"I haven't thanked you."

"Yes, Miss Harvey. I know," Lucien said with a smile, bowing to her yet again. He had embarrassed her, and he thoroughly enjoyed putting her to the blush.

When she had gone, her spine regally straight beneath her serviceable brown kerseymere gown and homey shawl, Lucien noticed the book Kate had been holding, the one she had placed on the stone bench while they were speaking. He picked it up, intent only on returning the volume to her, until he recognized the hand-printed cover.

The book contained the Tremaine family history, dating back to the day Hollis Tremaine had relocated himself in Sussex, and seemed a decidedly odd sort of reading material for a family servant. He must keep a close eye on Miss Kate Harvey, for many reasons. She was not only beautiful, but perhaps ambitious as well.

Holding the book against his body, Lucien approached Pamela Tremaine's headstone, for the first time noticing the sprig of wild roses on the grave. He had heard the servant addressing his mother in a friendly, familiar manner when he entered the cemetery. Did he have Kate Harvey to thank for this remembrance? He sincerely hoped not. Lucien did not wish to be in anyone's debt, especially emotionally.

He dropped to his knees on the soft sod, heedless of his clothing, and reached out a hand to touch the cold stone. Remembering his weekly visits to this cemetery in his youth, Lucien recalled the prayers his mother had offered for the happy repose of the souls of those buried here, but none seemed sufficient to express what he felt.

Pamela Tremaine did not lie in this cemetery, locked moldering beneath this damp, impersonal earth. Pamela Tremaine lived in every rose that dotted the meadow, each fragrant breeze that rippled through the trees, in the songs of birds that took wing through the sunlit sky.

He had long ago forgiven her, long since ceased including her in his litany of sorrows, refused to name her as one of the causes behind his altered circumstances. Without question, Pamela had loved her son. She had loved her husband, Edmund. Whatever her long-ago sin, whatever terrible reasons lay behind it, she had lived a good life for as long as he could remember, a meaningful, loving life, and she deserved to have her son cherish his memories of her.

Lucien stood, anxious to leave this place. He felt nothing here. No sorrow. No pain. His mother's body might lie here, but he carried her spirit with him, within his heart—deep within his heart, directly alongside the powerful, abiding hatred he harbored for Edmund and Melanie Tremaine.

How dreadfully bored Melanie felt, cooped up at Tremaine Court as yet another season was about to get underway, Edmund's fierce hold on the purse strings keeping her from renting a house in London. If only he would die, useless old man that he was. But then she would be forced by convention to go into mourning, staying away from the Metropolis, from Lucien, for yet another dreary year.

Unless Edmund were to die now, of course, in the early spring. The war with Napoleon had been all but won, everyone had heard that, even in this benighted backwater. Soon the troops would come home, and there would be

celebrations, balls, routs, and dancing in the streets. By next spring London would be the center of the entire world. Ah, to be a part of such gaiety!

But, no. Edmund would never be so considerate. She had to stay here forever, chained to Tremaine Court and that sniveling infant Noddy, waiting for her selfish husband to breathe his last. She had to remain in near penury, funneling whatever funds she had been able to get her hands on these past interminable years, funds better suited for clothing and jewels, to that miserable society bitch who so wisely kept silent as long as her supply of blood money arrived promptly on the tenth day of each new quarter.

The polite world knew what the bitch was, but the polite world turned a blind eye because of her birth, her breeding, her station. Threatening to expose her meant nothing, less than nothing, while Melanie knew that she herself, who had not been born into that exalted society, could not survive a similar revelation.

If only she could get her hands on the woman, but Sussex and London were worlds apart, so distant from each other that they might as well be situated at opposite ends of the universe. She could not count the nights she had lain awake, planning her revenge. How twisted the world could be, that the bitch and Lucien were both free to enjoy London while she, the innocent victim, remained helpless, locked away at Tremaine Court.

Could Lucien and the bitch have met? Could they have attended the same party, the same reception? Could they have spoken, exchanged confidences, destroying Melanie's dreams for all time?

The questions tormented her so. Not knowing wreaked havoc in her mind, causing her to wake late at night, trembling, in need of release from her ever-growing anxiety, her mushrooming fears.

She shouldn't be made to suffer these torments, but all her life she had been persecuted, misunderstood, and hated, yes, hated, by every woman she met. Because she possessed such

great, heartbreaking beauty. Because she was so truly lovable. Because men found her irresistible.

Lucien had once believed her irresistible, although he was proving maddeningly stubborn now, even though Moina had promised just last week that he would soon return to Tremaine Court. Had it really been more than a year? Time seemed to pass her by in fits and starts at Tremaine Court, with whole months flying past unnoticed, living from one of Moina's potions to the next, while single days could last forever.

Days like today.

Melanie paced the main drawing room, wringing her hands, her mind once more occupied with plans for ridding herself of the invalid Edmund before Lucien returned. How unattractively strong the weak were, ruling from their beds, demanding in their frailty, their mere existence hanging like a pall over every corner of the house, even though they were not there.

Weak Edmund ruled through his solicitor, a bloodless old stick who had emerged the only male within miles to be immune to Melanie's charms. The rules had been made painfully clear to her within a week of Edmund's first episode.

His new ground-floor apartments in the south wing had been declared out of bounds to her, so that she had not seen her husband above a half dozen times since his illness began. She smiled, thinking of that particular stricture. Edmund had certainly changed. She could remember a time he had wept, on his knees, begging for the pleasure of her company, the touch of her hand, the sight of her supple body reclined, naked, in his dead wife's bed. He would have killed for her then. If only he would die for her now.

Her smile faded as she remembered the remainder of Edmund's rules.

She had been barred from entertaining guests at Tremaine Court, could hold no house parties, nor could she attend more than one local party a month—as if there were any

real entertainment to be found in Sussex. Bath in the off-season was a mecca of activity compared to Sussex.

Shopkeepers and tradespeople waited upon her at Tremaine Court, with bills for everything from her most personal items of apparel to the food in the kitchens sent to the solicitor for his examination, leaving her with nothing save a small quarterly allowance—funds that went straight to that London bitch. Even these would halt immediately if she dared to set foot off the estate for more than a half dozen hours at one time.

Lastly, visits to the nursery had been strictly limited to three per week, with either Moina or that upstart trollop Kate Harvey to remain in attendance at all times.

Melanie pushed at her blond curls as she thought of Edmund's final command, believing it to be the one grace he had shown her. What need had she of a drooling infant? Surely no more than she had of a withered, crippled, impotent husband.

Yet, with all his strictures, and all his purported love for his heir, Edmund had allowed Tremaine Court itself to fall into disrepair, the estate now a fitting reflection of its crippled master. The comparison amused Melanie and her good humor returned, her growing tension easing slightly as she brought herself back to the problem at hand.

Edmund. Edmund dying. Edmund dead. Edmund lowered into the ground, dirt piled heavily on top of him, holding him down, worms feeding on his eyes. Edmund erased from her world forever. Now, before he summoned the strength to alter the will he had signed just after Noddy's birth. Now, while he still clung to the conventions enough to know that it was only fitting that his wife be placed in charge of his son's inheritance. Now, before she found it impossible to continue to be good, before she found it impossible to stay away from London.

Her smile grew, her pleasure intensified, as her dream took her beyond Edmund's death and to that longed-for removal to London. The child could not stop her. Noddy

held no power over her. Moina could not keep her, for, with Lucien once more in her bed, there would be no further need of Moina's potions.

A year. More than a year. Time and enough for him to miss her, time and enough to make him willing to listen, to understand, to forgive. She'd had thousands of hours to work out a plausible story, one that did not mention the society bitch, her sudden, crushing need for money three years ago, and her solution to a problem that had threatened to destroy Lucien's love forever.

Edmund would take the blame. A dead Edmund would have all the blame neatly tucked up alongside him in his grave, to molder there with him through eternity. A dead Edmund. A dead Edmund.

Melanie felt her throat grow tight as her senses stirred in familiar yet always welcome sexual arousement. She lifted a porcelain figurine from a nearby table, her sensitive finger-tips absently caressing the dainty shepherdess as a familiar tingling sensation grew between her legs. *A dead Edmund. A dead Edmund.*

"There you are, a living portrait of youth and innocence. It must be witchcraft, darling, for you do not age."

The figurine dropped to the floor, the impact neatly decapitating the shepherdess, and Melanie's hands flew to her mouth. God did love her! She whirled about to face the French doors that opened onto the terrace, following the sound of that special, beloved, never-to-be-forgotten voice. *"Lucien!"*

Thank heavens she had worn her new gown today, for Lucien had always liked her best in blue. The color brought out her eyes, he had told her, eyes he had said any man of sense would willingly sell his soul to have gaze into his. Had he noticed the clever way the dressmaker had designed the bodice—at her direction, of course—tucking a mere wisp of finest ecru lace into the nearly nonexistent center, to lovingly caress the high, firm swell of her breasts?

And her hair! She knew it to be shiny with health and most flatteringly arranged, for she had spent an hour before

the mirror this morning while one of the maids had combed it over the curling stick. She smelled of Lucien's favorite floral scent, the same sort she had been wearing when they met, the identical evocative perfume she had surrounded herself with ever since, waiting impatiently for the day he returned to her.

Melanie felt her hands begin to tremble as the sheer power of her happiness kept her immobile. A single tear escaped her eyes and she held out her arms, wordlessly begging him to take her into his embrace. How handsome he looked, how elegant—how virile. Her gaze went swiftly to the crotch of his well-tailored buckskins and the enticing bulge of his confined manhood, then traveled back to his face.

She realized she had grown suddenly hungry, almost ravenous.

Had he always been this handsome? His hair so dark? His skin so tanned? His body so wondrously formed? He was older now, six and twenty, and in the full flower of his masculinity. Together they would be so exquisitely perfect that when they went to London people would have to turn away as they walked by, shielding their eyes from the dazzling light of their combined beauty.

She loved him so much her heart ached with it.

"Oh, Lucien, my darling Lucien, I had almost given up all hope," she exclaimed, sobbing, as she broke free of her thoughts and ran toward him, no longer able to be ladylike, no longer capable of waiting for him to make the first move.

A moment later she had launched herself against his chest, standing on tiptoe as she rained small kisses along his cheek, the side of his throat, her fingers spread wide as her nails dug into his upper arms.

"I knew you'd come back for your Melanie, darling, I always knew," she explained between kisses, her words coming so quickly they tumbled over each other. "Moina promised me you would, even though she called me naughty for going to you too soon. You do forgive me for that, don't you, darling? I should have waited, but I needed you so. I positively *ached* with it. I should have given you time to

recover your strength, then you would have listened to my explanation. You would have understood, and I wouldn't have been so awful to you, screaming like some shameless Billingsgate fishwife. I've been so ashamed of myself! But that's all over now, isn't it? Over, and forgotten. I've been patient, I've been good, and now you're back, my darling, as my reward. You're back, and now we will be together forever, just as we always planned!"

Slowly Melanie realized that Lucien had not moved, had made no effort to hold her, to return her kisses. Fear invaded her mind, fear and a sudden pique. Could it be that he would prove mulish—after all she had been through for him? How ungrateful of him, and how inconvenient! Stepping back a pace, she looked up into his shuttered eyes, her head tipped to one side coquettishly, questioningly. "Lucien? You have forgiven your darling Melanie, haven't you?"

He raised a hand to his cravat, the strange ruby ring on his last finger seeming to throb malevolently as it captured her reluctant attention. "Forgive you, darling? Please, if you will, refresh my memory. What would this forgiveness be in aid of, as I cannot remember at the moment."

His tone. Had it ever before been this cold, this detached? Melanie's bottom lip began to quiver as pique dissolved into panic. She reached out to touch his forearm, her entire body tingling in reaction to his proximity, his scent, the promise of delights too long delayed. She hastened into speech once more. "But you must forgive me! I said some terrible things, did some terrible things, darling, that last night—things I regret more than you can ever know." The quiver re-formed into a pout. "But you were so horrid to *me,* darling, as well, when all I wished to do was love you."

"Really? How perfectly brutish of me, to be sure." Lucien stepped out of her embrace, straightening his lapels, as if the state of his jacket were more important to him than savoring the delight of Melanie's embrace. She experienced a brief, uncomfortable memory of his last homecoming, and her

complaint that he might muss her gown, and she allowed him his small, silly revenge. After all, Lucien had come back to her. She could afford to be magnanimous.

He walked past her, picking up the ruined shepherdess and placing it on a table before standing in front of one of the striped satin couches that were arranged around a low, circular table.

"I was quite ill, you know, and my recollections of that time are dim. But wait! Ah, yes, a slight, faintly unpleasant memory niggles now at the edges of my mind," he said, motioning for her to be seated so he could do likewise. "But that is all ancient history, Melanie, and best forgotten—especially as I have torn myself from the gaieties of London and driven down to the back of beyond for another reason entirely." He hesitated, raising her hopes, only to dash them by asking, "Tell me, Mrs. Tremaine, is your husband at home?"

Melanie sat on the very edge of the couch facing Lucien, avidly drinking in the sight of her beloved. He was punishing her, yes. But she could tell, she could see it in his eyes, in the way he looked at her—he loved her still. No man could touch her, no person at all, and ever be free of the passion they felt for her. No one. Not Edmund. And not Lucien. Didn't he understand that? How could he just sit there, outwardly so composed, and not want to hold her? Her own heart pounded so fiercely she could scarcely breathe, let alone conduct a polite conversation. What had he asked?

"Edmund?" she questioned warily. "You've come to see Edmund? But why, darling? He is nothing to you. He is nothing to either of us, save a temporary inconvenience. Please, Lucien, if you must talk, let us talk of you and me. There is so much you need to know. I cannot begin to tell you how unhappy I have been."

Lucien extracted an enameled snuff box from his waist-coat pocket, expertly flipping it open with one hand. Melanie fought the urge to applaud his elegant dexterity. Raising a small pinch of the special mixture to each nostril

in turn as she watched, he said, "Truly, darling, I'd really much rather you did not. I have discovered I can scarcely bear listening to other people's trials and tribulations. To be brutally honest, I have always found them fatiguing in the extreme. Tell me, please, do you by chance serve refreshments to your guests at Tremaine Court, or has such a quaint custom fallen into disuse?"

Melanie eagerly jumped up from the couch, feeling unaccustomedly gauche, and raced to the bellpull, summoning one of the servants and imperiously ordering that refreshments be brought at once. Mr. Tremaine must have been on the road since before dawn, and had to be near to perishing with hunger!

Once she had dismissed the servant she turned back to Lucien, half afraid he would be gone, that she had been dreaming his return. But no, this couldn't be a dream. In her dreams, Lucien had never been so cold to her, so unforgiving.

This new Lucien frightened her even as he aroused her. Loving her, he had been wonderful; aloof, he became irresistible. If she had wanted him before, she wanted him twice as much now. She wanted him as he had once wanted her, as much as he would want her again. She had only to be patient. He had come back, hadn't he?

She simply needed a little time, and he would be hers. Everything would be hers.

"Lucien, you will have to forgive me for a moment. Promise me you won't move! I really must search out Beasley and have him prepare your old rooms for you. They are directly next to mine. Isn't that above everything wonderful? Please, you are staying here with me, aren't you? You wouldn't be so cruel as to tease me with your presence, just to leave me alone once more."

She took a small step in his direction. Her voice shook, but she couldn't rid it of its tremor. "I would wither and die if you left me again, darling. Truly, I would."

She tensed, nervously awaiting his answer as he unfolded his long body gracefully, rising to walk past her in the

direction of the hallway. He stopped just at the door, turning to smile back at her.

"Poor little Melanie. So endearingly helpless, so easily flustered—so endlessly appealing. I remember her well. Yet I seem to vaguely recall another time, and another Melanie, a cold, grasping woman whose methods and morals would put Prinny to the blush. These faint memories we spoke of earlier continue to tickle at the edges of my brain, to confuse and confound me. I must put them down to the delirium of my illness, and forget them.

"But, to answer your question, as I am well aware of your agitation—yes, darling. I will be staying a while at Tremaine Court. The time has come for me to seek out the answers to some very important questions of my own, and I have come to the conclusion that those answers lie somewhere in this house."

"Yes! And I can give you those answers, Lucien." She rushed over to him, staring up at him intently as she lifted his right hand to place a kiss in his palm, before pressing that palm to her nearly bared breast. "For now, remember only this. My heart is pure and chaste with love for you, darling. Feel it, just there, beating for you, living for you. We have been victims, you and I—and dearest Pamela as well—victims of the lust of a wicked, *wicked* man. You will learn the whole truth now that you are back where you belong, now that you have come home to Tremaine Court, to your darling Melanie."

Lucien withdrew his hand, although she felt convinced he did it only reluctantly. Her nipples, hard as small, rounded pebbles caressed by the cascading waters of an icy stream, strained against the thin material of her gown, begging release.

She suppressed a laugh as she watched him watch the rapid rise and fall of her breasts.

"The truth lies with you, darling? Then my journey has not been in vain," she heard him say quietly, his words fighting their way through her sensual fog. His gaze returned to her face, his dark eyes shuttered so that she could not read

the thoughts he hid so well behind meaningless, unnecessary words. "How wonderfully gratifying. I believe I shall begin my search for this truth of yours with Edmund, however, as I presume he must be the lustful ogre of whom you speak. Please see that my refreshments are brought to wherever that 'wicked, *wicked'* gentleman might be found."

"Edmund has taken up residence in the south wing, darling," Melanie explained quickly, taking Lucien's arm as she walked with him down the hallway, leaning her tingling body into his, reaching yet another level of arousal. She felt so ready for him, so weak with love, that she needed his support in order to remain erect.

"That terribly plain, terribly boring Kate Harvey guards him night and day," she said, her ragged breathing making speech nearly impossible. But she must keep on speaking, delaying the moment, holding him close by her side. "In his sickness, Edmund has begun to believe my presence serves only to advance his myriad infirmities. It's just as well, though, as the sight of his wasted body sickens me. In truth, darling, I have had no husband since Edmund forced himself on me while you were not here to protect me. I have spent these last years as chaste as any nun, praying nightly in my lonely bed, beseeching God for your quick return."

She stopped, turning to face him, pressing her head against his broad chest. "Oh, darling, hold me, love me— pinch me so that I know I'm real, that you are real. I am so happy, so very happy!"

"Very well, darling, if I must." Melanie felt Lucien's hand on her hair, rhythmically stroking her perfumed curls, finally sensing his body relaxing against hers, accepting of her fevered embrace. An involuntary sob tore from her throat as the last of her fears dissolved, to be replaced by a nearly overwhelming ecstasy.

Even when he did not kiss her, but only gently disentangled himself from her clinging arms to walk into the south wing, his tall, strong body a symphony of perfection, Melanie's optimism did not waver.

She watched as he knocked on Edmund's door and, a

moment later, stepped into the room, closing the door behind him.

"Moina!" she called joyfully, hitching up her skirts as she ran back to the foyer and the wide, divided staircase that led to the first floor. "Moina! Dearest creature! It is just as you said! My darling Lucien has come back to me!"

CHAPTER 9

∽

But all was false and hollow. . . .

John Milton, *Paradise Lost*

*T*he south wing composed the most recent addition to Tremaine Court, being no more than seventy years old, and the windows here were larger than in the original structure, although just as deeply set in the three-foot-thick walls. The room Lucien entered had been closed against the sunlight, the heavy velvet draperies drawn tightly over the windows so that he had to stop, waiting for his eyes to adjust to the dimness, before he could go on.

He moved through two sparsely furnished, high-ceilinged connecting chambers, his footfalls muffled by plush Aubusson carpets, before detecting the sound of voices coming from what had once been a good-size reception room, now, obviously, converted to another use.

Approaching quietly, uncaring that what he was doing was not particularly honest, he stopped just outside the open door to listen.

"Edmund, please, do not carry on so," he heard Kate Harvey implore, her tone anxious, as if speaking to a fractious yet well-loved child. "Lucien has not been home

above an hour. I know you're happy to have him back. We all are, aren't we? He will come to you soon, I am sure of it. I wouldn't have told you, not if I had known it would upset you so. Now please, let me wipe your face and hands with this damp cloth, and brush your hair. You cannot want Lucien to find you looking this way. He will see you soon, you'll talk, and everything will be wonderful again. I promise."

Her words were followed by a gutteral male moan, and a small, pathetic whimper.

Outside the room, standing in the artificial darkness, Lucien closed his eyes, his head dropping to his chest. He should have remembered—eavesdroppers often heard more than they wanted to know. He felt physically ill, and utterly defenseless. Kate's letter had warned of Edmund's unexpected relapse, his increasing frailty—but Lucien had chosen to disbelieve her claim, deciding to see the truth for himself. Damn it! Word of Edmund's decline was occasion for celebration, not concern. And concern for Edmund's condition had not brought him back to Tremaine Court.

The attempt on his life had done that. Only that, even if he had tried to make Garth believe otherwise in order to keep the stubborn, well-meaning man from accompanying him.

Now if he could only discover some way of making his heart believe the story his mind told.

Lucien took a deep, steadying breath, clasping his hands together, to rub at the smooth ruby ring—his talisman, his curse—before knocking on the partially opened door and entering the room.

"My, my," he said brightly, deliberately taking out his handkerchief as he struck a pose and allowed his gaze to stray about the candlelit room, deliberately avoiding the large, heavily draped tester bed that looked so out of place among the walls and tables laden with Pamela Tremaine's most prized possessions.

Lucien swallowed down hard on the need to cry out in agony, in denial. He had envisioned this meeting a hundred

times, from a thousand perspectives. He, dealing from strength, would wound Edmund with his tongue, destroy the man with his accusations, his revelations. But never had he envisioned a scene such as this. As he looked about the room, helpless to do otherwise, shock after shock assailed his senses.

Oil paintings of his beautiful, smiling, dark-haired mother, more than a few of them depicted with her young son at her side, took up the majority of one wall. He remembered posing for several of them, his mother speaking to him as Kate Harvey had just spoken to Edmund, promising a reward if only he would stand still another few minutes.

Pamela's extensive collection of porcelain roses crowded a half dozen tables, nearly making up for the absence of fresh blooms. He had given her the delicate spray of yellow roses supported in a small gilt basket the summer of his sixteenth year, the piece purchased with money saved from his quarterly allowance. The blood-red roses had been a gift from Edmund as she recovered from a terrible chest cold that had frightened the Tremaine men by its intensity. The delicate pink rosebuds had been Lucien's attempt at appeasement as he had announced his purchase of a commission in his majesty's service.

The mantel clock that had been Lucien's present to his mother on the last Christmas they had spent as a family graced the Inigo Jones chimneypiece, flanked on either side by Pamela's well-worn prayer books and her prized rose-crystal-and-silver rosary that she had sworn had been personally blessed by the Pope.

There was more, much more, but Lucien knew himself to be in no condition to consider mounting a more thorough inventory of Edmund's hypocrisy. A sudden, sharp anger, overwhelming in its intensity, cleared his mind of these reminiscences and blinded him to anything save punishing his late mother's husband.

He took another three steps into the room, placing himself a good ten feet from the foot of the heavily draped four-poster bed. When he spoke, it was to those velvet

draperies. "Your loving wife said you had taken over the south wing, Edmund, but I had no idea you had converted the place into a shrine. How overtly maudlin—and yet so strangely unaffecting."

The sound of Edmund's unintelligible groans came to him through the velvet.

He touched the handkerchief to the corners of his mouth as Kate Harvey stepped out from the draperies on one side of the bed to glare at him, her distaste clearly mirrored on her beautiful face as she approached, her gray eyes sparkling with anger. What a striking female! Melanie had called her plain, he remembered as he glared at Kate, hating her for the loyalty to Edmund he saw displayed in her stiff carriage, but then Melanie had eyes for none save her own pink-and-white beauty. Otherwise, Kate Harvey would not be within fifty miles of Tremaine Court.

"You're a bloody fool, Lucien Tremaine," Kate said quietly, forcefully.

Her frank speech delighted him, for now he knew for certain that his words had drawn first blood. Edmund must be cowering behind those velvet draperies, no longer certain he wished to see Pamela's son. "So now I'm a fool, am I? How that assessment would wound me, Miss Harvey," he drawled, openly baiting her, "were I to value your opinion. As I don't, please step aside. I am here to visit," he hesitated, merely for effect, "your master."

He moved to his left. She moved with him. He moved to his right, and she was there before him, blocking his way. He stood his ground, raising one eyebrow as he looked down at her. His reading of her anger had not been wrong. Edmund had found himself a veritable dragon in his defense. Did she honestly believe the man worthy of her protection? What a pity. Lucien's opinion of Kate Harvey's intelligence dropped a notch. "Dare I be rude, darling? You begin to annoy me."

Her chin came forward in an attitude of belligerence as she countered swiftly through clenched teeth, "Annoyance does not begin to describe your affect on me, Mr. Tremaine,

and personally, I shouldn't care if you stood here all the day long and made an utter ass of yourself. However, I have my patient to consider. Edmund has been quite ill this past week, as I wrote you, and word of your arrival has greatly upset him. If you cannot be civil, I suggest you leave— now."

Lucien noticed the way her hands had drawn up into fists, as if ready to fly at him in defense of her employer. "I should like one day to introduce you to my man Hawkins, Miss Harvey," he remarked in real amusement. "You are much of a pair. Please, forgive my boorishness. I am perhaps so overcome with emotion at this pending reunion that I have become somewhat silly."

He deliberately schooled his features into an attitude of penitence. Kate continued to glare at him a moment longer before stepping to one side. "Don't stay too long. Edmund tires easily."

The woman was a true Original. "Your courtesy, Miss Harvey, fair bids to unman me." He made her an elegant leg, employing his handkerchief to advantage as he swept his arm wide, then watched as she exited the room, sure she would go no farther than the other side of the door she had left open in her wake. He silently vowed to make her regret that decision.

Lucien's smile faded, as he had been brought back to the matter at hand, the long-overdue, endlessly rehearsed, yearned for yet at times feared confrontation with Edmund Tremaine.

He remained standing, unwillingly immobile, searching inside himself for the elation he should be feeling at this moment, this long-awaited moment of truth, if truth could be considered the correct word. The man in that bed had brought Lucien low, had betrayed him, had all but destroyed him, in mind as well as spirit.

Now, if Kate Harvey's letter could be believed, it was Edmund who had been brought down, all the way down, to the point of desperation.

Edmund Tremaine had cost Lucien his mother, his fian-

cée, his name, his innocence, his thirst for life. But he had also cost Lucien his father, the only father he had ever known, had ever wanted.

At this man's knee Lucien had learned to ride, to shoot, to love the land they had ridden across together, land he had believed would one day be his. At this man's side he had grown to manhood, listening to him speak of honor, politics, crops, gifted writers and poets, and—most important and, considering the man's actions of three years ago, most contradictory—the difference between right and wrong. From this man's example Lucien had cut the pattern for his own life, believing that no man could dream of a more perfect happiness than that shared by Pamela and Edmund.

Lucien had never longed for the gaiety of London, for pleasure-filled nights spent in gaming parlors, ballrooms, playhouses, or the beds of willing women. He had wanted what his father had already possessed in abundance, what his mother had given her husband. Lucien had wished nothing more from life than love. Love, and peace, and a family of his own.

What he had found was Melanie, war, and the ultimate betrayal. Edmund Tremaine had taken everything, leaving him with nothing.

He turned on his heels, intending to quit this room, this house, these sanity-destroying memories. He had been lying to Garth, perhaps even to himself. He *had* come here in answer to Kate Harvey's letter, using the excuse of that letter to see his "father," talk to him before it was too late—and he had been a fool to come back. What had he hoped to gain? What could seeing Edmund Tremaine do for him now?

Or had he fallen so low that he believed it possible to take comfort from another man's pain? Had he become no better than this man he hated?

The sound of agonized sobbing came to him from the bed, halting him just as he had been convinced his speedy departure from Tremaine Court would be best for everyone.

He inhaled deeply through his nose, drawing in the sickeningly sweet scent of illness, of decay, that permeated the chamber, when he had hoped to breathe in courage.

Why did he feel pity for Edmund? The monster in that bed had cursed him for a bastard, helped to make him an orphan. Had Edmund used Pamela's deception in order to rid himself of a wife he'd tired of, in order to take the young, beautiful Melanie into his bed? And if he, Lucien, truly believed that, if several hundred endless days and nights of thinking and wondering had brought him to that single damning conclusion, why did he long to do nothing more than throw himself across Edmund's bed, begging the man to love him again?

Lucien distrusted Melanie, could never forget his last macabre night at Tremaine Court, dismiss her terrible, twisted logic and her taunting screams, but now that he had seen her again he could not entirely discount the notion she could be as much victim as villain in the piece. She had been recently orphaned when they'd first met, alone in the world except for a reclusive aunt in Bath, and so achingly young when he'd left for the Peninsula. So much the innocent, so sweetly confused and vulnerable.

His lips drew into a thin white line, his fingers curling into his palms. Melanie had been so innocent and vulnerable that he could not bear for her to remain in Bath with her uncaring, bedridden aunt—a woman who had not even deigned to meet with him. No. He had made arrangements for her to arrive at Tremaine Court the very day after he had gone off to war, where she and Pamela could plan the wedding that would take place upon his return, where she would remain safe, under the watchful protection of his loving "father."

Pity? He had none. Not for the man, not for the wife.

Lucien turned back, walking to the side of the bed to ruthlessly pull back the draperies, to stand looking down at the man who had said the sight of the bastard Lucien Tremaine disgusted him.

"Hello, Edmund," Lucien said, his smile wide, steadfastly

refusing to see the man as he appeared now, but only as he had looked the last time he'd seen him, frantically trying to cover his wife's naked body with his robe as he ordered the bastard Tremaine out of the house. "Oh, happy day! Your bad penny has come back."

Lucien Tremaine had only been back in residence a few hours, and already Kate had a lengthy list of grievances against him. Calming Edmund after the man's visit took nearly an hour, and yet another hour had passed before she had felt it safe to leave him, so that, in the end, she had entirely missed luncheon.

Stealing an apple from the kitchens in the hope it would ward off hunger pangs until the dinner hour, she went in search of Lucien, fully prepared to tear a verbal strip off his hateful, arrogant hide.

Fifteen minutes later she found him standing outside the ruined greenhouse, staring up at the broken panes. The sight of his well-tailored clothes and calm, unruffled demeanor only intensified her anger.

"You miserable popinjay!" she said by way of preamble.

She could have said more, if she were not so thoroughly put out with him. She would prefer to have said less, hitting him squarely between his shoulder blades with the apple core to gain his attention.

Lucien turned slowly, leaning on the elegant malacca cane that he carried, she surmised, because it had become the vogue to have one. She thought he would most probably take up wearing pink stockings and a feather in his nose if fashion dictated he should.

"Miss Harvey," he intoned languidly, his words accompanied by a slight, openly mocking bow. "We meet again. How perfectly delightful. Are you aware there is smoke coming from your ears? And you have called me a popinjay. Should I take that to mean you do not care for my ensemble? My tailor would be sadly crushed to hear so. But perhaps you would prefer I wore a hair shirt? No, I have it—sackcloth and ashes!"

Games! He wanted to play verbal games with her. Well, she was having none of it! She tossed the apple core over her shoulder with more force than aim, to have it land somewhere in the nearby bushes, advancing on him as she spoke. "How could you have been so cruel?"

He extracted an enameled snuff box from his waistcoat and opened it with an expertise that galled her, going so far as to offer her some before taking a pinch for himself. If there were any justice in this world, he'd sneeze all over his pristine waistcoat. But he didn't, of course. Kate found herself disliking him more with each passing moment.

"Cruel, darling? Are you perhaps referring to my meeting with Edmund? Surely you are in error. I am never cruel. In fact, I was goodness itself. I believe I should be rewarded, rather than condemned. Even you, with your dainty, shell-like ear pressed against the crack in the door, must acknowledge that I behaved most civilly, passing a quarter hour with amusing chatter of this and that, a few anecdotes concerning the goings-on of the *ton* sprinkling the conversation, and taking a timely withdrawal, per your command, so as not to tire your patient unduly."

She longed to slap—no, punch!—his handsome, grinning face. "Gibberish! Not a single word of comfort, of reconciliation. Not a hint of love or forgiveness. You offered him nothing but gibberish! Have you no eyes? Are you blind to all but your own consequence? The man is desolate, despairing."

He seemed to hesitate a moment, lending her some scant hope she had reached him, but when his answer came it came fast, delivered in staccato tones as brutal as iron striking against vulnerable flesh.

"The man, darling, is a vegetable—with a head no more capable of conversation than a cauliflower, a cabbage. His body is as shrunken and shriveled as a dried bean; half his face droops in the way of a wilted lettuce leaf pushed to the side of a dinner plate in distaste. If I should ever wish to make my confession, or if I should ever feel a compulsion to

either implore or offer forgiveness, I would not seek to do any of those things at the bedside of a bloody botanical garden."

He raised the cane so that it rested lightly on his shoulder, leaned forward to look into her eyes, and smiled as he added in a very different voice, an almost kindly voice, "There, Miss Harvey. Have I shocked you? Would you like to slap me? Will you turn on your heel and go away? That would be most gratifying. Or will you perhaps burst into maidenly tears? Edmund cries, you know. He cries, and he drools. They seem to be his only parlor tricks. Both are rather off-putting, don't you agree?"

"My God, how they have hurt you!" Kate exclaimed before she could guard her tongue, before she could harden her heart to his obvious pain. She could not afford to feel sympathy for this man. She could not afford to feel *anything* for him.

Lucien straightened, his smile intact, although it did not reach his dark, unreadable eyes. "Your letters to me to one side, I hadn't seriously considered you to be the sort prone to melodrama, Miss Harvey."

He flipped the cane forward and then sideways, to tap one end of it rhythmically against the palm of his hand. "Miss Harvey. Miss Kate Harvey. Surely you weren't christened something so ordinary as Kate. Could it be Kathleen? No. You don't look in the least Irish. It must be Katharine. A Greek name, I believe; its meaning, 'pure one.' Are you pure, Katharine?"

She knew his intention, damn both him and that cane he used to such advantage. He wished to divert her attention, knowing she had hit on the truth behind his cold, unfeeling exterior, the reason for his studied ruthlessness.

But she was not to be dissuaded, even if his words caused her to flinch inwardly. "I know Edmund has hurt you, Mr. Tremaine, Edmund and Melanie alike. But you must have retained some compassion. They cannot have beaten all of your mother's gentleness out of you. My letters explained

why you are needed here, remember? The man is dying. He desperately needs your forgiveness. Is that so impossible? And if it is—why did you come?"

As Lucien took her bare arm to leisurely lead her toward the broad steps that led up to the terrace, she visibly flinched, and hated herself for this easily read reaction to his touch.

"There was this man, Katharine," he began, his tone conversational rather than instructive. "A good man, not without his little vices, his small failings, but basically good. For the sake of argument only, we shall consider that man to be me. Then one day a trusted friend—someone like Edmund—told this man something, some terrible half-truth, or possibly a whole truth, but yet an unnecessary unburdening concerning the man, that so sickened him, so destroyed him, that he lost all will to live."

Kate fought for control, Lucien's nearness unexpectedly affecting her, causing her to react in a way she could not understand. In short, and to her immediate shame, she liked the feel of his hand on her arm. "I don't quite see the point of your story. Edmund is dying, Mr. Tremaine, not you."

"Hush, Katharine. The man I speak of wasn't really dying, unless we consider the death of the spirit. We are dealing in a sort of parable, you understand. But to continue; upon hearing that the man lay dying, the friend rushed posthaste to his bedside, begging forgiveness for the terrible thing he had done."

As Edmund longed to beg forgiveness of Pamela's son. Kate nodded as she picked her way across the unscythed grass, supported by Lucien's strong grip on her arm, her gaze returning again and again to his handsome, impassive face while he told his story.

"The dying man told his friend, 'Take this pillow from behind my head. Carry it to the very top of the tallest building in the town, slit it open, and let the feathers fly away into the wind. Once that is done, collect up all the feathers, every last one, put them back inside the pillow, and

return it to me the same as it was before. Then, and only then, will I forgive you.'"

Kate felt her hopes for Edmund plummet to her toes. "But that would be impossible!"

Lucien smiled down at her. "Very good, Katharine. Have you by chance heard this story before? That is exactly what the friend said. 'That is impossible!'"

They had reached the terrace and he released her arm, stepping away from her, so that she felt suddenly, strangely lonely, when she had never felt lonely before, only alone. She longed to retire to her room to think, to ponder, and, perhaps, to weep—for what, she did not know.

He spoke again, reclaiming her attention. "To which, I must add, the dying man replied, 'Just as it is impossible for you, my friend, to give me back what you have taken from me, the life I had so loved.'" He bowed to her formally. "And that concludes today's lesson in absurdity. Good day, Katharine."

Kate watched him walk away, swinging his cane as he went. She knew what he had meant. She had suffered a similar disillusionment. Like feathers on the wind, blown thither and yon, her own dreams had been scattered. Lucien could have been speaking about her, about her life, the security and happiness—the innocence—she had lost, never to be regained.

She remained frozen where she stood, unable to do anything but press her hands to her mouth, watching.

She must have been out of her mind to believe bringing Lucien back to Tremaine Court would make any difference, to think he would care. To believe he still retained the capacity to care any more than she had retained it when her world had been shattered.

Kate had long ago compared the occupants of Tremaine Court to the shadows she sometimes watched at night through her bedroom window, shadows of trees blown by the wind so that they appeared to be scurrying from the light, hiding from the moonlight in dark corners of the gardens, afraid of what that light might reveal.

Now Lucien Tremaine had returned, to be added to the list of shadowy creatures, alongside Edmund, Melanie, Moina, and herself.

They all resided here in their own separate hells, but at least they had chosen to do so. But not Noddy. For the love of heaven, not Noddy. Please, not Noddy. Edmund's son was no more than a baby, totally innocent, yet forced to exist in the shadows, away from all hope of light.

"Damn you to hell, Lucien Tremaine," Kate cursed quietly under her breath as she watched him walk toward Melanie, who had drifted out onto the terrace from the drawing room, "you were our only chance, our last chance! My pain was as great as yours, my heartache as terrible, but I have learned what you refuse to learn, what you refuse to face. The sun still comes up each morning, Mr. Lucien Tremaine, whether you deign to notice it or not, and the birds still sing, which you would know if you'd just take the time to listen. A time must come when you put the past, and the blame, behind you and rejoin the world. If you refuse to learn that, you might as well be dead!"

As she saw Lucien open his arms to Edmund's wife, as Melanie, laughing, flew into those arms, pressing her blond head against his chest, Kate grimaced, sickened by the sight. He was playing with Melanie, playing with them all, in order to watch, laughing, as they desperately struggled to gather up all the feathers and put them back where they belonged.

And, even worse, he seemed to be enjoying himself.

Kate turned away, heading for the privacy of her room in the south wing. "I may as well have hung my hope on the devil."

"We'll have a party to welcome you home, of course," Melanie told Lucien, having already worked out all the plans in her head. "No one of any great importance lives nearby, but there is the squire, and Sir Henry, and a few others. There is even a French comte in the neighborhood, although I believe he will be removing to Paris soon. I see

them but rarely, you understand, yet I am sure none would dare refuse an invitation to Tremaine Court."

"A comte? Such an unexpected delight. Yes, Melanie. I think I should very much enjoy a party."

She clapped her hands, delighted he was proving so amenable. It would take several weeks to organize a proper party, weeks during which she would daily draw him closer to her—and damn Edmund's strictures. Surely even he would have nothing to say against a party in Lucien's honor. "I shall set Beasley to getting the house in order while I draw up a guest list."

"You've changed, Melanie."

"Changed?" She looked up to see Lucien gazing down at her as they strolled the length of the long terrace, arm in arm, her happiness immediately replaced by panic. "Please, darling, don't say that. I know more than a few years have passed since first we met—long, horrible years—but I have done my best to stay beautiful for you."

"And so you have, darling," Lucien answered, guiding her to a nearby stone bench that sat outside the gazebo situated at the south end of the terrace, near Edmund's quarters. "I merely remarked on your change of gown. You wore blue at luncheon, as I recall. You look even lovelier in this color, rather like a dainty flower just coming into bloom."

Instantly diverted by his compliment, Melanie giggled girlishly, stroking her hands over the skirt of her sunshine yellow gown. "Then you have noticed! Today is your homecoming, darling, your real homecoming. I couldn't bear to celebrate such a glorious event wearing that tired old thing you found me in this morning."

She leapt eagerly to her feet, holding out her skirt as she twirled about in a slow circle, looking back at him over her shoulder, eager for his approval. "You do like it, don't you, darling?"

"I cannot believe you have lived without compliments all these years, Melanie. Does my paltry opinion really matter?"

Her smile vanished in an instant, to be replaced by an earnest expression devoid of all pretense. Dropping daintily to her knees at his feet, so that her skirts swirled around her, pouring a puddle of sunshine on the bricks, she placed her hands in his lap and squeezed her upper arms against her sides so that the bodice of her gown fell forward, nearly exposing her breasts.

She smiled triumphantly, regaining her confidence as she reveled in his sharp intake of breath.

"Yours is the only opinion that has ever mattered to me, Lucien," she told him earnestly, tears forming in her eyes. "I had so feared I had grown old and ugly, and you would return at last, only to look away from me in disgust."

A handkerchief appeared in Lucien's hand and he raised the pristine white cloth to his nostrils. "Never old, darling, and never ugly. I have been in London this year and more, and have yet to discover your like. Your beauty is quite singular. However, if I might make one small recommendation?"

She cocked her head to one side, anxious to hear what he had to say. A small frown ruined the perfection of his face, and that frightened her. "A recommendation? Is it my hair? Are London ladies wearing it cropped this season? I try to keep up to date with the fashions, but it is so difficult, darling, stuck away here in Sussex. I must look dreadfully out of date to you."

"Oh, dear. This is plaguey difficult for me, I fear," he answered, returning the handkerchief to his pocket as she waited, nearly sick with apprehension, for him to explain. "It is not your hair, but your scent that is outdated. How do I say this politely? It *cloys*, Melanie, clinging to everything, blocking the mind to any thought save the desire to stay on the leeward side of it. Truly, could you not find something more suitable, even locked as you are in this backwater? But not roses, darling. Anything but roses. Ah, poor lamb. I have insulted you."

"No! No, you haven't, truly, darling," Melanie answered

swiftly, averting her eyes. She wore this scent for him, in memory of him and the nights they had spent in each other's arms. How could he have forgotten? How could he be so cruel? How could she be so stupid! "I—I can only thank you for pointing it out to me. I shouldn't wish to have you distance yourself from me because of my cloying perfume. I shall dispose of it at once!"

She nearly fell as he rose unexpectedly, and without holding out a hand to help her to her feet.

"Good girl!" he said, smiling. "That is rough ground gotten over very neatly, isn't it? I cannot tell you how I have fretted, unable to muster the courage to confide in you. Now, give me a kiss to prove you have forgiven me, here, on my cheek if you please, before I go off in search of Moina. I'm quite convinced I should present myself to her before the day is out. That dear woman delivered more than one sharp cuff to my ears when I was a child, and I would not put it past her to repeat the punishment if I am remiss in my manners. Old family retainers seem to believe they are expected to take certain liberties, you know. Will I see you at dinner? Hawkins shall have arrived by then, so that you won't be forced to endure me in my travel dirt."

Moina? Lucien was going off to see Moina—leaving her here, to bleed over him, wounded by his censures? Melanie saw him through an angry red haze. How dare he toy with her like this! One minute hot, one minute cold, accepting her kisses, and then insulting her with his references to cloying scent. Her smile actually painful, she stood on tiptoe to kiss his cheek.

"Moina is usually in the nursery at this time of day, darling," she informed him, maintaining her composure only at a tremendous cost. "I will be waiting for you in the drawing room at six, as we keep country hours here at Tremaine Court."

She watched him leave, hating him, loving him. Her entire body shook with mingled rage and desire. Patience. She must have patience. She must allow him his small darts,

his veiled insults, his little hints of revengefulness. They would make him feel safe, protected from his feelings for her.

But not for long. He might strain against the golden leash she had slipped over his heart, but he would never break free. Soon he would realize that. They needed each other. They had been fashioned by God to be together, now, and always.

She looked up at the sky, checking on the position of the sun. It must have passed two o'clock. She was late today, but then she held the position of mistress of Tremaine Court, and if she wished to be late, so be it. He would wait.

She turned and began to walk rapidly down the length of the terrace that spanned the entire rear of the house, until she reached the small enclosed gazebo that stood across from the north wing.

Extracting a small key from her gown pocket, she unlocked the door and stepped inside, shivering slightly in the absence of the sun, for all the draperies in the small octagonal room had been pulled shut.

The room she entered was paneled, each separate panel displaying a pleasant country scene, the ceiling painted in a typically bucolic manner, full of half-naked cherubs, their hands outstretched as they reached for the forbidden apple. There were several pieces of furniture in the room, illuminated by two lit candelabras, the flickering light dancing against the walls.

Melanie noticed none of this before locking the door again from the inside. Her attention was drawn immediately to the low bed placed directly in the center of the room, and the youth of no more than twenty who sat, fully dressed, on the edge of that bed, his hands twisting in his lap, abusing his swollen manhood through his worn breeches.

All rational thought ceased, her cares and worries pushed to one side as Melanie gracefully glided into the wings, there only to direct the action—and Melly took center stage.

"You were to have everything ready for Melly," she scolded softly, wagging a finger at him, "and not amuse

yourself in her absence. I should punish you for being naughty. Where is it?"

The young man raced to a side table to produce the long clay pipe for her and quickly set about preparing it.

She had forgotten this one's name—and what did his name matter, when there would be a different young man next week, next month? No, not next month. Next month, perhaps sooner—please, God, make it sooner—there would be Lucien, and she would have no more need of these callow, clumsy boys.

The bowl of the pipe had begun to smoke invitingly and he brought it to her, offering it as if it were the grandest gift on earth, which it was, except for Moina's lovely potions, or Lucien's even lovelier body. She inhaled deeply of both the pipe and her companion's musky scent.

This one had a beautiful, strong body, tall and lean, and a pleasant, not totally vacant face. No. Not his face. She must concentrate on his beautiful body.

She felt the familiar welcome throb begin between her legs, so that she pulled down the bodice of her gown, her breasts released to perch themselves pertly above the tightly stretched material, her nipples hard, aching to be touched. She swayed forward, lightly rubbing the very tips of her nipples against the youth's slightly rough homespun white shirt. It felt good. It felt very good.

Yet something was still wrong.

She felt strange, tense. Yes. She remembered now. Something *was* terribly wrong. She didn't accept the pipe again, but only stepped back a pace to inquire, her full bottom lip thrust forward in a pout, "Melly's perfume, boy—do you like it?"

"Yer perfume, ma'am?" he asked on a gasp, gulping so that she giggled, watching his Adam's apple climb halfway up his throat. He dared to reach out, unbidden, to touch her breast—but with reverence, just as he ought, for she was not some blowsy slut for him to tumble in the stables. She was a lady, mistress of Tremaine Court, and the most beautiful, the most desirable woman ever to walk this earth. He should

be on his knees, weeping with joy at the sight of her perfection.

"Yer perfume smells jist like heaven, ma'am, truly it does!"

"Idiot!" She slapped his hand away, so angry she could kill him, if only to wipe that imbecilic grin from his lying lips. Her head pounded, and tears stung her eyes, making it difficult to see. "It is a terrible scent! Melly reeks of barnyards, the dung heap, and running gutters—like you!"

She stepped forward, grabbing the pipe from his hand, drawing soothing smoke deep into her lungs several times. There. That was better. The opium soothed her taut nerves, so that she offered him a turn. "Never lie to Melly, little man. When you lie it makes Melly so very, very sad." She stroked his cheek lovingly, cupping his chin with her palm. "But never fret. I will allow you to make her happy again."

The pipe regained her attention and she placed it to her lips once more, an airy sensation entering her brain, her weightless body beginning to mimic the sweet, swirling smoke that filled the air, feeling light, and capable of floating above the floor.

She handed him the pipe, drifted to the side of the bed, and stood there, swaying gracefully as she slowly inched her skirts higher and higher, so that he could see she wore no undergarments. She stared at him as the middle finger of her left hand slid between her thighs, to begin stroking her silken skin. She smiled as he gasped, his eyes dark with hunger.

Lifting her hand, she licked her glistening finger with the tip of her tongue, drawing out the action as she watched the bulge of his manhood strain against the buttons of his breeches.

"Let me see your mouth," she ordered as the youth approached to stand in front of her, his hands on her waist, steadying her. "Remember? I warned you to have it clean this time, with none of the mutton from your meal hanging between your teeth."

Her jaw grew tight, her heart thudding in her ears. Her

words came quickly, tumbling over themselves as she hastened to say them before the mushrooming fog of pleasure concealed them from her brain. "Ah, your teeth, darling. Remember? Gentle nips, small bites, sweet nibbles to tease Melly's most secret places. Your tongue hard, flicking, moving, drawing small tantalizing circles . . . as your lips pout, sucking the honey into your mouth. Remember, darling? Remember what I've taught you?"

Her eyes widened, the periwinkle blue nearly lost outside the dark, dilated pupils, the whole entirely surrounded by dazzling white. "Open your mouth!"

He did as she said, which pleased her, but then he put his hands to the top button of his breeches, preparing to open it.

"No! Not that way. Not yet!" She shook her head, nearly toppling over, for she had grown so dizzy. She felt otherworldly, and very, very powerful. Very in control of her life, of him, of her future. Her eyelids grew heavy, and she allowed them to close.

How dare this upstart boy presume to attempt such a liberty? He was just like Lucien! Taking, taking, and never giving. How dare he tease her, toy with her, torment her with his flattery one moment and his denunciations the next? Lucien. Lucien. An image of his face floated in front of her closed eyes and she smiled, welcoming the dream that became her only reality. Darling, ungrateful Lucien! She had played by his rules long enough. For more than a year she had played by his rules, even by Moina's rules. Now she would call the tune—and they would all dance to it!

"On your knees, bastard!" she ordered, pushing the youth who had become Lucien—who always became Lucien, who always would be Lucien—to the floor, before she collapsed onto the edge of the bed.

She lay back on the mattress, her skirts hiked up above her flat, white belly, her legs spread wide, her fingers digging into the soft golden curls as she opened herself to his gaze. "Now, darling. Now it is time to pleasure Melly!"

CHAPTER 10

The childhood shows the man,
As morning shows the day.

John Milton, *Paradise Regained*

The first things Lucien saw as he entered the schoolroom
were his tin soldiers, a vast collection abandoned by him
years earlier, but never really forgotten. A smile tugged,
unbidden, at the corners of his mouth. There were some
good memories left. Not everything had been destroyed.

He walked over to see that the brave soldiers of King
Henry V had been neatly arranged on the soft wool carpet,
the French once more aligned against the English. It wasn't
quite as stirring as the battle at Agincourt, but it would do.

He picked up one of the pieces, remembering how the
paint on the soldier's jacket had chipped the day it had
tumbled to the floor in the midst of a cavalry charge.
Confined to his bed by some childhood illness or another, he
had passed the time staging mock battles on his rumpled
coverlet, some of them fairly pitched battles, as he recalled.

Those had been carefree days, long before the realities of
war, of life, had intruded.

He replaced the soldier, noticing for the first time that the

troops were not only set up in neat rows, they were positioned correctly, ready to engage each other in battle, cannon and foot soldiers in their proper places while senior officers hung back, to direct operations.

The English had split their cavalry, however, which Lucien did not consider to be a good strategy, as it left their right flank unprotected. He squatted down on his heels, unmindful of his clothing, his consequence, and began redeploying the pieces.

A quarter of an hour later the carpet had become littered with soldiers, cannon, and several small building blocks Lucien had unearthed from a nearby cupboard to employ as hills and boulders, better defining the perimeters of the battlefield.

Lucien was on his knees now, lost in play, his comfortable position making it easier for him to move the pieces. There was a lull in the battle and the time had come to remove the dead and dying from the field. The French had proved worthy opponents, but not strong enough to withstand a lightning charge by the Staffordshire brigade, a fierce bunch of fighters who had shown no quarter and asked for none in return.

Master killers.

As he had been in Edmund's mausoleum of a bedchamber two hours earlier. Lucien knew he had behaved badly, spouting nonsense—gibberish, Katharine had called it—mercilessly disregarding Edmund's tearful, pleading eyes, his heart-clutching moans.

Lucien gathered up a handful of soldiers and slowly, almost automatically, replaced them in the leather case that had been specially fashioned to hold them, a vision floating before him that contained nothing but Edmund's ravaged face, half of it sagging, the once handsome features now vaguely grotesque.

But what else could he have done? To acknowledge Edmund's startling condition, his obvious deterioration, would be to open the door to the notion that he, Lucien, had not been the only one to suffer the torments of hell this

past year. He wasn't ready to admit to any pain save his own.

Why should he? Had the world turned so topsy-turvy that he, the victim, should be expected to feel sympathy for the man who had been the instrument of such appalling destruction? Edmund wanted his forgiveness? Edmund, who had surrounded himself with relics of his life with Pamela, as if this action would somehow absolve him of blame, while the woman lay prematurely in her grave? It was preposterous.

And then there was Melanie. Sweet, clinging, cloying Melanie, who possessed the face of an unpolluted angel, the body of an accomplished sinner, the fascination of an entrancing siren, and—his jaw tautened, his lips thinning—no more sense of ethics than a loosed cannonball. If he had arrived at Tremaine Court still harboring some faint hope that Melanie had married Edmund only because she had been caught up in circumstances beyond her control, that hope had died the moment she had opened her mouth.

Still beautiful, more exquisite than any woman he had met before or since, more seductively powerful, more arousing to his senses, it had taken every shred of his hard-won composure not to push her away from his body, sickened by the touch of her. Yes, that was it. Melanie was a sickness. He saw that now, as he never could have three years previously.

The green-as-grass Lucien Tremaine of three years ago had been captivated by her air of vulnerable innocence, caught up by her beauty, mesmerized by the undeniable power of her perfect, eager, nearly insatiable body. But two months of courtship, two months of carnal delights he hadn't known existed, and two years of remembering those months while in the Peninsula could not stand up to the misery of the more recent past, the memory of his final night at Tremaine Court.

Yet she seemed to believe that he had returned to Tremaine Court to claim her, to pick up where they had left off. The convoluted workings of her mind, coupled with the seemingly simple logic of her speech and her eagerness to

please, fascinated him, as a swallow might be fascinated by a snake.

"Here you be, Master Lucien, makin' a fine mess, as usual," Moina said, taking him by surprise as she entered from the nursery, her footsteps as silent and devoid of warning now as they had been the day she had come into this same room to discover him sneaking his dog Hero into one of the cupboards even though the animal was not permitted in the house.

Habits learned early die hard, and Lucien scrambled to his feet, a ready excuse springing to his lips before he caught himself, remembering that he had long ago outgrown the strictures of the schoolroom. Just as he had long ago outgrown Moina even if he had found it impossible to maintain his anger at the woman's defection. She was just too simple to have hurt him purposely.

"You've found me out, Moina," he admitted wryly, crossing the room to lean down, kissing the old woman's papery cheek, a duty kiss, for he had years ago figuratively tucked Moina away in this same nursery as completely as he had packed away his toy soldiers. Now, all grown up, he looked at her with adult eyes. Never tall, Moina seemed to have shrunk in stature as well as in importance. Her shoulders stooped, her neck and head thrust forward like the figurehead on the prow of a ship, as if to help the rest of her to navigate through the sea of life. "Does this mean I shan't be allowed a pudding with my evening tea?"

He watched as she progressed past him to a nearby chair and sat down, ignoring his joke.

"I'd all but given up on you, Master Lucien," she said, employing the steely glare that had once possessed the power to reduce him to knee-knocking terror. "At first, I told myself you'd come back, just to see me at least, but you didn't. I told myself over and over again that you was sulking, 'cause it was me what sent the packet to the Fox and Crown, 'cause it was me what knew it all and didn't tell you. But I also told myself you was a good lad, and you'd get past it after time."

She looked up at him searchingly, so that he noticed for the first time how really ancient she had grown, how very frail. "But it took that last letter from the gel, didn't it, Master Lucien? She came begging me for your direction in London town as soon as you'd run off, so I know about them letters. All them letters. Even the one what she wrote after that little spell Edmund took last week brought him low again. Shame on you, Master Lucien. It took Edmund to get you back, and not me—the only one here what really loves you."

"Love, is it?" Old habits and long-ago affection fled unlamented at her last words as those words reminded him of her seeming defection of a year ago. "And was it also this great love that kept you silent when I needed answers? This same love that caused you to send Kate Harvey, a stranger, to me at the Fox and Crown with the message that I was the living spit of my father—not to mention gifting me with a miniature of that same unknown father? Silly me, not to have seen it earlier. It was your love for me that prompted your actions. I should have known."

She pointed a finger at him, her hand trembling, her rheumy eyes filled with quick tears. "Don't you dare! Don't you dare talk to me like that, my boy. You don't know what it is you're saying. You didn't have to do the choosing. You were sick, sick to dying. I had to get you gone, get you away from this sinful place, so you could grow strong and come back to settle everything. It near broke my heart. But I couldn't let you die, not like your mama died. You—you were all I had left of her." She covered her face with her hands as sobs overtook her. "All I had left of my sweet baby."

The Moina of Lucien's childhood had never cried, never shown any emotion although, deep inside, he had always known she loved him. He knelt at her feet, thoroughly ashamed. In his anger, his disillusionment, he had chosen to forget Moina's intense devotion to Pamela. He had never really looked at the events of the past through Moina's eyes. His sorrow had been too selfish, too one-sided, to include

any one else's. "Moina, I'm so sorry. You're right, of course. I never thought it through. When Katharine brought the packet and your message to the Fox and Crown, I simply began to hate you along with everyone else. You had to have known all along, known all about my real father. Yet you never told me, not even when I lay in the north wing, not yet fully aware that my world had exploded. I should have realized you only acted as you thought best. It hasn't been pleasant this past year, Moina, becoming accustomed to the fact that I am a bastard Tremaine. It seems I am now twice the bastard, cutting you out of my life as well."

He laid his left hand on the woman's lap, squeezing the gnarled fingers she held out to him. "God, Moina, what a mess I have made of that life."

Moina took a deep, shuddering breath and he watched, amazed, as she brought herself back under control. "I'll be the judge of that, Master Lucien. I see you wear Christophe Saville's ring."

Her severe tone told Lucien that Moina regretted her tears and wished to return to her former position of power, that of a long-time servant who had no qualms about speaking frankly to the son of the household. He looked intently into her face, his eyes deliberately shuttered. "I wear my father's ring, yes. It serves as a reminder, and keeps me humble. You knew him, didn't you? All I've been able to figure out is that he lived somewhere near Paris. What was he like?"

"What is a man? They wear breeches, talk too loud, and drink too much. A man is a man, and they all been cut from the same cloth." The old woman shrugged, saying nothing more, and Lucien knew there would be no more said about his real father, at least not now. Moina could be as silent as the tomb when the mood struck her. After the events of the past, who should know that better than he? Yet he wanted to know, needed to know. Who was Christophe Saville? Had his mother truly loved him, or had he simply used her? How had Edmund been duped into accepting Lucien as his own child? Why had all of this happened?

"Tell me about my mother's death, Moina," he asked at

last, hoping to learn something, anything at all, that might help answer his questions. "You were right. I wasn't ready to hear about it before. I'm ready now. I've already learned that she became lost in a storm, fell sick, and died a few days later. The innkeeper at the Fox and Crown mentioned how he had made up one of the party sent to search for her, not aware that I hadn't known any details of Mother's last days."

Moina's eyes shone with tears once more. "Those were terrible days. It's my own fault, and I can't forgive myself. I been punishing myself for them these past three years and more, punishing myself in ways you can't never know, ways what are for sure going to send me to that everlasting hell your mama always told me about. I tried everything I knew, I swears it, everything I ever learned, but I couldn't save her. She didn't want to live no more, Master Lucien. He broke her heart."

She stared at him intently, her eyes dry, yet eloquent with pain. "They *both* broke her heart."

Lucien frowned at the woman's distress and said, "I know, Moina. Both Edmund and Christophe hurt Mother. But that's all I know. Even Hawkins couldn't tell me more, although he did say that you were the one who sent him to await my arrival at the mansion in Portman Square.

"Christophe Saville may have left my mother, but he provided his bastard son with a London house and a not inconsiderable fortune. Another man would have walked away from it all, I suppose, called it conscience money and scorned it—but we bastards are not given many chances, Moina, and must take what we can get."

The vehemence with which he spoke those last words surprised him. How long had he been this disgusted with himself, with his actions? He squeezed the old servant's hand again. "Please, Moina. There's so much I need to understand if I'm ever to have any peace."

Moina rose from the chair to go to one of the windows that looked out over the rear of the house. Lucien followed,

standing behind her as they both stared down at the terrace that lay three floors below, Lucien impatiently waiting for her to speak.

As he watched through the windowpanes the ground-level door to the gazebo at the north end of the terrace opened and a tall, young farm laborer walked out onto the grass. He looked left and right before turning back to lock the door with a key he pocketed, then retrieved a rake that had been propped against the wall and moved quickly away. Lucien thought the young man's appearance and actions strange, but quickly dismissed them as none of his business.

What did it matter to him if the lad had been tumbling one of the kitchen wenches in Edmund's north-wing gazebo? "Ah, Moina, did you see that? Springtime and young love. Even here at Tremaine Court, life goes on."

Moina sniffed and turned from the window, only to return to the chair, seating herself once more. She picked up her knitting and began working the needles with a dexterity that belied her badly twisted fingers. When she spoke again, it was to tell Lucien some of Pamela Tremaine's history, her simple country speech lending an air of believability to a story that seemed too bizarre to be creditable.

For Pamela, the end had come not six weeks after Lucien had departed for the Peninsula, even if the seed that marked the beginning of that end had been planted almost two dozen years earlier.

Lucien learned that Edmund had somehow discovered a small collection of letters and official papers, communications from Christophe Saville to Pamela Tremaine. Some letters had spoken of the great love they had shared one long-ago summer, others of Christophe's plans for Lucien, his son.

"She only kept them for you, Master Lucien, not out of any love for that fast-talking, pretty Frenchie. She tried to tell Edmund as much, but he wouldn't listen. You know Edmund. Proud. Stubborn. All he knew was that she had betrayed him, stomped all over his love and trust, he said. I

heard him. All the servants heard him. You could have heard him on the moon!"

"That doesn't sound like Edmund, Moina. I can't remember him ever raising his voice to me, to Mama, to anyone." Lucien recalled Edmund had always shamed him into owning up to his misbehavior. Edmund must have been devastated, to have lost control like that. Poor Mama, Lucien thought; having never seen him like that before, she could never have known how to deal with such anger.

The knitting needles continued to fly, taking up lengths of yarn from the great ball that sat in a basket at her feet. "My baby was so young when she was promised to Edmund Tremaine, too young. Her papa saw it as a way to get the Kingsleys back in their house, in their proper station before he died with your mama left alone and near penniless. He meant well, I suppose, but your mama didn't hardly know Edmund, let alone feel affection for him. Talked about running away, she did, to a nunnery.

"But she couldn't do it. She couldn't disappoint her papa. When that Frenchie came along unexpected-like, it was like a second summer had come that year for my baby. She was so happy, she was, the two of them laughing and singing—such pretty children, looking enough alike to be two peas in a pod. Oh, I should have stopped it, Master Lucien, but my baby was so terrible happy. How could I have broke her heart?

"Then he sailed for home, to tell his papa how he wanted to marry. There was a storm in the Channel, and the local fishing boat he hired went down, losing most all the hands that sailed on her. My baby made herself sick with crying when she heard the news. Not only was her Frenchie with the fishes, but no one was left to save her from being married off to Edmund."

Moina laid down the needles, staring into the middle distance, as if reliving all that had happened.

"My poor baby cried so that first night, Master Lucien—on her weddin' night—still lovin' that Frenchie the way she

did," Moina explained, her voice a dull monotone that made Lucien's flesh creep. "Edmund had to believe he wuz beddin' a virgin. It wasn't until her time come, when we saw your sweet face, Master Lucien, that we knowed the Frenchie had left behind more than that-there ring you're wearing. Your mama couldn't tell Edmund then, not when she had grown to love him, for he was proper good to her. Even cried, so happy he was to have a son."

It was then, the servant said, that Pamela, with Moina's blessing, had decided to live with her lie.

According to Moina, the only problem had been Christophe's miraculous return to Sussex about six months after Pamela had given birth. It seemed that he had been rescued by another boat, one bound for Calais. It had taken him all the ensuing time to recover his health and gain his father's permission to return to England. The man's anguish at learning Pamela had married nearly destroyed her new-found peace, as did his entreaties for her to leave Edmund and flee with him and their child to the continent.

But his pleas had been to no avail. Pamela loved Edmund now, and Lucien was the world to her husband. She could not leave, would not leave. At last, Christophe had retreated to the continent, vowing to return one day and claim his son. The year had been 1788, and France was already beginning to rumble with warnings of the coming Revolution.

Christophe Saville never came back to Sussex again, nor, after the papers detailing his gifts to Lucien had been delivered, had there been any more letters.

"I told her he must have lost his head in that Terror business, but she wouldn't hear none of it. Her Frenchie had done the right thing, she swore to me, that's all, and loved her enough to leave her in peace." Moina shook her head, smiling. "A bit of a dreamer, your mama, you know. Didn't like thinking about anything dying, not even one of her precious posies. And you were her proudest creation, Master Lucien—her most perfect rose. When you growed up

and went tripping off to war your mama cried and cried, sure you'd end up staring across a battlefield at your own papa."

Lucien returned once more to the window, to stare out over the gardens. "I can barely wait for this miserable war to be over, so that I can travel to France to learn Christophe's fate for myself. But I have to agree with you, Moina. I too think the man is long dead."

"Not that him being dead could have made it any the easier for your mama," Moina said, frowning as she dropped a stitch. "Nothing she said that day made it easier for my poor baby, and she said plenty, begging for Edmund to believe how much she loved him. She should have walked away from him, you know, waited for him to remember how happy the three of you were. But she was too overset to think straight, I suppose. She just let him rant and rave until he ran like a coward into his study with a bottle, then she took herself off, out of the house—just before that storm come blowing in off the Channel.

"I almost found it in my heart to forgive him when he come home carrying my baby in his arms, tears streaming down his cheeks, begging for me to help her. He didn't have no pride then, Master Lucien, not nary a drop. He just sat right next to her bed, holding her hand for three days and nights, begging for her not to leave him."

Lucien turned away from the window. "I find that hard to believe, considering he married Melanie within a few weeks of my mother's death."

Moina smiled. Lucien was sure it was a smile, and it struck him as odd, considering her next words. "When my baby breathed her last, just as dawn was trying to save her from the dangerous hours of the night, Edmund stopped his crying soon enough. I can see him yet, grabbing your dead mama's shoulders, shaking her, shaking her hard, and yelling and screaming at her for leaving him. Cursed her something awful, he did, saying she had left him to live without her, to live with all she had told him. Said he hated her for what she done to him. Wouldn't even go to the

funeral. He took that white-haired bitch into your mama's bed that same night, before the dirt was settled on the coffin. No, I'll never forget that, Master Lucien. Never forgive none of it, neither."

Lucien dropped his head into his hands. He had wanted the truth, and now he had it—and that truth was worse than anything he had imagined.

"I guess you could say he lived to feel right bad about what he said, what he did, but that makes no difference to me. He said it, and I heard him. There's more to tell, I suppose, much more, but I'm old now, and tired. You'll have to learn it for yourself, because I'm through talking. You have come back, Master Lucien, and not beforetimes either, for I'm fast getting past it. You ain't the only one what hates him, you know. The times I've itched to end it, you can't know. But I've made him suffer, in my own way, made all the guilty suffer, just like we ought to, just like my poor baby suffered. Now you have to finish it."

"Finish it, Moina? What do you propose I do—call him out? The man can't even walk. It's over. My mother's dead. Edmund is married to Melanie, which seems to be enough punishment for any man. What else could you possibly want me to do?"

"Don't you listen? It ain't over. Not yet. You have to put the finish to the thing. Just like it's up to you to figure out the rest of it, for there's more trouble brewing about now, ready to strike you down. I seen it already, and so has Edmund. Nearly did him in last week, which ain't fitting, as the end has got to come from you. And don't go asking me what I mean, 'cause I ain't going to tell you. You owes it to your dear mother, for it's you what stirred it all up, you know. Ain't knowed a man yet what didn't live between his legs."

Lucien leaned against the window frame, his heart heavy with all he had heard. "I started it all, Moina? Is that what you mean? Oh, of course. I see. You mean it all began with my birth."

"Do I? Mayhap. Mayhap that's only a part of it." Moina carefully put away her knitting before rising. "You'll be

supping alone this night, Master Lucien," she said, a faint hint of amusement creeping into her voice once more. "Mrs. Tremaine won't be joining you."

"Really, Moina? She seemed so eager to have a welcoming dinner with me. Has she taken ill?"

Lucien had answered automatically, not really paying attention, not really caring. His old nurse had raised more questions than she had provided answers, and he needed time to think. Melanie's absence at dinner tonight, the lack of her distracting presence, could only be considered a blessing.

"No. She's not sickening for something, Master Lucien," the servant answered obliquely, her laugh a dry cackle. "At least, no more than usual. Besides, she's just now got a good dose of her medicine." Her head turned to the right, toward the door to the nursery, and she put a finger to her lips, as if to warn him against speaking.

"Kate Harvey's coming, Master Lucien, to bring the little one back from seeing Edmund. Guards that baby like a tiger, she does, so be careful. She's a strange one. Keeps her door locked up tight at night, and carries a knife in the pocket of her gown. A good gel, though. Took fine care of you when I needed spelling."

Lucien had been about to inquire about this new danger Moina had spoken of, but at the woman's last words his head snapped up. He hadn't been dreaming it after all. Katharine had been in his sickroom when he had come back from the Peninsula. The body he vaguely remembered pressed against his had been her slim form, the lips he had kissed had been Katharine's full, pouting, yet obviously disapproving lips, so different from Melanie's demanding mouth.

He smiled in rueful realization. If he hadn't been convinced earlier of the extent of his delirium, he knew better now. It would have taken either a very brave man or one half out of his head with fever to attempt to kiss Katharine Harvey without her permission.

"The formidable Katharine seems to have made herself

quite indispensable at Tremaine Court, hasn't she, Moina?" he asked now. "It's Edmund's doing, of course. The man lives through his women, you know. Yes, Moina, it's sadly true. I've thought about it hard and long this past year, and I am certain of my conclusion, even without knowing what you've just told me. Without a woman by his side he is no more than a cipher, a shell.

"No wonder he hated Mother when she died. To his twisted way of thinking, she had done far worse than betray him, she had deserted him, leaving him aware of his own mortality. No wonder he married Melanie, who is an expert at causing a man to begin believing himself nearly godlike. And no wonder that now, in his physical weakness and fear, he has called upon Katharine Harvey to be his protector. Had Wellington two hundred like her, the French would have been vanquished long since."

"I like her well enough, Master Lucien, for all her taking care of Edmund," Moina said. "Don't go poking her head in where it ain't needed. Minds her own business, and don't cry about her own troubles."

"Which, my dear Moina, makes Miss Harvey either a very intelligent young woman, or one who has her own secrets to consider. Actually, with Miss Harvey, I would say both descriptions probably apply."

He began walking toward the door to the nursery. "Excuse me, Moina, if you please. I am feeling particularly brave this moment, and have decided it is time I met Edmund's heir."

Kate enjoyed her time spent with Noddy more than any other. The child's trusting, unconditional love had brought her out of herself, rescued her from the emotionless limbo she had existed in, first from choice and then out of necessity, since leaving The Willows.

She watched him now, sitting so straight and tall in his little chair, his blond curls mussed, his angelic blue eyes drooping with fatigue, as Edmund had proved particularly reluctant today to let his son go. Noddy had been very brave,

not recoiling from his father as Edmund cried, clutching the child to him with his good arm, refusing to let Kate take him away at the usual time.

"Tea, Mama?"

Kate had long ago given up attempting to stop Noddy from addressing her as his mother, and only replied automatically, "Yes, sweetheart. Noddy will soon have a lovely tea, with a very special bread pudding, just as you asked. And then it's a bath for you, my fine young man, and a bed. You've had a busy day."

"Indeed, yes, Katharine." Lucien Tremaine's cultured drawl came from somewhere behind her, shocking her into immobility. "But not nearly as ambitious as yours. Avenging angel, protectress, devoted nurse, and now loving *mother*, all between a single sunrise and sunset. Turn around, Katharine, to see me standing before you in awe. Is there to be no end to your talents?"

She refused to do his bidding, keeping her back to the man as she swiftly responded to his softly delivered insult. "Noddy. Stand up, sweetheart, and do just as I have taught you. Say how do you do to your half-brother, Lucien."

"Hardly his brother, darling," Lucien responded, his voice so close to her ear that she could feel his breath, warm against her neck, and so in contrast to the coldness of his tone. "As I recall, the word *bastard* dribbled most smoothly off your tongue not so many hours ago."

She turned to face him for just a moment, knowing he was near, yet still unable to keep from flinching as the movement brought her within easy touching distance of his powerful body. She whispered her answer, her eyes on Noddy, who stood in the center of the room, looking lost. "It is Edmund's wish that his scandal stay inside the family. You still use the name Tremaine. The estate is not entailed, so that Noddy is to be Edmund's heir, but the proprieties must be upheld. Now, please, say something to Noddy."

"There are so many titillating snippets in your words, Katharine, that I don't know which to address first. The word scandal is used as if Edmund, rather than I, had

something to hide, for, after all, he is happily wed once more, while I will always be a bastard. If only I were a royal bastard. Why, I might even then be able to garner a title out of the business.

"But to continue. You speak of family as if you are included in this particular one, although why anyone would wish for such a dubious distinction I cannot entirely fathom. Lastly, you seem so curiously familiar with Edmund's planned disposition of Tremaine Court. Truly, the mind boggles. But all this must wait, mustn't it, for the child cannot. Edmund's child. Melanie's child. Gracious, in some strange way, I do feel a slight kinship with the infant."

Kate watched, her heart beating at a fearsome pace as Lucien walked past her to perch with nonchalant ease on the side of a table, one leg swinging back and forth freely as he spoke. "Noddy, is it?" he asked, looking down at the sturdy, rosy-cheeked child. "You may not believe this, but once upon a very long time ago I lived in this nursery. I sat in that same chair, just as you were doing when I came in, impatiently awaiting my tea. Did you know, Noddy, that just as soon as you grow another inch or two you can push the chair beside that window over there, stand up very tall on its seat, and see over the tops of even the tallest trees, all the way to the pond?"

Noddy approached Lucien, smiling up at him as he reached out to touch the tassel on the man's riding boot. "Noddy see?"

Kate stood quietly, unable to decide if she should be happy or sad. Noddy's world had from birth been extremely insular, so it pleased her that he should react so well when confronted by an unfamiliar face. She also knew herself to be grateful for Lucien's apparent kindness toward a small child. Yet the poignancy of the scene struck her forcefully.

This had been Lucien's nursery. Tremaine Court had been Lucien's legacy. This child, this usurper to all that had been Lucien's, represented a union between the man he had believed to be his father and the woman he had chosen for his wife. Kate wouldn't have blamed Lucien if he had turned

on his heel and left the nursery, leaving her to deal with Noddy's questions.

Lost in her own thoughts, what happened next took her totally by surprise. Noddy's small hand slipped into Lucien's large outstretched one and the pair disappeared into the schoolroom, Lucien saying something about toy soldiers. Intrigued, Kate followed, to stand just inside the door, watching as Lucien sat on the floor, explaining his arrangement of the English and French troops.

What followed was a half hour Kate knew she would never forget. Noddy, a bright child, but a child just the same, soon lost interest in the soldiers and began arranging the blocks in small piles, just to knock them down again. Lucien seemed to understand, leaving the soldiers to begin rummaging through the cupboards, at last unearthing a battered wooden puzzle of the British Isles, and the two, dark head close to blond, lay belly down on the carpet, inserting the pieces as Lucien put names to each.

"This is Wales, Noddy, a lovely place where everyone's name, by law, must include at least three *L*s and four *W*s, and the people are usually very short, most probably from carrying such heavy names around with them all of their lives. And this green piece, well, this is Ireland. When you are all grown up, Noddy, I suggest you visit this place. Most especially a city called Dublin." He looked up at Kate and, to her amazement, winked at her. "There are some very friendly young ladies to be found in Dublin."

Kate allowed herself to be amused. She jammed her fists onto her hips, leaned forward and asked, shamelessly imitating Maureen, one of the maids from The Willows, "And is it corruptin' the lad you'd be about then, Master Lucien? Ah, sure and it's the divil himself at work, don't you know."

Lucien looked up at her, laughing, a lock of midnight black hair falling onto his forehead. "Cheeky miss," he said before Noddy, pulling at his sleeve, called his attention back to the puzzle.

His eyes. Kate leaned against the doorjamb, her knees

threatening to buckle beneath her. Lucien had smiled at her with his eyes. What manner of man was this? She had seen him purposefully cruel, so frigidly detached, that she had despaired of his capability to show any human emotion save suppressed rage. Yet now, only a few hours later, he had given her a fleeting view of Pamela's child, the caring youth whose copybooks filled with poetry written in his own hand she had discovered stuffed into the rear of one of the nursery cupboards.

Kate suddenly knew that, illogical as it seemed, she would do anything to have him smile at her that way again, to catch another glimpse of the Lucien Tremaine who had grown to manhood beneath this roof.

She stayed very still, watching as Noddy, usually a well-behaved child, stood up, only to straddle Lucien's back, begging him to play "horsey." It was a game she and the child often played in the nursery, and one that had a lot to do with romping and very little in common with any notion of decorum she would associate with Lucien Tremaine.

"But then, I've been wrong before," she told herself quietly as Lucien rose to his knees, his hands spread on the floor, and began walking about the room, a giggling Noddy holding on by the simple expedience of grabbing two fistfuls of his "horsey's" hair.

After Mary had come into the room with Noddy's tea tray and Kate had kissed the top of his blond head, promising to be back later to tuck him up, she followed Lucien out of the room, into the hallway.

"You were wonderful in there, Mr. Tremaine," she said as they headed for the stairway leading to the first floor. "Thank you."

"Yes, darling, I was, wasn't I? Tell me, what sort of monster did you believe me to be, that I might consider punishing the child for the sins of the parents?"

So much for her hopes. The flat tone of his voice effectively brought Kate back to reality. What had she been thinking? That Lucien Tremaine had turned from angry

avenger to cuddly lapdog in the space of one short half hour? That he had become human again thanks to the influence of an innocent child?

"Forgive me, Mr. Tremaine, I overstepped myself," she said as they paused at the landing, directly in front of a blatantly flattering portrait of Hollis Tremaine that had been banished to the nursery floor decades earlier. "But I promise, I shan't compliment you again."

"Or thank me."

She longed to push him headfirst down the stairs. "Yes, Mr. Tremaine. *Or* thank you. Now, if you'll excuse me?"

"No, Katharine, I'm afraid I can't do that. Amuse me, if you will. I find that there is something I must know, a missing puzzle piece I may have discovered just today— something to do with a certain disturbing incident during my recuperation that I have just now learned may have included you." He took a firm hold of her arm at the elbow just as she was about to turn away and pulled her along with him, down the steps. He steered her along the first-floor hallway, down the wide, divided staircase to the ground floor, past the clearly astonished Beasley—who had been pretending to dust a wall-mounted silver candle holder— and out into the late-afternoon sunlight.

Kate felt panic rising in her. He had to have been referring to the night he had pulled her down into his bed, the night he had held her, kissed her, run his hands so intimately over her body. Surely he was not trying to recall his memories of the nights she had forced gruel through his lips or the times she had helped Moina tie him to the bed to keep him from hurting himself while he thrashed about in delirium.

"This is an outrage! Where do you think you're taking me?" she asked, trying to catch her breath.

"I'm taking you somewhere that we can be outrageous," he answered, wry amusement evident in his tone, giving her arm another tug.

By the time they reached the open gates of the forecourt, Kate's breath was coming rapidly, partly from exertion, but mostly from fear. Fear also kept her silent, as did a tingling

anticipation. Did he mean to thrash her for what he might believe was her impertinence—or did he mean to kiss her again, as if for comparison?

Lucien turned to the left, Kate pulled along in his wake, continuing on until they were beyond the iron fence of the forecourt and standing amid a small, deliberately planted stand of beech trees.

And then she knew. He meant to kiss her.

Without another word passing between them, without any sort of preamble, Lucien pulled Kate against his body, his dark gaze centered on her eyes. She felt his intensity piercing straight through her, penetrating all the way to her soul. A moment later he lowered his head, his mouth claiming hers.

Why hadn't she put up more of a protest? Why hadn't she applied to Beasley for help? She had known all along that Lucien meant to kiss her. Had she really thought herself ready for this? Had she actually been foolhardy enough to believe she had at last succeeded in banishing all those terrifying memories of The Willows, so that she considered herself ready to begin a normal life once more?

If she had, she had been wrong.

Panic, not passion, flared fully into life, to become her primary response, Lucien's preemptive possession catapulting long-suppressed horrors suffered at The Willows to the forefront of her mind. She struggled with fierce determination, repeatedly beating her fists against his strong, broad chest, desperate to be free.

He made no move to release her. He did not hurt her, not physically, but just kept on kissing her, as if oblivious to her fear. This was no weak Lucien, sick and clearly inferior to her in strength. She could not escape him now as she had done that night in his room.

Kate's mind whirled. The memories continued to flood into her consciousness, taking control.

Strong hands had held her fast like this once before—before pawing at her, ripping at her gown, touching her where no male hand had touched her before or since.

Another's lips had once claimed hers in this way, punish-

ing her with their fierceness, then invading her mouth with a savage, plundering tongue—taking, taking, taking. Screaming had been an impossible solution then, and most probably useless even if she had been able to find her voice. Her strength had not been equal to *his* strength either, as it diminished to nothingness now beneath Lucien's strength.

Yes, she had lost this uneven battle between man and woman once.

But she had learned. Panic would not help her. She had to help herself.

Kate summoned all her cowering will, all her strained sanity, and forced herself to relax in Lucien's embrace, her mouth still his possession, her eyes open wide as she looked into his face, at his closed eyes—assuring herself he had become too engrossed to notice that she had figuratively stepped away from him, removed her inner self from the scene, beyond his physical domination of her person.

Slowly, and staring at him all the while, her right hand moved down, down, to slip into the pocket of her gown. Her fingers closed on the hilt of the small silver knife, her private symbol of security, that rested there. Willing her mind to blankness, she raised her hand once more, freeing the knife from the pocket.

She closed her eyes—and brought the blade down.

Lucien's hand closed around her wrist, stunning her with both its swiftness and its viselike strength, squeezing, until the knife dropped from her nerveless fingers. Still holding her wrist, Lucien raised her arm upward, placing her hand on his shoulder before, his mouth never leaving hers, he gathered her even more closely into his arms.

Tears stung her eyes, so that she closed them, unable to summon the courage required to keep them open. Her body sagged slightly against his, admitting defeat, even as she breathed a small, silent sob into his mouth.

Then, quietly, and so subtly that it took her several moments to notice, Lucien's kiss changed, no longer searching, but resembling a gentle persuasion. His mouth no longer took, but gave. His arms did not imprison her now,

but cradled her gently, supporting her as if he knew, as she knew, that she could not stand on her own.

Panic receded, to be replaced by a curious awareness. She had been wrong. This was no assault; this had never been an assault. He had made no move to touch her breasts, her body, no attempt to squeeze or fondle or probe. He was simply there, against her, with her, surrounding her, pulling her back inside herself, banishing her terror, making her aware. Aware of him. Aware of herself. Her own body.

Now it was that body that betrayed her, moving against his without the courtesy of asking permission, her lips softening, opening, allowing his tongue free entry.

He instantly took up the invitation.

Still the fear did not come back, the horror did not return to rear its loathesome head. In their place came wave after wave of the most disturbing sensations Kate had ever experienced.

Her throat tightened, making it difficult to breathe, impossible to swallow.

Her heart pounded, not in fear, but with an eagerness that hinted that her body knew more than she about what was now happening to it.

Her arms and legs became almost weightless, strangely bouyant appendages reminiscent of long-ago days when she had floated on her back in the pond at The Willows, the summer-warm water soothing her into a near slumber. Her arms floated now, to come to rest around Lucien's shoulders, her palms anchored against his back.

Yet she felt far from soporific, for she couldn't ignore the growing ache low in her stomach, the unfamiliar heaviness that mimicked hunger, a gnawing yearning that could never be satisfied by mere food.

Lucien's lips left hers at last, to travel along her cheek, her chin, the side of her exposed throat. She took a deep breath, in hopes a gulp of fresh air would clear her muddled thoughts and banish the bright stars now floating before her eyes.

She heard his soft chuckle of laughter. "Well, that answers

my question, doesn't it? I had occasionally thought you might be the one I kissed that night, but you can understand my inability to reconcile that memory with the young woman who wrote me such disconcerting letters. You see, that kiss was my first real memory of those weeks I spent at Tremaine Court. I had to know whose generous gift helped to bring me back when I was so lost in the shadows."

Kate took another deep breath, looking up at the trees above them, at the last, lingering, dusty rays of the sun as they filtered down through the leaves to sting her eyes, to lend a softening glow to Lucien's dark hair. She shook herself and stepped away from him. "It was no gift. And I rather think it was my *knee* that lifted you from the shadows, Mr. Tremaine," she dared to say, beginning to tremble again as she realized how nearly lost she had become in his arms. "And don't do that again. I do not like to be touched."

"Really? What a pity, dear lady, for you are so very touchable." He chuckled softly as he took her in his arms again, his teeth gently nibbling on her sensitive earlobe, the feel of his exhalation tickling her even as it fanned the smoldering hunger in her belly into a small yet steady flame.

She could barely make out his words, for his lips were pressed against the sensitive base of her throat. "Now there's the Katharine I've grown to know her letters. I suppose I could have asked, avoiding upsetting your sensibilities. But then could I have counted on you to answer truthfully? Somehow I doubt it. And I had to know it wasn't just another dream. There were so many dreams, you understand, most of them not very pretty."

She didn't want to hear this, didn't want to remember how lost he had been, or pity him again. Kate moved her head away, then placed her hands against his upper arms, pushing herself free of his embrace. He didn't try to hold her this time. "Now that you have satisfied your curiosity, Mr. Tremaine, please allow me to return to the house. Edmund will be wondering where I am."

She watched as Lucien bent to pick up her knife. His eyes

were shuttered now, as if their kiss, so devastating to her, had been nothing more than an experiment to him. "It's a good thing Moina warned me about this little toy of yours, darling," he said, holding it out in front of him, hilt first.

He was giving it back to her? Didn't he understand? She had planned to use the knife on him. Kill him, if necessary. Surely he didn't believe she had been about to martyr herself, to perish protecting her innocence like some heroine from the Minerva Press?

Kate took the knife, replacing it in her pocket, intent only on quickly putting as much space as possible between herself and Lucien, so that she could think about what had just happened between them. Right now, she hated him so much she couldn't be held responsible for what she would do if he didn't let her leave. She did hate him. Didn't she?

"Shame on Moina. Next time I'll use a pistol."

Lucien laughed out loud. "I'll keep that in mind. Moina also told me that you are a very closemouthed person, Katharine. I must admit, this—among other things—makes me somewhat curious to know more about you. Please, if you will, tell me how you came to be at Tremaine Court in the first place."

Kate felt sure this was no idle question. Lucien had decided to make sure he had not wasted his time in traveling to Tremaine Court. But if it was an amorous dalliance he was looking for, he would have better luck applying to his stepmother, for she would be more than willing to accommodate him. But not Kate. Never Kate. She had to make that clear to him.

Now, unknowingly, he had given her the opening she needed. If she didn't want a repetition of what had just occurred—and she didn't, truly she didn't—she could save herself a lot of trouble by telling him the truth. Far better, she thought, to suffer his disgust than his advances.

Raising her chin so that she looked him straight in the eyes, she announced baldly, "Of course I'll tell you. It's no great secret, and at least it was honest employment, the first in which I actually earned a steady wage. I came here to act

as wet nurse to Noddy when my own child died—my child, who had been conceived, to put it politely, on the wrong side of the blanket. Like *you*, Mr. Tremaine."

And then, before she could see Lucien's reaction, witness his sure revulsion, watch the light of humor dim in his dark eyes, she turned, head held high, and began slowly, deliberately to walk back to the house.

CHAPTER 11

And princely counsel in his face yet shone,
Magestic though in ruin.

John Milton, *Paradise Lost*

Melanie had said she would direct that Lucien be installed in the bedchamber next to hers, a notion that had caused him to wonder if she had any inkling of the definition of the word subtle.

But he also knew he had nothing to fear, if fear was the correct word. For Lucien had Hawkins, and Hawkins was nothing if not astute. In the house less than a day, he had already decided that Melanie had resumed her pursuit of his master.

Just as he had supposed, the ever-protective servant had firmly bolted the connecting door on the far side of the dressing room from the inside long before his employer disrobed for the night. Hawkins had also informed Lucien that, as he had no desire to sleep in the male section of the north wing with the rest of the servants, having once lived in the more respected butler's chamber on the ground floor, he had ordered a cot installed in that same dressing room.

"So you are to be my duenna, the guardian of my chastity," Lucien said, sitting on the edge of the high tester

bed to allow the man to remove his boots. "Isn't it odd, Hawkins? I believe I am disappointed in you."

"Disappointed, sir?" Hawkins asked, rising, still puffing a bit from the exertion of separating his employer from the custom-fitted footwear.

Lucien stood, removing his pantaloons. He had long ago put a limit to what assistance he would allow the endlessly helpful Hawkins to offer.

"Yes. You see, I had so hoped you would boldly inform me you planned to spend the night on the floor stretched out on a blanket in front of the connecting door, a blunderbuss tucked under your pillow. You are getting old, my friend, to demand the comfort of a cot."

His shirt and the remainder of his clothes were removed and handed to Hawkins, so that Lucien stood, unashamedly naked except for the miniature of Christophe Saville that hung halfway down his chest. "Now, if you'll excuse me, I believe I should like to crawl into my own bed before I drop from fatigue. It has, all in all, been quite a day."

Lucien awoke with the dawn after an uneasy night's sleep, to order his bath and tell Hawkins to see to it that his horse was saddled and waiting in front of Tremaine Court within the half hour.

He needed to get out, to escape Tremaine Court for a few hours, before he suffocated. An unwilling guest in the unfamiliarly familiar house that had once been his home, deprived even of the solace of his former bedchamber, beset on all sides by memories better left dead and new realities that sickened him, he had spent the night dreaming of a tall, unyielding young woman with eyes as gray as a stormy sea and a reluctantly yielding mouth that promised, if not salvation, at least a momentary forgetfulness—and damn that business about being Noddy's wet nurse!

Once astride Caliban, a big-chested, savage black beast whose unlovely appearance, nasty disposition, and blazing speed had already reached legendary proportions in Mayfair, Lucien's full attention became concentrated on show-

ing the stallion who was in charge of this particular expedition before they set out across the fields at a gallop.

A quarter hour later, the cobwebs effectively blown from his mind, Caliban's head tossing from side to side as his exhaled breath issued steamlike from his nostrils, Lucien slowed the stallion to a barely controlled canter, noticing that a horse and rider approached from his left across the field, the rider waving frantically to catch his attention.

The horseman had a fine seat, Lucien noticed idly, his concentration more on the superbly fashioned dappled gray mount that all but floated over the ground than on the man.

"Bonjour, monsieur! It is a lovely day for a ride, yes?" the rider called across the rapidly closing distance, tipping his hat as he approached, neatly turning the gelding at the last minute to ride beside Lucien as if he had been invited to do so. *"Nom de Dieu!* That is a most large, ugly horse you have, I think."

He stripped off one glove and held out his hand. "I am the Comte Guy de la Croix, if it is true and the filthy Corsican has been all but vanquished, so that my title will once again have meaning and, if it please the Virgin, substance. But no matter. I am simply *Monsieur* de la Croix now, aren't I, which is so much the better than *Citoyen* de la Croix, yes? Who knows, if you are to remain in this dreadfully dull neighborhood for any length of time, I might even suggest you address me as Guy, as I so dislike the formalities since coming to this soggy island. I have, you see, the lease of a most charming cottage not two miles from here. And you, *Monsieur,* are—"

"Tremaine. Lucien Tremaine," Lucien answered, shaking the comte's hand, although he did not remove his glove.

He looked closely at the man, judging him to be at least a half foot shorter than himself, though elegantly handsome and quite well muscled, even if he would not see forty again, for there were several silver hairs mixed in with his dark brown locks. The man's dress was impeccable, his riding clothes expertly tailored and without ornamentation, which

might have been just as well, for the black patch—covering the area where his left eye might or might not still be—tied to his head with a matching riband, appeared to be all the embellishment the man needed.

Lucien smiled in genuine amusement at the comte's eager friendliness. Addressing his remaining blue-green eye, Lucien said, "And unless you tell me you had nothing to do with the gelding of that fine animal, sir, you may address me as Mr. Tremaine. Otherwise, I believe Lucien would do, as we are in the country and away from the rigors of polite society."

The Frenchman gave a bark of laughter, the sound scattering a few birds that had been napping in a nearby tree. "You English, so in love with your horseflesh. So, please, Lucien—a fine French name, if I may be so bold—would it be wrong of me to believe you are attached to Tremaine Court and, perhaps, even to the lovely Mrs. Tremaine?"

Lucien directed Caliban onto the roadway, with de la Croix following behind, much like a hungry puppy would tag along after a friendly butcher. "She is my stepmother, *Monsieur*. I know you will pardon me for my own inquisitive phrasing, but do you always ask so many questions this early in the morning?"

The Frenchman laughed again. He seemed to laugh quite a lot. "Morning, noon, evening, what does it matter? Talk is wonderful, yes? It fills up the silences so very neatly. We French excel at chatter, and gossip, and romantic scheming which, alas, may explain how we could have been caught off guard by the so bloodthirsty *canaille*. We were much too busy peeking into one another's boudoirs, *mon cher*, eager for some titillation. So the delicious Melanie is your stepmother? Such a beautiful, fragile creature. Ah, what a fortunate man you are, to be sure!"

Lucien refused to be baited. As a matter of fact, he didn't care one way or the other if the man had become enamored of the "delicious" Melanie, for he, thank God, had at long last been cured. "May I then assume you have met my stepmother?"

The sun had risen higher in the sky, so that a few farm wagons passed them, heading in the opposite direction, on their way to the local market. He should be getting back for breakfast. Melanie was sure to be waiting for him, impatient to prove her love yet again. It might prove amusing to fence with her for a few minutes. He might even learn something important, some clue that could eventually serve as the key to the workings of her mind and unlock more unanswered questions from his own past.

De la Croix spoke again, reminding Lucien of his presence.

"Met her, Lucien? Ah, I have met her, danced with her—but that is all, as she is allowed out so seldom, you know. So dedicated she is, to her husband, her small son. I am of the nobility, you understand, and while romantic intrigue is like air to me, necessary, I would not so abuse the hospitality your England has shown me. And this nobility is much of a pity to me, for Melanie is so young, so eager for life. In my weakness, I dared to visit her one day last week, a paltry nosegay clutched in my paw, that is all—but, alas, it ended badly. Her husband, your fine father—he is better now, *n'est-ce pas?* Very frightening it was, to see a man struck down that way, just as we were speaking."

Lucien busied himself with controlling Caliban, who seemed to have decided he fancied having a piece of the gelding's ear for breakfast. "You were present at Tremaine Court when Edmund—when my father suffered his most recent attack?"

"Oui! He was there, on the terrace, sitting in the sun in that curious chair with wheels for legs, and nobody else about. I approached him, mumbling some pleasantry. I cannot remember my words exactly—but, no matter—when suddenly his eyes tried to turn about in his head, showing almost entirely white, and he slipped from the chair onto the stones at my feet. The pandemonium that followed! Ah, *mon cher,* it is so very good that you are here. Fathers need their sons at times like these, yes?"

Lucien raised a hand to his chest, touching the miniature

that lay behind his shirt, and succumbed to sarcasm, although he felt sure it was lost on the comte. *"Certainement,* Guy. Fathers need their sons. As sons need their fathers."

"Exactement! I have only a father myself, and he grows very old, very frail. Yet the old can prove so stubborn. He never left France, through it all. I, on the other hand, soon wearied of the hiding, and then, later, of the fighting. An eye is enough to give for a war that was never mine, yes? You have seen a gaggle of us washing up on your shores these last years, as we, I pray, will see you English in Paris very soon, to help us celebrate our freedom. But I shall wait here, on this safe island, bored but still reasonably whole until I am sure the Little Colonel is vanquished, before I return to my homeland. I only pray my dear intractable father, and our lands, will be waiting. But I should not tell you this or you will think me a coward."

"Not at all, Guy. An eye is enough to give." It would be so simple for Lucien to write this man off as nothing more than yet another dispossessed, displaced French nobleman, and a boring one at that. Simple, if it weren't for Jacky and his friends, and the knife that had nearly found its home in Lucien's back. Moina had warned of new trouble, and the affable *monsieur le comte* was, after all, a stranger.

"Perhaps I could assist in alleviating some of that boredom, Guy. Would you do me the honor of being my guest for dinner Friday evening at Tremaine Court? I'm sure my stepmother would be happy for the diversion."

"Diversion, Lucien? That is a very apt word. It all but rolls off the tongue. Diversion! *Oui, mon cher,* I should be most pleased to join you!"

Kate smiled at one of the servants as she entered the morning room, her good humor fading like the fleeting morning mist as she turned her head to see Lucien already seated, several empty dishes on the table before him, sipping coffee.

The sun shone against his back, throwing his face some-

what into shadow, but not completely hiding the handsome, powerful features. Had she ever before seen such piercing dark eyes, such finely sculpted cheekbones, such a noble nose? He sat so still, so at ease, and yet his body radiated a carefully leashed energy, giving her the impression that, if he wished it, he could leap across the table at her without effort before she could even think about mounting a retreat.

As he had leapt at her yesterday, beneath the beech trees. No. She was being unfair. Lucien hadn't leapt at her. His actions had been totally unlike that terrifying time at The Willows, that horrendous interlude that had changed her life forever. She had known yesterday that Lucien would kiss her, had somehow sensed it the moment he'd taken her arm to lead her down the stairs and outside.

She had known, and she had allowed it. Perhaps even wished it. She simply hadn't admitted the entire truth to herself until this morning, after spending a sleepless night reliving those last, confusing moments of his kiss, the moments after her immediate, reflexive, panicked response had faded and she had allowed herself to feel, praying that Lucien, this one extraordinary man, could somehow replace her long-standing revulsion at physical contact with something more normal, more human.

And he had. His touch had begun the important healing of a long-festering sore, yet it had opened another deeper, unexpected wound. The entire exercise had been a dreadful mistake. Now she would go through life knowing what she was missing, for Kate Harvey, that soiled, despoiled woman, had no right to dream of happiness with any man. If she had ever, even for a moment, hoped to believe otherwise, Lucien had given her the answer to that dream when he had not followed after her, telling her that he, a bastard, and as tainted in his own way as she, didn't give a tinker's damn about her past—it was her future that interested him.

Kate moved to the buffet table, pointedly turning her face away from him, even as she felt the heat of his gaze burning into her back, warming her. She had never been so aware of a man in her life.

"Good morning, Katharine. How nice to see you again— unarmed, I hope."

"It's almost ten. I thought you would have eaten and gone by now," she said, goaded into speaking before she could guard her tongue.

"Haven't you learned yet, Katharine? I never do as I ought." He stood, motioning her to a chair once she had finished filling her plate. He lifted the coffee pot. "Shall I pour? I'm feeling magnanimous this morning."

"Thank you, no. If you're waiting for Melanie to appear I'm afraid you're in for a disappointment. She never rises before noon." Kate looked down at her plate, discomfited to see that she had ladled two coddled eggs onto it. She loathed coddled eggs. Picking up her knife and fork, she sliced off a bit of Tremaine Court's own sweet pink ham and held it in front of her, unable to put it into her mouth. "Will you be visiting with Edmund this afternoon? He's most anxious to see you again."

"I have no doubt he is, Katharine. It positively devastates me to disappoint him. However, I have scheduled an appointment with the estate manager, a long-overdue meeting that will most probably carry me straight through to dinner."

She couldn't have been more surprised if he had said he planned flying once around the moon on a broomstick, waving his hat in the air. "You're meeting with Jeremy Watson? Why?"

He poured a cup of coffee and placed it before her. "Oh, dear. Must I really explain myself? It's so wearying, darling."

Kate bristled, biting down on the piece of ham so that the fork caught noisily between her teeth. She may not have believed herself to be the most astute person ever born but it had not taken her long to discover that, to Lucien Tremaine, the word *darling* was as good as a curse. She made him wait until she had thoroughly chewed and then swallowed the ham. "Forgive me. I've overstepped my bounds."

"Yes, Katharine, you have, and not for the first time. My

compliments. I didn't think you were aware that a person in your singular position should observe any boundaries." He leaned against the back of his chair, lifting a serviette to delicately dab at the corners of his mouth.

"My singular position?" Really! What was she, a parrot, repeating everything he said? And she knew what he referred to, knew it as well as she knew he was holding on to his temper, his studied air of indifference, with great difficulty. As she held tightly to her own. What had he expected of her this morning, that she would launch herself into his arms, begging for a repetition of yesterday's embrace, perhaps quoting him a price as she did so? A gold bracelet for a kiss? A diamond necklace in exchange for a more passionate encounter? Or did he think she gave it away for nothing, as did his dearest stepmother? "Am I to feel insulted, Mr. Tremaine?"

"I don't know, Katharine. You see—how do I put this delicately?—I have never before breakfasted with a former wet nurse who has risen so high. I can only wonder that you were not seated at the head of the table last night at dinner."

He wouldn't look so handsome with coddled egg dripping from the end of that aristocratic nose! He wouldn't be so droll once the coffee pot had been emptied into his lap!

What was his purpose? Why this attack? Surely her admission—worse, her bald *declaration*—hadn't been that important to him, that earth shaking. Did he have to sound so disappointed in her, so disapproving? Who was he to look down on her? Well, she'd choke before she'd explain that she took luncheon and dinner with Edmund and only ate breakfast in the morning room to give Edmund privacy during the time a footman bathed and dressed him for the day. And she'd be damned if she'd return to the servant's hall for her meals; retreating from Lucien's pointed barbs. The move to the morning room had been symbolic as well as actual, and she had done with retreat!

"Katharine?" His voice came to her from a distance, filtering through her anger. "I have formulated a theory. Humor me if you please. This theory concerns how you

came to know Edmund, how he came to know about your child. You fit yourself into this household with the ease of a hand inserted into a tailor-made glove. The entire arrangement seems so suspiciously coincidental, don't you think?"

Her head jerked up as she stared at him in openmouthed astonishment. It was incredible! Lucien thought she had known Edmund before coming to Tremaine Court. Intimately. He might even be putting forth the notion that she had borne Edmund a child! Could he really believe such nonsense? What else could he have meant? Of all the sick, twisted—

"Your silence betrays you. Answer me, Katharine." Somehow he had risen without her being aware of it, so that now he stood directly behind her, his hands pressing on her shoulders.

"You're mad!"

"Am I, darling? Consider the matter from my point of view for a moment. You exhibit exemplary table manners, although I still question your presence in this room. Your unaccented speech reveals your birth, as does your intelligence, and even your arrogance. Yes, darling, your arrogance. You may make a wonderful nurse, a pleasing companion, but you fall sadly short of being an acceptable servant. You don't have the humility for it."

He began massaging her shoulders, then moved so that his thumbs were at either side of the base of her throat, his fingertips slipping ever lower, to skim the first soft definition of her breasts.

"So where did Edmund find you? On that trip he took to visit his London solicitor shortly before I left for the Peninsula, perhaps? I have never been much for Cyprian Balls myself, but I understand many of the muslin company could easily pass for society ladies. And to think that Edmund set himself up as the arbiter of my mother's morals. Amusing, is it not?"

"How dare you accuse Edmund of anything so base?" She struggled to rise, but his strong hands held her in the chair.

"And may I remind you that I don't have to answer to you, Mr. Tremaine."

"Ah, darling, but you do. And it was you who pointed it out to me. You've been very helpful, Katharine, very helpful. As you yourself reminded me, I—in the eyes of the world—am the eldest son of Edmund Tremaine, his heir, his good right hand now that he is, shall we say, indisposed. This afternoon I shall see Jeremy Watson and allow him to explain to me the reason behind the current poor condition of Tremaine Court. It is my duty, you understand, as a loving son."

He sighed, overdoing it a bit, she thought, before continuing. "I have so many pressing duties. Primary among them, darling, is to ascertain whether or not my dearest, yet now woefully inarticulate *father* has set up one of his former mistresses under his roof."

Before she could consider the consequences of her action, she picked up the fork once more, jabbing the tines solidly into the back of Lucien's hand, causing him to loosen his grip. In a moment she was on her feet, facing him, her hand raised to slap his face.

Again she was to be thwarted. The man had the reflexes of a panther—swift, sure, and deadly. Pinning her hands behind her back with one of his, he pulled her against him, to punish her with his kiss, plunging his tongue into her mouth again and again as his other hand played intimately over her body from neck to thigh, rudely caressing her.

Before she could react, he pushed her away, his dark eyes bleak, his expression so coldly disgusted that she shivered. "Sweet Jesus! Am I never to have anything but that man's leavings?" She knew he was not speaking to her, but to himself. "Is that to be my punishment for being born?"

Kate wiped at her mouth with the back of her hand, shaking so violently her teeth chattered. "You don't deserve the truth, Lucien," she managed to say, "but Edmund does. I never met him until the day he came into the village looking for a wet nurse, as Melanie refused to feed her own

son. My child had been born dead, and I needed money to pay for my lodging at the Fox and Crown, as well as a place to bury my child. Edmund took me in, trusting me with his son, and now with his own welfare. I owe that man more than I can ever repay. And so do you, although you're too pigheaded, too intent on your own selfish pain, to see it!"

She watched as her words seemed to penetrate his anger, his desolation. Slowly, his eyes cleared, as if he now saw something he had been blind to until that moment. He moved toward her, his hand outstretched. "Katharine, I—"

"No!" Kate knew she couldn't bear it if he touched her again. She just couldn't. She had been used for the last time. "No," she warned him again tightly, her head moving slowly back and forth as she backed toward the door, her arms wrapped protectively around her waist. "Don't touch me! Don't you dare touch me ever again!"

And then, for the second time in twenty-four hours, she turned on her heel and slowly, deliberately, walked away from her traitorous heart.

CHAPTER 12

What in me is dark
Illumine, what is low raise and support.

John Milton, *Paradise Lost*

*L*ucien tied Caliban's reins to a nearby tree and walked to the edge of a small rise overlooking the pond that lay in a small dip of land some three hundred yards below him. He had made short work of his meeting with Jeremy Watson, his mind incapable of focusing on leaking roofs, ailing livestock, or eroded fields. All he could think of, all he could concentrate on, was the expression on Kate Harvey's face as she had stood toe to toe with him in the morning room and answered his violent verbal attack with one of her own.

No. He wasn't being entirely honest. That wasn't all he could think of. The memory of their kisses, both of them forced on her against her will, were also impossible to banish from his mind.

What was the matter with him? What perverse maggot had he taken into his head that made it imperative for him to attack the woman whenever they met?

And then he remembered.

She knew his past. Knew it, and was not afraid to throw it

in his face in order to help Edmund, whom she had championed. That's what rankled him. She had been there from the first to witness his downfall, his disgrace, and had gone so far as to taunt him with it in her audacious letters to him in London.

Where the *ton* had been neatly cowed by his carefully cultivated, high-handed manner, his purposely cutting wit, his aloof disdain—even his funereal wardrobe, for pity's sake—Kate Harvey had seen past the whole of it in a moment, to exclaim, "My God, how they have hurt you!"

How dare she see what he had allowed no one else to see? How dare she take him to task for Edmund's infirmities, Edmund's regrets? Who was she to pity him, to censure him?

A wet nurse. Kate Harvey was, had been, a wet nurse. She had lain with a man, given birth out of wedlock, and sold her mother's milk for a roof over her head and a quarterly wage.

Rather a case of the pot terming the kettle black, he would say.

No, he wouldn't say that. He couldn't. Not and be honest with himself. If her disclosure had shocked him it was because he could not bear to think of her as soiled goods. There had to be some reasonable explanation for the child. She had been betrothed to a soldier, now dead in the war. She was the daughter of an impoverished clergyman, forced to make her own way in the world as a governess, seduced by the master of the house and then turned away when her pregnancy became obvious. Something, *anything,* to explain away her lost virginity.

For one thing was certain. Kate Harvey was a lady. Her aristocratic features hinted at it, her speech and manner whispered of the quality, and she wore her arrogance as naturally as a queen wore her ermine robes.

Perhaps that was why he continued to be drawn to her. They were kindred spirits, both lost to the lives they had once enjoyed, cast outside the world they had known, to wander on their own, seeking a new identity.

He hadn't lied when he said he remembered her. But he

had remembered her eyes much more vividly than he had
the kiss he had stolen from her. Those strange gray eyes that
now sparkled with intelligence had been cold and blank the
first time he had seen them. Whatever happened that had
eventually led her to Tremaine Court, she had still been
fighting its effects when he came home from the Peninsula.

Had Edmund figured in her recovery? Had her work with
Noddy proved an answer to her loss? Or had the mere
passage of time healed her hurts, her despair? He had to
know. For if Kate Harvey could fight her way back from her
unhappiness, her disillusionment with the world, perhaps
there was hope for him as well.

But not as long as he remained at Tremaine Court,
surrounded by the memory of all he had lost.

Moina might have hinted at some sort of trouble at
Tremaine Court, but he couldn't bring himself to put any
real credence in her fears. She had become strangely prone
to melodrama when she spoke of Pamela's death. Yet she
couldn't really wish for him to kill Edmund for her—"finish
it," as she had termed it. That was only the prattling of an
old, still-grieving woman.

Jacky and his companions, the attempt on his life, he
would have to write off to either a quickly thought-up lie to
protect that fool Orton, or a coincidence—unless he wished
to consider that Moina had hired the clearly inept assassins
in order to shock him into returning to Sussex. Melanie
certainly didn't wish him dead. The vain, silly woman still
believed he had come to declare his undying love for her.
And Edmund? No, not Edmund. All that man wanted was
absolution, not another mortal sin on his soul.

And what did he want? What did Lucien Kingsley
Tremaine want? What had he hoped to gain by coming back
to Tremaine Court? Vindication? Revenge? The chance to
show the inhabitants he'd left behind that he hadn't been
crushed, that he had survived? Was it for the supreme
indulgence of dashing Melanie's hopes forever? Or perhaps
the self-serving thrill of watching a beaten man breathe his
last?

God, no. Please—he couldn't have sunk that low. He had come back because, damn him for his weakness, he still cared. Beyond the knife attack, beyond the possibility that Edmund might be dying, had lain the taunting truth of the condemnation of one Kate Harvey, a near stranger who had dared to confront him with the knowledge that he, Lucien Tremaine, had not become immune to the plight of the people who still lived at Tremaine Court.

Again, as if preordained, his thoughts had returned to Katharine.

Yes, Lucien told himself. His interest in Kate Harvey must in some twisted, some terribly convoluted way, be academic. And now that he had come back, now that he knew for certain that she too had suffered in some way, he might be able to learn from her. If she could regain her fire, if she could break free of the enervating shadows of a tragic past, perhaps he too could hope to find his way back to life.

And if he found that her way could not be his way, if he discovered that he had been wrong to believe that she, like he, had been one of life's victims, there was always the tantalizing prospect of stealing another kiss or two from her sweet, unexpectedly enticing lips.

After all, he thought, smiling as he looked down at the sunlight reflected on the surface of the pond, his visit to Sussex shouldn't be a total loss.

The surface of the pond rippled as he watched, its former stillness broken by a movement in the water, the source of which was hidden behind the small stand of trees to his left. Idly curious, and wishing to distance himself from his jumbled thoughts, he retrieved Caliban, mounted, and urged the horse into a canter down the grassy hillside, sure he would find that yet another generation of snow-white geese had made their home in the rushes that bordered the pond.

"So much for idle conclusions," he murmured appreciatively a few moments later as he smiled, watching as Kate Harvey's head and shoulders appeared above the water, her black hair sopping and flowing back from her forehead as

she pushed her hands across her face, wiping droplets of water from her eyes. "Hallo there!" he called jovially, standing in the stirrups as he waved to her. "One never knows whom one might meet when out for a ride, does one, Miss Harvey?"

He watched as she immediately sank back into the water, until her chin all but disappeared. "What are you doing here?" she asked, her hands visible as she crossed her arms, placing her fingers on her bare shoulders. "You're supposed to be closeted with Jeremy Watson."

Lucien dismounted, careful to tie Caliban's reins to a nearby branch, for the stallion had a mind of his own and was prone to indulge the whim of the moment, that whim usually taking him anywhere but back to the stables. "So I am, Miss Harvey, so I am. And where should you be, I wonder? Reading psalms to Edmund, or playing spillikins with Noddy in the nursery?"

"Your man Hawkins has kindly volunteered to sit with Edmund. It appears they know each other. As for Noddy, he is napping, with Mary in attendance." He saw her eyes dart in the direction of the bank and the clothing she had neatly folded and placed on a large, smooth rock. She appeared, to his amusement, to be judging the distance between that stack of clothing and herself.

"Feeling chilly, are you, Katharine?" he asked, walking over and seating himself on the edge of the rock, directly beside her folded gown. "Why not come out of the water, and we can talk more about your daily schedule. I'm above all things interested, truly I am. For instance—do you bathe here often? I would have thought Edmund would provide you with a tub."

A cool breeze whispered down the hill and across the pond, so that he could see Kate begin to shiver. "I have a tub, Mr. Tremaine. However, I became accustomed to bathing here when I could while I lived in the servant's quarters, and have not entirely given up the habit."

Rising, he walked to the edge of the pond and dipped his hand in the water. It was just as he remembered it from his

youth—not frigid, but still decidedly cool this early in the spring. He looked at the nearby ground, and then across the water to Kate. "I fail to see any soap, Miss Harvey."

Oh, dear. Was it really fair of him to be enjoying himself so much at her expense? Yes, yes it was. And the slight, nearly infinitesimal chance that he might yet be gifted with the sight of her unclothed body made him believe he was capable of almost anything.

"Of course you don't! I don't bathe in the pond any more. I merely swim in it. Have you no imagination, Mr. Tremaine?"

He threw back his head and laughed out loud. "Oh, my dear Katharine, you should be careful of what you say. I possess a very fertile imagination. For instance, at this precise moment my imagination is exploring the possibilities of what will occur if I were to remain on this bank until you come to the realization that it is impossible to remain submerged forever in that cold water."

She glared at him for a long moment, her eyes sparkling with suppressed fury rather than sliding from his in shame. "I could with great ease grow to loathe you, Lucien Tremaine," she bit out at last from between clenched teeth. Clenched, *chattering* teeth.

Her anger, and her struggle to control it, cheered him no end. "Yes, Katharine, I can see why you might say that. And you could grow *old* waiting for me to play the gentleman and turn my back while you exit the water. But I have just realized something. We have progressed, you and I, haven't we? Again you have addressed me as Lucien. Does that mean we might yet cry friends?"

Her hands rubbed furiously at her bare shoulders, so that he entertained the thought of stripping—with the idea of joining her in the water. He dismissed the notion just as swiftly, for he could not be that cruel, just as he could not have taken advantage of Susanna Orton in his Portman Square drawing room, no matter how low he believed he had sunk. What a damnable curse it was, being a gentleman.

"You've already proved to be far too aggressive with your casual acquaintances, Lucien. When I consider the liberties you might believe inherent in friendship, I don't think I wish to be your friend," she answered uncompromisingly, although it seemed to him that she had taken several steps toward the bank. Her shoulders, formerly only slightly visible, were now fully above water, so that he could see the faint shadow that marked the swell of her breasts.

He pulled a cheroot from his inner pocket and lit it. Blowing out a pale blue cloud of smoke, he said, "You're referring to my stolen kisses, I presume."

"There is that, of course. However, I'm referring—" she began, pausing only to look down at her chest and prudently sink another few inches into the water "—I'm referring more to the liberties you have taken with my character and your assessment of it. I did not appreciate being labeled as Edmund's former mistress."

Lucien tossed the barely smoked cheroot into the pond. Did she have to bring up that exercise in stupidity? It was bad enough that he had even thought of such a thing, let alone put his thoughts into words. "That remark was unreasonable, Katharine, and I apologize for it. I do not, however, intend to say I am sorry for stealing those kisses."

He rose, smiling at her as inspiration struck. "And, frankly, Katharine, I don't think you want me to apologize for them. Do you?"

She hid her expression behind lowered lids. "You're not completely unattractive, Lucien," she said, her voice so low he barely heard it, "and not nearly so pathetic as you were a year ago, when we first met. I've since had time to read the poems you wrote before you went off to school. And Edmund has told me so much about you, stories about your childhood, so that in some ways, I feel I know you."

She raised her chin, the fire back in her eyes. "But that doesn't mean you can kiss me again. I don't like being kissed. I don't like being touched."

She had read his poems? Listened to stories of his

childhood—including, most probably, Edmund's favorite story, a description of how a ten-year-old Lucien had loosed a frog at Squire Easton's spotty daughter's birthday celebration. Lucien scratched at a spot behind his left ear. Lord, what an embarrassing notion.

He saw that Kate's lips had taken on a faintly bluish hue and he actually began to feel slightly sorry for her. Not that he believed she would complain to him, not if a shark were to be somehow transported from the Channel into the pond and begin nibbling at her toes. "You don't like being touched? Yes, I had rather supposed as much when you drew your knife on me. I'll tell you what, Katharine—if you promise to give me that knife, I will walk to that large yew over there, and then turn my back while you get out of the water."

"Turn your back? I believe I'd rather you mounted your horse and rode off."

"Yes, I'm sure you would, but a friend would trust a friend to keep his word, wouldn't she?" Not giving her time to answer, he headed for the yew, convinced she had grown too cold not to take advantage of his offer.

As he stood staring up the hill he cursed his imagination for the images it projected in front of his eyes, images of Kate moving through the water, more of her slim body exposed to the sunlight with each step she took along the soft, muddy bottom of the pond. How he envied each droplet of water that would cling to her skin, only to run in small rivulets down the slope of her shoulder, over the swell of her breast, along the flare of her hip—

"You may turn around now."

He did as she bid, to see her standing on the rock along the grassy bank, her ugly brown gown sticking wetly to her body in several places, her hands lifted high as she twisted her wet hair into a tight bun at the back of her head. The knife lay at her feet. She looked as darkly exotic as a painting he had seen of an American Indian princess, except for the contrast of her curiously liquid eyes against her lightly tanned skin.

"You could have taken enough time to dry yourself," he said, walking back down the hill to her.

She lowered her hands, bending to reach for her jean half boots. "Even friendship has limits, Mr. Tremaine—Lucien. I thought it best not to test ours this early in the day."

"Good choice," he admitted, sitting himself beside her as she pulled on her boots. He picked up the knife, measured its balance in his palm, then pocketed the thing before she could change her mind. "It was the frog story, wasn't it?"

She turned her head away from her chore and smiled at him. "The frog story? I admit to having heard it, but it was remembering Edmund's description of the surprise you planned for your mother's gift one Christmas that proved to me that, no matter what, you couldn't be totally unlovable. Whatever possessed you to think you had any chance of having the Pope visit Sussex?"

Lucien shrugged, the memory of writing that letter and asking Edmund to post it for him coming back to him as clearly as if it had happened only yesterday. "In the end we settled for a book of the lives of the saints. She seemed pleased enough." He noticed that Kate was still shivering. "Here, now," he said, slipping his arm around her shoulders, "you must be chilled to the bone."

She shrugged off his arm and leapt to her feet, her movements so swift he was left sitting on the rock like some statue, his arm still outstretched. "I should be getting back to the house. Noddy will wake soon."

Lucien looked up at her, saying nothing, still trying to understand why he had behaved so well, when he had longed to be very, very naughty. He went to Caliban, taking the reins in his hand and following after Kate on foot. "I was remarkably good to you, you know," he commented after they had been walking together in silence for several minutes.

"You wish to be rewarded for being a gentleman?"

Her question stung at him, for he knew he deserved her censure. "We both know the answer to that. Bastards are

never gentlemen. Why did you write to me? Even if Edmund filled your head with rose-colored stories of my youth, you knew the circumstances of my homecoming, and what had transpired in my absence. How could you believe I would give a tinker's damn about what happened to Edmund, to anyone at Tremaine Court? And why, after I was so cutting to you in my letters, did you continue to write to me?"

He watched as a drop of water slid down her nape, to become lost in the growing damp stain that ringed the top of her high-collared gown. "Why? I'm not really sure. I only thought that time and distance might take the edge off your pain, your anger, so that you might remember all the happy years that preceded your breach with Edmund. His discovery, and your mother's subsequent flight and death may have been partially his fault, but he has had a long time to repent of both his treatment of Pamela and his hasty marriage to Melanie. I—I suppose that—if Edmund really is dying—I just want him to die happy."

They had reached the gate at the bottom of the garden and Lucien could take Caliban no further. "Time and distance, Katharine? Is that the answer? Is that what it took to put the light back into your eyes? You must know that you've changed. You must know that you're no longer the colorless cipher who opened the door of Tremaine Court to me a little over a year ago."

She lowered her head, flinching as he dared to put a finger beneath her chin, raising her face to him. "Yet you're not completely happy, are you? You don't like to be touched? No, Katharine. This has nothing to do with likes and dislikes. You are *afraid* of being touched. There is a difference. Perhaps you're wrong, and you don't hold all the answers. Perhaps time and distance are not quite enough. Perhaps you, like me, must still confront the ghosts from your past before you are truly free to face the future. It's an interesting theory, and one I think you and I might investigate further in the coming days."

She stepped through the gate, closing it behind her. "Then

you plan to remain in Sussex for a time? Will you visit Edmund again?"

He nodded, knowing he would lose everything he had just gained if he refused. "I'll visit the man, Katharine," he said, adding on a sigh, "but I won't make any promises. I'm not sure if there has yet been sufficient time, sufficient distance —not for me."

CHAPTER 13

*In naked beauty more adorn'd
More lovely, than Pandora.*

John Milton, *Paradise Lost*

*M*elanie raced down the wide staircase a scant quarter hour before Beasley would announce dinner. How could Moina have allowed her to oversleep on this of all days! By the time she had descended for luncheon Lucien had been long gone, riding the fields with that dull-as-ditchwater Jeremy Watson or some such stupidity, leaving her behind, with no way to fill yet another endless afternoon.

If she had not sneaked into his room when Hawkins had gone off on some errand for his master, to lie between the covers of the high tester bed, rubbing her nose against the pillows, luxuriating in the well-remembered, well-loved scent of him, she would have believed she had dreamed his homecoming.

Well, he was back now, for she had heard him moving about in the next chamber, talking to his valet for this past half hour or more before his footsteps had passed by her chamber on his way downstairs.

Naughty boy. He hadn't even knocked to ask if she might be ready to accompany him. She'd be cool to him for a

while. Yes, that's what she'd do. She'd hang back, tantalizing him with her bewitching presence without a hint of her eagerness to have him back in her bed—punishing him for not seeking her out himself.

But perhaps it was just as well. There would be time and enough later for him to see her bedchamber, to be overwhelmed as she led him through the small antechamber and he was met by the dozens of fat sandalwood-scented candles she had ordered Moina to light without fail at nine o'clock, before he was drawn to the shimmering expanse of lightest pink satin that invited him to lie down beside her on the wide bed, before they could watch their bodies move together in that most elemental, erotic dance beneath the large mirror that lined the underside of the satin-draped canopy.

How she would enjoy watching his face as he came to her, slowly unbuttoning his shirt, his eyes clouded with passion. But enough of that! She had had enough of fantasy. The reality awaited.

Counting to one hundred as slowly as possible before rising from her dressing table, Melanie at last followed after Lucien. Just before she left, she reminded Moina about the candles, the final service she would be requiring from the old woman for the remainder of the evening.

Now she crossed the tiled foyer on tiptoe and stopped just outside the closed doors of the drawing room, pressing ice-cold fingers to her throat in an effort to marshal her composure. She must remember her reserve; it wouldn't do to allow Lucien to believe he had her completely at his beck and call, even if he did, her darling boy. Turning about, she inspected her reflection in the pier glass that faced her from the opposite wall.

She had spent the entire afternoon preparing for this moment. Her hair, her crowning glory, had been pulled up and away from her perfectly oval face, the curls captured in a blue satin band, with only a few tendrils left free to tease at her temples, tickle her nape, entice a man to near madness. Lucien had once told her she had just the correct tousled

curls and profile to put him in mind of a particular handcarved cameo his grandparents had brought back with them from Capri. It would do no harm to remind him of that observation.

The gown she had chosen, a soft, periwinkle blue, had been fashioned in a more modest cut than anything she had worn in years. It dated, in fact, from her days in Bath, being the one she had been wearing the first time she had espied Lucien Tremaine—standing transfixed, openly staring at her from across the assembly room dance floor as if she were some sort of goddess come to earth—and there and then decided that *he* would be the one.

Surely he too would remember, be gratified by her sweet sentimentality. And reward her for it.

She turned her head this way and that, squinting slightly as she inspected her reflection, for her eyes were not at their best for distance, assuring herself that the dewy, limpid-eyed beauty she had seen looking back at her from her hand mirror a minute ago had not been jeopardized by her anxiety to see Lucien again.

Satisfied, and giving a last pat to the double string of Pamela's pearls she had chosen over the flashier diamonds Edmund had given her, she turned back to the closed doors, agitatedly shooing away the idiot footman who had come to open them for her—as if she had included him in her plans! Placing a trembling, expectant hand on each brass lever, she took a deep breath, smiled, angled her chin just so, and pushed open the doors.

He stood at the drinks table, a half-empty goblet of claret in his hand. Dressed from shoulders to below his knees in finely fashioned, funereal black, his linen so white it dazzled the eyes, Lucien looked every inch the fashionable London gentleman. His only ornament remained the ruby ring on the little finger of his left hand, and it throbbed intriguingly as it caught the light from one of the nearby candles.

Beautiful. So beautiful. The perfect male animal—well muscled, sleek, and quietly powerful. The boy had held such wonderful promise; the man delivered it, in abundance.

Melanie's petite nostrils flared as she let go of the handles, giving up her pose, and walked into the room, the provocative, mingled male scents of wine, cologne, and a hint of tobacco assailing her senses, muddling her resolve, fanning her need.

"Melanie," she heard him say as she stood very still, waiting for his greeting, his compliments, longing to see the hunger that would surely leap into his eyes. He did not approach her, make any move to bow over her hand. "I had begun to wonder if I was to dine alone again this evening. I can only hope you have sufficiently recovered from your indisposition to join me at table, although you do still look a trifle peaked, darling, don't you?"

He turned back to the drinks table. "Perhaps a small glass of sherry will put the roses back in those cheeks?"

Melanie felt tears stinging at the back of her eyes, her confidence of a moment earlier flown to the far winds. When had the base of power shifted, so that it was he that called the tune and she that danced? "If you say so, darling," she answered, woodenly walking over to accept the glass he held out to her.

After she took it, Lucien stood back, his dark gaze traveling the length of her person with a lazy insouciance that told her she had overreacted. He could not know how his last words had hurt her. After all, if he knew, and had wounded her deliberately, she would have to hate him. She couldn't hate Lucien. Hating Lucien would be above everything ludicrous. She loved him!

"I met the most droll Frenchman while I was out riding the other morning and took the liberty of inviting him to join us at dinner tomorrow evening in the hopes of enlivening our meal. You never were much for conversation, as I recall. Ah, well, you have only to be beautiful. A woman such as you would only find a brain to be a hindrance, wouldn't you? Though perhaps, darling, you will be able to search out a gown more suitable for entertaining our guest than that faded thing you're wearing?"

Stupid! She had been wrong. She had gifted Lucien with

attributes he did not possess. Like gentleness. Like forgiveness. Like understanding of her unremitting pain these last interminable years. Every single day she had labored over what she would say, what she would do when he finally admitted he belonged to her, when he at last came back to claim her.

He had to be made to understand.

The moment had come to play her trump card. The time had arrived for her to move back into the position of power. *Then* they would see who danced!

Stepping back a pace, and lifting her chin a daring fraction, her heart pounding in anticipation, she announced baldly, "He's yours, you know."

Lucien motioned her to a nearby striped satin chair, waiting until she had sat down to take up his own seat across from her. "Comte Guy de Lacroix is mine? Hardly, darling. I encountered him for the first time only recently, and have formed no great desire to adopt the fellow. As a matter of fact, I believe he could be yours, if you want him. He seems quite enamored of you, you know. But, no, that would be impossible, as you are already overburdened with involvements. A husband, doggedly clinging to life. A stepson whom you claim to love. Poor Guy, I fear he is destined to be disappointed."

Melanie's hands twisted in her lap, wrinkling the fine cloth of her gown. How could he be so deliberately obtuse! She leaned forward, her eyes narrowing, longing to shock Lucien from his good humor.

She spoke quickly, so that he would not be able to interrupt. "Noddy, Lucien. *Noddy* is yours. Why else do you think I so eagerly accepted Edmund's proposal? How droll it is, darling. The fool has been cuckholded not once—but twice! *Now* do you understand? *Now* can you appreciate how I have suffered, living with that horrid old man touching me, clumsily pawing my body—while all the time you were off playing at soldier, giving not so much as a single thought to me, or to the seed you so carelessly planted

before you left? You do remember our last night together, don't you, darling? That last, wonderful, endless night."

Her announcement made, Melanie sat back at her ease, watching him, prepared to be magnanimous when he fell at her feet, begging forgiveness. "Now, my darling Lucien, what do you have to say to that!"

"What do I have to say? Why, nothing." He lifted his left hand to his mouth to stifle a yawn. "And if by some chance you're waiting for applause, darling, I fear you will be sadly disappointed. I've seen much better on the London stage."

No! She flew to her feet, only to collapse on her knees beside his chair. Hadn't he understood? He couldn't have heard her correctly.

"But you must believe me, darling. Noddy is yours. Listen to me! I realized I was pregnant just after Pamela died. *Think*, Lucien! You can only imagine how *frantic* I became! With Edmund so distraught, how could I possibly tell him? How could I announce that I carried the bastard child of his dead wife's bastard son."

He pushed her hand from his knee, then clasped his hands together, fingering the ruby ring on his little finger. The blood red stone fascinated her and she envied the ring, for it flattered the hand that had once touched her. Touched her deeply. Intimately. Lovingly.

His next words brought her back to the matter at hand. "You do have a point, darling. I doubt Edmund would have sent out announcements to the London dailies. Let me see—how would he word it? Mr. Edmund Tremaine, of Tremaine Court, proudly announces the delicate condition of Pamela Kingsley Tremaine's bastard son's fiancée, Miss Melanie—no, far too convoluted, isn't it?"

"Stop it!" She could feel herself becoming more anxious by the moment. This wasn't the way this scene was supposed to be played out. This wasn't the way she had planned it. What a fool she was! Once again she had rushed her fences, spoken too soon, only to face possible disaster.

"Listen to me, darling, for it is all true! I was pregnant

with your child. Edmund would have thrown me out, to fend for myself, to do my best to survive until you returned from the war. *If* you returned from the war. I didn't know where to turn, what to do. When Edmund came to my room the night of Pamela's funeral, drunk and nearly out of his mind, I tried to fight him off."

"To your room, darling? I had heard, I disremember where, that you went to his rooms, the ones he had so lately shared with my mother."

She pressed her hands together, wringing them. "His room, my room—what does it matter? Edmund wanted me, had always wanted me, from the first day. Pamela's death couldn't have been more convenient for him. I—I've always wondered about that, haven't you?"

Lucien lifted an enameled box from his waistcoat and proceeded to take snuff. "Please, darling, I am but a simple man. One tragedy at a time, lest you confuse me. You were saying?"

He was weakening, she was sure of it. "Yes, of course, my darling. Let us get back to the point. As I struggled against him, I suddenly realized I could use his lust to help you, to help us. This was the answer to my prayers! If I allowed Edmund to make love to me, allowed him to believe he had fathered a child with me, he would most certainly marry me, and *our* child would be protected. The child would have the protection of the Tremaine name, just as Pamela would have wanted and, eventually, the three of us would have Tremaine Court as well."

Lucien stood, and she rose with him. Now! Now he would take her in his arms!

"I see. It is all so plain to me now. So strangely simple. Perversely so, some might say. You did it all for me. Such a supreme sacrifice! How endlessly selfless you are, to be sure. There should be a statue commissioned in your honor."

Her hands closed convulsively around his forearm. "Yes! Yes! I did it for you, darling. For *us*. Just as I told you when you first came home, although I am sure I muddled the telling of it in my eagerness to be with you again. But Moina

was right, the news proved too much for you, and I became hysterical when you rejected me—after all I had suffered for us. I said some terrible things then, I know, but I had to protect my position at Tremaine Court. I had to protect our dearest, dearest Noddy. Moina promised that in time you'd be back for me, and now you have come. Only it isn't like Moina promised, darling. You hate me now, while I—I still love you so!"

Her voice broke as she concluded her story and she turned her head into his shoulder, sobbing in earnest. Her world depended on what he said next. Her sanity. Her hopes for the future. Her whole life!

He remained silent for a long time, allowing her to snuggle against him but, to her chagrin, making no move to hold her. At last—a moment later, a lifetime later—when she had all but given up hope, he slid his arms around her back, beneath her knees, to carry her toward the doorway.

She clung to him tightly, her flesh tingling wherever his warmth touched her, sure that he would take her upstairs, into her bedchamber where all had been prepared for this wonderful moment, and work his special magic on her eager body. What if there were no lit candles? They would light up the room with the raging fire of their love! She felt the first sweet wetness between her thighs as her body prepared his welcome.

But suddenly, before they had even reached the doorway to the foyer, her shoes touched the floor. Lucien's hands held her shoulders, steadying her, then were removed, leaving her unsupported, bereft in her unexpected despair.

"Lucien? What's wrong? Aren't you taking me to my bedchamber?"

"Poor, deluded Melanie. You honestly believe I would have taken you upstairs and made love to you, don't you? Actually, I had momentarily considered taking you to Edmund, as I did once before, so that you could repeat your touching story to him. But I have just this moment thought better of it. I have thought *myself* better than that."

The reality of his rejection hit her with stunning force.

She looked up into his face, his achingly handsome, expressionless face, his cold dark eyes, and recoiled in fear from this indomitable man she had always believed hers for the asking.

Genuinely frightened, she pleaded, "Lucien? Darling? You still don't believe me, do you? I know all this has come as a shock, but you *must* know I love you, that I'd never lie to you. Haven't I proved it to you yet?" Clasping his lapels so fiercely her knuckles whitened, she gave him a single, convulsive shake, as if to drive home her point, her childlike voice high and shrill in her mounting terror. "Look at me, damn you! Don't you understand? Noddy is yours! Now you *have* to love me! What must I do to have you believe that?"

"There you be, Mrs. Tremaine. Dinner is served, madam, sir."

"Get out, you stupid ass!" Melanie ordered without turning to look at Beasley, who had entered the drawing room through another doorway.

"You do seem to have a considerable servant problem here at Tremaine Court one way or the other, don't you, darling?" she heard Lucien say as Beasley left, some small part of her brain acknowledging the impersonal tone she had learned to hate with a white-hot passion in the short time he had been back at Tremaine Court, back in her life and yet not really a part of it.

His hands came out to encircle her neck, and a moment later he withdrew them, Pamela's pearls now in his possession, leaving her feeling oddly naked. "I could not help but notice that the clasp on this necklace is faulty," he said, slipping the pearls into his pocket. "I wouldn't wish to see such a beautiful piece lost, would you?"

Her hands went to her bare throat before returning to hold his lapels once more, anger loosing her tongue and banishing her last remaining caution. "There is nothing wrong with the clasp. You just don't want me to have it because it was once your mother's. Well, your whoring mother is dead. Those pearls are *mine* now, Lucien. *All* her

jewels are mine. I've *paid* for them! Dear God, how I've paid for them!"

The pearls remained in his pocket.

"Yes. You have, haven't you? But you must please excuse me now, darling. Much as I would adore continuing this discussion, I awoke with the faint suspicion of a sniffle this morning, but ignored it, to find that it has returned this evening with a vengeance. I believe I shall dine in my bedchamber, allowing Hawkins the great joy of tending me. Perhaps we shall meet again tomorrow, to take up this discussion again where we left off. You will remember where we were, won't you—I believe you were protesting your unselfish, undying love for me."

While she stood there, incapable of further action, unprepared to fight what she could not understand, he removed her hands from his lapels as if her touch defiled him. "Or perhaps not."

Melanie stepped back, put her hands to her cheeks, her mouth opened to a small circle, her breathing uneven, tearing at her lungs, unable to believe he could have heard what she said and still walk away from her. "Lucien, don't, I beg you. I love you, darling. The jewels mean nothing. Nothing means anything if I can't have you. Please don't leave me like this! You can't know what you're doing! I'll *die* if you don't forgive me. Truly I will. You *can't* leave me again! *It isn't fair!*"

His head swiveled gracefully so that he looked back at her over one broad shoulder, one finely drawn eyebrow raised as if mocking her passionate appeal. His words bit at her, stinging like icy sleet slapping against her tender exposed flesh. "*Fair,* darling? After what you have revealed to me this evening I most seriously doubt you are even remotely acquainted with the meaning of that word. Goodnight."

"*Lucien!* Don't leave me!" Melanie watched him go, hating him, loving him, needing him so that her body ached with it.

The enormity of her defeat nearly overwhelmed her. All

her hopes, all her dreams, all those long years—wasted. Her darling Lucien hated her.

Nobody had ever hated Melanie before. Nobody. Even the thought was an impossibility. Everyone loved Melanie. Some had been jealous, of course. Like Felicia. Felicia, who was still making her pay and pay for their time together in Bath. Her time before Lucien, when she had used her body as her entrance to at least the fringes of society.

But everybody loved Melanie—even Felicia. Beautiful Melanie. Sweet Melanie. Irresistible Melanie. Men, women —no one was immune to her beauty. Even Edmund loved her. She could have him again, in a moment, if she wanted him. Yes. Yes, she could! She could have any man she wanted. But not Lucien. Not her darling, darling Lucien. She had given him what she had given no other man, her love.

And he had ground that love beneath his heel.

She turned away from the foyer to wander aimlessly through the drawing room, feeling empty, bereft, yet at the same time nearly choked by a multitude of pent-up emotions that must somehow be assuaged, familiar physical longings that mercilessly clamored for immediate attention.

Would this aching loneliness never be filled? Was she destined to have this gnawing hunger inside her until the end of her days, daily demanding to be fed, yet never again fully satisfied, never comfortably sated?

Damn Lucien Tremaine! Damn him to eternal, burning hell! He held the power to save her. Only Lucien. Everything, everyone else, before him or since, had served only as temporary solutions, leaving her exhausted, yet incomplete. She had to have Lucien's love. Only his love, joyously joined with his passionate loving, held the power to cure her needs.

But he had refused. He had deserted her, not once, not twice, but three times. He would be made to pay for that desertion, she swore it. She would make him pay!

She whirled about, striding to the drinks table, thinking to

find some comfort there, but the last tenuous, frayed shreds of her composure snapped even as she lifted the heavy crystal decanter.

A moment later thousands of thin slivers of glass littered the floor, a watery red splash dripping down the imported Chinese wallpaper.

Beasley came rushing into the room a few moments later to find Melanie kneeling on the floor, her legs tucked under her, her knees close together beneath the concealing skirt of her gown so that her right heel pushed against the door of her sex. Her arms were tightly wrapped about her waist as she rhythmically rocked back and forth faster—ever faster —her bottom lip caught behind her front teeth.

"Send for him, Beasley," she ordered tersely. There was no need for further explanation. Beasley knew what to do, what she paid him to do.

Turning her head, she looked up into Pamela Tremaine's mirror to see Melly looking back at her, her eyes wide and hungry, her complexion ashen, yet the whole still achingly, heartbreakingly beautiful. She looked like a glorious summer bloom, plucked at the height of her flowering. It was the same. It was always the same. The beauty was still there, mingled with the hunger, the promise. How could Lucien have seen her and not loved her?

"Tell him to come to me now!"

Convulsive shudders cascaded through her lower body as she stared at her reflection, the tremors signaling her self-induced climax. But no real release accompanied those sensations. No lasting satisfaction. Just this hunger. And this unremitting ache. The hunger and the tension wouldn't leave her alone. Only Lucien had left her, left her to fend for herself. Again. Poor Melly. Poor, poor Melly.

"But, madam—the dinner?"

Was she to spend her life surrounded by idiots? Imbeciles? Dolts? "Do as I say or you'll be scratching out *your* next meal in some barnyard!"

She stood, not without effort, her forearms still spanning

her waist, as if protecting a recent wound, and staggered toward the French doors leading onto the terrace. "Hurry, Beasley! Tell him Melly will be waiting in the usual place."

Comte Guy de la Croix tied his horse behind a large tree a prudent distance from Tremaine Court and approached the garden-level entrance to the north wing gazebo just as the moon broke through the clouds. All his senses were alert, on the lookout for any movement that might signal someone observing his progress.

Extracting a small key from his waistcoat pocket, he made quick work of entering the small stone building, careful to lock the door again from the inside before climbing the steep stone steps that led to another door and the elegantly furnished room where Melanie Tremaine undoubtedly lay waiting for him. Or in wait for him. The two were much of a piece.

He could smell the sickening sweetness of opium before he fully entered the room, and he smiled to think that she had begun without him. She was insatiable, this beautiful blond bitch, and so extraordinarily talented.

And there she lay, sprawled naked on the tumbled covers, her back to him, her legs thrust partway up the paneled wall behind the bed, her clever hands busy between her thighs. The small room reeked with the musky smell of sex. How many times had she brought herself off while he finished his dinner at the cottage, deliberately making her wait? Two? Five? A dozen? She would be ready for a little diversity, some game of his making.

The thought inflamed him.

He greeted her in French, knowing she did not understand the language. That made it easier to curse her in the midst of their love play. He felt himself grow hard, his body not nearly as fastidious as his brain.

There were no preliminaries. Why waste his talents on arousal when she was already leagues ahead of him? Quickly stripping to the buff, and without another word to her, he climbed onto the bed. Kneeling, sharply slapping her hands

away as he swung her legs down from the wall and turned her onto her stomach, he pulled her buttocks up and away from the bed.

She cried out as he took her from the rear, plowing into her as his hands ripped at her tender, mounded flesh, forcing it apart, pinching the soft fullness of her.

She tried to prop herself up on her hands, but he pushed her down, flattening her face into the covers, muffling her impassioned pleas for more, always more. He could not promise himself he would not kill this beautiful, mesmerizing witch if she addressed him as Lucien again tonight. A man could only stand so much!

Reaching around her back, sliding his fingers along her sleek rib cage, he took her creamy white breasts in his hands, testing their fullness, squeezing the slack nipples between thumb and forefinger. They grew stiff beneath his clever touch. He twisted them hard, so that she moaned low in her throat. He knew what she needed, how she needed it.

He rode her harder, and harder, her body moving beneath his with such force that he could barely hold onto her nipples as her full breasts swayed with each new assault—until she cried out with her release, just as he collapsed on top of her, his seed shooting high into her womb.

Guy didn't linger on the bed, but rose, naked, his body slick with sweat and the mingling fluids of their lovemaking. No, never love, he cautioned himself swiftly. Their animal mating had nothing whatsoever to do with love. It couldn't. He had many plans for Melanie, for his own future, but none of them included love. That tender emotion, so alien to him, could not be allowed to enter into those plans.

He crossed to the table to prepare another pipe for her. He had to keep her occupied or else she'd be clawing at him in another minute, eager to try yet another game. He possessed great talent, yes, but he was more than twice her age. His recuperative powers were not those of a man in his twenties.

Melanie turned onto her back, the palm of one hand lifted to her forehead, her legs limp and spread wide apart, totally open, totally vulnerable, eminently distasteful. To the

comte, there was nothing more unappetizing than the sight of a naked woman after he had done with her. He must keep this image always in the forefront of his mind. Then he could do what he had to do.

"Guy?" she asked, looking up at him with confusion-clouded eyes, as if surprised to find him in the room. "Oh, I remember now. I sent for you, didn't I? How lovely of you to *come*, darling," she trilled in that little-girl voice he alternately adored and loathed. Now, at this moment, he loathed it. She giggled at her own joke, so that he clenched his teeth, longing to slap her.

Her hands slipped down to tweak at her nipples as she raised her slowly undulating hips from the covers, inviting him back into the bed. And then she grinned. She had the teeth-baring grin of a wolf, bestial and hungry. This smile was nothing like the one she employed to such advantage outside this room, the sweet, innocent one that resembled the expression carved into the statue of the Virgin in his parish church of Sainte Thérèse. And nothing like his own carefully cultivated, ingratiating smile.

They were much of a pair, he and Melanie Tremaine, enough alike that they had recognized each other at their first meeting.

He turned away, unable to hide his disgust, for at times like this she showed him a part of his nature he did not wish to acknowledge, even to himself.

Yes, they were alike, he and Melanie Tremaine. Only he was more clever than she. Much more clever. He knew how to use the user.

He waited for what would come next. She always wanted something from him, as if he had not already sacrificed enough. But his turn would come. Already his plan had been set in motion and was beginning to bear fruit. Soon he would not need her any longer. Soon he would claim the ultimate prize. A pity. He had at times so enjoyed their nocturnal interludes.

She abandoned her seductive pose, to lie on her side, plucking at the covers. "I have a surprise for you, darling

Guy. I have ordered dozens of invitations sent out for a dinner party to welcome Lucien home. But the guest list is not limited to country bumpkins. I have *personally* invited a woman who will be traveling here all the way from London."

"How lovely," he answered automatically, barely paying attention.

"No. No, it is not. She's a most horrible woman, darling. But I have planned a lovely surprise for her. No one else is to know she is coming, you see. I wish us two to deal with her on the road, before she can arrive at Tremaine Court. She has made Melly very unhappy for a very long time, you understand. In truth, I cannot even love Lu—love you as I wish until this woman is dealt with, gone from my life. She is too distracting, and has been the cause of all my problems. You will help your sweet Melly, won't you?"

Guy inhaled the thin smoke deeply into his lungs, then handed Melanie the pipe, sitting down beside her on the bed, keeping his expression blank. She had nearly slipped, nearly said Lucien's name. What maggot had she taken into her head now?

He exhaled slowly, savoring the moment, allowing the drug to soothe his jangled nerves. "Lie very still while we talk, little one, so that the opium can do its lovely work. What do you plan for us to do with this so horrible woman, Melly? Beat her soundly, so that she goes away, never to bother you again? You do not need me to do that. You can hire for yourself some locally grown thugs, *oui?*"

She took a deep pull on the pipe before handing it back to him, leaving her hands free as she ignored his directions and slithered toward him on her belly, the snake invading the Garden of Eden, promising unheard of delights in exchange for his immortal soul.

Taking his still soft manhood between her hands, she flicked at its moist tip with her tongue as she smiled up into his eyes. His blood heated slightly and he moved languidly within her grasp, secretly pleased to learn he had not grown too old. He smiled, realizing he would miss this cunning

little whore just a bit when it was all over. Oh yes, there were times he could almost love her. Then he would deliberately harden his heart, remembering that she only wished to use him.

"Thrashing her would not be enough, darling. She would only cause me more trouble."

So? What did he care if this unknown woman from London made Melanie's life a living hell? The world was littered with eager women, his brain told him, eager, talented women who did not expect more from him than the occasional bauble. And as soon as he discovered why he came running each time Melanie called, why he did not seek out one of those so willing women, he would be a happy man. But wait. He might learn something valuable if he just listened. He had a mission to perform here at Tremaine Court, a battle he must yet finish, and a man could never have too much ammunition.

Guy forced his features into a concerned frown even as he joked with her. "How extremely awful for you, *ma chienne enragée!* You obviously need a more permanent solution. I must kill this so horrible creature for you, *n'est-ce pas?*"

"Yes! Oh yes, darling Guy," he heard her purr as she slid off the bed, to kneel between his legs, her long blond hair tumbling about her shoulders, streaming like warm, liquid gold across the tops of his thighs. Silly chit! She had taken him at his word. She really wished for him to kill this woman for her. What a preposterous, vaguely exciting thought!

Melanie pressed his manhood between her breasts, inching forward to lick at his stomach just below his navel, so that he felt a convulsive rippling of his sensitive skin. She had done it again. Yes, he would miss her.

He placed his hands on either side of her head, tilting it up so that he could look into her beautiful, innocent face. Love her? Love Melanie Tremaine? He would have to be quite mad! "You mean it, don't you, *ma pervertie louve.* You really wish for me to kill her?"

That grin was back—wild, teeth-baring, ravenous. "Ah,

Guy, I knew you would understand. But I have planned it so that you may enjoy yourself first, my darling. She will adore someone of your talents. Hurt her for what she has done to your poor Melly, make her beg for mercy. Hurt her terribly, *use* her. And then you must kill her for me. Only promise me something, my darling, darling Guy."

"Another promise, Melly? You would make me a murderer. What else could you possibly want?"

She ran the tip of her pink tongue around her full lips, then said, her voice at last as he liked it, low and husky, "Promise you will let me watch."

A moment later she caught his spurting juices in her mouth.

CHAPTER 14

No light, but rather darkness visible.

John Milton, *Paradise Lost*

Good morning, Edmund. My, but you're looking well today." Katharine nodded to Hawkins, who had just completed shaving the master of Tremaine Court and was in the process of removing the washbasin from the bedside. The chamber, wrapped in gloom for over a year, was filled with sunlight, the velvet draperies banished from both windows and bed. "I should be jealous that Hawkins has fit so neatly into the role of your companion, except that I am too thrilled with the rate of your recovery to do anything but be thankful for his presence."

"It's my pleasure, miss," Hawkins said, bowing. "Mr. Edmund and I go a long way back. Boys together, we were, my father serving at the Court before me. This is my home. There's no sense in carrying bad feelings anyway, I say. It wouldn't be fitting for me to be in this house and not take care of Mr. Edmund. Besides, Moina said it was all right."

Kate smiled. "Well, that settles it then, doesn't it? I'm not so new to the Court that I haven't learned that Moina's word is law. But I'm surprised you've spoken with her. She seems

212

to have locked herself in her room in the north wing this past week, although the maids assure me her appetite remains good, and her tongue as sharp as ever. Perhaps she and Miss Melanie are suffering the same illness, although Moina still seems able to visit her mistress at least once a day. Edmund —what's wrong?"

Edmund Tremaine, who had been lying quietly in his bed, propped up by pillows, began to moan, thrashing his head from side to side. It had been so difficult to watch him these past weeks, ever since the spell he had taken on the terrace that had resulted in his loss of both his speech and the use of his left side. "Moina? Are you asking for Moina?"

Edmund became even more agitated at the question, shaking his head as drool slipped from the corner of his slack mouth, so that Kate quickly assured him that he did not have to see the old nurse if he did not wish to do so. "I don't blame you for not wanting any more of her medicines. They taste vile, don't they? Perhaps it is Lucien you wish to see?" She called after Hawkins, who was about to leave the room. "Hawkins—has Mr. Tremaine been in to see Mr. Edmund this morning?"

"No, miss. He's late today. But he comes by every morning," he added, his tone defensive, "has all this week. I think he might be out riding with that French fellow again. Seems to have taken a shine to him."

"A shine to monsieur le comte, Hawkins? Really? That sounds ominous." Lucien entered the room in his riding clothes, still carrying his leather crop. "Heavens, my good man, will you soon be announcing the banns? Good morning, Katharine—sir."

Kate nodded perfunctorily, avoiding his eyes. Lucien had barely spoken to her since that embarrassing incident at the pond, and she no longer knew how to react when in his presence. He had said they should cry friends, but he seemed to have a vastly different definition of that term than did she. He ran so hot and cold—mostly cold. It was for the best, she told herself nightly as she lay awake in her bed, remembering how she had felt in his arms—remembering

the fear, the ecstasy. No good could come from a friendship between Kate Harvey and Lucien Tremaine.

Yet she couldn't regret his kisses, even if he had hurt her more than he could know. Should she have been more honest with him, telling him secrets only Edmund knew? Should she have been less honest with him, hiding the fact that she had borne a child? And did it really matter either way? Her future did not include Lucien Tremaine, any more than she had a place in his tomorrows. All that mattered, all that really mattered, was that he had lived up to his promise to visit Edmund, and that Edmund had been showing a slow but steady improvement with each passing day.

She looked to Edmund now, to see that the right side of his mouth had curled up in a smile, his expression openly adoring as Lucien propped himself familiarly on the side of the bed. Dear God, please don't let Lucien be toying with the man, building him up only to destroy him with a single, damning remark.

"So, sir, have you breakfasted yet?" Lucien asked Edmund. "I should imagine you have, for everyone seems to keep dashed early hours here at Tremaine Court—except for your wife, that is. Such a shame that she is feeling under the weather, isn't it? Ah well, it leaves me more time to enjoy the countryside, and to make certain Jeremy Watson implements the improvements I have directed. As I told you yesterday, the south fields are coming along nicely. You were a good teacher, sir, and I can only hope I learned my lessons well."

Edmund murmured something entirely unintelligible to Kate's ears, but Lucien nodded as if he had understood. "The workers begin on the chimneys tomorrow. It wouldn't be pleasant to light a fire in one of them and have this whole pile go up in smoke, now would it, sir? Let me see, there must be something else. Oh yes, now that the lawns have been scythed, I've set some workmen to repairing the front gates."

Katharine ceased to listen as Lucien's voice droned on, talking of this and that, without really saying anything. He

spoke today as he did every day, giving a cataloguing of things, like a child called into company to recite. He was pleasant enough, unfailingly polite, but he never spoke of anything even remotely personal, never made the smallest push to open a dialogue—albeit one-sided—on the reasons behind his long absence, the events that had caused his and Edmund's estrangement.

She tried to tell herself that Edmund was responding, that it was early days yet and that there was plenty of time for Lucien and him to come to terms with the past, but she did not know how long Lucien would stay at Tremaine Court. The Season was underway in London and, according to Hawkins, Lucien had already been making noises about missing some ball or other he had especially promised to attend.

He was still playing at friendship, she was sure, both with Edmund and with the rest of them. His games had already reduced Melanie to hiding in her chambers—a development that Kate could not look upon without charity—and his treatment of Kate herself had pushed her to the point where she had begun to studiously avoid him.

One certain way, she had found, to stay out of Lucien's path was to spend as much time in the nursery as possible. Although they seemed to have gotten along famously the first day Lucien had come back to Sussex, he had not returned to visit Noddy in the schoolroom. She had found it increasingly difficult to make excuses for him when Noddy questioned her as to the whereabouts of "Lu-cien," and her heart went out to the child.

". . . and once the field has been sufficiently drained we shall have to see about finding a crop that can be sown this far into the growing season," Lucien ended as Kate reluctantly pulled her attention back to what was going on in the room.

Drainage! Crops! Was that all he could think of to discuss with the man who had nearly died grieving over the walls that had been thrown up between them? Kate longed to race over to the bed and box Lucien's ears!

"Here, here now," she said, forcing a light tone into her voice as she walked to the far side of the bed, across from Lucien. It was time she took matters into her own hands. "Can't we find something more pleasant to discuss? Lucien —Edmund and I spent a pleasant hour yesterday afternoon pouring through a small box of trinkets I found tucked up in one of the drawers in his sitting room. Most of the items were self-explanatory—except for this." She turned to the table beside the bed, opened the drawer to extract a small packet and placed it on the coverlet. "Edmund appeared most cheered to see it, but I cannot figure out what it is. Do you know?"

Avoiding his dark, warning gaze, she lowered her head and began unfolding the tissue wrappings that held a small silver cup, badly dented on one side. She lifted it from the paper and held it out to Lucien, daring him to take it.

"My dear girl," he said, his voice an insulting drawl as he looked at the object without taking it, "surely you recognize the piece. I believe it is used for drinking purposes."

"I know that," Kate said, trying not to see the hurt that had stolen, certainly unbidden, into Lucien's dark eyes. "But what is its significance? It's badly tarnished, but I can make out the letter *L* on the dented side. It was yours, wasn't it? How did it get this way? I'm convinced there must be some story behind it or else Edmund wouldn't have saved it." She looked down at the man lying in the bed between Lucien and her. "Would you, Edmund?"

He looked up at her, his eyes shining with tears, but still smiling.

Suddenly the cup was ripped from her hand. "I used it to crack walnuts, as I recall," Lucien snapped, snatching up the paper and wrapping the cup away from sight. "If you look closely, you might see that I also teethed on it, or so I'm told. Happy now, Miss Harvey?"

"Deliriously so, Mr. Tremaine," she said, looking at him levelly. "Now, if you'll excuse me, I have duties awaiting me in the nursery. You do remember the nursery, don't you, Mr. Tremaine?" She looked down at Edmund, to see that he

had reached out with his right hand and brought the tissue-wrapped cup to his tear-wet cheek. "Oh, Edmund," she said, sighing, "I'm so sorry. I didn't think. It's just that I was attempting to—"

"Never point out the obvious, Katharine, especially now that you have succeeded so admirably," Lucien said, his voice devoid of rancor as he extracted the cup from the tissue before handing it back to Edmund, who sobbed and clutched it to his chest. "If you'd leave us now?"

Kate nodded, unable to find her voice, and quickly took her leave, offering up a silent prayer that her impulsive action had done more good than harm.

The afternoon sun filtered down through the beech trees, dappling the wooly blanket spread over the newly scythed grass where Noddy lay napping, his thumb firmly stuck in his rosebud mouth. Kate sat quietly, watching him sleep, her back against one of the tree trunks, unable to keep from smiling. How she loved this child.

Lying on his stomach, Noddy had tucked his knees up under him, his small round bottom thrust into the air so that a large painted lady butterfly had perched there, slowly opening and closing its wings, as if preening. Her fingers itched for her sketching paper, one of the many things she had left behind at The Willows, as she longed to capture the moment in watercolors.

Somehow a perfect, warm summer's day had sneaked itself into the usually watery Sussex spring, so that she had stolen a few precious, uninterrupted hours with the child, knowing that Hawkins would sit with Edmund until she returned.

What a wonderful change there had been in Edmund Tremaine! Kate no longer feared for the man's life, nor did she look forward to his death as a happy release from an increasingly intolerable existence. Just the thought that she had ever believed Edmund's death to be an answer to all their troubles distressed her. Why, only yesterday he had said her name, not very clearly, and not without a terrible

expending of his small energy—but he *had* said it. In another week, a month, he might be back to where he had been before this last episode. Lucien's arrival had wrought a near miracle.

Lucien. Kate's smile faded and she bit her bottom lip. She hadn't gone back to Edmund's rooms to see how he had fared after she'd left the two of them alone. Had she done the right thing, to force Lucien into acknowledging Edmund on more than an impersonal level? She had seen Hawkins in the hallway and he had told her Edmund was napping comfortably, so at least her impromptu interference had not had any immediate ill effects on their patient.

How her actions had affected Lucien, however, was another matter, as was her undeniable anxiety as to how he now felt about her.

Friends. That's what he had said, that they should be friends, perhaps even help each other as they seemed to be kindred spirits. And in a way he was right. But true friends didn't have any secrets from each other, a condition Lucien seemed to consider important, probably because he was aware that she knew his secrets while she had only given him snippets of her own past, bits and pieces of information he could have learned from any member of the Tremaine Court staff.

She might have told him. A week ago, after he had proved so gentlemanly—if only slightly naughty—at the pond, she might have told him. But the week had passed without his seeking her out again and her courage had failed her. Now, if only she could banish her memories of the embrace they had shared beneath this very beech tree . . .

"As the poet John Heywood said, Katharine, 'A penny for your thought.'"

A penny for her thought? Kate *thought* she would jump out of her skin. Literally. Not only had Lucien crept up behind her, to stick his head halfway around the tree trunk, surprising her, but he had said the one thing certain to infuse her cheeks with guilty color. Attempting to regain her composure, she answered swiftly, "Heywood was not a poet,

Mr. Tremaine, at least not in the classical sense. He was more an epigrammatist, and a particular favorite of Queen Mary, I believe."

She watched as the remainder of Lucien's body appeared from behind the beech tree. He folded his long form onto a corner of the blanket, his legs crossed in front of him, his elbows on his knees, and his chin in his hands. He had changed out of his riding outfit and was casually dressed in buckskins and a flowing white shirt, the collar of which he had unbuttoned, revealing a tantalizing portion of his broad chest. She could see the glint of a slim gold chain peeking out from beneath the shirt and wondered what sort of bauble hung from it. But not for long. Her attention, which he had gotten the moment he spoke, quickly focused on his dark, smiling eyes.

Obviously he had forgiven her for shoving that silver cup in his face and demanding that he remember his happy childhood. Indeed, he looked almost childlike now—a young boy ready for mischief.

"Katharine!" he exclaimed, his tone lightly teasing. "I had no idea we were harboring a bluestocking here at Tremaine Court. You see me prostrate before you, eager to catch each pearl of wisdom as it dribbles from your sweet lips. Tell me more, I beg you. Do you have a copybook about somewhere, perhaps? I should take notes."

"Hush, Lucien," she warned, her tone scolding, although her heart wasn't in it. No, that was a lie. Her heart, for her sins, was very much in it. "You'll wake Noddy."

His smile faded momentarily, his eyelids coming down to hide the expression in his eyes, the action reminding her that he seemed to have been studiously ignoring the child this past week.

"He's a pleasant enough child, isn't he?" Lucien said, looking over at Noddy, his words polite, his tone conveying to her that the subject of Edmund's son was unpleasant to him.

"Edmund adores his son."

"Yes. I had supposed as much."

Kate frowned. If someone were to come down the avenue at this moment, some stranger who had lost his way, Lucien, Kate and Noddy would appear to be a family taking advantage of a lazy afternoon beneath the trees. But they were not a family, no matter how that far-fetched dream plagued her at night. They were as mismatched a trio as could be imagined: the disillusioned bastard, the soiled woman, and the innocent child.

"Lucien, you've made quite an impression on Noddy. He has been asking when you'll be coming back to the nursery to play with him." Kate knew she was taking a chance, daring his anger for a second time in less than three hours, inviting an abrupt end to this unexpected, friendly inter-lude. But he had been so good to Noddy. Something must have happened since that first afternoon, something that kept him from the nursery.

He smiled at her, although it was his old smile—the one that didn't quite reach his eyes. "Lucien. Have I told you that I like the way you say my name, Katharine? Your inflection reveals a background in the French language. Edmund will have no need to engage a tutor for the boy as long as you are here, will he? Someday, when you have truly forgiven me for my dreadful assumptions, perhaps you will tell me more of your history."

Kate sighed. He might not have sought her out this past week to discuss what he considered to be the change in her outlook between the time they had first met and their reintroduction last week, but he still seemed inordinately interested in learning her background. "It would make for very boring listening," she told him, watching the butterfly as it rode up and down with each rise and fall of Noddy's even breathing, like a cork bobbing on the surface of a breeze-ruffled pond.

Lucien changed his position, moving closer to her, to lie on his side, with one hand propping up his head as he looked at her. A lock of black hair fell onto his forehead and she longed to run her fingers through it, smoothing it away from his face. Did he know the effect he had on her? She imagined

he did. He had to have become accustomed to his power over women. She couldn't be the only female who found his curious mix of cynicism and vulnerability irresistible.

"Boring, Katharine? You are an educated woman, more so than most. You have the air and breeding of a gentlewoman. Yet you feel it necessary to lock your door at night, even at Tremaine Court. You carry a knife for protection—or at least you did. I cannot tell you how much safer I feel now that the knife is in my possession. But to continue—you kiss, if you'll pardon my candor on a subject I know you would much prefer I keep closed, like a novitiate pressing her virgin lips to the cross on her rosary. Yet—again forgive me—you've borne a child. So many contradictions, sweet Katharine, are hardly boring fare for a story."

"Perhaps someday I'll write a book and become famous," Kate offered shortly, leaning forward to shoo the butterfly, moving only because it had become impossible to remain still.

Lucien's hand came out to grasp her wrist, not tightly, as it had the day she'd pulled the knife on him, but gently, as if fearful he might bruise her tender skin. His touch did something strange to her equilibrium and she feared she might topple forward, into his arms.

"Katharine, I'm sorry," he said as she looked into his eyes, searching them for the secret to her fascination with this man. "I was being petty—striking out at you because you dared to push me beyond the inane prattle I've employed in Edmund's rooms, and made me face the fact that I do have happy memories of the man, for all the good they do either of us. I only go to his room to please you, you know. Oh, dear, I imagine saying that earns you another apology. It seems I'm forever apologizing to you for one thing or the other." He released her wrist, only to take hold of her hand, the pad of his thumb lightly stroking the soft center of her palm, sending small shivers racing up her forearm.

"It's your own fault, you know. If you wouldn't insist upon being so contrary you wouldn't have to spend so much of your time apologizing," she offered weakly, ignoring his

admission while wishing she had the strength to move away from him, and knowing she didn't.

Laughing, he pressed his lips to the back of her hand, then released her. She conquered the urge to press her hand to her cheek. "Touché, Katharine."

He sobered just as quickly, his dark eyes staring at her with an intensity that frightened her. "It is my own fault. I've learned caution this past year, most especially here, as if nothing good could ever again come from Tremaine Court. I have tried letting my guard down a time or two since your last letter all but dared me to come back, perhaps even allowed myself to hope, just a little. But each time I do life deals me another unexpected hand, so that I find myself forced to raise that guard again. Has life ever bested you, Katharine?"

He shook his head. "Silly question. You wouldn't be hiding here in Sussex if it hadn't, would you? You'd be in London right now, breaking hearts from one end of Mayfair to the other. You don't have to answer, but please don't deny it either, Katharine, for I won't believe it."

She watched as he looked past her, at the trees, the bright sunlight, the bluer-than-blue, cloudless sky, his dark eyes slightly unfocused, as if he saw something invisible to her own eyes, something that made him unhappy. "Everything seems so beautiful here, Katharine, so peaceful," he said at last. "Odd, isn't it? Tremaine Court doesn't outwardly resemble the sort of place where souls come to die."

He sat up, grinning at her, his mirthless smile clutching at her heart. "Oh, dear. What could have prompted that, do you suppose, darling? I waxed almost profound for a moment there, didn't I?"

Darling. He was being so open with her, so honest. He had spoken of dashed hopes—and now he had thrown cold water all over hers. Why did he have to spoil everything? *Darling.* There was no denying it. The shutters had come slamming down. He was pushing her away. Impulsively, she reached out a hand, touching his shoulder. She had felt so close to him, so needed. She wouldn't let him destroy the

moment. "Don't, Lucien. Don't raise your guard again. I like you so much better when you're human."

He covered her hand with his own. "Human, Katharine? I would have said I was being maudlin, perhaps descending to the openly mawkish. Yet even you, my dear, must admit that this is not a happy household. Edmund is a little better, yes, but it can be only a temporary improvement, no matter how much you may have counted on my presence making a difference."

"I know." Kate spoke softly and only because she sensed he needed to hear her agree with him. His dark eyes, that she had seen shuttered, hiding from her, and blank, as hers had been a lifetime ago, and even eloquent with pain, were now clouded with confusion. He might continue to protest that he only visited Edmund as a favor to her, his new "friend," but she was convinced his reasons were far more personal than that. If Kate had learned nothing else she had discovered that it was easier to forgive the unforgivable than it was to doggedly cling to hate. After a year of living in the shadows himself, a year spent laying stones for the wall he had attempted to build around his emotions—keeping hurt out and leaving his anger no way to escape—she believed Lucien was now learning that lesson as well.

"And then there is Melanie, poor, twisted Melanie," he continued some moments later, bringing her back to what she believed to be the matter at hand—Lucien's struggle to regain control over his own life. He squeezed Kate's hand, hurting her, although she felt sure he was unaware of it. "My God, Katharine, to think that I loved her! That sad, sick creature. What is wrong with me, what fatal flaw do I carry, that I should ever have loved her? When I first came home Moina told me that men have always lived between their legs, if you'll forgive yet another crudity. She also said that the trouble at Tremaine Court had all begun with me. At the time I thought she referred to Edmund, and to my natural father. That wasn't quite right, Kate. Moina was talking about me. *I'm* the guilty one. I'm the one who brought Melanie to Tremaine Court."

"No! Moina's wrong. She only said that because she despises Melanie, although she continues to serve her. You're forgetting that your mother and Christophe Saville began it all, even before you were conceived." The moment she spoke she knew she had made a mistake.

He pushed her hand away with an abrupt movement, sitting up very straight on the blanket. "My, my, darling, you weren't exaggerating in your letter, were you? The one that hinted at your knowledge of the Tremaine history. You are exceptionally well informed, right down to the names of the cast of characters. Tell me, what other small confessions has Edmund seen fit to make to you over the years?"

She refused to allow him to bait her. "Edmund told me how he stumbled across the love letters Christophe Saville had written to your mother—about the deed to the house in Portman Square. He told me everything, Lucien, including some things you probably don't know, although I think you've begun to guess at them now, and even marvel at his sacrifices, no matter how ill-judged they might have been. He begged me to write it all down, all about his marriage to Melanie, so that you could read it after he died. He said he couldn't go to his grave without assuring himself you would one day know everything that had happened. I wanted more for him, wanted him to have some peace now, while he's still alive, which is why I kept writing to you in London, asking you to return to Tremaine Court."

"And I did return, to find that Edmund can no longer say *anything* to me. This story he dictated to you—will you allow me to see it?"

She looked away, unable to meet his eyes. "Edmund gave it to his solicitor. You will only be able to read it after his death. But trust me, Lucien, you can't blame yourself for what happened. You can't feel guilty because your mother died, or because Melanie took advantage of Edmund's despair. Melanie is a greedy, grasping woman, I agree, but she hides it well. No one can blame you for falling in love with a beautiful woman."

"How wonderful, darling. Does this mean I have been

absolved? I cannot tell you how that relieves my mind." He turned his back to her, looking down at Noddy's sleeping form. "Yet I cannot help but ponder yet another question," he said softly, so that Kate had to strain to hear him. "Would our good friend Edmund be so generous, do you suppose—would his sympathies remain so staunchly in my favor, his concern for my welfare continue to be uppermost in his mind—if he were to somehow learn that I just might be the true father of this child?"

"What? Oh, God—that *bitch!*" Now, at last, Kate understood. No wonder he had been avoiding her, avoiding the child. She closed her eyes, the sun suddenly too bright, too revealing of all the ugliness that hid beneath the beauty of Tremaine Court. She heard a bird singing on a nearby branch, the buzzing drone of a passing bee. The air hung so still that she imagined she could even hear Noddy's quiet breathing. She knew she could hear the beating of her own heart.

"Katharine? Katharine, open your eyes. It is possible, you know, although I'm not proud of the fact that I may have fathered a child and then blithely gone off to war, leaving Melanie behind to deal with the consequences. Melanie says it's true, and she only married Edmund when the opportunity arose, to give our child a name. She too tells a good story, perhaps even better than Edmund's, although I must confess I was not tempted to write it down, to record such a tale for posterity."

"She's lying, Lucien," Kate said earnestly, hoping he would believe her, daring to be brutally frank, even at her own expense. "Listen to me. I *nursed* Noddy, remember? I was frantic when I first saw him, sure he wouldn't live out the day. He was so small, smaller and more frail even than my own child, and my baby had been born nearly two months before he should have been. Noddy was born too soon as well, which was why Edmund had not as yet engaged a wet nurse. Moina told me Melanie had brought on the birth by taking some sort of physic because she had tired of carrying the child. She and Edmund had been married a

little over eight months when Noddy was born. *Eight months!* If he had been yours he would have been much bigger, much stronger. Now, I may not know everything there is to know about babies, Lucien, but I *can* count. Noddy is Edmund's son."

She must have raised her voice in her urgency to reassure Lucien, for Noddy began to move about on the blanket, screwing up his features as he slowly stretched himself awake.

Lucien and Kate were silent, both watching the child— the small miracle that had been born of such selfishness and tragedy. Kate silently prayed that Lucien believed her. She hadn't lied to him; she felt sure Noddy was Edmund's child. How could Melanie have been so cruel as to suggest otherwise? With all the men she'd had, all the lovers she had taken to her bed since Noddy's birth, why was Lucien important enough to her that she would lie about something so easily disproved?

And the physic! Kate had often wondered how Melanie could have done such a thing, jeopardized her child for her own convenience. Had that been the real reason? Or had she deliberately brought on her labor early so that her claim naming Lucien as the father would hold more credence? She dismissed that last thought at once. Melanie was not the sort to plan ahead, Kate thought, but acted recklessly, selfishly, on impulse.

If Kate's conclusions were accurate, if Melanie truly was capable of such desperate acts, was anyone at Tremaine Court safe now that Lucien had reappeared in her orbit?

At last Noddy yawned and opened his eyes—his clear blue eyes that were so like his father's—and smiled up at Kate. "Mama?"

"Yes, sweetheart, it's Mama," Melanie said from somewhere behind Kate, her tone so cloyingly sweet that Kate felt her flesh crawl. "Did you miss me, darling? I was so lonely without you while I was ill. Give Mama a kiss. I've come to take you into the gardens. Lucien, darling, do you wish to join us for a family stroll, or would you rather stay here,"

her voice deepened fractionally, "lying about with the hired help?"

Melanie swept by Kate on a wave of flowery scent, scooping up the suddenly shy Noddy, who strained against her hold, reaching out his arms to Kate.

"Mama!" he cried, the fear in his voice ripping at her heart. He struggled so violently that Melanie put him down, not wasting time with gentleness as she did it, grabbing the child's arm so that he couldn't run away.

"Mama!"

Melanie could not have heard what Kate said to Lucien, or else she wouldn't still be trying to maintain the absurd pose of loving mother. She would have flown at Kate, tearing at her face with her long, carefully manicured nails, screaming invectives. As much as that thought repelled her, Kate would rather have suffered Melanie's anger than watch, helpless, as Noddy became a pawn in his mother's latest terrifying game.

Kate looked to Lucien, sending him a silent message with her eyes, wordlessly imploring him to do something, *anything,* to keep Melanie from taking Noddy.

"Join you, darling? Now, why would you think I would do any such thing?" Lucien questioned at last, his voice a lazy drawl as he moved to recline on his back, laying his head in Kate's lap as if the action was the most natural thing in the world. "Frankly, I'd as lief you took your whining brat away, so that Katharine and I might be alone. Isn't that right, my sweet Katharine?" he asked, raising a hand to cup the back of her neck, deliberately drawing her head down close to his.

"Lucien, stop," Kate hissed under her breath, sensing what he was about to do. This was no way to handle Melanie—exchanging hurt for hurt. Hadn't he learned anything?

"We're friends, Katharine, remember?" he whispered quietly, so that Melanie did not hear. "Friends help friends."

And then he kissed her.

His lips were compelling, insistent, and Kate knew better

than to struggle against him. Several moments later, when she could raise her head, her mouth moist and swollen from Lucien's stirring, deliberately invasive kiss, she saw Melanie looking at her with such undisguised hatred in her eyes that she flinched.

Games. Everyone at Tremaine Court played games. Dangerous, self-serving games.

"Mrs. Tremaine—" she began quickly, but Melanie cut her off, her childlike voice high-pitched, and reflecting a level of hysteria greater than Kate had ever heard in all her years at Tremaine Court. The birds flew from the trees, escaping the unnerving sound.

"Slut! Whore! Slattern! You'd spread your legs for a penny, wouldn't you? Now that my husband is too weak to poke you any more, you have set your sights on something else that is mine. I see it now! You've made them all hate me, you wanton witch, you evil trollop! *You* are the cause of all my problems. I won't have it, do you hear me? I am mistress here! Pack up your things at once—I want you gone from this house!"

Noddy, clearly terrified, cried even louder, pulling free of his mother and pushing Lucien aside so that he could crawl into Kate's lap, hugging her tightly. Kate guided his head into her shoulder, instinctively cradling him against her, protecting him, and glared at Lucien. "Now look what you've done," she said angrily, hating him for exposing Noddy to such a terrible scene only in order to extract some petty revenge on Melanie. "Are you happy now?"

"Melanie, I believe that will be enough, thank you." Lucien looked at Kate as he spoke, his voice low, controlled, and—to Kate's immense surprise—instantly effective.

Melanie fell silent.

He stood, turning his back on Kate. "I'm sorry I did that to you, darling, but I thought you needed a small dose of your own medicine. You see, I've been busy counting on my fingers since last we spoke. You really shouldn't have left me to my own devices for so long. I know the truth now,

Melanie, all of it. What kind of woman are you, to brand your own child a bastard—just so that you could have your own way? Did you really think to win my love with such a lie? Such a long, sad string of lies?"

His tone softened as he stepped closer to Melanie, employing the same gentleness Kate had heard when he had spoken to Noddy that first day in the nursery. "You know, I'd dislike you more if I pitied you less. You're ill, Melanie, truly ill, and I feel somewhat responsible. I did leave you to go off to war. You were fine until I left you. I didn't help you then. Let me help you now."

Kate shushed Noddy as she watched, fascinated. Melanie changed in front of her eyes, as a caterpillar might emerge metamorphosed from its ugly cocoon, transformed from screaming fishwife into the beautiful, innocent creature whose appearances had been becoming increasingly rare over the past months.

"Darling Lucien," Melanie crooned, stroking the front of his shirt with her small, white hands. "You do still care for Melanie, don't you? I knew you did. That girl, that devious Kate Harvey, means nothing to you." She smiled, and a single tear appeared, to course slowly down her cheek. "It's true, I have been ill. But I really am much better now, I promise. Only walk with me in the gardens, darling, and we'll talk. You'll see, darling, I am much better."

Kate pressed a hand to her mouth, appalled. Did the woman have no shame, no shred of self-respect? Lucien had as good as said he hated Melanie, pitied her, and considered her to be ill, if not completely mad. He had spoken to her condescendingly, as he would to a child he wished to soothe, and not as a lover. Hadn't she heard him? Or did the woman only hear what she wanted to hear, comprehend only what she wished to believe? For all Melanie had heeded him, Lucien might as well have not spoken, nor used Kate to act out his impetuous revenge.

After two years of wondering, Kate experienced a blinding flash of insight, understanding Melanie Tremaine at long

last. It was all so simple. Where Kate—or any reasonable woman—would have been crushed, even destroyed, by Lucien's words, Melanie couldn't be hurt by anybody or anything. The woman existed in her own private world, an insular place where her own wants and needs were the only realities, where everything was wonderful, and everybody loved her. This heartbreakingly beautiful woman who stood inches away from Lucien—smiling up at him with a radiant expression so free of guile that she looked as young, as innocent, as Noddy—would consider any means justified if they achieved the end she craved, the end she believed she deserved.

And right now, heaven help him—heaven help them all—Melanie Tremaine wanted Lucien.

Lucien slid his arm around Melanie's small waist and Kate swallowed down hard on the bile that rose in her throat.

"Yes, Melanie," she heard him answer, the two of them moving off in the direction of the gardens, Melanie's head pressed against Lucien's shoulder, as if Kate and Noddy no longer existed. "We'll walk among the flowers, just the two of us, and you can tell me more about this dinner party you've planned. Guy is looking forward to it with the greatest anticipation, and has even ordered a new suit of clothes from London just for the occasion."

When they had turned the corner of the house, gone out of her sight, Kate at last relaxed her hold on the child, catching her breath on a silent sob. She had to control herself. It wouldn't do to break down in front of Noddy.

She knew she had just been witness to a bizarre form of insanity, a dangerous, obsessive madness. And now, thanks to Lucien Tremaine—who either arrogantly or naively seemed to think himself capable of handling Melanie—she no longer felt safe at Tremaine Court.

All these years she had tried to remain as invisible as possible to Melanie Tremaine. She had bitten her tongue, bided her time, and tamped down her naturally strong

personality, not always successfully, but at least well enough to keep her post, to remain close to Noddy, to help Edmund.

But now Melanie had to see her as a threat to Lucien's affections. Even if Lucien had been able to divert the woman, defuse her anger, Kate was convinced it was only a temporary reprieve. Melanie wouldn't rest until she had banished Kate from Tremaine Court.

CHAPTER 15

So dear I love him. . . .

John Milton, *Paradise Lost*

*L*ucien entered the south wing from the terrace, gratified to see Edmund propped in his Bath chair near the French doors, awaiting him. The man had his back to him, so that Lucien could stand unobserved and indulge his thoughts for a few minutes. Their twice-a-day duty visits had begun on a shaky note, with Lucien belligerent and Edmund prone to melancholy tears, so that he had resorted to talking of nothing but everyday things in the hope of avoiding further outbursts—by either of them.

Kate had effectively put a halt to that particular form of evasion just that morning by preemptively thrusting that damned silver cup—another reminder of his past—in his teeth. He hadn't known whether he wanted to strangle her or kiss her, convinced she believed she was helping him as well as Edmund. And Noddy. How could he forget Noddy, the child he had almost begun to believe he had fathered?

What an interfering woman! Without permission, without so much as a by-your-leave, she had charged into his life

with her letters, and then taken control of his will by the simple means of her honesty and concern for the inhabitants of Tremaine Court. The worst part of all was that she was making progress. She was making him feel, forcing him to confront truths he had spent so many long months trying to avoid. He could not forget Tremaine Court. He could not forget the nearly two dozen years he had looked upon Edmund Tremaine as his father, the years he had spent loving that supposed father.

The devil of it was that, even now, he could do nothing to right all the wrongs that had been done. He could not turn back time, erase the reality that he lived in and pretend that things would ever truly be the same between Edmund and himself. His mother was dead. His father had banished him from his home. Melanie was now mistress of this sad household. All the happy memories in the world could not block out these truths.

How was he supposed to live? How was he supposed to go on, looking for a future that held no shadows, that offered him some hope of happiness, of peace? Kate Harvey seemed to have found some semblance of peace, which was perhaps why he felt so drawn to her. He had even suggested that she might help him, that they might help each other. For, no matter how far she might have come since first he looked into her blank gray eyes, she still had some distance to go. Otherwise, she wouldn't flinch from human contact, he was convinced of that. Would she ever be able to forget the father of her child, bury the past, and find a life for herself that did not depend upon living that life for the people of Tremaine Court? So far she had let none save Noddy get physically close to her—a child, whose call on her affections was not romantic, but motherly.

Lucien looked toward the oil painting that hung over the fireplace, a painting that had been commissioned when he was five, a portrait showing his mother sitting in a chair in the garden, Lucien at her feet. *Motherly.* Pamela's life had been a living definition of that word.

And then he looked once more at Edmund. Slowly, and

initially very much against his will, Lucien knew he had begun to rediscover much of the affection he had once felt for the man whom the world still recognized as his father. They might not share the same blood, the same heritage, but they did share two things: their memories of happier days, and their love for Pamela Tremaine. If only Pamela's healing love could reach out to them from beyond the grave now, reestablishing a bond she had never meant to see broken.

Kate had spoken earlier of sacrifices Edmund had made for Lucien, and he thought he knew what she meant. Unbelievable as it seemed to Lucien, Edmund had married Melanie, had remained married to Melanie, in order to keep her away from his beloved Pamela's son. Whether he had believed this action might somehow make up for his poor treatment of Pamela, Lucien could not hope to know. He only knew that he could no longer enjoy the thought of Edmund's suffering. The need for revenge had been outstripped by his need to put the past behind him and get on with his life. Like Kate.

Lucien saw Hawkins enter the room and silently motioned for the man to leave again. Telling himself that he was taking this next step for his mother, he took a deep breath and walked toward Edmund. He could see, hanging at the back of the chair, the tied ends of the length of soft cloth Hawkins had secured about Edmund's waist beneath the blanket that covered his knees, the cloth securing him to the chair. Hawkins, the perfect gentleman's gentleman, could be counted on for his ingenuity as well as his discretion.

"Hello again, sir," Lucien said by way of greeting. He could not bring himself to address Edmund as Father, so he skirted the issue, uncomfortable with calling the man by his Christian name. "I see that our devoted Hawkins has cut your hair. The man's a master with the scissors, isn't he? And he has dressed you very nicely, as well. Who knows, perhaps one day soon we will see you at the dinner table, sitting once more in your proper place."

Edmund's eyes widened and he began to babble incoherently, as if Lucien had said something that frightened him. His hand fluttered over the arm of the chair, as if waving away an attacker.

Lucien was at his side in a moment, kneeling beside the Bath chair, fearful Edmund would hurt himself. "What is it, sir? What did I say? Don't you wish to go to the dining room?" He smiled, relaxing. "Of course. You're fearful of your table manners, aren't you? Obviously it has been some time since you've been to London. I've supped with many finely dressed dandies who would be better served taking their meals from a trough, and they had full use of their hands. Believe me, sir, it would not bother me in the slightest to have Hawkins nearby, assisting you, not if I were to have the pleasure of your company."

Edmund did not appear placated by Lucien's attempt at humor, but continued to wave his hand about, spittle dripping from his slack mouth.

"I haven't got the right of it? It's not the difficulties with feeding yourself that bother you? What else could it be?" He closed his eyes a second, shaking his head as another possibility struck him. "It's Melanie, isn't it, sir? You don't wish to see Melanie. How could I have forgotten? Katharine told me you have rarely seen her since you first became ill. It still boggles the mind to believe you inhabit the same house without speaking to one another."

He took hold of Edmund's hand. "I'm right, aren't I, sir? You don't want to see Melanie."

Edmund became very still, his head leaning to one side against the pillows Hawkins had used to prop him in the chair, and squeezed Lucien's hand a single time. He relaxed his grip for a moment and then squeezed again, his faded blue eyes staring imploringly at Lucien.

Lucien returned the look, genuinely trying to understand. Slowly, as if he were watching for the morning sun to peek up over the horizon, he felt a light flicker to life inside his brain. "Sir!" he exclaimed, taking Edmund's frail hand in both of his. "How could I have been so stupid, so blind! Just

this afternoon I lamented to Katharine that you couldn't tell me anything I needed to know. But you can, can't you?" He raised Edmund's hand, still clasped within his two strong ones, and shook it gently. "You *can* talk to me—with this hand you and I can talk to each other!"

Tears ran unchecked down Edmund's thin cheeks. "Lu-luu-cie—"

"Shh, sir, don't try to talk. Katharine will have my liver and lights if she comes in here to see that I've excited you. Speech will come in time, I promise. Every day you're getting stronger. Moina's medicines will yet prevail. For now, let us be happy with what we have."

Lucien kept hold of Edmund's hand with one of his own as he reached out to snag a small tapestry-covered footstool, pulling it over beside the Bath chair so that he could sit down. He was reluctant to release the man, break the tenuous line of communication they had established. "We'll start slowly, sir, with small questions. Just until I can be sure you are strong enough. All you have to do is squeeze my hand if you wish to answer yes. If the answer is no, do nothing. There is no reason to exert yourself any more than necessary. Do you understand?"

Lucien held his breath, waiting. A moment later, Edmund squeezed his hand.

"Wonderful! Splendid!" Lucien grinned, realizing that he had been speaking to Edmund as if the man were a child. He might be greatly immobilized, he might be extremely frail and unable to speak, but Lucien had every reason to believe his brain was still sharp. "Forgive me, sir. I'll try to contain myself. You've known all along that you could communicate, haven't you? I'm only surprised the fair Katharine didn't figure it out before this."

Edmund squeezed Lucien's hand again.

Lucien looked at him owlishly. "She knows? Why, that clever minx! Why didn't she tell me? Did she think I'd abuse the knowledge, pestering you night and day for answers to questions that have been plaguing me half out of my mind?

Does she really believe me to be that selfish? And, I warn you, sir, don't you dare squeeze my hand, for I already know the answer. And she told me we were friends. Ah, women. There's no way of knowing just how their minds work, is there?"

He looked at Edmund and smiled. "Although, much as we have been as oil and water at times, we have had our moments, so that I do believe she is beginning to like me, if only a little bit."

Edmund made a sound low in his throat as he squeezed Lucien's hand. The sound much resembled laughter.

Lucien smiled. "That amuses you, doesn't it, sir? I know how fond you are of her. Just this afternoon she told me that you have dictated a letter of sorts to me, explaining everything that happened while I was on the Peninsula. You wouldn't trust such knowledge to just anyone, would you? I'm not sure she knows everything, if any of us will ever know all of it, but she does understand enough to recognize where to aim her darts whenever I've angered her. She's a strange lady, your Kate Harvey. But I am willing to wager you know all her secrets and still approve of her. You wouldn't have trusted her with Noddy otherwise."

He pulled a face, if only to entertain Edmund. "Oh, dear. You will forgive me if I'm feeling slightly left out, won't you?"

Lucien was certain the sound he now heard coming from Edmund was a genuine chuckle of amusement.

He looked inquiringly at Edmund, unaware that his expression spoke volumes to the older man. "I don't believe I like this, sir, much as you are enjoying yourself. I have the strangest suspicion I'm being managed. Have you hand-picked Katharine for some devious reason of your own? Chosen her for me, perhaps?"

Upon feeling Edmund's answering pressure on his hand, Lucien smiled, his heart suddenly light. He had been entertaining thoughts much along those same lines himself this past week. As a bastard, he could not aspire to any great

heights, not and be true to his conscience, but Kate already knew the truth about him. They were, as he had been careful to point out to her, two like spirits, damaged goods, as it were, but not unsalvageable. He didn't wish to spend the remainder of his life alone. Besides, he liked the feel of her in his arms. He even liked the way she fought with him, how she ignored his moods and lifted them at the same time. "Ah, sir, where were you when I first met Melanie?"

He shouldn't have said such a thing, even jokingly, for Edmund seemed to shrink in the chair, the tears that always seemed so close to the surface spilling once more, coursing down his papery cheeks.

"Forgive me, sir," Lucien hastened to apologize, longing to kick himself. "That was unfair of me, as well as unbelievably stupid. I promise you, we won't speak of Melanie. Not today. Not until you're stronger. You're looking tired, as well you should, for you've had a busy day. Let me go in search of Hawkins, and he'll help you back into bed. All right?"

Lucien didn't wait for Edmund's answer, but left the room quickly, knowing there was no way he could remain in Edmund's presence and not ask the questions he burned to put into words. Most important among them was: did Edmund know that Melanie, his beautiful young wife and the mother of his son, exhibited unmistakable signs of insanity?

Lucien closed the door to the south wing behind him, heading for his own bedchamber, where he felt sure Hawkins would be, another question tugging at the corners of his mind. After everything that had happened, and with the way to his future becoming clear in his mind at last, did he really need to know any more about what had happened three years ago, when his mother died?

"Hello, darling. How long has it been since our last little visit? A month? Two? But not to worry, darling. I often listen outside your door, as I have been forced to go to great

lengths in my attempts to ease the tedium here at Tremaine Court. I was bored again today, darling. Wasn't that fortunate?"

Melanie stepped in from the terrace, her chin held high, deliberately avoiding looking at Edmund's contorted face, knowing the sight would sicken her. She had, after all, certain sensibilities.

Had she really allowed him access to her body? How had she borne it? Would Lucien ever realize the extent of her sacrifice for him, the agonies she had suffered?

But now was not the time for reflection, for self-pity. There was something she had to do. Something important. Oh, yes. She remembered now.

"You and Lucien have had a pleasant coze, darling, if I can believe my ears, and an informative one as well. Yes—I listened, heard every word. The entire scene was beautiful, Edmund, and quite affecting. You must be ecstatic. Truly, I nearly wept. I'm so happy for you, and for dearest Lucien. He seemed thrilled to be with you, and after the terrible way you treated him. I hadn't counted on that, and I really believe I don't like the thought. If you were truly to reconcile it could prove dangerous to me. But, wait. I have a thought! Think about this, darling. Wouldn't it be a pity if, after all this time, Lucien would have to lose you? Poor man, he'd be so upset."

She sneaked a quick look at Edmund out of the corners of her eyes, smiling as she saw him shrink against the pillows. Walking completely around the Bath chair, she ended by standing in front of him. What had she been afraid of? She wasn't sickened by the sight of Edmund's thin, wasted body. As a matter of fact, she was delighted.

"Tied you up, have they? Trussed you, like a chicken about to be led to the chopping block. Poor darling. Shall I loosen those bonds for you? No? Ah, yes, of course. You'd crumple to the floor if I did that, wouldn't you? But Edmund, darling, I've always liked you best when you were at my feet."

She wrinkled her nose in distaste. "Oh, really, Edmund, stop that whining. It's so pathetic. But enough of this chatter, amusing as it may be."

Her hand snaked out, catching at his right wrist. "You and Lucien have discovered a way to communicate, haven't you? How enterprising," she said, squeezing his wasted flesh with all her might, "and how woefully *stupid!*"

She released him, flinging his arm down onto his lap as if it were a particularly vile scrap of garbage. The entire man had been reduced to garbage, useless rubbish, but still capable of assaulting her, hurting her with the suffocating stench of his life.

Kneeling beside him, she leaned forward until her mouth was close to his ear. "Listen to me, old man. Listen well. You've been in my way for a long time now, but I've put up with you because Moina says I have to. But now you're becoming dangerous, while Moina is fast growing superfluous. You know what that means, darling? Do you remember what I do when someone gets in my way? Let me explain, shall I? If you say a word to Lucien, one single word about what happened after he left Tremaine Court, or what is happening here today—" She hesitated, smiling, confident she had gained his complete attention.

"Well, face it, Edmund," she continued when she was ready, only when *she* was ready, "you are quite helpless here in this chair, aren't you? It would be easy for me to dispense with you. There are so many *lovely* ways I could kill you. I've spent whole days thinking of them. As you know better than most, darling, Melly can be *very* inventive. Why, I tingle all over, just talking about it."

Strange, she concluded idly, Edmund's impassioned love words had never possessed the power to move her, yet now his incoherent babblings, his weak tears, his frightened moans, all but transported her to ecstasy. She leaned in even closer.

"And do you know what would happen then, darling? Let me tell you. Then there would be no more time with your

precious Kate Harvey. No more time with Noddy. And most importantly—no more private conversations with Lucien. There would be nothing. *Nothing.* Do you understand, darling? Do you understand what nothing is? Can you envision it—being lost in an endless nothing? Does the prospect frighten you?"

She placed her hand flat against his chest, smiling as she felt his heart racing in fear, watching as his eyes widened in terror. Her blood sang in her veins as the heady sense of power nearly overwhelmed her. Her hand slowly slipped upward, so that her thumb pressed hard at the base of his throat. His pulse beat there as well, but only because she allowed it to. If she were to push a little harder, hold her thumb there a while longer . . . "Ah, my darling, darling Edmund," she breathed passionately. "The possibility of your death excites me so."

Her mind was seized with sudden inspiration. With her free hand she pulled down the low bodice of her gown, exposing one perfect breast, cupping its weight lovingly in her palm. Rising up, she touched the nipple to Edmund's slack mouth, moving it side to side, pushing the rosy tip between his spittle-dotted lips. "Remember, darling?" she crooned softly, watching his eyes, exulting in the difference between her young, firm flesh and Edmund's wrinkled, wasted skin.

His head moved against her nipple, and she gasped in pleasure, believing he had become aroused. He wouldn't be trying to push her away. How could he, when she was giving him such a gift? "Yes, darling. Feel it. Feel me bloom for you, flower beneath your touch. Remember how you once wanted me—how you still want me?"

Pulling back, straightening her bodice as she stood, she looked down at him, her own power making her dizzy. "Shall I raise up my skirts, darling, so that you can nuzzle the rest of me? So that you can taste Lucien's seed on my thighs? Oh, yes. We were together this afternoon, darling, in the gardens."

She leaned down, bracing her hands on either arm of the chair, her face close to Edmund's as she whispered softly, sweetly, confidentially, "Shall I tell you what we did, darling? Lucien's such a naughty boy, he can barely keep his hands off me." A stab of real, physical sorrow caught at her as she knew, somewhere deep inside her, that what she was about to say would be a lie, it would all be lies. Lucien had taken her into the gardens, that was true, but he had only talked to her, helping her to plan the dinner party while cruelly fending off her advances. And then he had left her, to come here, to visit with her husband—this sad excuse for a man.

But Edmund didn't have to know the truth. Besides, if she said it aloud, if she did her best to believe what she was about to say, maybe she could make it true, just by wanting it to be so. She closed her eyes as she began to speak. "We had barely gotten out of sight of the house, darling, when he pulled me down onto the soft earth. Oh, it was wonderful! His mouth hotly pressed to mine as we clung together, our tongues entwined, dueling, his eager hands roving everywhere, seeking, probing, finding—"

"Melanie!"

She straightened, smiling in real happiness as she turned to look at Lucien, her husband forgotten, the mental picture she had formed behind her eyelids still playing out to its glorious climax.

Her smile was adoring, and totally satisfied. Dearest Lucien, he couldn't bear to be out of her sight for more than a few minutes! "Hello, darling. Isn't it wonderful? Edmund has progressed to sitting in his Bath chair again. I was passing by outside after you and I parted on the steps, and couldn't resist coming in to congratulate him."

She turned back to Edmund, her smile still in place, her eyes narrowed in warning. "We've been having the *loveliest* visit, haven't we, Edmund?"

Lucien's hand grabbed painfully at the tender flesh of her upper arm, whirling her about to face him. His dark eyes looked murderous, so that a shiver of apprehension skipped

down her spine. "Darling? Whatever is the problem? I vow, your expression is positively fierce."

He disappointed Melanie by not answering, but only turned to that womanish Edmund, who had slumped against his pillows, weeping. She watched, admiring the width of Lucien's shoulders, longing to run her hands down his back, and lower.

"Sir? Are you all right? Hawkins! For God's sake, man, get over here. Take him back to his bed!"

Lucien turned back to Melanie as Hawkins pushed the sobbing Edmund to his chamber, shaking her so that she was certain her neck would snap. What had come over him? "Darling, stop! You're hurting me!"

"I don't have time to bandy words with you, Melanie. And I'll do more than hurt you if you don't answer me. What were you saying to him? Damn it, Melanie, *what* were you saying to him?"

Her chin quivered, and tears welled in her periwinkle blue eyes. How dare he distrust her, believe the worst of her? She fought back her tears, finding strength in righteous anger. "What was I *saying* to him, Lucien? Edmund is my husband. What should I say to him? How dare you ask such a question? My God, Lucien, what sort of heartless creature do you think I am?"

"That, darling," he answered, so coldly she believed— only for a moment, but a very unsettling moment—that she did not really know him, "I am still in the process of discovering. Now get out of here." He pushed her toward the door to the terrace. "And Melanie," he added as she staggered away, crying in earnest now, for his harsh words had hurt her beyond belief, "don't come back. If I ever find you near Edmund again I might just kill you!"

Lucien closed and locked the French doors behind Melanie's departing back, shutting out her impassioned pleas for him to understand that she had done nothing wrong, then pulled the heavy draperies shut so the sitting room was plunged into unnatural darkness.

He hadn't known he could be so suddenly, violently angry, so devastated by the sight of Edmund's tears, Edmund's obvious fright. If he had questioned his feelings for the man before, those questions had all been answered in the instant he had come into the room to see Melanie hovering malevolently over Edmund's chair.

Hate, it would seem, could only be maintained while one remained objective, coldly detached.

And Lucien now knew that he was no longer objective. He had chosen his enemy in that instant, narrowed his field of blame, and if it was revenge he still wanted, still craved, his efforts were no longer directed toward Edmund. No matter how he tried, he could no longer hate his mother's husband, even if he had lost the right to call the man his father.

He hurried after Hawkins, reaching the bedchamber just as the servant had finished undoing the cloth restraint and was about to help Edmund into bed. Motioning the man to one side, Lucien slid his arms beneath the older man's frail body, doing his best not to wince as he lifted, and discovered that Edmund weighed little more than Melanie, painful as it was to make such a comparison.

Settling Edmund gently onto the bed, he tucked the covers around him and was about to step away when the other man's good hand reached up to clutch at the opened collar of his shirt.

Lucien watched as Edmund's mouth worked, painfully trying to form words. "I—I lo—" Edmund said, one side of his mouth refusing to cooperate. Tears continued to run down his cheeks, into his mouth, as he struggled to continue, his breathing rapid and shallow. "Son. M-my s-son. I—I love. *Y-you.*" His grip tightened on Lucien's shirt. *"Son!* I—I lo-lov—"

Lucien could stand it no more. Whatever his failings, whatever his sins, this man had suffered enough. They had both suffered enough. Burying his head against Edmund's chest he whispered hoarsely, meaning the words with all his heart: "Oh, Father, and I love you!"

He had what he wanted now, what he remembered

longing for on that endless journey back from the Peninsula and now realized he had been looking for ever since—the only thing he needed to heal himself, to make him whole again.

Lucien Kingsley Tremaine's father had at last welcomed his son home.

PART THREE

THE JOURNEY
1814

What if earth
Be but the shadow of heaven and things therein
Each to other like, more than on earth is thought?

John Milton, *Paradise Lost*

CHAPTER 16

Her virtue and the conscience of her worth,
That would be woo'd, and not unsought be won.

John Milton, *Paradise Lost*

Kate removed the wilted daisies and laid freshly picked roses at the base of the headstone, then stood, sucking at the tip of her index finger where one of the thorns had pierced the skin. She looked down at the dead blooms in her other hand, realizing that it had been some time since she had visited Pamela's grave.

"Not since the day your son came home, as a matter of fact," she said, looking at the headstone. "But I do bring good news, Pamela. Lucien and your husband seem to have found a measure of peace with each other. Hawkins is very closemouthed about it all, but something slightly wonderful must have happened the other day, for Edmund is actually trying to get well and Lucien—well, let me just say that your son has a very lovely smile."

She walked over to the stone bench that stood in the shade of the high wall, laying the daisies beside her as she sat down. "Ah, Pamela, how is it possible to be both happy and sad at the same time? I have what I've wanted now, what

you and I both wanted. But is it enough? Melanie still reigns as mistress of the house, although I believe her days are numbered. Noddy will be provided for, even if Edmund does not recover, for Lucien is an honorable man and could do no less than care for Edmund's son. In short, Pamela, I am no longer needed here."

Kate picked up one of the wilted blooms and began stripping off the petals, one by one. "You know that I never really felt comfortable with the terms of Edmund's new will, naming me guardian of Noddy, and I am sure Edmund will be equally uncomfortable when he has to inform me that he has decided to name Lucien in my place. Lucien, I suppose, will fly completely into the boughs when he hears of Edmund's secret arrangement with me—for surely he will believe me to be a scheming, opportunistic woman out to feather her own nest. In his place, I might think the same thing. So there is nothing else for it. Not only am I free to leave, but I must leave.

"But that is how it should be, Pamela. I was no more than a necessary substitute. Noddy's future is Tremaine business, and Lucien is once again a Tremaine, in all but his bloodlines. Besides, his Kingsley blood ties him to this land. He quite obviously loves it here."

She raised her head to look out over the cemetery, to the small, unmarked granite cross off in one corner of the graveyard and the dainty spray of fresh roses that were propped in front of it. *Poor unwanted, dearly loved baby. Will Edmund take his turn at this ritual when I am gone, laying flowers on your grave?*

Kate looked down at the mess she had made in her lap, shaking her head as she stood up and brushed at the petals that clung to the front of her gown. "And so, Pamela, it is almost time for me to go, time for me to get on about the business of rebuilding my own life. Lucien may even find it easier to control Melanie once I am out of the picture, for the woman is extremely suspicious of me, and jealous as well—not that she has any real reason."

Kate stood silently beside the grave for another five

minutes, her mind purposely blank, avoiding thoughts of the one piece of news she could not share, even with Pamela. Leaving Tremaine Court, the safe haven where she had been given the luxury of recovering from her personal nightmare, would be difficult. Saying good-bye to Noddy would be even more so. But walking away from Lucien Kingsley Tremaine, from the promise of happiness his kisses had shown her, would be the most difficult thing she would ever do in her life.

"Two bouquets, Katharine? You must have something very important to discuss with my mother today."

Kate whirled about to see Lucien standing at the open gate, his horse behind him, tied to one of the posts, grazing in the tall grass. Had he tied rags to the horse's hooves, to muffle their sound? How else could she not have heard his approach? She turned her head away to quickly wipe at her wet cheeks, then said, "Only one bouquet is from me. The other is from Moina. I saw her in the kitchens as I was leaving and she asked me to lay flowers for her. It's strange—she has always known I come here each Saturday, but she has never asked me to bring flowers for her before today."

Lucien's sudden frown showed her that he too found the old servant's request odd. "How very interesting," he said, approaching to lay a small bouquet of wildflowers next to the bunches of roses. "And they say old dogs don't learn new tricks. I'd ask her why, except that I doubt she will answer. Moina never explains anything. She only hints, and then sits back to wait while you chase yourself in circles, trying to figure out what she meant. Katharine—will you walk with me?"

He didn't wait for her answer, but only took her hand and led her out of the cemetery, leaving his horse tied to the post. She felt curiously calmed by Lucien's touch, even as her heart began to beat at nearly twice its normal rhythm.

They walked in silence for several minutes before, coming to a halt at the crest of a small hill, Lucien turned to her, taking her other hand in his as well. "You didn't flinch,

Katharine. Not at the cemetery, and not now. Does this mean you're no longer afraid of me?"

She looked into his eyes, those dark, formerly unreadable eyes that now sparkled with amusement. "You read too much into things, Lucien. I hardly feared you would throw me to the ground and ravish me within sight of your mother's grave." She pulled her hands free, folding her arms tightly around her waist, and turned to look out over the meadow. "I saw Edmund earlier. His recovery over the past two days is nothing short of remarkable, even if he cannot talk as yet and his left side is still weak. Hawkins tells me he is eating everything put in front of him, and all but demands to be put in his Bath chair."

"He also has refused to take any more of Moina's medicine," Lucien told her, his voice so close that she knew he was standing directly behind her—close enough to touch her, close enough to slip his arms around her and draw her back against his strong, broad chest.

She swallowed down hard on sudden nervousness, not totally unmixed with fear, and said, "It does have a vile smell—the medicine, that is. I can hardly blame him for refusing it, especially since even Moina now agrees it has not done him much good. That's why she was in the kitchens. She has thought of another potion, some sort of restorative tonic, she said. I wish her luck with it, for I believe it smells even worse than the first medicine."

She inhaled sharply as Lucien slipped his arms around her waist, his hands covering hers as he rested his chin on her shoulder. "Thank you, sweet Katharine."

"Th-thank you? I don't know what you mean."

"No?" His lips brushed at the side of her throat and she thought her knees would buckle. "Then you don't recall standing across Edmund's bed two days ago, brandishing my infant cup as if challenging me to a duel? You are a stubborn little bulldog, aren't you, once you've gotten your teeth into someone? For more than a year you've been hounding me, and now you have what you wanted. What we

all wanted, although I refused to see it. And so, whether you wish it or not—thank you, Katharine."

She could barely concentrate, barely hear him for the sound of her blood pounding in her ears. He wanted her to accept his gratitude? She didn't want his gratitude! She wanted his love. Dear God—she wanted his love! "You—you're welcome."

His soft chuckle melted something deep inside her. It would be easy, so wretchedly easy, to relax against him, to build on his offer of friendship, to take advantage of his feelings of gratitude, to believe that his happiness could become her happiness as well.

The bastard and the wet nurse. The outcast and the soiled woman. Both of them injured. Both of them bruised by life, by circumstances. Kindred spirits, with much in common, much more than just their love for Edmund, even their concern for Noddy. Kate knew how Lucien saw them. As two of life's victims, now given a second chance. He may even have conjured some mind-easing daydream as to how she had come to bear a child in the first place.

Yes, that's how he, if applied to, would describe the two of them. Two like souls who, knowing each other's secret shame, might have a reasonably good chance for salvaging something from life in each other's arms.

She had worried how he would react when he learned that Edmund had secretly named her Noddy's guardian? How ridiculous. That fear crumbled into dust and blew away when she considered her other secret, the one that, once revealed, would in turn destroy the premise upon which Lucien had built his arguments. He might consider them both to be disenfranchised, but there were some things that can not be either taken or given away.

The circumstances of a child's birth, for instance. Lucien should be able to understand that. He had not chosen to be born a bastard, any more than she had asked to be born Katharine d'Harnancourt.

And no matter what their present circumstances, he

would always be the bastard Tremaine, and she would always be Katharine d'Harnancourt.

Lucien might be able to cope with the thought that she had borne a child—and she could only love him for that. But could he live with the reality that she, far from being disenfranchised, could trace her family directly to the man who now sat on the throne of England? That was asking too much of a proud man like Lucien, a man who had already proven to her that he could not forget he was a bastard.

"Katharine? Where have you drifted off to this time? I asked you a question."

Summoning all her strength of spirit, Kate disengaged herself from Lucien's embrace, realizing that she had indeed unconsciously allowed her body to rest against his. "I'm sorry," she apologized, turning to face him. "You're right. My mind was several miles away." *As far away as The Willows.* "What did you ask?"

Lucien laughed, flicking at the tip of her nose with his finger. "I asked if you would like to go swimming in the pond—which was my second question, meant to startle you back to attention when my first question went unanswered. But never mind, you don't have to answer. Your pretty blush has done that for you."

Did he have to be so happy, so carefree? If his cynicism, his swiftly changing moods, had intrigued her, his good humor bid fair to destroy her. It was like watching a birth, the emergence of a new life from the darkness, and she knew herself powerless to fight the attraction she felt for him. The love she felt for him.

"I see," she said, keeping her voice firm, and faintly disapproving. He was giving her too much credit for his figurative rebirth, his newfound optimism causing him to build castles in the air. That he might wish her to live in one of those castles with him nearly broke her heart. "And what was your first question?"

He sat down in front of her, leaning against the trunk of a tree. "It wasn't precisely a question, I suppose, but more of an observation. I spent the morning reading the London

papers I have been ignoring this week or more. The news is sadly out of date, but it would seem that Napoleon is on the run. Murat has actually deserted and joined with us. It's difficult to believe the war might be over soon, after all these years."

Kate sat as well, careful to keep her distance, spreading out her skirts as a sort of barrier. "Do you miss it? Not the war, for no one could possibly miss war and still be sane—but do you miss being in the thick of things, fighting alongside your men? Edmund showed me some of the newspapers he'd saved, where your name appeared in dispatches. You were quite the hero."

"War has no heroes, Katharine," Lucien said, picking up a long blade of grass and slowly ripping it in half lengthwise. "Garth and I found that out soon enough. I wanted to go back over there, you know. I wanted to throw myself on some Frenchman's saber to get back at Edmund—or make him happy—or some such nonsense, but my wound didn't permit it. Instead I took to wearing black, in mourning for my mother, my lost innocence, and all the men who were dying in my place—and then stalked around London in a foul mood, hating every man who wasn't over there with Wellington, fighting for his country."

He threw the grass down and looked at her, his grin sheepish. "What an absolutely splendid piece of work I was, Katharine! I believe Garth thought I had run mad when we met up again in London a few weeks ago."

Katharine fought back tears, instinctively knowing Lucien was talking to her as he had been unable to speak with anyone for so long, freely, openly, and without fear of censure. She felt honored and shamed at the same time, knowing she had not trusted him with her own innermost thoughts, her own truths. "Tell me about Garth, Lucien," she said, wishing she could confide in him as well, but knowing that she had left it too late, and that if she spoke now their tenuous bond would be broken. "You mentioned his name several times in your delirium."

Lucien smiled, leaning his head back against the tree

trunk, looking up through the branches, his eyes squinting against the sunlight that filtered down through the leaves. "Garth? Ah, now there is a truly fine piece of work, Katharine. We met when I went away to school—two scared little boys barely out of leading strings. We went our separate ways after a while, with me coming back here and him going to cut a dash in London. But we were thrown together again on the Peninsula. It was as if we had never been apart. I think we took turns saving each other's hide over there. A man couldn't ask for a better friend than Garth Stafford."

Kate felt her blood run cold. "Stafford?" she blurted, then bit her lip to stop from asking if Garth Stafford happened to live anywhere near Wimbledon. "Um—do you think Mr. Stafford will be visiting Tremaine Court any time soon, or is he still intent on cutting a dash in London?"

Lucien tipped his head forward, looking at her quizzically. "Garth? Come here? I hadn't really considered such an event. But, now that you mention it—I'm surprised he hasn't come bounding down to Sussex before this, with fire in his eyes. You remember that I told you I was attacked in London? Garth was with me at the time. One of the attackers mentioned Sussex, so that we thought—but I have decided my conclusion was in error. I believe I owe that attack to an idiot boy who has not yet learned how to lose gracefully at cards. But, yes, now that I think on it, I shouldn't be surprised if Garth were to find some excuse to barge in on me here at Tremaine Court."

Kate scrambled to her feet. "I'm sure that would be lovely, Lucien," she said, turning to walk back to the house. "I think it might rain soon, so I suggest we head back. You'll have to retrace your steps in order to retrieve your horse, but I can cut across the meadow. It's time I relieved Hawkins, anyway. I do have to earn my keep, you know."

She didn't wait for his reply, but began to walk away, taking no more than three steps before Lucien's hand came down on her arm, holding her fast. "What's the matter, Katharine? You're running away faster than Caliban when

he realizes I've forgotten to tie up his reins. Surely you're not afraid of getting wet on such a warm day? Especially as there is not a cloud in the sky. Is it something I've said? Some memory of someone you knew who went off to war and didn't come back?"

She frowned, thoroughly confused, then stiffened her spine as something in his tone alerted her to a deeper meaning in his question. She would settle this now, once and for all time! "My lover, you mean? Is that the story you have conjured up to explain away the reason behind the fact that I gave birth without the sanction of wedlock? That I flinch when someone touches me because I wish to remain true to that dead lover? Would that make everything all right in your eyes, Lucien? Would such a sad tale make living with my lack of virginity more palatable—perhaps even vaguely patriotic? Well, I'm sorry to disappoint you, Mr. Tremaine, but it didn't happen that way. I've cried no tears for the father of my child. The only tears I've cried are for that child, and for myself—and I haven't done that in quite a long time!"

He pulled her, struggling, into his arms, pressing her head against his chest. "Katharine, I'm sorry. You're right. I have been weaving plausible explanations in my head, like cobwebs, lacking in substance. Perhaps I even thought we could trade a secret for a secret, the way friends often do. But you already know all my secrets, don't you? Please forgive me. I promise not to force anything again, to wait until you're ready. I'm only grateful that you let me talk to you."

Putting a hand at either side of her head, he lifted her face so that she had no choice but to look into his eyes, no choice but to let him see her tears. "Are we still friends, Katharine?" he asked, his voice husky and rasping on her jangled nerves.

"Friends," she whispered, unable to stay angry with him, unable to hate him for caring about her. And then she allowed her eyelids to flutter closed as he leaned down and pressed his mouth to hers.

Her lips opened on a sob and allowed him entry, her tears

prompted by the overwhelming emotions that seared through her with the white-hot heat of a lightning bolt. This was what it meant to be a woman, this feeling of complete love, unconditional surrender, total and utter trust in the much stronger man whose hands molded her gently, without force, without having to show their mastery over her. Lucien may have been taking from her with his kiss, drawing her ever closer into his life, but he gave as well as took, surrounding her with his love, his sweet tenderness, and the promise of untold happiness.

Kate felt no fear as he drew her down on the soft, long grass, as he lay close beside her, as his fingers began to loose the buttons at the bodice of her high-cut gown. She experienced only a nagging sorrow that she would not, could not, have this wonderful man beside her for a lifetime.

His mouth moved from her lips to her throat, pressing small kisses down its length and then on the sensitive exposed flesh above her breasts. She felt no fear, and smiled weakly as she realized that she would never be afraid as long as Lucien held her. And he did not rush her, his fingers never pushing aside the fabric of her gown, never fully exposing her breasts or daring to touch her intimately. He only raised his head, looking into her eyes as if he saw something wonderful there, and then captured her mouth once more.

To show him she was not afraid, to prove to him that she had accepted this deepening of their relationship, Kate threaded her arms around his back, to hold him tightly against her. The warmth of his firm flesh throbbed beneath her hands. Holding him felt so wonderful, filled her with an emotion so overwhelming that she had only experienced it once before—the moment she had first held Noddy in her arms. Kate knew she was touching love. Complete, utter, eternal love. And more. She felt the first wild stirrings of passion.

And then he was gone. So swiftly that she could not immediately understand what had happened, she had been lifted to a sitting position, and then deserted. Lucien stood above her, breathing heavily, looking out over the meadow.

"I thought I heard a rider approaching," he said, slicing a look toward her before taking two steps down the hill. "It's Guy. From the route he's taking, it would seem he has just come out the rear path leading away from Tremaine Court. Strange. I thought he said he would be away from home for a few days, so that we had to postpone his invitation to dinner. Stay very still, Katharine, and he may not see you. I'll go down to meet him."

Katharine nodded, unable to answer, for the abrupt change in Lucien's mood had taken her quite by surprise. She watched as he strode down the hill, back toward the graveyard, waving at the comte, the sound of his voice if not his words floating back up the hillside to her.

She sank back against the tree trunk, closing her eyes as she fumbled to close her buttons, not knowing if she should curse the comte or thank him.

CHAPTER 17

All seem'd well pleas'd, all seem'd but were not all.

John Milton, *Paradise Lost*

*L*ucien walked back from the stables whistling snatches of some tune or other whose title escaped him at the moment. He had spent another pleasant morning putting Caliban through his paces, with the always amenable Comte de la Croix in tow, Guy's inane chatter and faintly raucous jokes helping to pass the time between breakfast and the moment Lucien could go to the south wing.

The past few days had flown by as Lucien spent every possible moment with Edmund, holding the frail man's hand as he filled their hours together with lighthearted reminiscences of their life together at Tremaine Court. He spoke little of the years he had been away, both those spent with Wellington and his time in London, preferring to concentrate on fond recollections of his mother, of their happy family life.

Old wounds had healed, old scars faded beneath the joy he felt while sitting with Edmund, surrounded by memories of his mother. He spoke of his favorite pony, Jumper, and the summer Edmund had taught him to swim, and the

winter they had joined the servants for a special treat on Boxing Day, and the trip all three of them had taken one spring to the Lake District, his mother demanding the coach be stopped every few miles so that she might gather plants to take back to her greenhouse.

Lucien smiled as he walked along, rhythmically beating his riding crop against his leg. There weren't enough hours in the day to talk of all his memories, to recount all the wonderful events from their shared past.

Of Melanie, of Edmund's wife, Lucien was careful to say nothing.

Kate Harvey, however, had figured often in his one-sided conversations, for Lucien found it impossible to banish her from his thoughts, thoughts that centered on her intelligent eyes, the way her lustrous black hair might feel between his fingers if he were to loosen it from those confining, confounding pins, and the strange stirring deep in his loins each time he remembered the feel of her lips beneath his.

Yet of Kate herself, Lucien had seen little since that day on the hillside. Free to be with Noddy now that he spent so much of his day with Edmund, she had taken full advantage of the situation, confining herself to the nursery, emerging only for quick walks in the gardens early in the morning, before Melanie stirred from her bed.

Although Lucien had assured her that she would not be turned off, no matter how Melanie might wish it, it seemed apparent to him that Kate was not about to tempt fate by placing herself in Melanie's path. She did not even appear to bear him company at breakfast any more, so that Lucien had begun taking both that meal and his luncheon on trays sent to Edmund's bedchamber, trying to tell himself that Kate was not purposely avoiding him.

He would just have to give her time. He could wait. Now that he had found Kate, he could wait. Good things, it was said, came to those who waited.

If only he could be patient.

Thinking of patience brought him, reluctantly, to think-

ing of Edmund's wife. Only at dinner did he see Melanie, who seemed to have lost the hysterical edge that had prompted Lucien to seriously consider taking steps to have her removed to some local asylum where she could not present a danger to herself or anyone else.

Since that terrible scene with Edmund, Melanie had often closeted herself in her chambers for hours, being waited on by a procession of dressmakers, hairdressers, and local tradespeople. She had flung herself into elaborate preparations for the dinner party, seeming to have no time left for Noddy or Lucien or any thoughts of turning Kate out of the house. At the dinner table her conversation bubbled with enthusiasm for the fine time they would all have, and she had put the staff to work with a will, polishing silver, washing windows, and taking down the heavy velvet draperies, replacing them with light summer gauze panels that allowed the sunlight into the rooms, enhancing the satin and brocade furnishings.

No longer did Melanie's moods swing rapidly from delight to despair, from happiness to violent anger, from passionate jealousy to equally passionate desire. All her energies seemed devoted to the dinner party, to the heady powers and responsibilities of her position as mistress of Tremaine Court.

She appeared, as a matter of fact, to be perfectly normal —except for those few hours every day when she disappeared, to where, he did not know.

Lucien would be tempted to believe Melanie had been the victim of a temporary nervous upset, a transitory madness now behind her if not for Moina's warning, delivered late one evening when the servant came to his room to give him a potion she swore would help Edmund. "Remember this, Master Lucien," Moina had said in her usual cryptic way, "that-there woman is always at her best just before she does her worst."

Lucien knew he really had to have a serious talk with Edmund about Melanie—and he promised himself he would, soon. But not yet. Not now, just as he had rediscov-

ered his love for the man, not while they sought to heal the breaches of the past, and build on their future.

The future. Lucien's smile faded as he considered that evocative, tantalizing word. Consciously, realistically, he knew that Edmund might yet die, no matter how he lied to the man, telling him he looked stronger every day. He could not help deceiving himself for a little while longer, wishing things could be different, that they could have more time together.

Never had time been so precious to Lucien. He quickened his pace, eager to get to the south wing, to learn if Edmund had spent a peaceful night.

"Lucien! I say, old friend, what's your rush? I haven't traveled all the way from London just to see your departing back, you know."

"Garth, you sly dog!" Lucien wheeled about, grinning, to see his friend approaching across the neatly scythed lawns, obviously on his way from the stables. "What has brought you here? Running from somebody's husband, perhaps?"

Garth Stafford stopped five paces from Lucien, sweeping into an elegant bow. A light gray drab cloak hung from his left arm, a curly-brimmed beaver was clutched in his right hand, and he was dressed head to toe in elegant evening clothes, as if he had quit London in a rush the previous night. "Nothing like it, Lucien. I leave such things to scamps like you, who have shimmied down many a Mayfair drainpipe in the wee hours. You see me before you, the town crier, bearing wonderful news!"

Lucien chewed on this for a moment, considering the idea that Garth might have some ulterior motive. Knowing he had not been invited to Tremaine Court, had his friend trumped up some ridiculous story, just so that he could come checking up on him? Knowing Garth, it seemed possible.

A week ago, Lucien might have been angry. No, he most definitely would have been angry! Now, in his new happiness, he couldn't think of another person he would be more happy to see at Tremaine Court.

"Town crier? Gauche as it may be for me to point this out, Garth, you're rather overdressed for the role," Lucien pointed out cheerfully as the two of them proceeded to the main entrance. "What happened? Did you break the bank at faro? Or did that long-lived uncle of yours finally stick his spoon in the wall, and you are at last the Earl of Haslemere —which would be a good thing, as you've been living high on the expectation this age, and I've been daily expecting an urgent missive from you, begging me to bail you out of the River Tick."

"My pockets are deep enough, thank you. And my news is better than anything you can imagine." Garth flung his arm around Lucien's shoulders, giving him a congenial shake. "Much better! Word came from Dover just last night, while I was yawning my way through Lady Cornwallis's boring crush, as a matter of fact, and I called for my curricle at once, my first thoughts of you. We all knew it was just a matter of time since that ridiculous invasion of Russia, but now it's confirmed. Lucien, brace yourself. As of a few days ago, about the eleventh of April—Boney has abdicated! I hear Blücher's cavorting in Paris, Wellington has soundly routed Soult, and the Little Colonel is retreating to Elba with his tail neatly tucked between his legs. It's over, Lucien! *The bloody war is over.*"

"My God," Lucien whispered, stopping so abruptly he nearly stumbled, turning to grip Garth's shoulders. Had there ever been more welcome news? "I don't believe it! It's over? It's really over?" It took several moments for the enormity of it all to sink into his brain. "Oh, sweet Jesus! *It's over.*" He pulled Garth against him, hugging the man tightly, then released him, abandoning him where he stood, and began running toward the house. Here was news to cheer Edmund!

He burst into the foyer to see Kate just coming down the stairs, and raced over to grasp her at the waist just as she reached the bottom step, lifting her high against his chest. "It's over, Katharine!" he exclaimed, whirling her around in

a circle as she clung to his neck to keep from falling. "I told you it was only a matter of time. Napoleon has abdicated!"

He loosed his grip a fraction, allowing her to slide slowly down the length of his body, until her face was even with his. "Ah, Katharine," he said, seeing her tremulous smile and quick tears, "isn't life wonderful?"

The moment was almost too perfect; he felt nearly drunk with happiness. There would be no more fighting. No more fine young men lying broken and bleeding on the field of battle. No more pain, no more dying, no more senseless slaughter. No more grieving mothers, no more anguished widows, no more fatherless orphans. Only peace. Sweet, blessed, glorious peace!

Lucien spared a moment to remember Packer, and Hasbrook, and young O'Connor, and all the numberless others who had given their lives so that he, all England, all the world, could rejoice in this moment.

Kate opened her mouth, most probably to say something —to demand that he put her down—but he gave her no opportunity to speak. This was not the time for words. Wrapping his arms tightly about her waist, he lifted her feet fully off the floor once more as he took her mouth in an exuberant kiss, whirling the two of them round and round in the middle of the foyer once more, their bodies pressed tightly together, celebrating life.

"Here, here, now, Lucien, quit mauling the poor child and introduce me. After all, I am the bearer of all these glad tidings. Shouldn't she be kissing *me*? It seems only fair."

Lucien put Kate down, but only reluctantly, for he realized that, after Edmund, he had wanted to share his news with only her. Keeping a firm hold on her waist, as she had been doing an unhappily effective job of avoiding him these last few days, he turned her to Garth, who stood at his ease just inside the door, and made short work of the introductions.

"Miss Harvey, allow me to introduce you to Mr. Garth Stafford, good friend, fellow officer, and totally untrustwor-

thy when in the company of gently bred females such as yourself. Garth, may I present to you Miss Katharine Harvey, devoted companion to my father in his illness and," he smiled down at Kate, feeling happily proprietary of both her and the knowledge that he had so easily referred to Edmund as his father, "a lady not to be trifled with, if you value your hide."

"Miss Harvey," Garth said, advancing to bow over her hand before straightening, to say, "Have we met before? You seem strangely familiar. It's something about your eyes. They are beautiful, of course, and extremely unique. Yet I feel I have seen such eyes before."

Lucien felt Kate stiffen in his loose embrace, then begin to tremble. "I'm sorry, Mr. Stafford, but I believe you are mistaken."

Lucien gave a bark of laughter to cover her abrupt denial, looking at her intently. "Katharine, don't apologize to the bounder. And, Garth, cut line. She isn't about to be taken in by such an obvious lure. Save your pretty speeches for Almack's, where I am sure they are received with blushes, appreciative titters, and batted eyelashes. Now come, let me take you upstairs to Hawkins while someone rescues your baggage. You did stop to pack, I trust, or are you planning to spend your entire visit in that outrageous waistcoat? *Yellow,* Garth? What an unfortunate choice. You look like a canary."

As he guided Garth toward the stairs Lucien glanced back at Kate, to see her worrying her lower lip with her teeth, avoiding his eyes. His elation faded, to be replaced by a niggling feeling that his newfound happiness might somehow be in danger.

Garth stood at the mantel, surveying the drawing room from his carefully chosen vantage point, admiring the furnishings while at the same time trying to see some stamp of Lucien in them, and failing badly. The colors were all wrong, too feminine, too fragile, to have been the background in which his friend was raised.

Lucien's mansion in Portman Square suited him better, full of vibrant hues, rich woods, and an individual stamp of excellent taste in everything from the Chinese silk wallcoverings to the smallest trinket arranged on the tables.

Not that he was unhappy to be here. He had driven down to Sussex on impulse, not knowing whether his news would serve as entry to Tremaine Court, for the last time he had seen his friend, Lucien had made it plain he did not desire his company. But Garth's curiosity, and his concern, had fast become an obsession—not knowing how Lucien fared, worrying about that strange knife attack—and if Napoleon hadn't conveniently lost the war he would have found some other excuse to visit Tremaine Court, and damn Lucien's reluctance to see him.

Yet Lucien had greeted him with open arms, inviting him to stay for as long as he wished, even apologizing in advance for not being a good host, as he would be busy most days with his father. There was, however, Lucien had told him, to be a dinner party soon, which might prove enlightening. And tomorrow morning they were to go out riding, perhaps to meet the Comte de la Croix, a most amusing Frenchman residing in the neighborhood. The displaced aristocrat should be delighted to hear Garth's news.

Garth had lunched in his bedchamber before sleeping most of the afternoon away, and once his valet had arrived with his baggage he had soaked in a tub before leisurely dressing for dinner, not encountering Lucien again since that man had deposited him in a large guest chamber down the hall from his own.

Before falling asleep Garth had mentally reviewed his meeting with Lucien, marveling yet again at his friend's vastly altered appearance. Not only was the funereal black he wore in London gone, to be replaced by comfortable country clothes, but Lucien's face seemed to have lost its harsh planes, taking on a youthful handsomeness reminiscent of the man he had known so long ago.

Could the mysterious Kate Harvey have something to do with the change? Garth couldn't quite manage to place her

in the household, for she too didn't fit his image of Tremaine Court. She dressed plainly, without frills, yet Lucien certainly did not treat her as nothing more than Edmund Tremaine's paid companion—an odd enough occupation for a young, unattached female, even in Sussex.

Besides, Kate Harvey was a very attractive woman, tall, willowy, and with a uniquely beautiful, intelligent face. To Garth's way of thinking, such women did not serve as companions to ailing old men—and they most certainly were not kissed by the son of the household.

He shrugged, abandoning his pose at the mantel. Yes, servants were kissed by the sons of households—more than kissed—but he instinctively knew that Lucien and Miss Harvey were not engaged in that sort of arrangement. Indeed, Lucien had all but warned Garth off, staking claim to the young woman as if he had already spoken for her.

That was a pity. Garth, at loose ends at the moment, wouldn't have minded a flirtation while he remained at Tremaine Court. With Edmund Tremaine confined to a sickbed and, according to Hawkins—from whom Garth had only with great difficulty extracted this slight information—Lucien's mother dead these past three years or more, it would be a quiet household.

"My gracious, why was I not informed that we are to have a guest for dinner? Please, sir, won't you tell me your name?"

Garth turned toward the sound of the lilting, musical voice, to see a vision of such fragile loveliness, such exquisite face and form, that he had to blink—twice—to believe his good fortune.

The young woman who stood just inside the door was remarkably petite, a veritable pocket Venus, from her glorious halo of blond curls to the very tips of her satin evening slippers. Her skin, touchable, flawless ivory, was broken only by the softest pink flush of her cheeks and the crushed-rose color of the most intriguing mouth he had ever seen.

And those eyes! What color could they be? Was there ever such a glorious blue?

He found himself lost for something to say—but not for long. His face lighting in a broad smile, he crossed the room to bow over her gracefully raised hand, pressing his lips to the cool, scented skin. "My name, you glorious creature, is Garth Stafford, and I consider myself the most fortunate man in the world to be in the same room with you. If I were to perish this very moment, I would do so willingly, save for the fact that I could not be blessed to utter your name with my last, dying breath."

He made no move to release her hand, and she did not withdraw it, allowing him to prolong the moment. "La, Mister Stafford, I could not countenance such a distressing occurrence, any more than I should wish to have you expire at all. If I tell you my name, will you promise not to die?"

Garth pulled her arm through his, guiding her to a nearby settee. "You have my word, fair lady."

She giggled as she seated herself, the skirt of her low-cut sea-foam green silk gown spread around her on the striped satin so that she looked like a nymph rising from the sea. Dear God! Her beauty was such that he was finding himself poetic.

"In that case, Mr. Stafford, I will be most happy to tell you my name, although why you should not already know it, I cannot fathom. I am Melanie Tremaine, sir, your hostess."

Garth stood very still, looking down into her smiling face, and felt his heart stop.

"Ah, Garth, there you are. Please forgive my tardiness. Hawkins is such a stickler for perfection, you know, and did insist upon breaking out a fresh neckcloth even when I informed him that his third effort had been sufficiently magnificent. Have you introduced yourself to my stepmother?"

Garth looked from Melanie to Lucien and then back to Melanie once more, surprised to realize that his heart had survived the shock. Melanie? The adored fiancée Lucien had

spoken of almost hourly while they were on the Peninsula? Melanie had become Lucien's stepmother? How? When? No wonder Lucien had taken up residence in London—a city he had always shunned—refusing to speak of Sussex. No wonder he had become so hard, so jaded. He had done it to hide the pain. The man must have been devastated! To lose someone like Melanie, such a glorious angel, would be enough to send the strongest man over the brink. And to lose her to his own father? Unforgivable!

Garth felt the sudden need for a glass of wine. Several glasses of wine. Perhaps several bottles.

"We have met, yes," he heard himself say at last, wondering if his voice sounded as hollow to Lucien as it did to himself. "I—I had no idea—"

"I am assured you did not, my friend." Lucien stepped to the drinks table, pulling the stopper from a crystal decanter before pouring two glasses of port, offering the first to Garth. "When my mother suffered a fatal accident, shortly after I left to join Wellington, Melanie and my father were fortunate enough to find solace together. It was a natural enough thing, I suppose. They have a son upstairs in the nursery, Noddy, a truly splendid boy." He turned to Melanie, his tone deferential. "And you, Melanie—would you care for some sherry?"

"Oh, yes, Lucien. I should love that above all things. How thoughtful you are."

Garth stood very still, closely watching his old friend's every movement and finding nothing to fault until Lucien answered silkily, "Yes, of course, darling. You know I live only to please you."

Darling. Garth picked up on the term immediately, catching a quick glimpse of Lucien as he turned back to the drinks table to see that a slight tic had begun working in the man's cheek.

Garth felt he had been somehow set down on a stage in the midst of a play already in progress, not knowing his lines. What should he say? What could he say?

And, not knowing, he uttered the very worst thing he could have said had he chosen from any of a million topics. "Will Miss Harvey be joining us, Lucien? I barely got to speak to her above an instant this morning in the foyer, what with you kissing her senseless one moment, and then whisking me off upstairs the next."

He heard a sharp intake of breath from behind him and turned to see Melanie Tremaine's ivory skin fade to a sickly white. "Lucien!" she exclaimed, her musical voice rising an octave, to become shrill, and quite unlike the flattering picture of innocent loveliness she had projected when she first entered the room.

She sprang to her feet, trembling so violently Garth instinctively put out a hand to steady her, only to have it swatted away as she brushed past him to confront Lucien.

"Surely you haven't taken to tumbling that ungrateful doxy in this house? I won't have such lewd behavior under my roof, do you hear! How dare you defile this house—and with Edmund on his deathbed? Rut if you must, but take her behind the stables, where her kind feels more at home."

"Hush, Melanie. We will not speak of such things. You must control yourself. Otherwise you will make yourself ill and we will have to cancel the dinner party. You wouldn't like that, would you, darling?" Lucien's voice was low, commanding, while at the same time curiously gentle.

Garth watched, fascinated, as the woman seemed to obey him, her fingers uncurling from the small fists they had gathered into as she spoke.

"Garth brought good news this morning, news that the war is at last over, and I foolishly kissed Miss Harvey—out of the joy of the moment. Nothing more happened, Melanie. I promise."

Melanie raised her hands to cup Lucien's cheeks. "Oh, darling, I'm so sorry. What could I have been thinking? I should have known your taste does not run to rail-thin, dark-haired giants like Kate Harvey."

"Of course, Melanie." Lucien reached up to lower her hands from his face, his features an expressionless mask, and turned her back toward Garth. "Now you really should apologize to Garth as well, and then we can forget it ever happened."

Melanie apologized most prettily, as would a child directed to do so by its parent and, as far as it would seem Melanie and Lucien were concerned, the awkward moment had ended.

The butler rang for dinner before Garth could cudgel his brain for anything else to say. Dear God, what was going on?

Lucien motioned for his friend to take Melanie's right arm while he took her left, and Garth walked into the dining room with all the eagerness of a condemned man being led to the block.

The meal, simple country fare but splendidly prepared, passed without further incident, with Melanie's endless stream of questions concerning the goings-on in London neatly taking them from first course to last before she retired, complaining of the headache, leaving Lucien and Garth free to take their cigars onto the terrace.

Standing in the gray of twilight, Garth gazed out over the gardens, looking over a Tremaine Court that appeared to be a most congenial place, and envied Lucien's luck at having grown up amid such loveliness. Or should he envy the man? And, more importantly, was Tremaine Court the congenial, lovely place it appeared to be? It had seemed that way, until he had met Melanie Tremaine.

Perhaps he should concentrate on happier things. Garth leaned against the edge of the low stone railing at the end of the terrace, smiling at Lucien, who had taken up a stance several feet away, his long legs spread slightly apart, looking very much the lord of the manor as he stared into the distance. "Has someone already told you how changed you are, my good friend, or would you like me to perform that office?"

Lucien slowly turned his head toward Garth, smiling slightly. "Changed, Garth? For good or ill?"

"For the better, of course. You're no longer dark and brooding. There will be many a disappointed lady in Mayfair once you bring your smiling face back to town. They'll just have to make do with our dearest scowling, pouting Byron, I suppose, if you will no longer provide fodder for their fanciful dreams. However, I can't say that I shall miss the Devil Tremaine."

"Goodness, Garth, I never knew my happiness could be the author of such unhappiness. But, as long as I have somehow served to brighten your life, I suppose I shall be content."

They smoked in silence for several minutes, Garth becoming more uncomfortable with each passing moment, until at last Lucien, startling him out of his confused, troubling thoughts, said, "Out with it, old friend. I know you're close to perishing with curiosity. Ask your first question."

"My first question? Then you will agree that I might have several? All right—old friend, I'll ask. My first question is—will you answer my questions?"

Lucien threw back his head, laughing aloud. "I shouldn't, you know, for I am convinced your speculations would prove to be much more interesting. But, yes, I'll answer. If there is only one thing I've learned in the past year it is that secrets have a way of festering, only exacerbating the wounds they have inflicted. It's time you knew the whole of it."

Where should he begin? He longed to know more about Miss Katharine Harvey, not only because Lucien had kissed her, or because of Melanie's obviously low opinion of the young woman. He had seen Katharine somewhere before today, he was certain of it! Her quickly spoken denials when he had broached the possibility that morning had all but confirmed his suspicions.

But his first question had to be about Melanie. "Your

stepmother—forgive me, Lucien, but she is the most start-lingly beautiful woman I've ever seen—is she the *same* Melanie?"

Lucien blew out a cloud of blue-gray smoke before answering, looking at Garth owlishly, a hint of the old coldness in his dark eyes. "I had thought your questions would be less elementary. Do you honestly believe there could be *two* such creatures?"

CHAPTER 18

All hell broke loose.

John Milton, *Paradise Lost*

*K*ate walked out onto the terrace, lifting a hand to shield her eyes against the sun as she looked out over the gardens, searching for Lucien. She had gone to the nursery for a visit with Noddy only to discover that he had been there before her, whisking the boy off somewhere, promising to have him back before luncheon.

She frowned, remembering Moina's vague answers to her questions about where Lucien and Noddy might have gone. The old servant had seemed distracted, even dropping a stitch in her knitting as Kate thanked her again for providing Lucien's Portman Square address, as some of the credit for Lucien and Edmund's happy reunion surely belonged to Moina.

Perhaps she should not have mentioned the reconciliation. Kate already knew Moina's loyalties lay with Pamela Tremaine, for the woman had made no secret of her feelings, or the fact that she blamed Edmund Tremaine for Pamela's death. Yet Moina's devotion to Lucien could likewise not be

questioned. Surely she would eventually relax her hatred enough to rejoice with Lucien at his new happiness.

Only one thought jarred: Moina's supposed loyalty to Melanie, a woman whom the servant could only see as her beloved Pamela's usurper. Kate had often pondered at some length on that particular relationship without discovering a possible satisfactory explanation. Clearly Moina had long ago captured the dominant role, with Melanie taking on the outward trappings of mistress while Moina exerted a quiet, mysterious, yet obvious power over the volatile younger woman.

Kate would have spoken to Edmund about this seeming inconsistency if he had been stronger, asking his opinion, but by the time she had been assigned the position of his companion, Edmund had already become too frail for her to consider bringing up any subject that might alarm him.

She could, of course, mention her concern to Lucien. She had wanted to, more than once, but whenever she was with him all thoughts of Melanie, of anything save her love for him fled her mind. She was too busy storing up memories of him, of their time together, to keep her warm through all the long, cold years she would spend without him.

But would Lucien even listen to her if she were to tell him her fears? He seemed to think he could control Melanie, which Kate knew to be wishful thinking. Did only women really recognize the potential for deviousness of other women, with men destined to make all their judgments of females based only on the superficial, the easily explained, never troubling themselves to look deeper?

Of course, she should be grateful for small favors, shouldn't she? Lucien had seemed to accept her own reluctance to talk about herself, even going so far as to promise he wouldn't badger her any more but only wait until she felt secure enough to come to him on her own. Which, she knew, was something she could not bring herself to do. Already her bag was packed and tucked under her bed. She had to leave, tonight, before Garth Stafford made any confession superfluous and she had to face the disillu-

sionment in Lucien's eyes when he realized that she had not told him the truth on her own.

But she could not leave without saying good-bye to Noddy, without seeing Lucien one more time.

The enchanting music of a child's delighted laughter could be heard in the distance and Kate squared her shoulders and followed the sound, descending the broad stone steps at the center of the terrace, to enter the recently tamed maze Pamela's ancestors had ordered planted nearly one hundred and fifty years previously. The hedges were no more than chest high, so that it would be impossible to become completely lost, and Kate knew the twists and turns well, so that it did not take her long to reach the center, a large grassy square planted with trees.

She stopped at the entrance to the square, one hand raised to her mouth as she took in the incongruous sight that met her eyes. Lucien sat cross-legged on the grass, Noddy in his lap, while Garth, clad as casually as his friend in breeches and an open-necked white shirt, cavorted about, his hands raised on either side of his head, his index fingers jutting skyward. His booted feet pawed at the ground as he snorted fiercely, doing a splendid imitation of a bull preparing to charge.

She turned to leave, not wishing to encounter Garth Stafford yet again, but Lucien's voice stopped her and she stood very still, listening to him tell Edmund's son a story.

"And then, Noddy, as Garth finished gorging himself on the chicken leg and looked up to see the bull—snort for us again, will you, dear man, as you do it exceedingly well—he realized that he had foolishly stuffed his pistol inside his bedroll, out of reach. Not that a pistol would be of much use against such a fearsome beast. What could he do, Noddy, you might well ask? Challenge the bull to a duel—chicken bones at ten paces? I imagine not. Well, you must be thinking, that's the end of poor Garth. But have no fear, as our story ends happily enough, for I chanced to stumble upon the scene at that harrowing moment—immediately taking in the seriousness of the situation—and went hotfoot

to the rescue. Here, Noddy," he said, settling the boy on the grass, "you stay put while I modestly demonstrate to you how I effected said rescue."

Kate, sure she had not been observed, rolled her eyes at this obvious exaggeration.

"Now you're the hero of this story? I say, Lucien, I think you're taking this a bit far," Garth protested, abandoning his ferocious pose for a moment. "Don't listen to him, Noddy. He reacted purely from fright, as he couldn't allow me to die when I was the only one who knew where to get more chickens. And you know what, old friend? Upon reflection, if I had known you were going to crow so about it, I might just have let that bull gore me."

"Stop grumbling, Garth, and put up your horns. After all, I saved your life." Rising, and picking up his hacking jacket as he did so, Lucien struck a pose Kate had only seen depicted on a luridly graphic tapestry her father had imported from Castile. He stood at an angle, his arms outstretched to one side, the shoulders of his jacket held in his hands. "Now, *el toro,* charge at my cape!"

Garth lowered his head, his boots pawing the ground yet again, and ran forward, Lucien neatly stepping to one side to allow his friend to chase the gracefully maneuvered jacket as it whipped through the air.

Lucien then positioned the jacket once more, prepared for a second charge.

Only Lucien's bull seemed to have another plan in mind. His hands still raised to his head, Garth ran straight ahead until, at the last possible moment, as Lucien took one graceful step backwards, he redirected his charge, sending a surprised Lucien sprawling full length onto his dignity.

Kate bit on her thumb to keep from laughing out loud.

Noddy, giggling and clapping his hands in delight, watched as Garth tumbled to the ground on top of Lucien, then joined the party, throwing his small body on top of the pile, his chubby legs flailing as Lucien grabbed him, tossed him onto his back, and began tickling him.

"Ouch! Lucien, give over," Garth complained, somehow

now repositioned on the bottom of the pile. "I gave up rolling in the grass when I reached Noddy's age."

"So that's what caused you to be the way you are, Garth? I've always wondered. It must be burdensome, growing up at the tender age of two," Lucien observed as he sat up, releasing Noddy, who immediately climbed onto Lucien's back shouting, "Horsey! Horsey!"

"Nom de Dieu! May I believe my eye? The London gentlemen scramble in the dirt, *n'est-ce pas?"*

Kate, wiping tears of suppressed mirth from her cheeks, turned in surprise to see the Comte de la Croix standing directly behind her. The absurd sight of the nattily dressed Frenchman—with a patch covering one eye and a gold-rimmed quizzing glass firmly stuck to the other—succeeded in putting paid to her hope of not being discovered spying on Lucien by immediately reducing her to helpless giggles.

"It is *fort amusant,* yes?" he continued when Kate, embarrassed by her outburst but unable to check the flow of laughter, could not find her breath, yet alone her voice. "I so adore seeing infants at play. But you do not join them, *Mam'selle,* for which I cannot blame you. I too am reluctant, for I am wearing my beautiful new jacket, newly delivered just this morning."

"Guy!"

Kate turned to see an attractively flushed and rumpled Lucien approaching, his black hair stuck with bits of grass and his full-sleeved, once snowy white shirt pulled half out of his trousers. A worshiping Noddy seemed to be permanently attached to his leg, so that Lucien half walked, half dragged himself to the edge of the lawn, his right hand outstretched in greeting.

If he were any more handsome, Katharine felt her heart would have melted.

Lucien ran a hand through his hair, succeeding only in rearranging the disorder. "Has it gone noon already? How remiss of me to invite you to share our mutton and not be present to welcome you. Garth—where are your manners? Are you going to spend the entire day rolling around on the

ground? Pick yourself up and come with me. We have to deliver this monkey back to the nursery if we want to have time to clean up our dirt before luncheon."

Then, almost as if it were an afterthought, he turned to Kate, who had been wondering when he would notice her. "Good day to you, Katharine. I can only hope you enjoyed the show?"

Lucien's remark served to erase any lingering traces of amusement or warmth Kate might be feeling, replacing them with simple embarrassment. "You knew I was watching?"

His dark eyes took on a strange intensity belied by his broad smile and her toes curled deliciously in her half boots. "I always know when you are near, Katharine. I make it a point to know. How fares my father?"

"He's napping quietly," she answered absently, directing a quick, assessing glance toward Garth, who also looked at her with some intensity. She turned her head away, avoiding his inspection, and bent to hold out her arms to Noddy, sure that Lucien would like his leg back.

"Mama!" Noddy pronounced happily, and quite distinctly, as he allowed himself to be lifted, wrapping his legs about Kate's waist. "Play bull?"

"Shhh, sweetheart," Kate said, watching Garth as he seemed to silently mouth the word "Mama," a confused frown creasing his forehead. "Mary will be wondering where you are, with all your lovely food growing cold on the table while she searches for you. Gentlemen?" she questioned as she looked at each of the three men in turn, although she knew her tone to be more informative than inquisitive. "You will excuse us, I'm sure. Young Master Noddy is late for an engagement in the nursery."

Noddy, his stomach clearly not figuring uppermost in his mind, immediately proved difficult, struggling in her arms as he reached for Lucien. "Lu-cien! Lu-cien! Noddy play bull!"

"Later, Noddy," Lucien promised, shaking his head. "Be a good little soldier and go with Kate now."

Just as she believed she had gained a firm grip on the child Guy stopped her, putting a hand on Noddy's arm. "The child, he is of such a prettiness. He is Mrs. Tremaine to the life, *oui?*"

"Hardly, darling."

Kate looked quickly to Lucien, who had denied the comte's assertion with a quiet vehemence that sent Noddy's bottom lip quivering. Kate's heart dropped as she recognized Lucien's remark for the cut it was intended to be. *Please,* she thought, *don't let his dislike of Melanie goad him into saying something he'll regret.*

"Here now, little man," Lucien was quick to continue, lifting Noddy from Kate's suddenly nerveless arms, cradling him against his chest. "I didn't mean to startle you. Guy, forgive me. I must conquer this tendency to overreaction, mustn't I? But boys should resemble their fathers, don't you agree? Life is difficult enough for boys without hearing that they might appear feminine? Having only met Edmund the once, Guy, you might not have seen that Noddy has inherited his father's eyes, and once these blond curls are cut, the resemblance will become clearer."

As Lucien spoke, and Kate and Garth exchanged looks that told her he had not been surprised by his friend's outburst, Noddy busied himself playing with the gold chain that hung around Lucien's neck. Finally succeeding in tugging it loose from beneath the shirt, Noddy peered at the miniature strung on it intently for some moments before exclaiming, "Lu-cien! Lu-cien! Mama, look, look! Lu-cien!"

Kate didn't have to look. She knew. She had seen the miniature of Christophe Saville the night Moina had placed it in the packet, the night she had delivered that same, condemning packet to the Fox and Crown. So Lucien Tremaine carried two reminders of his true father—the ruby ring and the skillfully executed, illusion-destroying miniature. And a third reminder—one that never left him—his father's face, which peered back at him each time he gazed into a mirror.

She moved swiftly to snatch Noddy away. But she did not

move quickly enough, for Guy was there before her, his manicured fingers cradling the miniature. *"Sacré mille diables!* Dearest Lucien, who is this man? He could be a brother to you if but the clothes were different, *n'est-ce pas?* Garth—you must see this so incredible thing!"

Garth looked to Kate, for she could feel his level gaze on her, but she could not tear her attention away from Lucien.

Handing Noddy back to Kate, Lucien removed the medallion from Guy's possession, looking down at it as he held it between his fingers. "Amusing, is it not? I discovered the thing some years ago in an out-of-the-way shop—somewhere in Piccadilly, I believe." He turned to Garth. "You remember, don't you, old friend?"

"Indeed, yes," Garth replied at once, so hurriedly that Kate felt sure he had to make up his story as he went along. "As I recall, at the time we thought the man depicted in the painting must be some long-lost relative of yours. You took to wearing it around your neck when we went to the Peninsula, as a sort of good-luck amulet, not that it kept you from taking that cursed ball in your leg."

Lucien must have told Garth at least some of the truth, for his inventive lie about the Peninsula revealed as much as it concealed. Kate closed her eyes, offering a silent prayer of thanks that Lucien inspired such loyalty. She just as quickly amended it to include Garth Stafford as well, for the man was truly a most honorable gentleman.

If only he had not come to Sussex.

Guy murmured something in French, lifting his quizzing glass a second time, continuing his inspection of the miniature. "Amazing, Lucien. You spoke of males resembling their fathers a moment ago. This unknown man could well have been yours, *n'est-ce pas,* if it were not for the existence of Edmund Tremaine. You must resemble your mother, yes? Ah, well, enough of this. Lucien, as I recall, you promised me a meal. Shall we get on with it?"

"That's it!"

All eyes turned to Garth, who approached Kate, his index finger extended as he pointed to her face. She began shaking

her head in the negative, wordlessly begging him not to say any more. "Why didn't I see it before this? Guy, it was your observation that sparked my memory—with all this business about parents and children."

It had only been a matter of time before he placed her. Her bag packed, her plan in place to leave this very night once it was dark, Kate had made one single mistake. She had wanted to say good-bye.

She fought a sudden urge to scream, panic robbing her limbs of strength, preventing her from running as far and as fast as she could, away from Garth's words. She had no choice but to remain here, in the center of the maze, while he put the finishing piece in the puzzle that had obviously been tugging at him since their first meeting.

Noddy struggled in her arms and she put him down, desperately marshaling her strength as she rose to her full height to look at Garth, resembling nothing more than a prisoner staring down a firing squad.

"Remember, Lucien?" Garth asked, clearly too taken with his discovery to read the plea in her eyes. "It's those eyes. They are so unique, are they not? That exotic, elongated shape, that glorious near absence of color. Beautiful! But more than beautiful—for I have seen those same eyes in a man's face, and let me assure you that then they are most intimidating. I know you thought I was merely flirting when she was introduced to me, Lucien, but I meant it. I'd seen eyes like Miss Harvey's before yesterday."

"Darling Garth," Lucien said, his drawl pleasant, yet faintly warning. "Surely this could wait for another time? You're embarrassing Katharine."

Kate knew Lucien had spoken to protect her, just as surely as she knew he longed to hear what Garth had to say. But it didn't really matter how Lucien heard, or when—the moment he learned the truth any scant hope she'd harbored that flight was not the only avenue open to her would disappear. Not only would Lucien hate her, but she would have to go back. Back to the scene of her shame. Back to The Willows.

"It's all right, Lucien. Let him speak," she said dully.

Only a few more months and she would have passed her twenty-first birthday. Only a few more months and she would have been her own mistress. She might have to spend the rest of her life without Lucien, but at least she would have had her freedom.

But now the truth would come out. Now her father would know where she had gone, and he would descend upon Tremaine Court, breathing fire, demanding she be returned to The Willows.

How strange that Lucien's good and loyal friend should be the instrument of her downfall.

Garth's head turned from Lucien to Kate, and quickly back again to his friend, as if seeking further instructions.

Lucien sighed. "All right, if Katharine has no further objection. Guy, if you'll excuse us? Garth seems to have something stuck in his craw and I'd best allow him to cough it out before he strangles on it. We'll join you on the terrace in a few moments."

The comte spread his hands as if in benediction. "This I shall do, *je vous assure!* Come, *mon petit,*" he said soothingly, bending to take Noddy's hand. "We are decidedly *de trop, n'est-ce pas?* You would like for me to show you my watch?" he asked, pulling an elaborately decorated gold pocket watch from his waistcoat. "It does the most marvelous tricks!"

Silence reigned in the small square for a few seconds after Guy and Noddy departed, Garth hanging his head as if deeply ashamed of himself. "Kate—forgive me. I am not usually so prone to indiscretion. It's just that—"

"It's just that you were born very near to Wimbledon. I understand." Kate felt a sort of fatal unreality enveloping her, much like the absence of feeling she had known that first year after leaving The Willows, before she had forced herself to struggle back into the stream of life. She couldn't let that happen to her again. She had come too far. Life was too precious to give up feeling—even if all she could feel was pain.

Kate could not bear to prolong the moment. Besides, Lucien must be near to bursting with curiosity, for he had long hinted—more than hinted—that he wished to learn her history. She had never doubted his interest and, now, perhaps, his love—she had only feared his reaction.

"I've known that Lucien's good friend was named Garth," she remarked, forcing a smile, if only for Stafford's sake, "but only quite recently did I learn your last name. It is as I've heard said, passing strange—how the simplest thing can mean so much."

"Then I'm correct?" Garth took another step forward, shaking his head. "I thought—I supposed—but I left for school very young, you understand—so you would have been little more than an infant at the time—and then it was off to London, and then the war, with only flying visits back to see my mother. . . . My God! I remember the whole of it now! My mother mentioned it when I drove down to see her when I first came back, although I confess I didn't pay her much attention. You're supposed to be visiting somewhere in America—Boston, wasn't it?—and been trapped there since the beginning of the war! Yet here you are! How? Why?"

"Boston?" Kate smiled, oddly amused. "I always wondered how he would handle my disappearance. Inventive, my esteemed father, isn't he?"

Lucien stepped between them. "Fascinating as this garbled conversation is, darling, do you think you could possibly include me? I, like our friend Guy, am beginning to feel decidedly *de trop.*"

Garth grinned. Clearly he was enjoying himself, mentally patting himself on the back for successfully jogging his memory, and Lucien's confusion only enhanced his pleasure. Also clearly, Kate decided, Garth had no idea how Lucien would loathe hearing what he had to say, or otherwise he wouldn't be so eager to speak.

"This is slightly backwards in form," Garth continued blithely, "but, Lucien Tremaine—my dearest friend, bravest compatriot, and clearly besotted admirer—allow me the

inestimable pleasure of introducing you to Katharine d'Harnancourt. *Lady* Katharine d'Harnancourt, to be precise, of The Willows, Wimbledon!"

Kate felt Lucien lift her hand, his dark eyes on her—hard and unforgiving—as he pressed her suddenly icy-cold flesh to his lips. *"Lady* Katharine? This is indeed a distinct honor. You're full of surprises aren't you, darling?"

"Lucien," she began, not knowing precisely what she would say, what she *could* say, to make him understand. "I wanted to tell you," she heard herself lie, "truly I did. But the time never seemed right."

He straightened, looking cold and remote even as his tousled hair and grass-stained clothing gave the lie to the excruciatingly austere formality of his manners. "Of course you would have, darling. But when was the time to be right, what with your various duties occupying you from morning till night? Does Edmund know how very honored he is, being waited upon by the Lady Katharine? How condescending of you, dear lady. I confess I am all but overwhelmed to think that you tended me in my own illness. Nursed me. *Nursed* Noddy."

If Kate weren't so aware of his disillusionment, she would have slapped him.

Behind them, Garth cleared his throat. "Lucien, for God's sake, give the poor girl a chance to explain. It may not be as bad as you think. I knew her father, the Earl. He did not, as I recall, have a reputation as being the most convivial of men."

Kate began hearing a strange buzzing in her ears, as if a nest of bees had taken up residence in her hair. "You *knew* him? Mr. Stafford—Garth—are you saying that my father is dead?"

Garth quickly averted his head, but he didn't have to answer her, for she had already read the truth in his eyes. Her father was dead. Strange. She hadn't expected that, hadn't even hoped it. Would never hope it. She should be feeling something, shouldn't she? Grief? Relief? *Something.*

But she felt nothing, nothing at all. Only numbness, a rapidly spreading numbness.

The buzzing in her ears grew louder, more insistent, even as her vision narrowed, blocking out everything but Lucien's face. Suddenly frightened, she reached for him, only to feel herself falling.

The last thing she heard was Lucien's voice, calling her name.

CHAPTER 19

To know this only, that he nothing knew.

John Milton, *Paradise Regained*

Kate had partially roused from her faint by the time Lucien carried her into her bedchamber, although she would not speak to him, refused to look at him. It took the arrival of Moina, sent for by a weeping Mary, voicing fears of an onset of brain fever, to spur Kate into protesting that she was fine, although this assertion did not save her from a stiff dose of laudanum.

The Comte de la Croix, gracious and understanding in the extreme—and totally forgotten by his host—had been forced to return home for his midday meal, while Lucien left Kate's bedchamber only to quickly closet himself in the morning room with Garth, threatening imminent mayhem if his knowledgeable friend did not immediately share everything he could remember about Lady Katharine d'Harnancourt.

Lucien hadn't found Garth's story easy to hear.

After her mother's death, Kate had lived very much in isolation in her father's house, the man not leaving the estate in more than five years, preferring to mourn his dead

wife in private—and then, eventually, entertaining a long string of willing females imported from nearby London. As far as Garth knew, Kate's only companions while growing up had been her younger cousin, Roger, who lived nearby, and perhaps her governess, although that woman had most probably been dismissed when Kate turned fifteen.

Hearing this, Lucien said nothing, only thinking that there could be no one less prepared to set out on her own than the young woman Garth had described, no person less suited to deal with the harsh realities of life and poverty. Already knowing himself to be deeply interested in learning the name of the man who had taken her virginity, he was now totally consumed with discovering his identity.

But there had been more to learn. He had pushed his emotions to one side to press Garth for the rest of it, but only learned some of the details of the earl's death.

After visiting with Edmund for an hour, and keeping a bright face on things so that the man did not become alarmed by Kate's absence, Lucien was at last free to rush back to Kate's bedchamber, determined to remain there until she awoke.

His mind in turmoil, Lucien spent the next few hours reviewing everything he knew about Kate. After that, until the sun faded behind the trees, until Hawkins tiptoed in to light candles, and while Kate lay motionless, her complexion unnaturally pale, Lucien berated himself for a fool. A damned stupid, arrogant fool! Was this how Edmund had felt as he kept his vigil at his wife's bedside?

Had Lucien believed himself to have a corner on misery? If life had dealt him an unfair hand, he decided that his troubles were as nothing compared to the fate that had befallen Kate. After all, he was a man, and expected to be strong. Kate had been little more than a child when she must have decided it necessary to flee The Willows, friendless, penniless, and—he was convinced now, although Garth had not been privy to such information—pregnant.

How had she coped with the unbelievable terror of bearing and losing her baby? What store of hidden strength

had she called upon to retain her grip on sanity and, more importantly, her quiet dignity? Why, if it hadn't been for Edmund—and Noddy—she herself might have perished, or been reduced to earning her daily bread in a way women in her circumstances had been forced to earn it since time began, on her back.

He remembered his anger in the maze, and longed to kick himself for his reaction. Lucien took hold of Kate's hand, squeezing her limp fingers, willing her awake. He had to talk to her, had to beg her forgiveness. He couldn't block from his mind the terror mirrored on Kate's face as Garth had so proudly voiced his discovery. She had clearly been horrified to have been found out, obviously fearing she would be sent packing back to her father, to the scene of her shame. Had she really believed he would do such a thing, that he would betray her in that fashion? She had, of course, and that hurt. It hurt a lot.

He had never believed Kate to be a loose woman, only one who had loved unwisely. But she had told him that she had felt no affection for the father of her child. Now he knew her identity, and that information only raised more questions. Even pregnant, why would she leave her father's house? What possible reason could she have had?

He pressed his lips to her fingertips, her lengthy sleep beginning to worry him. He had gone along with Moina's desire to dose her with laudanum partially because he needed time to think, time to confer with Garth. But now he needed Kate awake, needed to speak with her, needed her forgiveness for his harsh words in the maze. Needed her answers.

The covers rustled as Kate moved on the bed. "Oh, my head! I feel as if it has been stuffed up with cotton wadding. Lucien? Let go!"

Refusing to release her hand, he leaned forward, whispering, "Katharine? Katharine, lie still. You're all right."

She lay quietly for a few moments, as if collecting her thoughts, then pulled her hand away, struggling to sit up in the bed. Pushing a hand through her long hair, which had

become unbound as he carried her through the maze and up onto the terrace, she answered angrily, if somewhat muzzily, "What a ridiculous statement. Of course I'm all right. Or at least I'm as all right as anyone could be after having been drugged. No wonder Edmund sleeps so much. Moina must dose him with twice the amount she gave me!"

He watched her as she looked around the room, frowning as she saw that, other than for the small circle of candlelight near the bed, the entire chamber was in darkness. "I've slept the day away, haven't I?" A pained grimace flitted over her face and she bit her bottom lip, her expression telling him the events of the afternoon had come flooding back into her mind.

"My father—" she began, looking not at Lucien, but through him. "I forgot. Papa's dead, isn't he? It's so strange. All my life I have thought him immortal. I believe I am almost more disappointed than sad." She struggled to disentangle herself from the cover Lucien had laid across her legs, her movements still slowed by the laudanum. "I have to find Garth—he'll explain what happened."

Lucien quickly sat on the side of the bed, pressing her back against the pillows. He could feel her body trembling beneath his hands, see the naked pain in her eyes. Where were the words he might use to comfort her? Why did he feel so damned useless? "Garth already told me everything he knows, Katharine. But any explanations can wait for another time. You've suffered a shock, whether you're willing to admit to it or not. Why don't I ring for some warmed milk, or burnt feathers, or whatever it is fainting ladies are supposed to require?"

"Burnt feathers?" Her daintily rounded chin jutted forward belligerently. "I am *not* some vaporish miss! It was just the shock of it, that's all. And I further assure you, Lucien Tremaine, either you will begin telling me what I wish to know within the next five seconds—or I will shout this house down searching for Garth!"

Lucien smiled, relaxing. "Ah, Lady Katharine," he teased, releasing her shoulders but maintaining his perch on

the side of the bed. "You have hidden that spirit well these years—with one or two notable lapses—but it is back in full force at the moment, isn't it? Very well, what do you wish to know?"

She reached her hands behind her head, deftly twisting her long hair into a thick coil before tucking the ends in at her nape, so that he marveled at her dexterity, and the remarkable change in her appearance. Where she had looked vulnerable, almost childlike, and eminently desirable with her hair loose, she became regal with her hair bound. She became, in short, Lady Katharine d'Harnancourt.

"Well? When did he die? How long have I lived in fear of discovery without need? And," she added, momentarily avoiding his eyes, "I imagine I should ask how he died, as well."

"Your questions seem fair enough," he answered, purposely speaking slowly, deliberately drawing out the inevitable. "But, if I am to answer these questions, can I be sure you will return the favor, for I have several of my own?"

That adorable, defiant chin lifted again. When it came to arrogance, he believed she could give the Prince Regent lessons. "Very well. I can see I shall get nowhere until I satisfy your curiosity." She lay back against the pillows, seemingly unaffected by the knowledge that they were alone in her bedchamber, with her tucked up in bed. Either that, or uncaring. "Besides, I believe I already know your first question. I suppose," she said boldly, "complimenting myself with the notion that I at least fractionally understand the workings of your mind, that your dearest wish now, as ever, is to know how I came to be pregnant."

Lucien smiled, happy to be able to shake her too-brittle composure. "Ah, my dearest Lady Katharine, I am already reasonably conversant with the mechanics of the thing. It is the *who* of it that continues to beg for an answer."

Lucien watched as hot color ran into her pale cheeks and longed to take back his words. Stupid! Why couldn't he have waited? Why did his male pride have to get in the way when

she was so vulnerable, so totally unprepared for his questions? He was going about this all wrong. He never should have come into her bedchamber. Not while his blood still ran so hot. Not while the need to revenge himself on whoever had caused Kate pain remained uppermost in his mind. Now he had insulted her, shamed her, when he had only wanted to comfort her, be with her, return the favor of her gentle nursing of him when he had been lost in a world of confusion and pain.

"Why would you still wish to know—although I suppose I should feel flattered that you, unlike your stepmother, believe I would even know the man's name."

His timing might be badly off, but now that he had broached the subject he wanted it finished, once and for all. Then, and only then, could they move on to other topics, such as why a young woman of her birth and station would choose to hire herself out as a wet nurse. "Humor me, Katharine. You have already told me that you no longer want him, but at least let me know the name of your disreputable lover."

"This discussion is over," Kate pronounced coldly, her lips pressing together in a thin line. "Now that I think of it, I can't understand how it ever began. Kindly leave my room. I'll seek Garth myself."

Damn! He had pushed her too hard. "Katharine, please—"

"No!" She slid away from him, tumbling off the far side of the bed, nearly losing her footing in her urgency to be away from him, then turned to face him. "What is it about you, Lucien? I thought you would hate hearing that I was the daughter of an earl, that you would despise me for letting you say we were kindred spirits when I have been damned with a title I neither asked for nor desire. But I was wrong. Not entirely, for you were quite angry with me, earlier, in the maze, and rightly so. But you got over that quickly enough, didn't you? You really don't care about my title. All you really want to know is the name of the man who got me with child.

"How far do you plan to take this concern of yours, Lucien? Should we marry, perhaps—although you would naturally first wish to ascertain whether or not I'd be tempted to put horns on you within six months of the wedding. My God, Lucien, you're as bad as my father. Worse! He at least listened to my story before condemning me!"

Lucien remained seated, trying to remind himself that he was the articulate Lucien Kingsley Tremaine—urbane, confident, respected and even feared by his peers. No one had ever dared speak to him this way, or else be exposed to his razor sharp tongue, his brilliant put-downs, his icy disdain. So where was that brilliance now? His wits had gone abegging, along with his consequence, so that he had been reduced to the role of scolded nursery tot, unable to defend an indefensible action.

He rose, walking around the bottom of the bed to face Kate. It still hurt that she hadn't trusted him enough to tell him the truth about her background, but it was time he pushed pride aside and moved on. "Am I standing close enough, sweet Katharine, or would you like me to move another few paces forward?"

She frowned, shaking her head. "What are you talking about? I thought I made it abundantly clear that I want you gone. Why would you ask if I want you closer?"

He smiled, for he believed he had defused her anger with his question. "Why, so that you might be able to pick up that heavy candlestick and repeatedly beat me over the head with it. That is what you'd like to do, isn't it? After all, I've taken your knife. I just thought I owed it to you to make myself an easy target. I'd seek out an old sword and go into the woods to fall on it, except I wouldn't wish to deprive you of the satisfaction of watching my death throes."

He reached out to take her hand, daring a smile. "Are you prepared to do the deed quickly and cleanly, or would you perhaps prefer that I grovel first? I'm amenable, either way."

"It's uncanny. You even apologize with arrogance." She shook her head again, unable to hide a smile, although her

294

amusement faded before he could appreciate it. "I don't want you dead, Lucien. I didn't want my father dead. I just wanted, still want, what I've always been denied—to be believed!"

She pulled away from him and crossed to the far side of the room, her hands twisted together and pushed against her flat stomach, as if she were in real physical pain. He loved her so much he believed he could actually feel some of that pain. If only he could carry it all for her, relieve her of a burden she had borne alone for too long.

Lucien watched as Kate paced the length of the carpet for some moments before she spoke again, and when she did it was as if she spoke to herself.

"How strange it all seems, even now. It would have been easy enough to prove my story. All I would have had to do was slit my wrists, or leap from the church steeple, or tie a large rock to my ankles and wade into the nearest rain-swollen river—then everyone would have believed me. Even the priest, the one my father called upon to coax a confession from me, while not going so far as to advocate suicide, a deadly sin, waxed poetic about women martyrs of the Church who had chosen death before dishonor. It was all rather heroic, I suppose. Of course, I would have been *dead*, but that would be just a trifling inconvenience to the rest of the world, wouldn't it, for at least I would have been vindicated. What a vindication!"

She stopped pacing and turned to face him. *"A Vindication of the Rights of Women.* Surely you remember, Lucien? I laughed from the beginning of that book until I had turned the final page. I laughed so that I wouldn't cry. Miss Wollstonecraft's lofty ideas are fine in theory, but they are somewhat difficult to put into practice when you are penniless, pregnant, and adrift in a world ruled by men."

Lucien winced. He had given her that book as a jest, to nettle her. Had he taken so much as one correct step since meeting Katharine?

"But I chose not to destroy myself," she said, bringing him back to attention, "and that, dear Lucien, turned out to

be my greatest sin. Selfish of me, don't you think? But how could I do otherwise? I did not need Miss Wollstonecraft's theories. God gave me a mind, and that mind told me that my only duty was to survive, no matter what the cost! After all, it wasn't *my* dishonor—it was his! The shame wasn't mine, but his. Yet the same world that condemned me didn't expect *him* to hang himself in his study, or blow out his brains with his fowling piece—a truly lovely thought I refined upon again and again, but useless. But then, *his* belly wouldn't balloon out, giving evidence to the world of what had happened, would it? God! How I despise being a woman!"

Lucien walked over to her, placing his hands on her shoulders. "You know, of course, that you're making precious little sense. Society's rules may be difficult, but they can be bent, have been bent. Surely your father attempted to bring about a marriage between you and the baby's father?"

"Marriage?" She struggled to free herself, but Lucien had had enough of chasing her about the room, and would not let her go. She pressed a hand to her mouth for a moment, looking up at him as if gauging his response to what she would say next. As if deciding whether or not he could bear it.

"Lucien," she began slowly, deliberately, "you seem to have confused my history with your own. Your mother, loving your father but believing him dead, was forced into a marriage with Edmund. That had been her father's solution and your mother took it. *My* father's solution, not quite so inventive as Pamela's, was to lock me in my room until I admitted I had lied. When I refused, he planned to have me installed in some convenient madhouse, hiding his shameful secret from the world. Do you think I wanted to run away from the only home I'd known? Do you think I enjoyed being on my own, frightened and weary until, only two weeks after fleeing The Willows, I gave birth in the Fox and Crown, with only a coarse-mouthed maid there to curse me for bloodying the sheets?"

She took a deep breath, then added, almost offhandedly,

"It's odd, isn't it, that having a daughter locked up as mad is less dishonorable in today's world than admitting that his only child had been raped by her father's best friend."

Lucien felt the blood draining from his face. His hands gripped her harder, willing her to retract her last words, all her words. He hadn't wished to face the idea that she'd had a lover, that she had lain with a man, sharing her body with him, giving to him what he knew he had wished to claim for himself—her virginity. But to believe she had been raped, violated—her body used against her will—sickened him.

"Oh, my God," he murmured at last, not knowing he had spoken. "I can't believe it."

Her bitter laugh interrupted his misery. She spoke quickly, each word inflicting a separate, searing pain, like the metal-tipped lashes of a whip cutting into his back over and over again. "Of course you don't! Why should you be any different? Perhaps if I described it for you? I'll say it to you the way I said it to my loving papa, the way it repeated itself in my brain night after night until I forced myself to forget. Until Edmund, who had learned to listen closely before passing judgment, convinced me that I had to forget.

"Listen well, Lucien, and then tell me if you believe me. I was raped—although I didn't learn the proper term for what had happened to me until much later. You'll have to forgive my ignorance, for I had no mother to explain such things to me. But I learned the word, all the words. Raped. Violated. Ravished. Defiled. Ugly, aren't they? They even sound violent."

"Katharine—"

"No! I want you to listen! I *insist* that you listen! He found me in the barn, Lucien, where I had gone to see some newborn kittens. I was so happy to see him, calling, 'Uncle, come look at the lovely kittens!' I called him uncle as a courtesy, you understand, for I had known him forever. The cat had taken the kittens into a low-ceilinged corner of the barn, high in the loft, so that I had to move to one side to let my 'uncle' close. He pulled me onto his lap and, together, we watched the kittens, so young their eyes were still closed,

hunt blindly for their mother. My uncle stroked my arms as he held me, telling me how big I had grown since last he saw me. And then, slowly, so that I didn't notice at first, his hands became more insistent—more familiar—until, frightened, I tried to move away."

"Katharine, stop. For the love of God, stop!"

She continued as if she hadn't heard him, her eyes dry, her face frightening in its lack of expression. She looked now as she had when he had first seen her, as he had hoped never to see her again.

"But he wouldn't let me go, Lucien. He only laughed, and pushed me down, so that my head became wedged in the corner between the sloping roof and the floor, the kittens just beside me. He pressed his mouth on mine, silencing my screams with his lips, his insistent, choking tongue, and he began loosening my clothes, pushing up my skirts—his hands everywhere at once. I fought him, but I only ended up rolling onto one of the kittens, nearly crushing it.

"The mother cat began to hiss, biting and scratching me before she gathered up her babies and deserted me, leaving me there while my 'uncle' ripped open his breeches and pushed his knee between my legs, telling me not to scream, telling me never to say a word about what he was about to do to me, explaining that he was going to 'broaden my education.' I still didn't know what was happening. I only knew I was embarrassed, so embarrassed and frightened.

"But I got quite an education that day in the barn. A very painful education. Do you want me to tell you what I learned that day; what I learned a few months later when my father came to my room, breathing fire, to accuse me of having a lover; when, in my appalling stupidity, *he* had to tell *me* that I was to have a child? Do you want to hear the names he called me when I at last understood, and told him my 'uncle,' his dearest friend and drinking companion, had raped me?"

She hesitated, sighing. "Or have you finally heard enough?"

Lucien pressed her unresisting head against his chest, his

fingers pushing through the twisted coil of her hair so that they tangled in the heavy warmth, his palm pressed against the nape of her neck, soothing her. He felt sick and angry at the same time, and fiercely protective. How could Kate's father have heard this same story and not believed her?

"Katharine, sweetheart," he breathed against her ear. "Forgive me. Forgive us all. Men are terrible creatures—violent, and selfish. But you must listen to me. Garth told me something this afternoon, something that suddenly makes sense to me. I hadn't wanted to tell you how your father died, give you even more pain, but now I believe I understand what happened. I think your father did believe you. In the end, and much too late for either of you, he believed—and protected you the best he could." He took a deep breath, then ended, "This 'uncle' of yours—was his name Eustace Langford?"

She lifted her head to gaze up into his face, her hands pressed against his chest. "How—how could you possibly know his name?"

A tic began to work in Lucien's left cheek. "Garth told me how your father died. He can't be entirely sure of the date, but it must have been shortly after you left The Willows, while Garth and I were on the Peninsula. It also explains why you were never found. Nobody knew you had run away. The world must still believe the story your father had circulated about your having gone to America."

He continued to hold her close, his free hand gently rubbing her back. "Katharine, you have to be brave. Your father challenged one Eustace Langford to a duel—called him out over something so trivial the whys and wherefores have escaped Garth—and shot him dead. Your father then went home to await the constable, but his heart failed him before he could be arrested.

"His brother is now the earl but, according to what Garth learned from his mother—a matchmaking mama who sees him as a prospective suitor for your hand once you return from America—your very considerable inheritance awaits you at The Willows."

He watched as his words slowly penetrated her mind. All these years she had hidden herself away at Tremaine Court, cutting herself off from everything and everyone she loved, believing herself unlovable, nursing her wounds, finding a measure of peace, and caring enough to reach out to Edmund, Noddy, and even himself, in their time of trouble.

She had been so strong for so long that he knew it would take her some time to recognize that her circumstances had been drastically altered the moment Garth Stafford had recognized her.

She was free now to leave Tremaine Court, leave him, free to return to The Willows and take up her life as Lady Katharine d'Harnancourt once more. She was free to travel to London, where, thanks to her name and fortune, she was bound to be an unqualified success in society, which knew nothing of the truth of her absence. She was free to turn her back on these past unhappy years as well as on Lucien Tremaine, the bastard who had no more right to her than did the man in the moon.

He held his silence as Kate's intelligent grey eyes showed him that she finally understood. He continued to watch as her bottom lip began to tremble uncontrollably, watched as the first tears escaped, to roll unchecked down her cheeks.

"Oh, Lucien," she said on a sob, her defenses down at last, her arms sliding around his waist, seeking comfort, causing sweet, nearly unbearable pain, creating hope when he knew he did not deserve to hope. "What will I do now? Papa's dead!"

CHAPTER 20

Demonic frenzy, moping melancholy,
And moon-struck madness.

John Milton, *Paradise Lost*

*M*oina's potion had begun to do its work. Melanie lay on her peach satin coverlet, the bed ringed with fat white candles that flickered mysteriously, the soft, warm light flattering her ivory skin. She smiled up at her reflection in the mirror, watching as her hands inventoried her body lovingly, caressingly, devoutly worshiping.

Perfection. Exquisite, heartbreaking touchable perfection.

Blond curls spilled over the satin pillows like warm gold. Unblemished skin, so creamy and touchable; dusky-pink-tipped breasts; the tawny nest at the juncture of her thighs, hinting of buried treasure; her minuscule waist, flowing out to lush hips and ripe thighs; had there ever been such beauty of form?

She frowned, but only for a moment. Kate Harvey possessed no such claims to beauty. Hair as unremittingly black as a raven's, her complexion touched by the sun and marred by freckles, her tall frame more angular than rounded, her hips narrow, her breasts—if, indeed, the slut

possessed such features—hidden beneath the shapeless drab gowns she favored. And those eyes, those odd, smoky, all but colorless eyes. Could even the most charitable call this beauty? Could Kate Harvey possibly be even remotely desirable?

Melanie's smile widened. Not to Garth Stafford. Garth Stafford knew real beauty when he saw it. Why, the man had all but flung himself at her feet last evening, to declare his undying love.

And Guy. How could she forget Guy? Ah, the French knew how to appreciate beautiful things. He might use her roughly at times, his English deserting him as he spoke to her in a strange, gutteral French. But his violent male love play excited her, teaching her again the consummate pleasure of carefully applied pain, loosing urges previously indulged only once before, a lifetime ago in Bath. No! She would not think of such things. Soon her nemesis would come, summoned not to a party but to a dance with death, and that chapter of her life could be closed forever—and her darling Lucien would never have to know.

The frown returned, this time to remain. She had Guy. She could have Garth with only the snap of her fingers. She could have anyone she wanted.

So why did she still want Lucien?

The man was a fool! He haunted Edmund's rooms nearly every waking hour, as if he actually cared about the wretched creature. And when he wasn't hovering over Edmund, he hung about in the nursery, visiting with that sniveling brat, Noddy, or teasing her by the attention he insisted upon paying Kate Harvey. Why, he was with her even now, fretting over her like a hen with one chick, all because the slattern had fainted in the maze. Ridiculous!

Melanie had tolerated his little games, his small revenges, but how much should she be forced to endure? She had made such elaborate plans, suffered for so many terrible, empty years in order that they could be together. The time had come for the games to end. Her nerves had been stretched nearly to the breaking point, so that she had

betrayed herself in his presence more than once, allowing Melly's passions to rule her head.

She could not afford any more mistakes. Lucien had to be brought under control soon, made to understand that he belonged to her, that they belonged together, now and forever.

But how? Edmund stood in their way. Kate Harvey stood in their way. Even Noddy, by his very existence, presented a problem. She had to rid Lucien's world of all these stupid distractions, put a period to all the vicious lies they must be telling about her.

She had been so good. For nearly a week, thanks mostly to Moina's potions, the opium pipe, and her visits from Guy, Melanie had been able to control herself. She had been the model of propriety. Until last night, when Garth said that Lucien had kissed Kate Harvey again. She had been startled into anger, into rash speech, so that Lucien had been forced to reprimand her.

How had she ever gotten through the remainder of the evening? If it hadn't been for the knowledge that Guy awaited her in the gazebo—Guy and his marvelous tricks, his increasingly intoxicating perversions—she might not have been able to force Melly's badly bruised sensibilities back under control.

Yet even Guy could not ease the burning for very long. Moina's potions could not ease the burning. Only Lucien. He held the key to her happiness. His hands. His mouth. His pulsing manhood deep inside her, driving her onward, ever onward, to the only real fulfillment she had ever known. If she lived another hundred years she would never forget the peace, the terror-banishing contentment she had so surprisingly, so unexpectedly, found in his arms the very first time they had made love.

The others gave her loving. Darling Lucien, and only Lucien, had offered her love. Now, damn him, he tried to placate her with pity, with reassuring words, with empty promises. She would still like to kill him, if she did not love him so. She would enjoy killing him, laughing as he begged

for his life, revenging herself for his callous dismissal of her love for him.

Her love for him. Damn him. Damn him! *Damn him!* Why did she have to love him so?

Melanie looked up at her reflection again, bending her legs, her knees spread wide apart, her hips slowly undulating from side to side as she admired the view. If Lucien could only see her like this, open, ready, eager.

If only she could discover some way to encourage Lucien to take that first step back to her, make him want her again, just a little bit. It would be impossible for him to treat her so impersonally then, not as memories of their time together came flooding back, entrapping him even as her hot flesh would envelop him, devour him, draw him deep inside her, making him hers for all eternity.

The way she had made Edmund hers.

Her gaze drifted to the goblet resting on the table beside the bed. It was still half full. She had been saving the remainder of Moina's potion, rationing it, wishing to prolong her pleasure.

Melanie smiled at her reflection as she slid her hands down her sleek stomach, her fingers tangling in the warm, moist, tawny nest. Ah, yes. She had made Edmund hers.

It had worked once. It would work again.

"Are you planning to crawl into that bottle alone or do you want company?"

Lucien looked up to see Garth standing at the door to the study and motioned for him to enter. "Only close the door behind you, if you please. A light still burned beneath my beloved stepmother's door as I came downstairs, more's the pity. We wouldn't want her wandering in here, now would we?"

Garth laughed, taking up a glass from the drinks table and pouring himself some wine. "Why do you think I've searched you out, if not for protection? Luckily for me, and with you sitting with Kate, Melanie seemed more interested in Guy tonight at dinner. I think he was pleased that you

invited him after robbing him of his luncheon today—
although he left quickly enough, his amusing tale about
going over some business papers ringing most pathetically
false. He's aware she's after him. I hadn't known a Frenchman to be so intelligent—or a beautiful woman to be so
unattractive. I'm still having some difficulty digesting all
you told me last night."

He sat himself down in one of the leather wing chairs,
sighing theatrically. "Have I only been in residence for two
days, Lucien? It feels like years."

Lucien looked at his friend from beneath lowered eyelids.
"You're free to leave at any time. I scarcely need a keeper.
Or have you decided to be a dutiful son and make a push for
our newly discovered Lady Katharine?"

"What? And have you slicing up my guts for garters? I am
not so brave. Besides, I'm enjoying myself here at Tremaine
Court. I rather like seeing you humble, for one thing. It
makes for a delightful change after the shock you gave me
when I returned from the Peninsula."

Lucien drank deeply from his glass, staring into the cold
fireplace. He was so weary. He and Garth had talked into the
wee hours last night, and for at least another two hours
that afternoon while Kate lay sleeping. Garth knew everything now, all about Melanie, all about Edmund, and *almost*
everything about Kate, believing she had run away from The
Willows to escape a domineering father. His friend had not
passed judgment on any of it, which was why Lucien
treasured his friendship. Of course, when it came to
Lucien's feelings for Kate, Garth harbored one small failing.
He wasn't above loosing the occasional verbal arrow, refusing to hide his amusement over Lucien's predicament.

For, unlike Lucien, Garth saw life in simple black and
white.

Melanie was a conniving bitch, and a bit unbalanced into
the bargain. Solution? Ignore her, for she had no teeth.
Besides, half of England was unbalanced. It had become
quite the accepted thing to have a relative just in or just out
of the local madhouse.

Edmund and Lucien had reconciled. Solution? None needed. As far as the world was concerned they were father and son. End of story.

Kate Harvey was really Lady Katharine d'Harnancourt, wealthy, lovely, and devoted to Noddy and Edmund. Lucien, bitten badly once but now older and wiser, had tumbled into love with the lady. Solution? Marry her. Now. Immediately. At once. Before anyone else could come steal her away.

And then, ah, here is where Garth shone—he had come up with a simple happy-ever-after ending. Then, according to Garth, Lucien and his beautiful bride would move into Tremaine Court, care for the ailing Edmund and his truly adorable son, Noddy, raise a half dozen or more of their own children, and "everyone would live happily ever after." Except for Melanie. But surely she could be given a generous allowance and the directions to France, where she would be bound to find accommodating companionship among all the happy revelers who would flock there now that the war was over?

It all seemed most satisfying, and almost easy. Except that Lucien did not see things in black and white. He could not help but notice all the shades of gray, including the troubled gray of Kate's eyes as he had left her an hour ago. He had no idea how long he would have to wait before he could go to her and declare his love without her concluding his declaration had been motivated by pity or, even worse, some ill-judged sense of duty.

Lucien knew that Melanie, who had cornered him only that morning in the music room, pleading with him to remember how much she loved him—a piece of information he had not shared with Garth—was daily slipping further into a world that had little connection with reality. The memory of Moina's vague warning of some days ago only reinforced his concerns, so much so that he looked forward to Saturday evening's dinner party with trepidation, unable to conquer the feeling that it could end in disaster. If only Moina would speak to him again, but she

had proved impossible to corner, hiding behind claims that her health was "poorly."

Lucien, remembering how neatly Garth had disposed of the future of the inhabitants of Tremaine Court, turned to look at his friend. "Tell me something, Garth. What do you think of our friend Guy? I mean—why is he staying here in Sussex while the rest of the world is undoubtably readying themselves to rush posthaste across the Channel? He has lands near Paris, and a father whose fate he cannot know. Why is he continuing to cool his heels here when he could be reclaiming his estates?"

Garth grinned at Lucien over his wineglass. "Guy? Let me see. He doesn't want to miss your beloved stepmother's dinner party Saturday night? After all, it should be the social event of the season. I'm sure Melanie said something about a squire being in attendance, as well as an Honorable. I tell you, the mind boggles! Do you think I should have sent to London for my court dress?"

Lucien shook his head, pulling a face. Perhaps he wasn't as far ahead of his friend as he thought in making inroads into the wine. "Keep talking like that, Garth, and I believe you'd feel more at home in a belled cap and pointed shoes, playing the fool. I'm attempting to be serious. Don't you think it even the faintest bit odd that he should still be in England, making no preparations to depart?"

Garth dipped a fingertip into the wine, then sucked on it, appearing lost in thought. At last he pronounced, his tone hinting that he was saying something profound rather than pointing out the obvious, "Guy is French."

"How astute of you, Garth," Lucien returned, rising to pour himself another glass of wine. "Please continue. You see me before you, hanging breathless on your every word."

Garth was quick to oblige. "*You,* my good friend, are half French."

"Correct again! Garth, you amaze me. Clearly a quarter of the English populace carries some French blood." He sat down. "But you do begin to interest me."

Placing his glass on the table beside his chair, Garth

pressed his fingertips to his temples, his eyes shut tight as if meditating. "I recall an evening in London, not so very long ago. I recall a man named Jacky who visited his mother in Sussex, only to return to London with a mission. That mission—to plunge a knife into the unsuspecting back of one Lucien Tremaine. He missed, alas, which is why I am here, playing soothsayer in the back of beyond, rather than watching the ponies race at Newmarket, a discreet mourning band pinned to the sleeve of my jacket in memory of a dear friend, cut down in his prime."

Lucien bit on his knuckle, considering Garth's words, then just as quickly dismissed them. "I have decided that Orton hired those thugs. There was something in their incompetence that put me in mind of the man. But even if I'm wrong, I fail to see any connection between that single, never-repeated attempt at murder and our dear friend the comte's remarkable reluctance to return to his homeland."

Garth abandoned his pose, grinning. "As do I, old friend, but it did serve to pass a few moments without your mentioning the fair Lady Katharine's name. You were sitting here pining for her when I came in, were you not? I'm not surprised if she's out of charity with you at the moment, considering your treatment of her in the maze this morning, cutting up stiff the way you did. Perhaps you might leave off lapping up wine and consider your evening better spent composing a poem in her honor? An ode to her glorious gray eyes, or some such rot?"

"You aren't amusing," Lucien said, his chin burrowing into his cravat. "I made an utter ass of myself over a woman once, and Katharine knows all about it. That's embarrassing enough as it is, without the knowledge that I have taken nearly every wrong step possible where Katharine is concerned. Besides, she has only today learned that she's an orphan, no matter that she left home years ago. I have to give her time, play by her rules—or at least I will, once I can figure out what they are. I doubt even she knows at this point. I'm convinced she'll eventually return to The Wil-

lows, and from there go on to London, under her uncle's protection. She deserves to be courted, wooed gently, and not frightened."

"And, in the meantime, you're going to stay locked up tight in this room, drowning your sorrows? So this is love? I shudder to think of ever finding myself in such a sad condition. Lucien, good friend, you are pathetic!"

Lucien tipped his glass in Garth's direction. "Friend Garth—I couldn't agree with you more!"

Some time later, the tall clock on the half-landing struck one as Lucien passed by, his steps steady although his mind was wrapped in a pleasant cloud thanks to the wine he and Garth had shared. He made his way up the left side of the divided staircase, intent on finding his bed and, hopefully, a good night's sleep before waking to the reality of the perpetual muddle his life seemed to be since returning to Tremaine Court.

Hawkins was not on hand to scold him for his drunken condition, or to help him fumble out of his clothing, for the servant had taken to sleeping in the small room beside Edmund's in order to attend him during the night if needed. Halfheartedly cursing this defection, and refusing to summon one of the footmen at this late hour, he placed one foot after the other into the bootjack, removing his Hessians.

Guided by the light of the candle he carried and the tapers that burned low in his bedchamber, Lucien located his bed and padded toward it, preparing to undress.

He had lifted a hand to the small onyx pin in his neckcloth when, not knowing why, he realized he was not alone. Turning slowly, he made out the approaching outline of a feminine form dressed in a flowing white nightgown, and the shapes of two identical crystal goblets, one carried in each hand.

Lucien voiced his first, hopeful thought. "Katharine?"

His only answer was a laugh, high-pitched, childish, and slightly hysterical.

"Melanie." He had refused to move to another bedchamber, not wishing to appear as if he were running away from the woman. But this was ludicrous! What did he have to do to keep her out—nail shut the connecting door to their rooms?

"Darling Lucien," she purred, entering into the halo of light thrown by the candles, so that he could clearly make out the rosy tips of her breasts and the triangle of golden curls barely hidden by the sheer nightgown. Her blond hair was unbound, flowing onto her shoulders, and her glittering blue eyes shone like stars in the night sky. "I've been waiting ever so long. I had begun to think you would never come to bed."

Lucien was suddenly and violently angry, and in no mood to measure his words. "Melanie—get out!"

She ignored his order, placing the goblets beside the candles before walking straight up to him, not stopping until she was only inches away, her heavy, cloying, once intoxicating scent assaulting his nostrils. She placed her hands on the lapels of his jacket. "You don't want me to leave, Lucien. You're only saying that because you want to tumble that slut, Kate Harvey. But she won't have you, will she? I was downstairs earlier and saw you go into her rooms—and I saw you come out again. It's true, isn't it? She'd lie in the gutter with the dregs of the earth, but she won't have *you*. That's why you were drinking tonight, isn't it, darling? How long has it been? How long since you've lain with a woman?"

He brushed her hands away, disgusted.

"Listen to me, darling," she persisted, her hands on his jacket once more. "I can help you. You're near to bursting, aren't you?" Her hands ran down either side of his jacket as she smiled up at him. "How I adore clothing, don't you? A woman's gown is fashioned low in the bodice, to display her jewels, while a man's jacket parts here, just so," her hands slid lower, following the flared cut of his coat, "to display *his* most precious jewels to the world."

Before he could stop her, Melanie's right hand slipped all the way down, to cup his manhood beneath the tight-fitting doeskin pantaloons.

"Ah, darling," she crooned, squeezing him gently, provocatively, her practiced touch making him respond in spite of himself, "it isn't natural to live with this terrible ache you must be feeling." She dropped to her knees in front of him, her face pressed against his thigh. "Don't send me away, darling. Let Melly stay. Let Melly help you."

He felt his own arousal and hated himself for it, hated her for it. Reaching down, he pulled her roughly to her feet, holding her at arm's length. "Melanie, have you no shame? Why must you force me to hurt you?"

Her face crumpled pathetically, ready tears running down her cheeks. She looked completely stricken, and totally uncomprehending that she had done anything wrong. "Lucien—darling—I only wanted to help. I made you exquisitely happy once, I know it. Moina has explained to me that you believe you no longer love me, and I can understand how confused you must be. But I still love you, and you need me right now. All I want to do is help you. Here, I even brought us each some mulled wine. If you want, we can just sit and talk."

She turned away quickly, before he could find an answer to this convoluted thinking, picking up the goblets and handing one to him. He took it, watching as she sipped from hers, smiling at him over the glass when she was done.

"Come, darling," she said, walking over to the bed and patting the space beside her. "Come sit down, and we'll talk. You think you're very much in love with her, do you not? I can't imagine why. Won't you explain it to me so that I can understand? It would make losing you so much easier for me, darling, truly it would."

The last thing Lucien wanted to do was plop himself down on the bed beside Melanie and indulge in a friendly discussion about Kate—especially with Melanie sitting there all but naked. He stood his ground, taking a deep drink of the

wine to steady his nerves, to give himself a moment to figure out some way of ridding his room of Melanie without rousing the entire household.

He took another drink of the mulled wine, cursing himself for believing he could control her, cursing his predicament.

Kate avoided the mistress of Tremaine Court as much as possible. She had recognized the danger. Why hadn't he? How stupidly blockheaded he had been, believing he could control Melanie, defuse her wild imaginings, circumvent her schemes meant to make him love her again. Wearing a gown that reminded him of their first meeting in Bath was harmless enough. Trying to make him believe Noddy was his had been a desperate move, yet easily disproved. But this time she definitely had gone too far. This time she would have to be stopped, dealt with, banished. But first he had to get her out of his room!

"Melanie," he began, taking a single step toward the bed, "this is insane. I know you're confused sometimes, but you have to realize that anything we once shared is over now. You've tried wooing me, even cornering me and, much as I'm flattered by your devotion, and feel somewhat responsible for not recognizing your problems earlier, I cannot allow you to sneak into my rooms and—"

What was happening? He already knew himself to be more than two parts drunk, for he and Garth had split nearly three bottles, but suddenly he felt extremely lightheaded, as if he might pass out. He shook his head, trying to clear it, then looked at Melanie.

God, but she was a beautiful creature. Had he ever before seen such full, red lips—parted now, the pink tip of her tongue darting out to trace a circle around the soft skin of her mouth. He swallowed hard, feeling himself being drawn to those lips, his own tongue pushing insistently against the back of his teeth.

He could see her narrow, almost nonexistent waist that flared outward into lush, inviting curves, making a perfect cradle for the treasure hidden beneath the soft, golden curls.

And her breasts. His hands itched to touch those perfect globes, watching as they strained against the sheer cloth.

He remembered as if it were only yesterday how she had felt, how she had tasted, how she had moved beneath him and above him, how her body had clutched him, held him, teased him, incited him to heights he hadn't known existed. He felt his body stirring, almost hurtful in its throbbing arousal, his blood pounding in his ears as he threw down the goblet and struggled to be free of his neckcloth, pulling loose the miniature of Christophe Saville as well. His shirt was next to go, the buttons ripped free of their moorings. His hands moved to the top of his pantaloons.

"My God!" His breath coming quickly, painfully, as if he had just run a long race, he watched as Melanie stood, draining her potion before throwing the crystal goblet aside. She stripped off her nightgown as she walked toward him, her wide smile strangely feral, her features swimming eerily in front of his eyes as if she were half human, half floating spirit.

Her hands reached out to skim his bare chest, to touch the buttons of his pantaloons. Her voice came to him from a distance, luring him like a siren song. "Melly's here, darling. Let Melly help you. Melly knows what to do. Only your darling Melly, who loves you. And you do love her, don't you, darling?"

Darling. What a sobering word. He looked down at the shattered goblets, the spilled wine, and then at Melanie, his eyes narrowed in his efforts to focus his mind. "The wine. Melanie. What did you put in the wine?"

"Shhh, darling," she crooned, her voice still coming to him as if from a distance, fighting to penetrate the insistent, intolerable pounding in his ears. "It's wonderful, isn't it? Moina always prepares wonderful potions for me—such a darling woman. I put this one in our wine. I didn't take much for myself, saving more for you—just for your pleasure. I don't really need Moina's potions when I can have you. I don't need anything else when I can have you."

Her arms slipped around his waist. "Oh, darling Lucien, I love you so. Love me, darling. Love me!"

Moina's potions? What had Moina to do with any of this? Lucien felt sick. My God—she couldn't have!

Melanie's small hands were busy at Lucien's waist once more and he roughly slapped them away even though he wanted nothing more than to throw her to the floor, spread those lush thighs wide, and ride her, ride her hard, until he collapsed in exhaustion.

"Damn you!" He pushed her violently away, so that she stepped squarely down on the sharp shards of splintered crystal, drawing blood, before tumbling backwards against the bed.

Lucien wrapped his arms tightly around his naked upper torso as if he could physically restrain his sudden, fierce lustful desires. As Melanie clambered to her knees on the bed, her hands cradling her breasts as if inviting him closer, smugly sure of her power over him, he deliberately concentrated on a mental image of Kate's beautifully serene, intelligent face. All he wanted to do, had to do, was think of his dearest, untouchable, unattainable Katharine.

"Listen to me, bitch," he hissed through clenched teeth. He had to say this quickly, before his body betrayed him. He had to leave, get as far away from Melanie as fast as he could. He picked up his shirt and threw it at her. "Listen well. Your foot is bleeding badly, not that you seem to have noticed. Bind it up with that shirt. Then I don't care if you impale yourself upon one of the bedposts. But you're not to leave this chamber before morning. You're not to raise your voice, or cause a scene, or mention one word of what happened here tonight to anyone. Do you understand?"

Melanie's full bottom lip came out in a provocative pout as she touched her fingers to her foot, then wiped the blood on her breasts. She seemed to have passed beyond reason, beyond any sense of decency. Her fingers slipped between her thighs as she deliberately teased him, incited him, lured him closer, even deeper into her depravity. Her feet moved on the sheets, staining them with her blood. Yes. She had

moved beyond pain, beyond anything but her own drug-induced passion.

"One word, Melanie," he warned, his breathing so ragged he was finding it difficult to speak. "One word and you're gone. I swear it to God, Melanie—I'll have you thrown out of this house! I'll have you locked away, where you can't hurt anybody but yourself."

His threat seemed to penetrate her sensual haze. She slid from the bed, her movements mimicking that of a drunkard, to fall to her hands and knees amid the shattered crystal, the sharp pieces inflicting more wounds. "No, Lucien!" she demanded, crawling over to him, her bleeding palms clawing at his legs. "You don't mean that. You can't mean that. Never that! I'm sorry! I swear it! I was naughty, darling, very naughty, but I only did it to prove to you how much you still want me. And you do want me right now, don't you?"

The smell of wine was in the air, choking him. The smell of wine, of Melanie's sex, of blood. Her hands were on his thighs now, the heat of them burning through his pantaloons, his every sense alive to carnal pleasure. "Christ, Melanie—right now I'd take Moina if no one else were available. I'd take the first disease-ridden slut I saw on the street. I'd take anyone or anything I could find."

His voice lowered, to lend importance to his next words. "I'd take anyone, Melanie—except you. Do you understand me now? Do you understand how much you disgust me?"

She fell to the floor, sobbing, but he didn't take the time to look back, turning to flee the room while he could still walk, while his mind still functioned a fraction above sheer animal lust.

Garth. He could go to Garth. Have him hit him on the head, knock him out until the drug dissipated in his system. Yes. He'd go to Garth. Garth would help him. He pressed his forearms against his stomach, desire building in him until it became an actual pain. A pain he could taste, feel, smell. An oppressive longing he would kill to satisfy.

He flung open the door to Garth's bedchamber, only to

find it empty. He had left his friend in the study, finishing his last glass of wine. Biting his bottom lip until he drew blood in order to fight back a groan, he stumbled further down the hallway, heading for the servant's staircase that was positioned closer to the study.

Help. Help. He kept repeating that single word inside his head. He had to find help. He couldn't fight this alone. Not while Melanie lay in wait for him in his bedchamber, holding the cure for his torment, a cure that would damn him forever. Dear God! Somebody had to help him.

CHAPTER 21

Freely we serve,
Because we freely love, as in our will
To love or not; in this we stand or fall.

John Milton, *Paradise Lost*

*K*ate had found it impossible to rest. Her father's death, the why and how of it, had shaken her more than she believed possible, now, after more than two long years and a small lifetime of shocks piled one upon another until she had considered herself immune. Dreams plagued her both waking and sleeping, terrible dreams, fanciful dreams, even bittersweet dreams in which she was a little girl again, safe and secure at The Willows, the beloved only child of her adored and adoring parents.

She had given up trying to rest sometime after one, deciding to retrieve her book from the library, hoping to read herself to sleep, yet she tarried now in the hallway leading back to the south wing, already certain that the book, no matter that it had thus far proved to be stultifyingly boring, would not help.

"Katharine!"

She halted immediately, clutching the book to her breasts, aware she was dressed only in a worn nightgown, one of

Edmund's cast-off dressing gowns hanging loose from her shoulders.

"Lucien?" she questioned, not turning around, refusing to face awake the one dream that would not leave her each time she closed her eyes. "Is something wrong?"

His laugh was hollow, haunting, painful to hear, and when he spoke again she knew he was just behind her, his warm, wine-scented breath caressing her nape. "Wrong, dearest Katharine? What is wrong? What is right? Is it wrong to want you until my very teeth ache? Is it right to deny myself the pleasures of your body, the sweet, soul-destroying ecstasies we could share?"

"You're castaway!" Hadn't she borne enough today, without this? How could he do this to her? She took one hasty step forward, then turned to confront him, more than prepared to tear a verbal strip off his insufferably arrogant hide. The words died in her throat.

He stood before her naked, or very nearly so, for he was clad in nothing more than pantaloons. There were smears of what looked like blood on his hose, yet she could see no sign that he had been injured. She stared, dumbstruck, at the sight of his bare chest, a broad-shouldered, muscular expanse that tapered to a narrow waist, the whole covered by a fine mat of black hair that formed a vee, the base of which she could only imagine—should never imagine—as it lay hidden behind the buttons of his pantaloons.

He put his hands out to her, reaching for her, then just as quickly drew back, his knuckles white as he closed his fingers into tight fists. Only then did she notice that he was bathed in sweat, his brow furrowed, his entire face a contorted mask reflecting some hidden torture. "Katharine, I'm sorry. God, you can't know how sorry. Let me pass. Christ! Do you have to be so beautiful? Run, Katharine. Run away. Now!"

She considered obeying him, but only for a moment. "You're ill. What is it—some strange fever you contracted on the Peninsula? I've heard such fevers can recur, even years later. You look much as you did when I nursed you."

She laid a hand on his forearm, unable to suppress a small shudder when she felt the burning heat of his bare flesh. "Let me help you, Lucien. You need to lie down."

"Help me?" he repeated dully, as if unsure of what she had said. "Yes, yes. Help me. That's what I need. I need help, Katharine."

She led him down the hallway and into her own bedchamber, fearing he would not be strong enough to climb the stairs to his own rooms. Besides, he seemed to be delirious. He needed someone to stay with him, so that he wouldn't wander about, possibly injuring himself.

A small part of her brain issued a warning as she closed the door to her bedchamber, knowing that Lucien stood directly behind her. That part of her brain nudged forth the memory of Lucien's delirium when he had returned from the Peninsula, and the night he had dragged her onto his bed in a blind attempt to make love to her.

Lucien was a strong man, stronger now than he had been that long-ago night. If he decided that he wanted her she knew she would be unable to fight him. More frightening was the thought that she couldn't be certain she wanted to fight him.

"Sweet Katharine," Lucien said from behind her, and she gasped as he took hold of the single braid that hung halfway down her back, roughly pulling her around to face him. "I want you, sweet Katharine," he rasped, his eyes dark, bottomless pools that seemed to see her without actually focusing on her. "I want your mouth beneath mine, your soft breasts pressed against my chest, your long legs wrapped high and tight around my back. I want to be in you, Katharine, with you, a part of you. I need you, sweet Kate, need you, need only you—"

"Lucien, stop!"

She pushed against his chest, her hands slipping on his sweat-slick skin, frantic to be free of him. Still he held her, his fingers digging into the soft flesh of her upper arms as he dragged her relentlessly closer. How could she have miscalculated so badly? How had she let her concern for him

override her common sense? He was out of his mind with fever, not responsible for anything he said, anything he did.

This time the blame *would* be hers.

Rape. That ugly, unforgettable violence. It would happen again. The unthinkable would happen again. And loving Lucien wouldn't make it any easier. It would only make it more difficult.

And then, suddenly, she was free. "Lucien—"

"No!" He had pushed her away, roughly, so that she stumbled over the hem of her dressing gown and went crashing to the floor. "Christ, no! Katharine, help me. You've got to help me. Hit me, tie me up—something. Damn Melanie! Damn Moina! How could she be a party to such madness? Why? What dark potions has she been feeding Melanie, potions that eat into the body, rousing the devils that hide there, destroying all the good?"

Kate remained on the floor, confused and horrified, her vision blurred by tears as she watched Lucien crash drunkenly across the room to pull down the heavy velvet draperies, wildly searching through the yards of fabric until he unearthed the long silken cord used to tie them open. He returned to her, flinging the cord into her face. "Here! Use it, Katharine. While I still have the strength of will to help you—*use it!*"

Guy sighed, wondering how he had come to this. Descended to this. Damn his father, who preferred a stranger to his own son. Damn Christophe for planting his seed in an English garden. Damn Lucien for sprouting from that seed. Damn Melanie, the convenience who had become a complication. Damn them all to the deepest, foulest regions of hell.

But for now, for this minute, damn Melanie! Why hadn't he been told precisely how the deed was to be done? Why hadn't he been more careful, knowing Melanie to be so unstable? And how could even the drug-ridden Melanie have been foolish enough as to have given Lady Southcliff *his* direction, so that the encroaching woman had shown up on his very doorstep this morning—totally unexpected and

unwanted—rather than at Tremaine Court, imperiously explaining that her invitation had stated that there were to be so many overnight guests coming to the dinner party that "Melanie's dear friend the comte" had kindly offered his own cottage to some of them?

The boorish woman had probably babbled that particular bit of information to all her friends before leaving London.

Stupid, stupid Melanie! Didn't the bitch know the rules? A wise bird never soiled its own nest.

Guy knew his eyepatch made him too easy to describe, to remember. He could only hope the hired coachman would disappear into the bowels of London, giving him enough time to rapidly complete his business here and return to France, long before anyone could point the finger of blame in his direction. In the meantime, as far as the world was concerned, Lady Southcliff had never arrived at her planned destination.

But he didn't like it. He didn't like it at all. He preferred detailed plans, carefully laid out, even more carefully executed. This whole affair had an air of the slapdash about it that worried him. He paced his small study, mentally ticking off his hastily organized preparations.

He had dismissed his purposely small staff of four for the day, neither the man of all work, his valet, the cook, or the simpleminded housemaid having seen Lady Southcliff before he had quickly ushered her to one of the spare bedchambers, suggesting she rest before tonight's party at Tremaine Court—the dinner party that was not really to take place for five more days, although she could not know that, would never know that.

The presence of Lady Southcliff's personal maid had been handled in the past hour. He would dispose of the body easily enough once darkness fell, for there would be no moon. By the time the Channel gave up the remains even the maid's own mother wouldn't be able to recognize her.

He poured himself a brandy, but only because he was thirsty, and not to steady his nerves. He had seen too much death during the Revolution and the years that followed.

The maid hadn't been human to him, only another potential problem, now solved.

He had summoned Melanie just before noon, to find that her mood was not of the best. One of her palms was wrapped in a bandage and she seemed to limp when she walked. Something had happened last night at Tremaine Court, something she refused to talk about with him. He only knew that she was on edge, which meant that today she would be insatiable.

She had gone upstairs a half hour ago, telling him she wished to confront Lady Southcliff alone, to talk to her, about what he did not particularly care. She had teased him before going in search of Lady Southcliff, showing him her toys: the ever-present opium pipe, some silken ropes, a dark, silver-handled dildo, even a curious decorated leather mask that had no opening except at the nose.

"They are all gifts from Felicia," she had told him, her mood improving with the display of each new piece. "I know she'll be so *excited* that I wish to return them. We used to have such fun, you know, taking turns with the toys."

He had murmured his appreciation. Perhaps the afternoon would not be a total waste. It might even prove to be an education.

He cared little why Melanie wished the woman dead. Lady Southcliff was lush, blond, and beautiful. That in itself could be motive enough for someone like Melanie. He also wanted the London society matron dead, but at least he understood his own motive. All his motives.

He sat at his ease in one of the leather wing chairs that flanked the fireplace, content to pass the time by throwing a pair of dice, one hand against the other, until Melanie summoned him to the bedchamber.

He did not have long to wait.

"You can come up now, darling Guy. She is ready for us."

He looked up to see Melanie standing just inside the doorway, her large blue eyes fever-bright with excitement, with anticipation and, most probably, some sort of drug. She wore a pale yellow gown that sported small puffed

sleeves and a deep ruffled hem—and she looked as beautiful, and as innocent, as a child of fifteen, even if the gown was unbuttoned, so that it hung on her loosely. Eve's face must have looked like this, he mused idly, just before she offered Adam that so tempting apple.

Today, however, Temptation held a long, thin silver knife in her hand.

"I had thought she would give me more trouble," Melanie said, "but I had forgotten how much dearest Felicia enjoyed the lovely games she taught me all those years ago. Ignorant, trusting cow. But she moves well. You'll have to be careful not to get blood on the toys, for I believe I should like us to use them again. You'd like that, wouldn't you, darling—like seeing your Melly bound, blind, open and helpless beneath your talented fingers? We could take turns, couldn't we?"

"I should enjoy that above all things, *ma propre petite maladie*," he answered tightly, replacing the dice in his pocket. Couldn't she keep her own pleasures out of the conversation for more than a moment? They had a job of work to do. Couldn't they just get on with it?

But it seemed that Melanie wanted to talk.

"She used to pay me, you know—lots and lots of lovely money—until she learned of my engagement to Lucien. How enraged she was that I would think to leave her, as if there were ever any doubt that I would better myself once I saw my chance. But it wasn't just the money, at least not after Lucien took me to his bed. Foolishly, stupidly, I told Felicia how I loved him, really loved him. Then, knowing all about my past—for I had confided in her in a weak moment—she made *me* pay, the ungrateful bitch. *Me!* I was the best she ever had!"

"How terribly ungrateful of her, my dear. You have been much sinned against, *oui?*"

"Yes! She is the beginning and the end of all my troubles, all that I've had to do to survive. With Lucien already gone off to that silly war, she would have gone directly to the Tremaines if I hadn't paid. How I once feared her. But not any more. Not after today. After today, and once I am rid of

that encroaching Kate Harvey, of course. Shall we use the toys on her as well? It might prove amusing. Then, once it is all done, nothing will stand between me and my darling Lucien. Nothing! Isn't that right, darling Guy?"

Kate Harvey? Why would he want to kill her? She was nothing to him, less than nothing. "That's right, Melanie. You won't have to be afraid of the wicked Felicia any more. Of anyone. Shall we nip upstairs now, darling, and do the deed? I wish to have time to bathe before seeking out my dinner at the Fox and Crown, as I have dismissed the servants for the day. You've greatly discommoded me, you know, *chérie*. I should be cross with you."

She glided gracefully across the room and pressed the knife into his hand. The flowery scent of her perfume reached him. That, and the sweet odor of opium, and the musky smell of sex. Only a half hour had passed, and already she was leagues ahead of him.

He looked down at the knife, absently testing its balance, then smiled. "Wherever did this knife come from, darling?" he asked, a fingertip lovingly caressing the initials *LKT* that were carved into the silver handle in a delicate script.

Melanie pouted. "I found it. In Lucien's rooms, I suppose. I have many of his things. I like to keep reminders of him close to me."

"In Lucien's rooms? When? And just what, pray tell, were you doing in his rooms?"

"I don't remember!" she asserted, her voice rising shrilly. "What does it matter?"

Was he always to come in second best to Lucien Tremaine? First with his father, and then with this lovely white witch? He fought a stab of jealousy, neatly turning his reaction into anger—and resolve. Guy ordered his features into an expression of bored disinterest. "You're right, *ma petite*. It does not matter at all where you got it. What matters, darling, is that you did. Shall we be on with it?"

She smiled again, placated. "But don't you want to know more of why I want Felicia dead, darling?" she asked as she began pulling the gown up over her head, to stand naked in

front of him, her only covering the pale white stockings that rode high on her thighs, a strand of emeralds around her slim throat—and bandages wrapped around her knees. What could the woman have been up to?

"Only if you find it necessary to your happiness, my so beautiful *araignée blanche,*" he answered silkily, once again, yet again, amazed by the singing perfection of her body.

She laughed as the gown was discarded, spilling onto the floor at his elegantly booted feet. For the way she used it, the way she abused it, her form should be wrinkled, sagging— repellent rather than provocative—but then excess had always warbled a more convincing overture than did virtue.

She turned, motioning for him to follow her to the staircase leading to the second floor of the cottage.

"It all seems so long ago now, darling," she said, telling her story in that rather high, childish voice he had grown to loathe. "It was in Bath, where I had gone to find myself some bored gentleman who wished companionship in exchange for a small sum of money, a few jewels, a place to lay my head. Only Felicia found me instead. At first I did not know what she was—for I was quite young—although I suppose all the *ton* did, for no one seemed to like her very much even though we were invited everywhere. She would accept no invitation unless I was included. She called me her ward. Sweet, considerate Felicia. Otherwise, I might never have met my darling Lucien."

Guy watched, entranced, as Melanie, her rounded buttocks unashamedly moving in an entrancing rhythm, preceded him up the stairs. He concentrated his mind once more on the bag of "accessories" she had taken with her to the room. Against his better judgment his blood began to run hot, his mind already traveling down the upstairs hallway, sensing what he would find waiting behind the closed door to Lady Southcliff's bedchamber. "I believe I already understand. She loves the women, your Felicia, *n'est-ce pas?*"

Melanie stopped when she had reached the landing and looked back at him over her shoulder as he stood below her

on the second to last step. "Yes, darling, Felicia loves women. Almost as much as she adores pain—almost as much as she detests men."

She threw her head back and laughed out loud. "This whole, long, delicious afternoon, dearest Guy, you and your darling Melly are going to give Felicia everything she loves, and everything she hates. Together we are going to make her weep with happiness and cringe with revulsion. And then—"

She hesitated, turning to rub the stiffened rosy tips of her bared breasts against his avidly seeking mouth, "—and then, dearest, sweetest Guy, you are going to fix everything, fix it so that Felicia can never hurt your darling Melly again."

Lucien had been awake for over an hour. Stoutly tied to the base of the heavy bedpost, his legs sprawled inelegantly in front of him, he looked up at Kate from the floor and grinned sheepishly as she entered the room and stopped some distance in front of him. "Good afternoon, sweet Katharine. What time is it? Lovely day, isn't it? You may untie me now."

"It has just gone two, and thank you so very much for pointing that option out to me, Lucien," she answered, her words slow and measured. "But I don't believe I will untie you just yet."

Lucien tried to free his wrists, but the rope held firm. At least Kate was obedient in some things. She had obeyed him to the letter and tied her knots well. "Katharine, enough of this. I apologize again for frightening you, for saying things I shouldn't have said, even if I was half out of my mind last night. But she has avoided me long enough. Half the day is gone. I have to go to Moina now. I must to talk to her."

Kate said nothing, but just continued to look at him levelly, as if assessing his mood. He felt ridiculous. He knew he must *look* ridiculous as well, stripped to his pantaloons, his hands tied behind him as he sprawled on the floor,

caught like a dog that has run in circles only to end with his leash wrapped tight around a chair leg.

"My dearest Lady Katharine," he reminded her, hoping to tease her into releasing him, "you've got a man tied up in your bedchamber. What if one of the maids were to come in? The mind boggles." When she still made no move to release him, his gentle taunting turned to impatience. "Katharine! For the love of heaven—*let me go!*"

"Lucien," she said at last, her solemn expression beginning to worry him, "you mentioned Moina while you were babbling. You said Moina had something to do with what was happening to you. You mentioned Melanie, and a potion."

Why did she insist upon telling him what he already knew? His temper flew into the treetops. "Well, thank you, darling, for that excrutiatingly pithy and yet totally redundant synopsis. Now will you untie me? Either that, or you could summon Garth in here, so that he can enjoy the spectacle. I imagine he hasn't had a good laugh yet today. And while you're about it, why not invite the entire staff? You could print up tickets, and charge admission, as they do at any farce!"

"Stop it!" She leaned over him menacingly, as if tempted to box his ears. He pushed himself backwards, toward the bedpost. Clearly he wasn't the only one in a temper. "Don't do that, Lucien. Don't you ever again call me *darling* in that insufferable tone of voice, for it has no effect on me at all! *None!* Just be quiet and listen, or I'll keep you trussed up here until Christmas, when I can hang holly around your head and stuff a spiced apple in your mouth. I'm trying to remain calm, Lucien, in order to find a way to tell you what you must know without having you go running off in a temper, causing even more damage. Moina has enough on her plate without you bursting in on her, angry as a baited bear."

"I'll be good, my lady." How he loved this woman! Really loved her. He had never loved Melanie like this. He had

desired her. He knew the difference now. Last night's potion, and his reactions to it, had delivered the final lesson, if one had been needed. Lucien pushed his own discomfort and embarrassment to one side. "If you want my promise, my word as a gentleman that I will not harm Moina, you have it, and I will bow to your wishes and not ask again to be released," he agreed in earnest tones.

"However," he added, grinning, "I *do* have an itch, my most earnest, overbearing Lady Katharine—quite a plaguey itch—just here, at my right shoulder, that I would dearly love scratched."

She laughed shortly, and he knew he had won. What would the world be without humor, even if at the moment he knew his was a form of gallows humor? "You're incorrigible!" she exclaimed, shaking her finger at him as if he were a naughty but well-loved puppy that had just been "nervous" on her carpet. She dropped to her knees and reached behind him, the clean, fresh smell of her reminding him of his own sourness. He turned his head away, longing to kiss her, yet refusing to dirty her with the aftermath of his feverish night.

A moment later he was free, his shoulders aching from their unnatural position, so that it took him a minute to find the strength to move his arms.

Standing, Kate quickly put a hand out to him, to help him to his feet. He took it, looking up at her as he remembered the other times she had begun to offer her assistance, only to withdraw it, as if afraid to become involved with him at any level even faintly personal in nature.

What a long way they had come, he and his Lady Katharine. How could he have feared that she might wish to leave him, to return to The Willows? If they could make it through the horrors of their separate pasts, and the potential catastrophe of last night, nothing could hinder their road to a shared future. It was a nice thought, comforting, and Lucien squeezed her hand in a silent promise before letting her go.

"I have a pot of strong tea waiting in the next room," she

told him matter-of-factly, handing him one of Edmund's shirts. "I'm sure you'll feel much more the thing after you have something in your stomach, although Moina said you shouldn't eat heavily until after you've had a good long nap."

He followed her into the small, comfortably furnished sitting room that Edmund had given over for her own use, struggling to push his arms into the sleeves of the shirt. "You are a veritable fount of useful information this morning, aren't you, sweetheart? What else did Moina have to say?"

"That's what I've been attempting to tell you, or rather, what I've been tempted not to tell you. Lucien—you're going to have to be very brave."

"Brave? I let you tie me up, didn't I? What else can I do to show my bravery?" He really wished she'd get to the point. He wanted a bath and a bed, and not necessarily in that order. He also wanted a drink, and tea was not his preferred choice. His head pounded worse than it had after his most crushing bout of drinking. No wonder Melanie kept to her rooms so much, if this bone-weary exhaustion was the normal aftermath of Moina's potions.

He watched as Kate seated herself in a blue velvet chair he could remember seeing in his mother's private sitting room and poured steaming tea from the silver pot that rested on a low table in front of her. Several unmatched vases jammed with freshly cut wildflowers filled the air around him with scent.

Lucien relaxed what remained of his guard, for the room seemed to welcome him, soothing his still-jangled nerves. He pulled a wooden side chair away from the wall, turned it backwards, straddled it, and accepted the tea Katharine offered, noticing that her hand trembled ever so slightly as she passed him the cup.

When she didn't speak, he repeated his question. "Brave, sweetheart? How so?"

She rushed into speech. "You have to understand, Lucien—I was frantic! You were out of your head, saying

the strangest things, your skin burning with fever. For all I knew, you could have been dying. When you said Moina's name I realized that she might be able to help me, give me something for you. After all, she has always been the one we turn to for medical answers. Once you let me tie you to the bedpost—Lord, Lucien, but I hated doing that—I went in search of her. I explained how you were acting, repeated some of what you said, and—well, Moina became agitated. Extremely agitated."

Kate looked up at him, her expressive eyes swimming with tears. "Lucien, Moina has been giving Melanie potions ever since Pamela died—blaming her for your mother's death. She is convinced that Melanie, out to better her own lot, had something to do with the discovery of Christophe's letters. I didn't ask her how she knows this, although I won't pretend, knowing Melanie, that such a theory doesn't make sense. Moina controlled Melanie with her potions. Potions, opium, sleeping draughts."

"Opium? My God!" Lucien could not decide which was worse, Kate's news, or the fact that it was so easy to believe. "No wonder Moina has been avoiding me, with a secret like that to keep. That poor old woman. Moina's a simple soul, although well trained in medical arts—I believe there is gypsy blood somewhere, or Russian, I disremember which. And poor Melanie. She needs help."

Lucien stood, intent upon returning to his bedchamber to summon Hawkins to help him bathe and dress. "There's nothing else for it, Katharine. I have to speak with Edmund this very afternoon. I believe even Melanie knows she needs help. I can remember now how agitated she became when I said something along those lines last night. Please excuse me now, Katharine—and thank you."

"Lucien," Kate called after him, "come back. There's more." Kate looked up at the ceiling, as if something she saw on the plain white plaster might help her. "Oh, God, Lucien, I feel so responsible. How could I not have known? Why didn't I guess?"

Lucien put out a hand, touching her arm, willing himself

not to shake the information out of her. "Katharine, if this is too much for you I'll go to Moina myself."

She began toying with a fold of her skirt, as if unable to keep her fingers still. "Did—did you ever wonder how Edmund could have married Melanie so soon after his wife's death? How he could have believed himself to be in love with her?"

Lucien could feel a tic begin to work in his cheek. He didn't think he liked the direction this conversation was taking. "Moina?"

"She gave Melanie a potion to take to him after the funeral, a potion much like the one Melanie brought to you, I suppose. As I already told you, Moina blamed Melanie for Pamela's death. Melanie *and* Edmund."

"I see," Lucien said softly. But he was lying. He didn't see. He didn't see at all. If only he had *seen*, damn it—if only he had really looked at Edmund, acknowledged the torment in the other man's eyes that last night instead of concentrating on his own pain—perhaps he could have done something to help!

"She never planned for it to go on this long—but when you first returned from the war Melanie slipped from her control long enough to chase you away. Besides, you had been wounded, and were in no state to become Moina's instrument of revenge. Moina's been impatiently waiting for your return ever since. But now that you have come back, and have reconciled with Edmund, she is confused, unable to understand what she should do next."

Lucien couldn't move, couldn't speak. His mind whirled back to the first conversation he'd had with Moina upon his return to Tremaine Court. If only he had taken the old servant's ramblings about guilt and punishment more seriously.

If only. The words pounded in Lucien's skull. Samuel Johnson was wrong. Hell was not paved with good intentions. It was paved with "if only."

"Lucien," Kate prompted, shaking him from his jumbled thoughts, "Moina knows now that she was wrong to have

done what she did. To prove it, to prove how sorry she is, she told me something else. Something that may help ease your pain."

"I seriously doubt that, Katharine." He had been right. Tremaine Court, the beautiful, carefree home of his childhood, had become a place where souls went to die.

"No, Lucien. Listen to me. I've already told you that Moina hated Edmund, truly hated him. She says she saw him as weak, unworthy of the devotion Pamela felt for him. She hated him for rejecting Pamela, for fathering a child with Melanie, for disinheriting you—even though she helped orchestrate at least a part of it. Moina has been using her potions to make them suffer all these years, waiting for you to come back, hoping you would then kill them both for what she believes they did to Pamela—and to you."

"I was to become their executioner? You're telling me this in the hope it might cheer me, Katharine?" he asked, unable to stifle his sarcasm. "I have to tell you, you've missed hitting that target by a wide margin."

He barely noticed that Kate had risen from her seat and come to him, sliding her hands around his shoulders as she ended quietly, "Lucien, I don't know whether this is good news or not, for Edmund may be too weakened at this point to meet the challenge. But at least now we know. At least now we can try to do something about it."

"Do something about what? It's over, Katharine, done with. There's no going back and changing what has happened."

"That's true. But something still might be salvaged from this whole terrible mess. You see, Edmund may have suffered some sort of seizure a few weeks ago, Lucien, but he was never ill before that. Not really. Moina employed more than love potions. All along, probably ever since Pamela died, and until just a few days ago, Moina has been slowly poisoning Edmund, crippling him, with carefully regulated doses of nightshade and some sort of snake venom."

PART FOUR

PARADISE REGAINED

1814

See golden days, fruitful of golden deeds,
With Joy and Love triumphing.

John Milton, *Paradise Lost*

CHAPTER 22

*I feel
The link of nature draw me: flesh of flesh,
Bone of my bone thou art, and from thy state
Mine never shall be parted, bliss or woe.*

John Milton, *Paradise Lost*

*H*e would come to her tonight. Their union was as inevitable as the sunrise, the changing of the seasons, the rising of the tide at the full moon.

Everything they had lived, every heartbreak they had experienced, separately and together, had brought them to this moment.

This afternoon they had acted as one, going to Edmund's rooms to throw out all of the small brown bottles filled with Moina's "medicinal tonics." Together they had slowly, laboriously explained everything to Edmund, whose tears had seemed grounded more in relief than a mute expression of frustration, or even anger.

Together they had searched for Melanie, only to find that, once again, she had disappeared. Lucien assumed she had gone off with one of the farm workers, as Kate had already explained Melanie's penchant for day-long rendezvous somewhere on the estate, a practice that had been common knowledge since long before Kate's own residency at

Tremaine Court. If she ran true to form, Melanie would only return to her own rooms just before dinner, retiring for the night without need of food, to sleep soundly until at least noon of the following day.

Over a late luncheon in the smaller dining room, a strange meal during which not a single fork was lifted, she and Lucien had brought his friend Garth up to date on all that had happened. Garth, whom Kate had grown to appreciate more with every passing moment, each succeeding crisis, listened intently, asking no questions, only offering his services in any way he might be needed. He did remark that he had thought to visit Guy later that afternoon, but had now changed his mind, instead volunteering to assist Hawkins with Edmund.

Only then did Lucien give in to the exhaustion Kate was sure he must have been feeling, retiring to his bedchamber for a well-deserved rest. She, in her turn, had stayed with Edmund for another hour, watching him sleep, reliving in real horror the times she had coaxed the sometimes reluctant man to take his medicine. Finally she called upon Hawkins to relieve her and returned to her own bed for a long nap.

And so the remainder of the day had passed quietly enough, with the dependable Mary in charge of Noddy and Moina still closeted in her small chamber in the north wing.

But now evening had come.

After nibbling nervously on the bread and cold roast beef Hawkins had been so kind as to personally deliver to her rooms, Kate had taken a lengthy bath, scrubbing herself roughly from head to foot, almost ritualistically washing away the past in the hope of making a new beginning.

Wearing nothing but Edmund's burgundy brocade banyan, she sat on the hearth rug, brushing her freshly washed hair in front of the fire one of the housemaids had lit for her. She smiled as the brushes moved through her long tresses, watching as the carefully polished silver rims shone brightly in the yellow-orange light from the flames. All the scene lacked was her dearly loved maid Amy, and Kate mentally

promised herself she would seek the girl out, inquiring after her at her parents' cottage in the village near The Willows. Amy was a part of her past, but that past had become bearable now, and she felt it right to have the young maid become a part of her future.

Her future. Kate smiled, mouthing the word silently.

Future. What a lovely word. The future belonged to her now, to do with what she wished. She could stay with Edmund, with Noddy, but only if she wished it. She could return to The Willows, visit with her uncle and cousin—or travel to Italy to see the Colosseum. She now had the freedom to do anything, go anywhere she wanted.

Freedom. Another lovely word. The freedom to choose. The freedom to give her heart, her love, body and soul, to the tortured stranger who had strayed into her orbit—unlooked for, unbidden, unwanted. As he had not looked for her.

But, tonight, healed of all his wounds, he would come to her. Tonight they would love. Of her own free will. If he left her tomorrow, never to see her again, hold her again, she could go on, could live her life, never to retreat again into the shadows. He had not given her that power, that determination to go on. She had given it to herself, just as he had fought his own battle, bringing himself back into the light.

They were complete by themselves, whole. Separately, they had each faced their own demons and, separately, they had fought them down. Separately, they possessed the strength, the will, to live.

Together, if they chose, throughout the years they would share, through the children they could bring into the world, they held the power to live forever.

The room faded with the oncoming of dusk, so that Kate sat illuminated in the soft glow from the dying fire, still brushing her waist-length hair, still dreaming her waking dreams—smiling, at peace, waiting.

Lucien stepped from the bath shaking excess water from his hair like a spaniel shakes itself after a swim, before

accepting a warmed towel from Hawkins. As he had bathed, Hawkins had informed him of Edmund's condition, which remained relatively unchanged, prompting the servant to suggest that it might take some time before the man's system would be cleared of Moina's potions.

He dismissed Hawkins, preferring to dress himself, choosing a pair of fawn-colored trousers and a plain white shirt opened at the collar. He combed his still-damp hair as he stood in front of the high dressing table, then picked up the ruby ring and slipped it on his finger.

Leaving his dressing room, he took up the glass of claret Hawkins had left for him and crossed to stand at the mantel, staring unseeingly into the middle distance.

Was it too soon? Was he moving too fast, pressing too hard, asking too much? She would have to be blind as well as deaf not to know how he felt, for he had been clear enough last night, while he was "raving," as she had termed his fevered declarations.

How long had he loved her? An hour? A week? Forever? Hers had been the first face he'd seen at Tremaine Court upon his return from the Peninsula, the first person whose presence he had cursed and come to hold somehow responsible for his altered circumstances, his pain. Hers had been the cool hand that had soothed him in his delirium. Hers had been the eyes that had haunted him, calling him back to the place of his birth, the birthplace of his shame. Hers had been the scorn, the righteous indignation, the fire and the spirit that had dared him to think, to feel, to question.

And hers had been the loyalty and the strength that had taught him to forgive, shown him that the only path to his future lay in coming to terms with his past.

Fighting her own devils, she had taken on the care and protection of Edmund, of Noddy, when a lesser female— anyone at all—would have run as far and as fast as she could, distancing herself from yet another potential tragedy.

And she had taken him on as well, standing toe to toe with him, not giving an inch, even as he had taken every possible

wrong step by forcing intimacies that must have frightened her to her very soul.

She loved him. There could be no other explanation, no other reason for her steadfast determination to help him last night, to help him every time he had asked, and even when he hadn't had the wit to ask.

Soon now it would be over. Melanie, that wretched, flawed woman, would be dealt with, painful as it might be to lock the beautiful, haunted creature away for the remainder of her days. Edmund would recover; he had to recover, for Noddy needed him. Edmund's son would give him the will to live again.

And Lady Katharine d'Harnancourt would be free to stay or go, as she decided.

Lucien knew he couldn't hold her, would not hold her even if he had the power to do so, for she deserved the right to form her own future. If she envisioned a life that did not include him, a life as distant as possible from her strange existence of these past few years, he would not attempt to dissuade her.

If she left him behind in order to exercise her freedom, if he were to find himself once more alone, he would not descend into black despair. Not again. Never again. He was wiser now; a hundred years wiser, a thousand years stronger.

But, ah, how he would miss her.

Placing the wineglass on the mantel, Lucien walked toward the door, knowing he had kept her waiting long enough. She knew he would come to her tonight. He had to go to her, just as he would have to live without her if she went away.

He wanted her forever, he wanted her love forever. But if the future he envisioned was not to be, at least they would have this single night.

Kate knew even before he said a word that Lucien was the man in her room. The doorway to her bedchamber had opened just as the clock in the hallway struck the hour of

eleven. She remained where she was, seated on the hearth rug, Edmund's banyan tied securely at her slim waist, her bare legs tucked to one side, her long hair loose and flowing down her back. And waited.

He came up behind her, his footsteps barely making a sound on the carpet. She didn't move, didn't turn her head.

"Katharine? It's all right, isn't it? I'll go if you want me to. Do you want me to leave, sweet Katharine?"

She couldn't speak, answering his question with a slight shake of her head, but it seemed to be enough. She heard his clothes whisper to the floor before he dropped to his knees behind her.

She held her breath as he pulled back her hair and placed his hands on her shoulders, his thumbs warm against the bare flesh of her throat. She moved then, arching her head backward, to rest against his bare chest, as he brought his head down, his lips nuzzling softly at the base of her throat.

She wet her suddenly dry lips with the tip of her tongue, then bit down on her bottom lip, to stifle a small sob of thanksgiving. She felt no anxiety, no inclination to pull the edges of the too-large banyan close across her breasts. All she felt was Lucien's presence, his closeness, his love. No fear. No repugnance. Only a melting softness, a willingness to offer whatever he believed he needed. He nibbled lightly at her tender skin, the movements of his teeth and tongue sending shivers of delight skittering up her spine.

"Katharine," she heard him murmur as his hands moved to push the banyan from her shoulders, exposing her breasts to the light from the fire, to his gaze. She swallowed at the lump that had risen in her throat and closed her eyes as his hands left her shoulders, to travel down her arms, then forward, to cup each breast, his thumbs lightly stroking her nipples. "My own sweet Katharine."

She sensed her body melting beneath his touch as she heard the sound of his uneven breathing, sensed his nervousness, his reluctance to rush her, to frighten her.

Tilting her head forward, she opened her eyes, to watch, entranced, as his right hand left her breast, to slowly travel

down her rib cage, to move in small circles against her flat belly. He seemed to be worshipping her, as if her body gave him pleasure. She hadn't expected it, hadn't even hoped for it, but soon she felt a pressure greater than that provided by his hand begin to build inside her, a curious, welcome warmth that spread lower, so that it seemed natural for her to relax her legs, allowing him access to every part of her.

Trust. She trusted him completely. Trusted him not to hurt her; not to rush her, and she had to let him know of that trust. She continued to watch, bemused, as his fingers disappeared between her thighs, resting against her most secret flesh, finding the moistness that had somehow formed there. His discovery did not embarrass her. It delighted her.

She turned as best she could, taking hold of his left arm, pressing a kiss against his shoulder, silently willing him to hold her. To hold her tightly. To teach her how to love him.

He turned her in his arms, gently pressing her down against the hearth rug, then stretched out close beside her, his head propped on his hand. He looked so handsome, so young, and so very much in love. "Hello, my sweet Katharine," he said, his dearly loved smile melting her heart. And then, to her surprise and shame, she burst into tears.

"Don't cry, my love." His voice was gentle as he traced the curve of her cheekbone with his fingertip, catching her tears as they fell. "I'd never hurt you."

Kate shook her head, sniffling, trying to explain. "I know that. It's just that this isn't fair to you. I should be a virgin. You deserve a virgin. I've borne a child, Lucien, a child I did not want but could not help but love, and mourn. You cannot forget that, even if you wished to. I carry the shaming reality on my body."

She knew her words had puzzled him, until she took his hand and laid it beside the two faint bluish lines that scored her belly near her right hip—the reality she had spoken of, the indelible mark of a woman whose body had grown to accommodate another life.

His gaze lingered on those marks for a long time, his fingertips tracing them, while she cringed inwardly. It was

one thing for him to say he understood, but it was another to watch him as he came face to face with the evidence of her past.

"You're wrong, Katharine," he said at last, his voice husky as he looked at her, so that she knew he had come to some sort of decision. "There is no shame to be seen here, just the fading scars of an old battle. I only wish I could have been there, to help you fight."

Kate's breath caught on a sob. Keeping his gaze locked with hers, he pushed himself to his knees, then bent over her, to place his lips gently, almost reverently against each of the marks, as if worshiping the evidence of her womanhood.

"I love you, Lucien Tremaine," Kate said as he came to her again, his mouth now inches from hers. She reached up her hands, any shame she might have rightly or wrongly felt forever banished by his healing words. She laced her arms around his back, pulling him down to her. "I love you with my heart and my mind. Now, please—teach me how to love you with my body."

Lucien took a deep, shuddering breath, and she sensed that he was as nervous as she. "The past is gone, sweet Katharine," he said, pulling her close. "You're my virgin bride, and I'll never hurt you, I swear it. Not tonight, not ever. I'll spend my life proving to you that you aren't wrong to trust me with your love."

Then he kissed her eyelids, her cheeks, the tip of her nose, the firm line of her chin, before at last claiming her mouth in a gentle possession that held more promise than passion. He smoothed his trembling hands along her shoulder blades, ran worshiping fingers down her body, as if committing each curve to memory, his every touch a blessing, a benediction.

By the glow of the firelight they moved together without words, each caress growing bolder, each kiss deeper, until Kate sensed that the time had come for Lucien to claim her as his own . . . for now . . . forever.

Raising himself above her as she opened herself to him, he came to her unhurriedly, banishing any lingering traces of her brutal introduction to physical intimacy with the heal-

ing power of his love. Loving him, wanting him, the excruciating pleasure she found as he moved deep within her body still took her by surprise.

Lucien's lovemaking was blessedly sweet, as much a communion as it was a union, so supremely spiritual that, when at last it was over, when they clung together, as if unwilling to be two people again, Kate knew the tears on her cheeks were not all hers.

"Lucien?" she asked once they were lying side by side, still locked in a tight embrace, as if each were the only solid thing left on the earth.

"Hmm?" He looked up at the ceiling, but she could see his smile. He seemed satisfied, as if a small part of him gloried in the fact that he had brought her pleasure.

"I have just realized something. It's not really important, I suppose, because you didn't have to say anything, not really. I did this of my own free will. Truly. It was my first real decision in a long time. But, I just remembered—you haven't said you love me."

He laughed, chuckling softly at first, and then out loud, as if she had said the most humorous thing he'd ever heard. "Love you!" he exclaimed at last, kissing the tip of her nose. "Madam, I more than just love you. I *adore* you! I'll adore you for the rest of our lives, if you'll let me."

"Adore me?" She sighed, laying her head against his chest, her arm draped intimately, confidently, across his waist as she smiled, thrilled that she felt so free to touch him. "I think I might be happier if you confined yourself to merely loving me for the rest of our lives. As I will love you. That way, dear heart, we can argue once in a while. You don't always make me happy, you know."

"Is that right?" He pulled her body completely on top of his, her long black hair tumbling all around them, blanketing them, blessedly taking them back into their own private world. "I could make you very happy right now if you wanted me to, Katharine," he suggested, cupping her smooth buttocks with his hands as he teasingly ground himself against her belly.

She moved her body against his, pleased to discover that lovemaking need not always be a serious undertaking. *"Very* happy, Lucien? How? Teach me."

His smile faded as he grew serious once more. "I've never really loved before, sweet Katharine. This is as new to me as it is to you. But I suppose we could learn together."

As the dawn slipped quietly over Tremaine Court, pouring warm, healing sunshine in through the windows of Kate's chamber, they finally slept, lying in the middle of the rumpled bed, still locked in each other's arms.

CHAPTER 23

Awake, arise, or be forever fallen!

John Milton, *Paradise Lost*

*K*ate woke shortly before noon, instantly attuned to the soft, even breathing of the man who lay sleeping beside her. Moving slowly so as not to wake him, she raised her head from its resting place on Lucien's bare chest to gaze at his profile in wonder, the finely chiseled features whose every beautifully sculpted plane had been indelibly imprinted upon her heart.

How supremely simple life had seemed before she had encountered Lucien again, lain with him, gloried in his sincere words of commitment. Simple, and empty. How laughably naive she had been to believe true happiness lay in independence. But how could she have known? How did you miss what you never had? Had there ever been an understandable definition of love, of the soul-searing intimacy of its sweet expression between a man and a woman, of the supreme freedom to be found in making a lifelong commitment to another human being?

Carefully slipping from the bed, she slid her arms into Edmund's banyan and walked to the floor-to-ceiling win-

dow to look out onto the overgrown gardens, to the wide fields dotted with wildflowers. Spring, the world's harbinger of rebirth and once a cruel reminder of her shame, had never looked so beautiful, been so welcome. She felt tears stinging at her eyes, overcome by her own happiness.

"Good morning, sweet Katharine." Lucien's voice came to her low and faintly husky as he pushed her long hair to one side and bent his head to nuzzle at her nape, his morning beard tickling her sensitized skin. "I awoke to find my arms empty and half of myself missing. Perhaps I should have you fitted for leading strings, so that you cannot stray."

"If I ever leave you, Lucien, it won't be of my own choosing. I would find it simpler by far to stop breathing."

He pressed his cheek against hers, and the two of them looked out through the windowpanes. "Strange," he said at last. "I would have thought there would be snow. It is Christmas morning, isn't it, with my most treasured gift at last unwrapped?"

She laughed throatily, pressing her head against his shoulder, relaxing against his solid strength. "If you could convince the good Hawkins to bring us our meals, I suppose we might consider remaining locked in here together until time and nature accommodate us. Or does that sound selfish?"

His hands gently kneaded at her shoulder blades, then slipped to grip her upper arms, turning her to face him. "Not selfish, Katharine, only premature. We have things to do first."

She looked up into his dark eyes, marveling at the way the skin around them crinkled boyishly when he smiled. Yet how could he smile, when his words had succeeded in bringing her crashing back to reality?

"Yes, we do have some full days ahead of us, don't we, Lucien? We must see to Edmund's recovery. We must deal with Moina. We must cancel that dreadful dinner party Melanie has planned. We must see Edmund's wife removed to a place where she can't hurt herself, or others."

She bit her lip, sighing, before adding, "Ah, poor Noddy

—that he should have to go through life deprived of mother love."

Taking Katharine's hand, Lucien led her over to the bed, seating himself beside her.

"First things first, I suppose," he said, kissing each of her fingertips in turn. "Noddy has never been deprived of motherly love, Katharine, for he has always had you, will always have you. Melanie has never been his mother. Secondly, while everything you said is true, and we do still have some difficult days ahead, may I refer you to other, more pleasant matters? For instance, my love—the matter of our marriage. I'd like the ceremony performed this afternoon, but I am amenable to some small delay. We also have to consider locating a place to live, for even though I consider my London house quite comfortable I should also like us to have a home in the country, near Noddy and my father. We must also select suitable names for our children—I propose a half dozen as a fine number, all of them with your wonderful gray eyes—"

"Three boys and three girls," Kate interrupted, laughing. Had anyone ever been as deliriously happy as she felt at this moment? "And the boys will have your eyes, Lucien. I must absolutely insist upon that."

He pressed her back onto the mussed covers. "Oh, you *insist*, do you, madam? I can see that you do not intend to be a conformable wife."

Kate giggled as his hands slipped to her rib cage and he began to tickle her. "Stop that! I *do* outrank you, sirrah," she reminded him with mock severity when she could catch her breath, "and, as I have been meekly *taking* orders for several years, I believe I shall discover infinite joy in *issuing* some for a change."

He brought his mouth within a whisper of hers as she lay back on the bed, her hair spread about her like a black satin waterfall, the banyan falling away from her so that his bare chest brushed provocatively against her breasts. "I see," he said, his voice an affectionate growl, "although I might take issue with your use of the word *meekly*. And what would be

your first order to me, Lady Katharine? Shall your lowly servant fetch you some morning chocolate, or perhaps you would rather I prepared your bath?"

"A bath sounds deliciously decadent, Lucien. And would you wash my back?" she asked, daring to reach up and nip at his bottom lip.

"Your back, is it? I suppose I might. Among other things," he replied intriguingly just before his lips claimed hers in a long, drugging kiss, and Kate gave herself up to his loving.

All good things may not necessarily have to end, but there had to be intermissions, Lucien acknowledged, even in the exploration of newly discovered love. Much against his will and inclination, he at last left Kate in her bed, hugging her pillow as she smiled in her sleep, and returned to his own chamber to bathe and dress.

He was met there by Hawkins, a hot tub, and good news. Edmund had begun to rally. Still paralyzed on one side, he had been awake when Hawkins went in to him that morning and had actually asked for food.

"Not that he doesn't talk slow-like, sir, and not that it didn't take me a devil of a time to understand him, but he did ask. Ate everything I brought him, too. And his luncheon as well, once I cut up the meat. Now he's asking for you and Miss Harvey and young Master Noddy. I swear, sir, it won't be long until he's up and about, spry as ever. I've got more than seven years on him myself, you know, so he's still a young man."

Lucien paused as he ran a brush through his towel-dried hair, considering the servant's statement. Hawkins' conclusions were reasonable; Edmund had only just passed his fifty-sixth birthday. He still had any number of good years left to him, God willing, years in which to guide Noddy through to young manhood, years in which he could watch Lucien's and Kate's children grow up, years they could all share now that they were once more a family.

Had life ever been this good? Had any one man ever been privileged to this much happiness?

"I have heard Miss Melanie up and moving about her rooms, sir," Hawkins informed Lucien, his expression dour as he helped him shrug into his hacking jacket. "She has called for her tub and something to eat. I suppose she'll be expecting to partake of dinner downstairs."

Lucien frowned into the mirror. Hawkins had succeeded in bringing him rudely back to earth, reminding him of unpleasantness still to come that seemed so alien to his present mood. "Hawkins, I have a particular favor to ask of you. Kindly locate Beasley—if you can, for a more sorry excuse for a butler I cannot imagine—and obtain a list of Melanie's dinner guests. There can't be more than a dozen, all within ten miles of Tremaine Court. Send out footmen to deliver Melanie's regrets."

He pulled his gold watch from his pocket and consulted it before saying, "I'll be with my father for some time this afternoon, Hawkins. When you see her, please ask Miss Harvey to join us at her convenience. I believe it would be best if we get the remainder of this distasteful business over with as quickly as possible."

"And Mr. Stafford, sir? He went out riding with that Froggie this morning, but he's back now, twiddling his thumbs in the drawing room. Excuse me, please, for bringing it up, but he *is* your guest, sir."

"Garth!" Lucien slapped a hand to his forehead and turned to face his servant. How could he have forgotten the man? "Hawkins, my good friend," he said, openly courting the man's favor as inspiration struck, "I've just had what I believe to be a splendid notion. How would you like it if I staked you to a few rounds of whist? Say a hundred pounds, just to start you off, and more to follow if your luck runs badly—returning only what I've advanced while you retain all your winnings?"

He grinned, recalling the older man's prowess at gaming, not that the servant had ever fuzzed the cards. Not the upstanding Hawkins! "You could perhaps purchase a small villa in Rome with your share."

The servant steepled his fingers in front of his nose,

staring at his employer. He looked like a naughty toddler contemplating a large, unguarded dish of sticky sugarplums. "Whist, sir? I do dearly love the game. I suppose I might oblige you, if Mr. Stafford proves agreeable."

"Oh, he'll be agreeable. Garth can always be counted upon to prove agreeable, if not always lucky." Lucien laughed out loud as he turned to leave the bedchamber. "Only treat him gently, my dear fellow," he warned half-heartedly in parting, "for Garth has long been a particular friend of mine."

Then he hurried down the stairs, all thoughts of Garth and Hawkins flown from his mind and already planning what he would say when he met with Edmund.

"Edmund looks wonderful, doesn't he? And so happy!" Kate linked her arm through Lucien's as they passed through the decorative lych-gate at the bottom of the garden and entered the wildflower-strewn field, the blooms bowing as if in welcome beneath the warm, perfumed breeze. "I'm sorry I cried, but seeing him with Noddy—watching his features lift in that heart breaking, lopsided smile—nearly undid me."

Lucien leaned down, brushing away a stray lock of her long, unbound hair. Her starched white cap, shoved into his pocket, would join the others he had taken from her room and already delivered to a housemaid along with strict orders to make a bonfire of them. "That's all right, Katharine. If I were not a grown man, and past such displays, I should have shed a tear or two myself."

"Wretch!" she countered, jabbing his ribs with her elbow. "Even Hawkins seemed misty eyed."

They walked in silence for a while, no particular destination in mind, stopping to kiss each other whenever the mood struck them, two contented people alone in a world that had been too long without love. At last, reaching the relative privacy of a small stand of trees atop a gently rising hill, Lucien pulled Kate down, drawing her into his arms as

they reclined among the tall grass and scattering of wild-flowers.

"I love you, my dearest Lady Katharine," he murmured solemnly into her hair before his fingers began working at the buttons of her gown. It had become as natural as breathing to touch her, to hold her—only more important. "I love you and thank you with all my heart. You've given me back my life."

She looked up at him, her expression equally earnest as she ran a fingertip along his lean cheek. "Given you back your life? No, Lucien. *You* did that. You alone. I'm only grateful you see me as a part of that life."

Lucien smiled, deliberately trying to lighten the mood, his fingers stilling on the third button of her gown. "You know, sweetheart, if Garth were ever to hear us dripping sentimentality this way he would run screaming into the pond. I suggest we get it all out of our systems now, before we meet him for dinner. Otherwise, he may just refuse to stand by me on our wedding day. Did I mention that I told Edmund our happy news before you and Noddy joined us? He seemed so cheered by it that I found myself announcing that the marriage would take place here, in my mother's private chapel, the first day of next month. By his reaction, I would say he'll make a supreme effort to be well enough to attend."

Lucien hadn't known how Kate would react but, from a multitude of possibilities ranging from delight to a typically female protest at not having a suitable gown for the ceremony, she chose the only one for which he hadn't been prepared.

"That's all well and good, Lucien—if you have reconciled yourself to asking my uncle for my hand *and* explaining how we met, since I am supposed to be languishing in America. I doubt my father told him the truth, you understand. Otherwise, we will have to wait until June, and my twenty-first birthday." She grinned, and he could see that her smile contained an element of amusement taken at his expense.

Lucien considered this new problem. "I have it!" he said

at last. "I could say I encountered you just as you disembarked at Dover, and immediately fell beneath the spell of your overwhelming beauty."

"That's very good, Lucien, as far as it goes, and I thank you for believing me to be beautiful. Naturally, I will assume you are also prepared to convince Uncle Frederick that *you* are a fine, upstanding man who has only his dear niece's best interests at heart. Then, of course, there remains the matter of a formal proposal to me which, *by the by,* has been conspicuous only by its absence. I should think I'd like you to go down on one knee as you declare your undying love. Having on occasion been on the receiving end of your arrogance, Mr. Tremaine, I suggest you strive to project an air of humble respectfulness. Yes, I believe I should like that very much."

"Oh, you do, do you, you little minx? Well, we'll see about that!" Lucien countered, pulling Kate on top of him as he began tickling her, delighted by her giggles as, together, like children at play, they began rolling over and over down the small incline, flattening the grass as they went.

They came to rest near the bottom of the hill, close beside a small spinney, Lucien grateful their exuberance hadn't propelled them into one of the many thorny bushes that ringed the thickly wooded area.

Still laughing, his long legs entangled in the skirts of Kate's gown, and with stray locks of her sweet-smelling hair clinging to his face, limiting his vision, Lucien raised his head to peer through the long grass and see exactly where they were. His smile froze into a grimace as his stomach threatened to turn.

"Oh, God. *Oh, sweet Jesus!* Melanie?"

The bloody, mutilated naked body of a blond female lay partially hidden beneath a thorn bush not five feet away, as if the person who had deposited it there had been less concerned over concealment than the possibility of being scratched.

Lucien pulled Kate close, convulsively pressing her face

against his chest as she struggled to turn her head. *"No! Don't look, Katharine. For the love of heaven—don't look!"*

Unable to tear his own gaze away, a part of Lucien's brain registered the fact that who he saw—what he saw—obscenely sprawled no more than five feet from him could not be the petite Melanie, but the body of an unknown female.

A woman likely destined to remain nameless both now and into eternity—for her face had been quite literally and most deliberately carved into nothingness.

CHAPTER 24

Our state cannot be sever'd; we are one,
One flesh; to lose thee were to lose myself.

John Milton, *Paradise Lost*

Kate looked down at her hands, wishing she could will them into ceasing their trembling, longing to bolster Lucien's confidence with a convincing show of her own. But that was nearly an impossible feat, considering the fact that Constable Clemens and his assistant were standing in the middle of the drawing room, both of them staring at Lucien as if he had the word murderer branded into his forehead.

Madness. What the constable was intimating was madness. What Lucien had seen near the spinney, what he had not allowed her to see, had been madness. Or the result of madness.

Everything had happened so quickly, too rapidly to give her time to adjust to the abrupt change. One moment she and Lucien had been so carefree, frolicking like children at play, and the next—

Dear God, would this nightmare never end? She shivered, fighting back tears.

Lucien had all but dragged her back to Tremaine Court.

He had deposited her with Hawkins, then ordered blankets brought to him before racing back to the scene of his grisly discovery with Garth and two of the older footmen.

An hour later they returned, accompanied by Constable Clemens, a loud overbearing man who belched with every second breath, and ever since that return he had been asking Lucien why a murderer would choose to deposit a body on the Tremaine estate.

It was a question for which Lucien had no answer. And how could he? Murder rarely arrived unaccompanied by some form of twisted logic, some motive, but the deliberate mutilation of a woman's body catapulted any notion of logic outside the realm of rational understanding.

Lucien had already put forth the theory that, while not overly concerned with the possible discovery of the body, the murderer had gone to great lengths to assure himself that his victim's identity remained a secret for as long as possible. In addition to the deliberate mutilation, the body had been stripped of all clothing, all jewelry. Two of the woman's fingers had been hacked off, as if to eradicate identifying rings that had been too tight to be removed any other way.

Katharine was still having a measure of difficulty recovering from that shock when the constable took up the story.

"So as I see it, we only have a couple of clues," Clemens said. "The victim's hair was dyed blond. Being as there is a lady present, I won't go into how I figured that one out. Second—and this is very important—her hands were soft with no calluses or anything. Indeed, Mr. Tremaine, I have decided this dead lady was no ordinary miss. Might even have been one of those fancy London ladies, traveling down here to visit someone she knew?"

"I must say, sir, I'm crushed. Truly crushed. When did I ever say anything untoward about you? You are pointing your finger back at me again, aren't you, my good sir?" Garth asked, folding his arms. He already had been questioned at some length as to his reasons for being in the

neighborhood, his answers more flippant than informative. Kate smiled at him, sure he had spoken only to divert attention from Lucien.

"Maybe. Maybe not. You don't seem the sort, for all your big mouth." Clemens turned his attention once more to Lucien. "Now you, sir, are a different kettle of fish. Ain't been around much lately, have you sir?" he asked, his tone totally lacking in respect, if not innuendo. "I'm new to this place myself, but I did manage to hear about some strange goin's on in this house a year or so ago, when you came back from the war. What did you do that your own pa threw you out? Well, I guess that's neither here nor there. Yet here you be, back again in Sussex not more than a month, lordin' it over the place while your pa lays dyin' in his bed. And here we be—findin' bodies everywhere we step."

"Bodies?" Lucien questioned, looking at Kate. She could only shrug, for the constable's words had also taken her by surprise. "You mean there's more than one?"

"Two. So far." The constable went on to describe another grisly discovery made by one of the local farmers on his way to market early that morning, the body of yet another young woman, this one still clothed. "London clothes, but not fancy, more like a lady's maid or some such thing, with strange designs carved into her arms and legs and her throat slit from ear to ear. Ben—that's the farmer, you know—well, he said he thought her to be smilin' real wide and invitin' at him, till he seen the blood soakin' her gown, o'course. Simple man, Ben. As if a woman could have two mouths. Anyway, this farmer, Ben, he found her propped against a tree along a cart path—one not far from Tremaine Court now that I recollect it. What do you think of that, Tremaine?"

"I think, my good man, that you have dangerously overstepped yourself, in many ways," Lucien answered coldly as Kate slipped her hand into his, squeezing it in warning for, to *her* way of thinking, it would be best to ignore the uncouth man's heavy-handed implications. "I

also believe justice might be better served if you were to excuse yourself and get on about your business before the murderer's trail grows cold—or he strikes again."

The constable scratched at his ample stomach, belching yet again. "Would that be so, sir? And here I am thinkin' that's what I'm about right now. You know, I've heard told war can do strange things to a man. Seein' all that dyin'. Might make him even like killin'—enjoy it. Tell me, Tremaine—where were you last night?"

Kate had had enough! Sure that Lucien would fly at the ignorant man's throat in another moment, she stepped in front of him, quickly, instinctively, to speak out in his defense.

"Katharine, don't!" Lucien warned, trying to pull her back. "The man's a born fool. This isn't necessary."

"On the contrary, Lucien," she answered, not looking at him but still staring at the constable, "I believe it to be extremely necessary, *because* the man's a born fool. I intend to speak with him in terms he seems to understand best. To answer your question—Mr. Tremaine spent last night with me, in my bedchamber. *All* of last night, and much of this morning. You do take my meaning, don't you?"

"Oh, good girl, Kate!" Garth exclaimed as he jumped up from his seat and struggled to hold Lucien back. "Pluck to the backbone! Lucien, marry her quickly, or I will, and never mind her inheritance! Oh, and by the way, I imagine congratulations are in order?"

"Katharine!" Lucien implored, shaking off Garth's grip as easily as he would a harness constructed of spring snow, to grab at her hand once again.

"Let the girl talk, Tremaine." The magistrate blew his nose into his fingers, then wiped them on his pants leg while he looked Kate up and down, clearly taking in her plain, grass-stained gown and slightly rumpled appearance. "With you, missy? Can't say as I blame him. And who would you be?"

She shook off Lucien's hand and took two more steps

forward, her chin lifted in open scorn, her nervousness forgotten. "I, my good man," she said, borrowing Lucien's phrase as well as his arrogant tone, "am the affianced bride of Lucien Tremaine. My name is d'Harnancourt. Lady Katharine Marie Elizabeth d'Harnancourt, of The Willows, Wimbledon, and the only niece of the Earl of Raynes. If you are not familiar with his lordship, I suggest you should apply to our dear Prince Regent, His Royal Highness being a particular friend of my uncle's."

Kate watched as the constable frowned, as if considering how much trouble a man could get into by insulting the niece of a man who was chums with the Prince Regent. "Well, now, we shouldn't be jumpin' to conclusions, should we, it being early days yet? I mean, I suppose if it's like that—" he began, only to be cut off as Beasley entered the room.

"Here you go, Constable Clemens," Beasley announced baldly, shoving a bundle of cloth into the man's hands as he looked daggers at Lucien. "One of the maids brought this-here shirt to me this morning. Found them stuck in some corner or other. Belongs to Mr. Tremaine here. There's hose too, and everything covered in blood." He leaned close to Lucien, so close that Kate, standing just beside him, sniffed the sour smell of ale on the butler's breath. "Make my Miss Melanie cry, will you? Well now, explain that away, if you can."

Kate closed her eyes, willing herself not to faint.

Beasley turned back to the magistrate. "He's a wicked man, sir. A wicked, terrible man. Hurt Mrs. Tremaine real bad the other night when she wouldn't let him have his way with her. Found her in his bedchamber, I did, and crying as if her heart would break."

The magistrate shook out the shirt, the material wrinkled and smeared with dark brown splotches that looked very much like dried blood. "All right, now! Here's something I think we ought to be talking about. Isn't that right, *Mr.* Tremaine?"

Kate watched as Lucien's jaw hardened and knew—just knew—that he would not explain how his clothing had become stained with blood. Whether from pride or some silly, high-flown interpretation of gentlemanly honor, she was convinced that he would refuse to defend himself against Beasley's damning evidence.

And that is when Kate let out a soft moan before deliberately, and with the utmost attention to being as clumsy as possible about the business, swooned into the constable's arms.

"Tell me something, my dear, if you will," Lucien said several hours later as he crept into Kate's bedchamber, a half smile on his face. "Is this only a passing fancy, or do you plan to make fainting a permanent part of your repertoire? I only ask so that I might prepare myself. Clemens nearly dropped you, you know."

Kate scrambled from her bed and into Lucien's open arms. "I was convinced he was about to take you off to the local guardhouse, Lucien," she said, pressing her head against his chest. "Thank heavens you knew what I was about."

Pressing a kiss against the top of her head, Lucien answered truthfully, "But I didn't, sweet Katharine. Much as it shames me to say this, it was Garth who picked up on your idea and pushed me toward the door before Clemens or his dolt of an assistant could stop me. I've been hiding in the greenhouse ever since." He sighed, guiding her to the bed and sitting down beside her. "So now I am a fugitive from the law. Do you think I should take up robbing stagecoaches, or would a flight to America prove more prudent? And please, don't take too long deciding, will you? After your declaration of this afternoon, your bedchamber will be the first place Clemens looks for me if he decides to return to Tremaine Court tonight."

Kate turned to grip his shoulders. "Stop feeling sorry for yourself," she demanded, so that he had to hold back a smile

at her vehemence. "You didn't murder those women. Garth and I spoke about all of this tonight at dinner. Thank goodness Melanie had taken to her bed again, or else there would have been the devil to pay. I doubt she'll much like hearing her 'darling Lucien' is running from the constable. As it is she will probably sack Beasley the moment she hears what he did. But that is nothing to the point. Now listen to me. It's simple, really. All you have to do is stay safely out of sight until Garth and I can uncover the real killer."

"Really? Is that all I'm supposed to do?" Lucien felt himself becoming angry, which was only one step up from the frustration he had been feeling all afternoon as he sat hunched in a corner of the abandoned greenhouse, with only the spiders for company. "How terribly clever of you both. I am to merely sit back and wait for you and Garth to solve my problems for me. I think not. And what of Edmund, Katharine? What of my father? This news will be the end of him."

Kate tried to take him in her arms, but he could not sit still, could not accept her comforting words, her optimistic predictions. Pacing the floor beside the bed, he averted his eyes, saying, "Katharine, I cannot stand by and do nothing while you and Garth put yourselves in danger. I've had all day to think about what has happened, how the first body was found on Tremaine property. Garth and I have talked about it as well tonight, while I bathed. Hawkins guarded the door, blunderbuss in hand. It was all most edifying. However, according to Garth, who says he spoke at some length with Clemens after my escape, he doesn't trust the man to find his own behind in the dark. So it is up to us to locate the murderer. *All* of us. And quickly."

"Because of Edmund," Kate said, looking very small as she sat on the bed, her legs tucked up beneath the hem of her nightgown.

"Yes," Lucien answered, going over to take her hand. "Because of Edmund, because of you, because of the children you and I are going to have one day—and because I

360

think I am being deliberately set up to be named the guilty party. Katharine," he said, watching her closely, "my knife is gone from my dressing table."

"Your knife? I don't believe I understand."

He sat down beside her. "Neither did I, I'm sorry to say, until Hawkins pointed it out to me. You see, since you were so kind as to make me a gift of your knife, I haven't carried my own. It had been resting most comfortably on my dressing table, alongside the miniature of Christophe Saville—which, by the by, has also gone missing. Several other items are missing—shirts, a neckcloth, a pearl stickpin—pieces of no consequence. Either Hawkins has become incredibly clumsy, or I have become the victim of a thief. Hawkins believes the knife at least might turn up soon, most probably near the place we found the body this afternoon."

"But I don't understand, Lucien. Why would anyone wish to have you arrested for murder? Why would anyone want to hurt you?"

"I doubt it is Orton, still smarting from the drubbing I gave him at cards," he said, trying for a little levity, and failing miserably. "All I can think of is that Moina told me there was new trouble here at Tremaine Court. I may be wrong, and I know that applying to Moina for answers would be a waste of time—but I believe that trouble has just found me." He smiled at her. "Have I thanked you yet for saving me from the hospitality of the local gaol? Of the two, I believe I much prefer the greenhouse. It has fewer spiders, I am sure."

He laid her back gently on the coverlet. "But more important, my sweet Katharine, I want to thank you for loving me, for believing in me, for not asking me how my shirt came to be smeared with blood."

"It's Melanie's blood, isn't it? I saw the bandage on her hand yesterday."

Lucien nodded, still reluctant to think about what had happened the night Melanie had come to his rooms. "Her

hand, her foot. I don't think she even felt the cuts. I didn't hurt her, you know. She sliced herself on some broken glass and I told her to wrap the wound with my shirt. Beasley must have found her and taken it from there by himself. It's strange. I didn't think Melanie could provoke loyalty, and I'm sure he isn't enamored of her for the fair way in which she treats him."

Kate lifted a finger and traced it down the line of Lucien's jaw. "Ah, Lucien," she said teasingly. "You must be tired. Otherwise you would understand. There are many men in the area who could be enamored of Melanie. Many, *many* men."

Lucien lay back on the coverlet beside her, closing his eyes. "Good God, Katharine. If I am to believe that, I would have to conclude that there are a dozen men in this neighborhood who could see a former fiancé as a threat for Melanie's affections. Any number of men who might wish to see me in gaol, and out of the way."

Kate laid her head against his shoulder, her fingers plucking at the buttons on his shirt. "But, Lucien—why not just shoot you and be done with it? Why kill two innocent women in the hope you would be blamed? Besides, Beasley has never impressed me with having a talent for inventiveness except, of course, in finding new ways to avoid performing his duties."

Lucien's head ached. There were so many questions, and so few answers. The identity of those two unfortunate women, one of them with soft, lady's hands and the other wearing the simple clothes of a servant, troubled him. Where were their coach and driver, if they had only been traveling through the area at the time they were murdered? Why had such pains been taken to conceal their identities? And—no matter where his mind traveled, it always came back to this—why had someone gone to such trouble to lead suspicion to his door?

He made as if to rise. "I must go now, Katharine. I've stayed too long as it is. Once it's light Garth and I are

returning to where we found the first body. But in the meantime, the greenhouse and the spiders await." She slipped her arms around his waist, and he allowed himself to be detained—for just another moment, he told his mind, while his heart prepared to mount a revolt. "Don't worry, Katharine, everything will be fine."

"Can you promise me that, Lucien?" she asked, and he heard the fear in her voice. "Can anyone promise that?"

He turned to look at her, really look at her, for the first time since entering the room. He hadn't wanted to look at her, had purposely avoided touching her. How could he look at her, touch her, kiss her—and then leave her? Her beautiful gray eyes were awash with tears. How could he leave her? He couldn't! "Ah, sweet Katharine," he whispered, pushing his hands into her unbound hair and drawing her mouth up to meet his.

They had loved each other in many ways that first wonderful night, he and his sweet Katharine; slowly, with reverence; laughingly, in the heady joy of discovery; quickly, with fierce, unexpected hunger.

Now their lovemaking took on yet another dimension, one of comforting the other, affirming life, their love—when there existed a very real possibility that this night could be the last they would ever share.

Lucien ministered to her, his every touch an affirmation, his hands soothing away the horror of the past few hours, to replace it with the promise of everlasting love.

Kate blossomed beneath his touch, her body tense and resistant at first, but then moving languorously as he removed her gown in order to worship her breasts with his mouth, his fingers gently stroking the silky skin at the apex of her thighs until her legs opened, allowing him entry.

He moved slowly, his lips pressing against her taut nipples, the full underside of her breasts, her sensitive navel, her soft belly. He kissed the bluish marks near her hip, the creamy skin of her inner thighs.

Kate moaned softly, attempting to close her legs, but he

persisted, moving his body so that he lay pressed against her right leg, his head level with the prize he sought.

She didn't know, in her innocence could not possibly imagine what he was about to do, how he planned to worship her, but he felt certain that the timing could not be more right for this most beautiful, intimate union, this unalterable pledge of devotion and commitment—and of trust.

Her trust, that she would allow him to touch her in this way. His trust, that she would understand that his actions sprang not from animal lust, but unconditional, everlasting love.

His mouth sought her, claimed her, his tongue stroking, delving, finding. She blossomed for him, her legs falling open completely, her hips rising slightly from the bed as she allowed him access, eased his search, abetted his every new discovery. Her gentle moans enflamed him to every intimacy; the wet heat of her response drove him to push for her ecstasy; the convulsive throb that came at last, over and over again, blending with the soft sounds issuing from her throat.

He laid his head against her belly, his breathing ragged, wondering at how complete he felt when he had not found his own release. Loving Kate, feeling her love, had brought a joy to him that he had never before experienced. If he could do no more than hold her throughout the rest of this long, historic night, he would be content, no matter what tomorrow brought with it.

But Kate, it would seem, did not share his feelings. He felt her hands on his shoulders, reaching for him, pulling him up to her.

Without a word, never looking at him, she pressed him against the bed and lowered her head to his chest, her mouth seeking and finding one soft male nipple and urging it erect. His stomach muscles grew rigid as her lips traveled lower, ever lower, her long hair teasing his sensitized skin, her fingers feather light as they molded his ribs, slid over his belly, and then raised his manhood between her hands.

He sucked in his breath at the sweet agony of her touch, her untutored loving that excited him as no expert at the art had ever done. When he felt her tongue touch him, when her lips sealed themselves around him, he could only close his eyes and arch his head back into the pillow, his hands reaching out blindly, seeking to hold her.

He had not asked for this, could not have hoped for this, but Kate was giving him a gift he would treasure for the rest of his life—the healing power of her love—complete, unconditional, all-encompassing.

Sitting forward, he lowered her onto her back, rising above her, his hands braced against the bed as he looked deeply into her eyes . . . as slowly, with infinite tenderness, he entered her, glorying in her sudden shyness that melted away almost instantly as he began to move, bringing her back to the very edge of ecstasy.

He tried to maintain his position but it was impossible, for he instinctively knew he needed to hold her as they climbed this particular mountain, as they inexorably moved together toward the dizzying precipice, as they tumbled off, to float slowly, rapturously back to earth, locked in each other's arms.

If they were ever to have a child together, he prayed it would be the fruit of this sublime, unearthly union, the lifelong remembrance of one glorious night of love.

"I love you, Lady Katharine Marie Elizabeth d'Harnancourt," he vowed at last, reluctantly letting her go to take the ruby ring from his hand and slide it onto the third finger of her left hand. "I will love you beyond death."

She blushed. It may have been dark in the room, but he was sure she had blushed. He felt his passions stirring yet again, for nothing in this world could be more exciting than his most adorable, prudish wanton. "And I love you, Lucien Kingsley Tremaine," she said, her tone low and fervent, humbling him. "Perhaps even more than I thought I did."

He said nothing more, but only smiled and drew her close, knowing the only thing that could destroy the singing

perfection of their most recent union would be to talk about it. The clock in the hallway chimed out the hour of two, reminding him that, like it or not, dawn would come.

"I have to leave you now, sweet Katharine. And you'd better try to get some sleep," he suggested prosaically, disengaging himself from her embrace to pick up his hastily discarded clothing. For with the dawn he knew—as Kate must know—the constable would return.

CHAPTER 25

Shortly after dinner the following day, after leaving a fractious Edmund in Hawkins's capable hands, a worried Kate was at last free to go in search of Moina, hoping the old servant might be willing to speak to her about this "new trouble" that threatened Tremaine Court. Garth had been gone all day, he and Lucien doing only heaven knew what, returning to report that they had come up with precious little information that might help Lucien's case. Lucien, Garth told her, could not chance another visit and remained in his new hiding place, out of sight.

She had just reached the landing outside the schoolroom when she heard the sound of Melanie's voice, shrilly raised in anger.

"Stupid old crow! How dare you deny me? How dare you refuse me? My head aches so terribly that I have been unable to leave my rooms all day. But did you come to me when I summoned you, when you knew how I needed you? No, you did not! I must have it! Don't you know yet why I allow you

367

to stay here? Refuse me again, old woman, and I'll wring your scrawny neck. *Do you understand?"*

Kate ran to the nursery, quickly looking in on the napping Noddy before closing the door in an attempt to shut out the hysterical sound of his mother's voice. Retracing her steps, she headed for the small chamber farther down the hallway that Moina used for her own sitting room. Entering without knocking, she saw Melanie standing over Moina, slapping at the woman who held up her arms in a vain attempt to defend herself.

"Stop it!" Kate, instantly incensed, grabbed at Melanie's wrists, earning herself a glancing blow on the cheek before gaining control over the smaller woman's wildly flailing hands. "Stop this at once, before I am forced to hurt you!"

"Let her go, Lady Katharine," Moina said wearily. "She can't hurt me any more. Nobody can."

Melanie went completely still, her blue eyes narrowed as she looked up into Kate's face. *"Lady Katharine?"* she questioned, all but spitting the words, the way a deadly adder might sound if it could whisper. Her smile widened slowly, the full measure of her disdain not lost on Kate, who had been nearly as shocked as Melanie. How had Moina heard of her title? When? Was there anything the woman did not know?

"When did this miracle take place, hmm? Well, that will teach me to sleep the day away, won't it? I've always sworn there had to be something havy-cavy about you, *Kate Harvey,* what with your high and mighty tone and your sly arrogance. So at last the truth comes out. Noddy suckled on titled teats? How very privileged. What happened? Did you spread your legs and let some well-hung village boy fill your belly—so that you were banished from the family estate? Poor, *poor* Kate."

Stung by her crudity, Kate relaxed her grip. Melanie pulled her hands free and walked a few paces away, then turned, the silken draperies of her sheer dressing gown swirling around her ankles so that Kate saw the bandage on her foot. "But why should I be surprised? I've always

wondered why Edmund championed you. Had you read to him. Had you put in the room next to him. And now I know, don't I? I considered you to be a convenience, keeping Edmund occupied, keeping him from bothering me. But *he* knew the truth all along, didn't he? The withered old bastard *knew!* How he must have enjoyed his little joke! You've both been laughing at me!"

What did it matter now what Melanie thought? When had it ever mattered? Lucien was in trouble, and Moina might be able to help. All Kate wanted at the moment was to be rid of Melanie so that she and the servant could talk. "Yes. Edmund knew, almost from the beginning. But believe me, Melanie, neither of us found the situation particularly amusing."

Kate watched as a variety of emotions flitted across Melanie's face, none of them appealing. "He installed you here for Lucien, didn't he? Oh, no, don't try to deny it, for I can see the truth in those sly, colorless eyes! Not content with the rules he laid down with his solicitor, keeping me tied here at Tremaine Court, Edmund cast himself in the role of pimp—buying himself a woman for his first wife's bastard with wet-nurse wages. I suppose the stupid fool is lying in his own disgusting slobber at this very minute, thinking he has had the last laugh after all."

She threw back her head, laughing loudly in the small room so that for the first time Kate noticed that Melanie wore the miniature of Christophe Saville around her neck. Melanie's laughter cut off abruptly and she glared at Kate through slitted eyes. "And you people call yourselves the *quality?* If you are one of the quality, Kate Harvey, then *I* should be Queen of all England! Well, let me tell you something, missy—it won't work! None of it!"

"Of course, Mrs. Tremaine," Kate agreed, still covertly eyeing the medallion. It would appear she had found Lucien's thief. But what did that mean? Melanie professed to love Lucien. Surely she didn't wish to see the man she loved hanged for murder?

Melanie advanced on Kate slowly, menacingly. "And do

you want to know why it won't work? It's because he's mine, *Lady Katharine*. Lucien belongs to me! I had him first. Has he told you how he loves me? How he loved me? Has he told you about our time together, how he worshiped my body, every inch of it, his hands trembling with need, all but weeping in his adoration? No? Then I shall tell you, for I remember it well. I remember it *all*. Oh, sweet God, how Lucien loved me! He must remember—*he must!*"

She whirled about to confront Moina once more. "Give it to me, you ungrateful bitch! I must have it. You know how Melly needs it!"

"And I say no to you," Moina answered, rising, her stooped body keeping her a clear half head shorter than Melanie. "No more potions, not ever again. You'll have to make do with them men you lay with, pretending they're my baby, my poor, motherless baby. Go to one of them iffen it's loving Melly needs, and see iffen they can help her now."

Melanie fell to her knees in front of the servant, to press her head against the woman's legs, childlike, pleading. *"I can't!!* It isn't the same. You know it isn't the same. There's no release, no rest. Only the heat, and the hunger. Over and over and over—until I believe I'm going to perish with it. I don't understand. I've been so good, suffered for so long. Where is Lucien, my darling Lucien? It isn't fair! Why has everything gone so wrong? Moina! You have to help me. Oh, dear God—*help me!*"

Kate found it impossible to move, unable to do more than stand as mute witness to Melanie's demented grief, a small part of her actually pitying the tormented woman, pitying the then younger Lucien for ever having met her. It was obvious to Kate that Melanie still did not know that Lucien was being hunted for murder, in part because of evidence Melanie had unwittingly produced for the constable. What would she do when she found out?

Moina reached out a hand and patted Melanie's golden curls. "That's it, you evil white witch," she said softly, almost kindly. "You cry now, like my poor baby did when

your poison touched her, like young Master Lucien did when you took away everything he loved. Now you can cry for everything *you've* lost. Cry to God. Cry to me. Ain't neither of us going to help you now."

Melanie crumpled completely to the floor, sobbing, her small body tucked in on itself protectively. Kate stood by, a hand to her mouth—remembering. Just as she had once discovered Lucien collapsed on the music room floor, bereft, confused, totally beaten; as she had witnessed Edmund, physically and mentally crippled; she now saw Melanie at the nadir of her life, open and vulnerable to pain, to loss.

Melanie's destruction appeared to be complete. It was a cruel justice, a crude justice, but it was Moina's justice. Not God's.

Kate finally reacted, holding out a hand to the old woman and leading her back down the hallway and into the schoolroom, locking the door behind them, shutting out the sound of Melanie's hysterical weeping.

She sat on the edge of the windowseat, fearful her legs might not be able to support her much longer. "You were very brave, Moina," she said, if only to fill the silence, "standing up to Melanie the way you did. I can only apologize that neither Lucien nor I foresaw what would happen once you denied her your potions. I dread the moment she discovers Lucien has gone into hiding. Poor Melanie. I imagine I should send for Beasley, or someone."

Settled in the rocking chair, her toes barely reaching the floor, Moina began to speak, an unmistakable lilt in her crackly voice. "Don't you go feeling sorry for that one, Lady Katharine. She can take care of herself. Always has, always will. It's because of her I'm going to hell. But that's all right by me, because I fixed that white-haired bitch now, you see, fixed her good, once and for all. She's suffering something terrible, without my potions. Isn't it a treat?"

The servant turned to look outside, into the darkness. "She killed her, you know. Told me she didn't really mean

for it to happen that way, but that little girlie killed my sweet baby the same as iffen she put a knife straight through her heart."

Kate left the windowseat to pull up a nearby stool and perched beside the rocker, grasping the servant's gnarled fingers in her own. She had come to the nursery floor to ask Moina about the trouble she had warned Lucien about but, as Moina seemed inclined to talk, Kate decided to learn what she could. "How, Moina? Lucien said you have hinted as much to him, and neither of us doubt you, but we can't quite understand how she accomplished it. Pamela's secret lasted for twenty-three years before Melanie arrived at Tremaine Court. Please, won't you tell me how you can be so sure she was involved?"

Moina smiled. "About time someone figured out where to start. Tell you what, Lady Katharine, I won't go telling you any long stories, for that's not my way. But I will give you something that will help you. I'm only sorry for those two ladies. I hadn't counted on anybody else getting hurt. I thought I had it all figured out. I thought he'd be happy enough killing—well, never you mind about that. It's all of a piece, you know. Melanie, Christophe Saville, the new trouble that's come to hurt my Master Lucien. All of a piece. Learn the one, missy, and you learn it all."

She reached out and took Kate's left hand in hers, fingering the ruby ring Lucien had placed there only a few hours earlier. "This-here ring surely gets around, don't it?"

Quickly. Quickly. Time had become of the essence. Improvisation had served him well enough thus far, but he knew it had never been his strongest suit, even though the local constable, who had shown up unlooked-for in his dining room today just as he had been about to sit down to a late luncheon, had already proven to be remarkably malleable, delightfully dim-witted, his questions so simply turned to Guy's own advantage.

Guy smiled, cheered by the memory of how easily he had maneuvered both the constable and the conversation. . . .

Does the esteemed comte—just then personally pouring his uninvited guest a glass of fine French brandy—have any private suspicions, any notion of who in the neighborhood might be capable of such heinous crimes, the magistrate had asked?

Suspicions? Well, yes, the comte does, possibly—although it is most impolite to speak badly of others when one cannot be quite sure there is reason to do so. Yet how can any gentleman of conscience be anything less than helpful when the constable is so clearly in need of guidance? Please, would the good sir have some more brandy? And could the constable possibly be more precise in his questions?

The constable could.

To begin, does the comte, by chance, know Lucien Tremaine?

Oh yes, indeed yes. It happens that the comte is very well acquainted with Mr. Tremaine, and has even been invited to dine.

Several well-chosen words, a smattering of innuendo, and a few eloquent Gallic shrugs convey the comte's misgivings about one Lucien Tremaine.

But the constable—just then indelicately wolfing down a heaping plateful of golden crusted duckling—must understand that the comte does not arrive at this sad conclusion on his own. Tremaine's own house guest, a Mr. Garth Stafford—and a delightful man, truly top-rate—has confided that Tremaine has made quite a reputation for himself in London.

Cold-hearted, mysterious, a bit dangerous, Stafford has said—truly, for how else would the comte have learned such things? Stafford has quite clearly admitted that Tremaine has made enemies, and that there has been at least one recent attempt on his life. Why, again according to Stafford, some in society even harbor the amusing notion that Tremaine has forged a pact with the devil. Has the esteemed constable perhaps noticed Tremaine's distinctive ring—the one Stafford mentioned is rumored to hold a petrified heart cut from a living dove in the midst of a black mass? Interesting information, n'est-ce pas?

What? The constable has discovered evidence? How perfectly wonderful! A shirt smeared with blood? And hose? Really. But then why does the constable come to the comte if he is already sure of his man? Why has he not alerted the countryside, calling upon every man of courage to hunt Mr. Tremaine down?

Of course the comte will not speak of Mr. Tremaine's escape. How very embarrassing for the dear constable, to be sure. But there can be no question of Tremaine's guilt—not now that he has bolted?

No! Surely this is a jest? This servant, this Kate Harvey— she has announced that she is in reality someone else entirely, a Lady Katharine d'Harnancourt? She swears he is innocent? Vraiment? And this is believed? Ah, such a trusting man, this guest at his table. Has the esteemed constable yet met a woman who would not willingly lie for love, even a titled lady, if she is to be humored in this fanciful story of willows and Wimbledon? Ah, a smile, a wink. Just so. How wondrously comforting that gentlemen of the world understand each other. Why, might the good sir explain, would Mr. Tremaine choose to flee, if he is indeed innocent?

But, please, enough of womanish alibis and botched arrests, and enough of stories about supposed gentlemen cowering behind female skirts. The dear constable must say more about these so terrible murders. Perhaps there can be found a most telling clue if the comte and constable but put their heads together, oui?

This is terrible! Carvings? Mutilation? How curiously distressing. It is possible that the constable indeed discovered his murderer. Now, if only he could catch him, oui, discover some more proof of a solidness that would defeat this Lady Katharine's protestations? Please, another serving of duckling for such a hard-working servant of the law? As the comte was saying—much as it is painful to mention—it is well known that such atrocities go hand in hand with devil worshippers. . . .

Yes, thus far improvisation had served Guy Saville extremely well, but he could not rely upon that bumpkin

constable to finish the job. Not without all but taking the dolt by the hand and leading him to Lucien's door. Then, and only then, would the man put aside his bucolic pride and announce a hunt that would surely ferret out the so elusive Lucien Tremaine.

The time had come to apply *le coup de grâce,* the brilliant finishing stroke, his well-planned finale in which the endlessly, unconsciously helpful Melanie Tremaine had been months earlier cast as the leading player.

He heard the sound of her key in the door, turned to welcome her to the gazebo—and to the last act of his little drama—his wide smile firmly in place until she launched herself into his arms, sobbing wildly.

"Oh, Guy, Guy!" she told him as he led her toward the bed. "It is so terrible. More terrible than you can know. They hate me! They all hate me!"

He felt her small body trembling beneath his touch, not with passion, but despair. Her hysteria did not augur well for his plan; indeed, this little feminine fit would make it that much more difficult to execute. *Exécuter. Très bon.* A good choice of word. An excellent choice of word.

"Who would dare to hate you, *ma petite?* You know yourself to be most eminently lovable." He tilted back his head and smiled at his reflection in the overhead mirror in appreciation of his wit. "After all, you have told me time and again how very lovable you are, *mon vaniteux pigeon.* You must tell me their names."

"Moina, who refused to give me my po—my medicine tonight. That horrible Kate Harvey, Edmund—all of them! But most especially, my darling Lucien. I did not tell you before, could not face it, but Lucien has rejected me. Totally! He even threatened to kill me, Guy—*me,* who loves him past all bearing!"

He pushed her down on the side of the bed, leaving her in order to prepare the opium he had brought with him, for he would get nowhere until she had lost the edge of her hysteria. He returned to the bed and offered her the pipe, noticing that her hand and foot were still bandaged. She had

been very vague about the source of her injuries. Perhaps Lucien had more spleen than he thought. "Threatened to kill you, darling? This sounds most ominous. Here, this will help banish those tears. Tell me—did anyone happen to hear him make this threat?"

Melanie looked up, taking the pipe from him. "Hear him? No, I don't think so. Oh, my head aches so." She drew the mind-dulling smoke deep into her lungs, holding it there for some moments before exhaling. "Wait! There was Beasley. Yes, I remember now. I'm quite sure I told Beasley. He found me in Lucien's rooms as I held the knife, preparing to slice Lucien's bed to ribbons. Why—why do you ask?"

So Beasley knew of Lucien's threat, did he? How accommodating of Lucien. How accommodating of both his dearest nephew *and* Melanie. The saints were indeed smiling tonight. He pressed the pipe upon her again. "No reason, darling, only a little idle chatter, to fill the silence caused by your despair. But, look—I have a special surprise for you this evening that is sure to cheer you. See, I have brought all your regretfully departed friend's clever toys, remembering how you said you had at times enjoyed this game of *esclavage,* this bondage. I have made you happy now, *oui?* Smile for me, my beautiful Melanie."

But Melanie did not smile for him. She only drew on the pipe yet again, almost desperately, as if seeking something she could not find. She did not even ask how he had disposed of Lady Southcliff's body. Details such as that seemed to elude her interest. Indeed, from the moment the deed was done, Melanie had put the dead woman out of her conversation, concentrating on how happy she would be once all the other obstacles in her path were removed and she and Lucien were free to love each other.

Guy could forgive Melanie for many things, but he could not forgive her that. He had killed for her, twice, and all she could speak of was Lucien? Was it then that he knew he could not love her? Had never loved her? Would love her forever?

At last, her high, childlike voice robbing her curses of all but the power to bring a smile to Guy's face, she flung the pipe from her and turned to sob into the pillows. "It's not enough, I know it's not enough! Moina refused me the potion. I must have Lucien! He is the only one who can help me now. But I cannot find him. Nobody will talk to me, nobody will tell me where he has gone, not even Beasley! Lucien can't leave me. Nobody leaves me. Everybody loves me."

Any niggling hint of remorse Guy might still have harbored at what he had planned fled at the mention of his nephew's name. No love. And now, no remorse. Never before had a woman complained that he, Guy Saville, had not proved man enough for her. His inborn caution, however, did not similarly take flight.

Fighting her would only make what he had to do more difficult. He had to divert her, get her talking of something else, and then ease her into helping him. "Of course everyone loves you. I love you with a great passion. Tell me who else loves you, Melanie."

She closed her eyes and picked up the pipe again, then giggled. "Papa loved me," she said after a few moments, rolling onto her back, this unexpected piece of information effectively gaining Guy's undivided attention.

"Your papa? Surely you do not mean that."

Melanie giggled yet again. "Don't I, darling Guy? Of course he did not like for me to call him Papa. He never visited when I was young. Gentlemen don't usually visit discarded mistresses and their bastard offspring, you see. But eventually he came, when my mother died—and when he saw me he fell in love. Everyone falls in love with me, darling Guy. Everyone."

Guy sat very still on the edge of the bed, barely able to breathe. "He hurt you, *ma petite?*"

She turned her head back and forth on the pillows. "Hurt me, Guy? Oh, no. He was good. He was so very good to me. He called me his pretty Melly. He petted me, and gave me

pretty things—and I let him love me. It hurt at first, but then I learned to like it. So many pretty things. I like pretty things, Guy. I like it when people love me."

Her smile crumbled and her bottom lip came forward in a pout. "But then he wanted to leave me, go back to London where he could go to parties and the theater—and have his choice of many women. Nobody should ever try to leave me, Guy. It isn't nice. I told Papa he shouldn't go, that he shouldn't stop giving me pretty things, but he only pushed me away. He didn't want to make love to me any more. He said I was a disease and I had made him sick. He said we had done what we did only because of my sickness."

Guy handed her the pipe and she drew on it deeply. She was still visibly upset, but her voice had begun to slow, to slur. It wouldn't be long now before she remembered the fever that always burned so closely beneath her skin. Still, Guy hesitated. He hadn't planned on loving Melanie Tremaine, and he most certainly had not planned on feeling sorry for her.

She handed him the pipe, smiling at him. Her feral smile, the one he had learned to mistrust. "Papa never did get to leave, darling Guy. But I did. With all my pretty things, and all his pretty money."

Guy's blood ran cold. "Why didn't your papa leave, Melanie? What made him stay?"

Now she laughed in real amusement. "Silly Guy. Because I killed him, of course. I asked him to love me one more time, then used his own knife on him as he slept. Why didn't he leave me? Because it is terribly difficult to get out of a coffin, darling Guy."

Guy looked down at her, into her innocent blue eyes, her heartbreakingly beautiful face, and shivered. And he had thought to change his plans, find another way to destroy Lucien and take this white angel of death back to France with him? May the saints preserve him from any such madness!

But Melanie was still speaking. "I left him and traveled to

Brighton, and then to Bath, to find someone else who had a lot of lovely money," she told him, running her hand along his thigh, inching toward the bulge in his pants. "There were many generous men in Brighton, but I discovered Felicia in Bath, and then Lucien. Lucien, who loved me. Ah, Guy, you cannot know how he loved me." Her fingers found him and squeezed, hard. "Felicia knew about Papa and would have ruined everything. So Felicia died. She died for Lucien. And now he does not want me! After all I have done for him, suffered for him! He can't leave me, Guy," she said, her voice breaking on a sob. "How can he leave me?"

Guy disengaged her hand before reaching for the satin ropes, then climbed further onto the bed, taking hold of Melanie's unresisting arms. It was then that he saw the medallion, the smiling face of Christophe Saville. It was so perfect a touch, so strangely fitting, that he had to smile, even as he continued to lie. "But you are wrong. Lucien is coming to you tonight, my darling Melanie," he crooned. "Did I forget to tell you? I have sent for him, and he will be here directly. Here, let me help you prepare for him."

She looked up at him, her pupils dark and wide, showing the effects of the opium. Moving quickly, he tied her left wrist to the bedpost. "Lucien?" she questioned, staring at him blankly, her limbs nearly dead weights in his hands. "Lucien? Coming here? My darling Lucien? I—I don't understand. When? How?"

The second wrist now secured, Guy slowly moved lower on the bed, taking hold of one slim ankle, continuing his sleek lie. "How could he not come? He loves you, Melanie. Loves you dearly. Remember?"

Melanie frowned for a moment, then smiled. "Yes. Yes, of course he does. I told that ungrateful Kate Harvey how much Lucien loves me, but she doesn't believe me. Filthy, impure gutter bitch. Leasing out her teats! How could he love her? No! He loves Melly, he has always loved Melly."

"Yes, yes, of course. *Certainement,* darling," Guy crooned, testing the knots that held Melanie's ankles, not

really listening to her slurred ramblings, for now they meant less than nothing to him.

Against his will, remembering Felicia Southcliff's cries of unsurpassed ecstasy, her moans of exquisite pain, he felt himself becoming aroused. It was a damnably inopportune time for him to feel amorous, but an extremely pleasurable sensation nonetheless. Perhaps he might enjoy himself first, ride this bewitching white bitch one last time—and then do the deed.

Melanie had begun to stir on the bed, tugging at her bonds. "Guy? I don't think I wish Lucien to see me this way, not at first. I need to hold him, touch him. Release me, Guy. Release me at once."

He didn't answer, but only began stripping off his clothes, his manhood swelling painfully within the confines of his buckskins, begging release. Reaching down, he took hold of Melanie's sheer dressing gown and, with one sharp motion, rent it from bodice to hem. He looked up at the overhead mirror, marveling at the alabaster perfection of Melanie's small body spread provocatively for his inspection. Lady Southcliff had been beautiful, stretched wide in front of him, but this woman was exquisite. The perfect vessel. Eager, adventurous, totally wanton.

But Melanie may have been correct. The opium did not seem to be enough tonight. She wasn't writhing in expected pleasure, mouthing sweetly obscene requests, instructing him in how to pleasure her. Instead, she seemed to be attempting to draw her thighs together, as if the word modesty had belatedly entered her vocabulary.

"Guy!" she ordered, her voice rising. "I don't like this. You must release me! Lucien! *Lucien!*"

"Be quiet!" The walls of the gazebo were thick, but he could take no chances, not with Lucien out there, somewhere, perhaps even now deciding one of the matching gazebos would make a good hiding place for the night. Grabbing the leather mask, Guy straddled Melanie as he forced the silencing leather over her head and laced it up

behind her, tangling a few strands of her long hair in the knots he made.

She still moaned, perhaps even began to cry once more, but now no one but he could hear her.

Out of breath, and even more excited by his exertions, he remained straddled across her waist, intrigued yet again by the unnatural sight of a faceless body, open and vulnerable to his every whim, his every new, exciting idea. He remembered her story about her papa. *Incest.* He was old enough to be her father. *Forbidden fruit.* The thought was repelling. The thought was exciting.

Slowly, and with infinite tenderness, he stroked Melanie's breasts, his practiced hands eventually soothing her until she lay quietly beneath him, allowing him to nudge her nipples into stiff erection.

"So beautiful still, this body of yours, my darling Melly. So very, very beautiful," he crooned in all honesty, repositioning himself between her spread thighs, to sink himself deep within her in one fluid stroke, effectively impaling her on the bed. He did not move, did not succumb to his passions. He preferred now to talk to her, to explain— perhaps even to gain a measure of understanding, if not forgiveness, for what he was now forced to do. After all, he was a French nobleman, a gentleman.

"I arrived on these shores a stranger, Melanie, knowing my goal but not how I should accomplish it. You remember, for you welcomed me. Didn't you, darling? You—you and your twisted love—showed me the way. I have planned this almost since the moment we met, definitely since the first day we coupled here, like wild animals, with you calling me Lucien just as I brought you to the pinnacle of pleasure. That insult, darling, became your first real mistake."

Still on his knees, he paused a moment, running his hands up and down her silken skin, watching as his swollen manhood slid slightly out of her, only to disappear once more, deep inside her body. "Poor Melly. Your old friend Felicia might yet have saved you, taken your place in my

plans, for I have to admit, I truly had become most fond of you. But it was not to be. No, you steadfastly refused to give up this mad love of Lucien."

Anger twisted cruelly in his gut. "And that, I'm afraid, became your second mistake. Your fatal mistake. I am sorry for you, Melanie, sorry for your wasted life, your unhappiness. But you are a stupid, stupid girl. A wise person loves only herself. But you'd hang in his place, gladly, and me with you, before allowing your darling Lucien to go to the gibbet. How does he inspire such loyalty? Even this woman you hate, this newly titled lady, has helped to seal your fate by swearing she shared his bed last night in an attempt to save him from the rope. Yes, my darling. Your Kate Harvey and the ungrateful Lucien in bed, loving—*together*. Oh, dear. Such a startling revelation could serve, one way or another, to put us both into a sad decline, *n'est-ce pas?*"

He withdrew from her to sit on the edge of the bed, his manhood flaccid, his passion dimmed by disgust. She remained still, barely breathing, but he knew she had heard his every word. How pitiful she looked, lying there. Now she had to acknowledge that all she had done, all she had risked, had come to nothing. Her elaborate scheming, her entire life, her reason for living—all had ended in abject failure.

He should feel no pity for her, especially now, knowing about her father, knowing that she was past all salvation. If he were to allow her to live she could only end in some madhouse, chained to a wall, her body used and abused by her keepers, her perfect beauty marred by filth and running sores. What he was about to do could only be termed a humane act, much akin to assisting a mortally wounded animal out of its misery.

"I helped you bury your old enemy, darling Melly, and now, through you, I will destroy mine. Not precisely a fair exchange, you might say, but then what in life is fair, *chérie?* Never fear, I will be quick about this, just as I had planned from the beginning. The rest will come later, all that distressing business with the knife necessary to fit the pattern your sweet sickness has already set. I detest it, but

the so stupid constable must be given ample evidence if your darling Lucien is to hang for murder."

Melanie's small hands clenched into fists as she came to life with a vengeance, trying to rip her wrists free of the ropes.

"Not one murder as I had planned," Guy continued, "but three. Enough to hang Lucien a dozen times over. Three, Melanie. Felicia, the maid—and now, at last *you*. You hadn't even thought of the maid, had you? Of course not. All you can think of is the moment. Your penchant for bloodletting did at least save me a midnight ride to the sea in order to be rid of Felicia's maid. Have I thanked you for that? No? Shame on me."

He straddled her once more, pressing her forearms to the bed. "So, now you understand at last, *n'est-ce pas?* You have perhaps even forgotten your love of the so unworthy Lucien as self-preservation has come once more to the fore. Or do you struggle only because you fear for your Lucien's fate?"

He moved away from her, for she had begun to sweat and he disliked the smell of her fear. It was contagious. "You realize now how I plan to make you useful to me, even if you do not know the why of it. Don't hurt yourself, darling, for to struggle against the inevitable can only cause you needless pain. There, that's it. Lie very still. You see how good I am to you—even though your insane clumsiness in sending Felicia to my door has robbed me of the leisure of remaining in England for the supreme satisfaction of witnessing Lucien's body dancing at the end of a rope."

He would have said more, explained more thoroughly—for he did so enjoy listening to his own brilliance—but Melanie began to strain against her bonds yet again, her frightened, muffled whimpers painful to his ears. Sighing, accepting the inevitable she refused to face, he leaned forward, grasping her head at forehead and chin, and with one quick, twisting motion, snapped her slim neck.

Shaken, his heart pounding, he climbed off the bed, backing away from Melanie's limp body as he reached for the still-glowing opium pipe, needing outside courage to

finish what he had begun. "A wise bird never soils its own nest, *ma chère,*" he said sadly, looking at the evidence of his handiwork. "We taught each other many things during the nights spent here together, you and I, but you refused to learn that one very important lesson from me. I, however, am a wise bird. I have fouled Lucien's nest."

He prudently moved his clothing out of harm's way, his hands trembling, his mouth twisted into an expression of revulsion for what he was about to do. Gingerly, he picked up the knife bearing Lucien's initials—the weapon Melanie had been so considerate as to choose for the instrument of Felicia's destruction—and approached the bed.

He had work to do. *Quickly. Quickly.*

CHAPTER 26

Morn,
Wak'd by the circling hours, with rosy hand
Unbarr'd the gates of light.

John Milton, *Paradise Lost*

The sharp, driving rain had dulled to a cold-as-charity drizzle by the time the assembled mourners hastily mumbled their last amens and turned to leave the cemetery, a small, silent group huddled beneath an anonymous canopy of large, black umbrellas.

Once outside the gate the canopy splintered, breaking into distinct clusters. Kate and Garth hastened directly for their waiting carriage while the servants made their way back on foot.

The sadly uninspiring minister, his lengthy graveside prayers already forgotten, lingered with a few curious neighbors to decry the barbarous notion that no one had been invited back to Tremaine Court for so much as a cup of hot tea with the grieving widower, while *monsieur le comte,* his valet struggling to keep up with his employer's rapid strides and holding an umbrella high to protect the man's head from the elements, hastened to his own rented coach.

Also just outside the gate, a dejected Constable Clemens

and his assistant stood in the rain, looking out over the countryside as if they had truly expected to see Lucien Tremaine at his stepmother's graveside and now were left not knowing what to do.

Inside the high walls two farm laborers who had been hastily pressed into service—soaked to the skin and grumbling at their lot—spat and cursed as they manned ropes to lower the casket into the deep, muddy trench, then picked up their shovels.

Only Beasley, standing unnoticed just inside the gate, his traveling bags at his feet, snuffled into a large white handkerchief as he heard the hollow, repetitive sounds of sodden clumps of dirt raining down on the polished mahogany.

As the Tremaine carriage moved away the heavy canvas side curtain parted for a moment and Lucien looked out toward the graveyard, then sat back against the cushions, holding tightly to Kate's hand, his lips drawn into a fine line. Melanie Tremaine had been granted at least one of her wishes. She had become a permanent part of Tremaine Court.

"Lucien?"

He turned to look at Kate, unhappy to see that she appeared to be exhausted, almost as exhausted as he felt after being in hiding for nearly five days. He hadn't seen her for the last three, unwilling to expose her to danger, as Constable Clemens had been a daily visitor at Tremaine Court.

"What is it, dearest?" he asked. "Surely you aren't surprised to see me. After all, you've been badgering Garth for days to set up some sort of meeting. It fit his sense of the dramatic to have me in the carriage, right under our dear constable's bulbous nose."

"Now, Lucien, I never said she badgered me," Garth protested from the facing seat. "Your Katharine is merely a most persuasive woman. It was she who convinced the local squire to order that same constable to put out the story that Melanie's death occurred as a result of a tumble down the stairs, assuring him it wouldn't do to alarm the entire

386

neighborhood. As for the rest, well, you may be right. I do enjoy a touch of theatrics. I have often thought I should like to tread the boards, if I were not heir to an earldom."

The carriage pulled up in front of the house and Lucien saw the confusion in Kate's eyes. "I thought we were going to talk, Lucien," she said as Garth opened the door. "We've barely had time to say a half dozen words to each other."

"That's true enough. But now you must say even less than a half dozen words to our dear friend Garth. May I make a suggestion? Say 'good-bye, Garth.' "

"No need," his friend said, leaping to the ground without waiting for the coachman to let down the stairs. "I'll be with Edmund, Katharine, when you get back."

The carriage pulled away before Kate could do more than ask who was sitting on the box.

"Hawkins, of course," Lucien told her, chuckling. "He wasn't about to let just anyone drive me, you know. Mary is with Edmund and Noddy, so don't worry." He took both her hands in his, then leaned forward to kiss her. He didn't think he could live another five minutes if he couldn't kiss her.

Several pleasurable minutes later, as the carriage rolled along the roadway, and with Kate now snuggled tightly against him, Lucien at last asked the question that was uppermost in his mind. "Does Edmund know?"

Kate smiled at him and nodded. "About Melanie? Yes, he does, although we told him the lie about her supposed fall on the stairs. I believe he is much relieved by the thought that he no longer has to fear her, even if none of us can be happy that she died. Nobody deserves such a death, Lucien, not even Melanie."

"And does he ask for me?"

"Hourly! He still believes you were called to London on business. You won't recognize him, Lucien, for that is how changed he is. It's only his speech and the weakness in his left side that still plague him. Moina's potions had nothing to do with his last attack, you know, the one that did this to him. She says he suffered some sort of shock, although I

haven't dared to push Edmund for an explanation. He has enough to worry about right now, without believing you are to be arrested at any moment."

"I can understand that. It is a thought that has crossed my mind a time or two and it's damned disturbing," Lucien admitted, slipping his arm around her shoulders, unashamedly seeking the promised comfort of her body. "Lord, Katharine, but I'm weary. Nearly too weary to consider laying you back on these cushions and making love to you. How long has it been since I've slept? A week? A month? I promise you, my sweet—once this is all over I shall make a more ardent groom than I do a fiancé."

He felt her hand, cool against his lightly bearded cheek. He hadn't been able to cater to his creature comforts since fleeing the constable.

"And I shall see to it that you keep that promise—the very moment Hawkins has finished shaving you," she said. "Is that shameless of me? I sincerely hope so. Poor Lucien. These past days haven't been easy for you. What a terrible man!"

"Terrible?" Lucien chuckled low in his throat. "You're speaking of our esteemed constable, aren't you, my love? If Garth hadn't had the presence of mind to hide my knife and medallion before he summoned the man to the gazebo I should have been hunted down like a fox by now and locked up in some damp cell, awaiting my trial. I could murder Beasley for putting Clemens on my scent in the first place. I caught a glimpse of our esteemed butler, back there at the cemetery, his packed bags at his feet. What happened? Did Hawkins forcibly strip him of his butler's keys now that Melanie is gone?"

"No. He is leaving of his own choice. He truly must have loved Melanie. Poor, unhappy Melanie. But everyone should have someone to mourn their passing, I suppose," Kate murmured, slipping her fingers inside Lucien's greatcoat to stroke his chest.

"I find it easier to believe he is mourning the loss of his position at Tremaine Court and the money Melanie must

have paid him to act as her procurer. Hawkins must be in his glory, though. I believe we shall have to engage another butler once we adjourn to London, not that I mind. Hawkins was like a fish out of water away from Tremaine Court."

He reached over to kiss Kate's chin. "If we ever get to London, that is." Frustrated, he sat forward, clenching his hands in his lap. *"Devil worship!* Garth says Clemens is convinced I committed these murders as some form of devil worship. Unfortunately, I have to agree with his deduction, if not his choice of suspect. But why would Melanie dabble in such a dangerous business, especially after the first two murders? With Moina's help I had already figured out that she was meeting at least one man in the gazebo—one of the farm laborers, and a harmless enough fellow it turns out— but what sort of dangerous, twisted games could she have been playing to have tempted that horrendous fate? I know you feel sorry for her, Katharine, but damn it, she won't leave me alone—even in death!"

Kate shook her head, her bottom lip caught between her teeth. He watched as tears gathered in her eyes and wanted to kick himself for speaking out of turn.

"Katharine?" he asked worriedly, realizing that he hadn't been the only one to suffer these past few days.

"Lucien, Moina and I were probably the last two people to see Melanie before she died—except for her murderer, of course. She had come to Moina's room to demand a potion. Moina refused, as we had told her to, and Melanie flew into a rage."

Kate's face grew pale. "I entered the room to see Melanie hitting Moina, furiously slapping at her. Anyway, when at last Melanie realized she would not get her way she collapsed onto the floor, saying no one understood and sobbing as if her heart would break."

"Melanie had no heart, Katharine," Lucien interjected, disliking the hint of sympathy he detected in her tone. "If your polite upbringing tells you to forget everything else, kindly remember that. Melanie had physical beauty, but she had no heart, no compassion, no sense of morality."

"I've often wondered if her great beauty was not also her greatest curse," Kate said. "But, Lucien, I left her there—without so much as a backward glance, without a thought as to what she might do next. If only I had stayed, tried to reason with her—"

"No! Don't think that way, Katharine," Lucien told her, cradling her against his body. "You wouldn't have changed anything, only delayed it." He closed his eyes and a vision of Melanie as he had last seen her burned behind his lids. Garth had come to his new hiding place in the loft of an old barn on the estate, and taken him to the gazebo. When he had entered he had immediately recognized Melanie's hair, a golden halo surrounding the garishly painted leather mask. Other than that, all he had seen was blood. Melanie's blood. Everywhere.

He lifted Kate's hand and kissed it. "I'm sorry, my love. This hasn't been any easier for you than it has been for me. Probably worse. Who knows what sort of madman we're dealing with. I've got to get you away from here, no matter how much I'll miss you. First thing tomorrow morning Garth will take you to safety at The Willows and—"

"Absolutely not," she interrupted, pressing her fingers against his lips, "I'm not going anywhere without you. Not now. Not ever. Don't even think of anything so foolish. We've only just found each other." He tried to move her hand away but she shook her head. "Lucien, I have something important to give you. Please, let me speak."

He kissed her fingertips, silently agreeing to listen to her, as he remembered that he had fallen in love with an intelligent, determined woman.

"Thank you." Sitting back against the leather cushion, refusing to meet his eyes, Kate sighed and said, "I don't know where to begin."

He gave a sharp bark of laughter and allowed himself to relax. "Isn't that just like a woman? You want to talk but you don't know what to say," Lucien teased, earning himself a sharp jab in the ribs from Kate's elbow.

"Be serious, Lucien! I've held this inside for three impos-

sibly long days and nights because you refused to come to me. I would have given it to Garth and had him deliver it to you, except that I selfishly wanted to be with you when you read it." She reached into her reticule and drew out several yellowed sheets of paper. "Here, Lucien. Moina wants you to have this."

He eyed the pages warily, as if they might somehow come to life and bite him. "What is it?"

Kate's eyes were filled with tears again. "It's a letter, my dearest. A letter from your mother."

He took the letter, his hands shaking as he unfolded the pages, recognizing his mother's neat copperplate handwriting, and then refolded them. He looked at Kate. "You've read it?"

She nodded. "And I've taken the liberty of reading it to Edmund. I didn't think you'd mind. He cried, but I think he's all right now." The carriage lurched to a stop and she pushed back the curtain and looked out the window. "Where are we?"

"Miles from anywhere, if Hawkins is as good as his word, and I've no doubt he is," Lucien said, looking past her to see that it had stopped raining. "We're reasonably safe, since Garth tells me Clemens has yet to mount an all-out search, still reluctant to say he had me and then let me slip through his fingers." He held out his hand to her. "Madam, would you care to walk with me?"

He assisted Kate from the coach, tipped his hat to Hawkins, and began walking toward a small stand of trees some distance away. The letter seemed to be burning into his fingers, but he was reluctant to open it again and read what his mother had written. "Why now?" he asked as he and Kate stopped beneath the trees. "Why did Moina give this to you now? Why didn't she give it to me when she sent you to the Fox and Crown with Christophe's letters?"

Kate shook her head. "I asked her the same questions. She told me she wasn't ready to 'end it' when you first came home. Now she says the time has come for you to know it all."

Lucien took a deep breath and unfolded the pages, holding them with both hands. Now, at last, he would know. He had waited for so long, wished for this moment a thousand times while believing it would never come. And now he was afraid to read the letter. In his own way, employing logic as it suited him, he had come to terms with his past, with his mother. He wasn't sure he could live with a truth different from the one he had imagined.

Closing his eyes, he handed the letter to Kate. "Read it to me, Katharine. Read it to me the way you read it to Edmund."

Kate took the letter, politely cleared her throat, and began to read:

Lucien, my dearest, darling child,

You left this morning, your head held high, the buttons on your lovely uniform winking in the sunlight, or in the reflection of my tears. I know not which. How proud I was of you, I am of you, my darling boy. You are, and will always be, the most perfect rose in my garden.

Yet I am so sad, feeling that I might never see you again, never watch you bow so courteously to me as you bestow a kiss on my cheek. Please forgive my silly tears, and forgive me for embracing you when I know you have grown too tall for such overt displays of affection, but I am a mother, and a mother sometimes does these things.

Do not fear that I think you might fall in battle, for I know this cannot be true. The Good Lord would not allow such a pain in my heart. No, it is my future that I cannot be sure of, for I have discovered a small problem with my health. It is a woman's problem and I will not discuss it with you for fear of putting you to the blush. Moina assures me I am fine, but I have known her too long, and she cannot hide the truth from me.

Lucien, you must be brave, for if you are reading this letter it will mean that I have been called to my

Heavenly Father. I am not afraid, but I cannot die with any real peace until my conscience has been cleared of a secret that has been kept from you for too long.

So now I will ask you to be brave again, my darling child. Oh, how terribly cold the words seem, written in a letter! If only I could hold you, my son, if only I were eloquent! Sweet Virgin Mary, help me to find the right words!

Lucien, you know that you are the child of my heart—but what you do not know is that Edmund is not your true father.

My darling, I know this revelation must come as a most unwelcome shock, and you must be saying, "No! That is impossible!" You are right to think so, for Edmund Tremaine has been a father to you since before you were born. He has been the best of fathers and the best of husbands, and I love him dearly. As you love him.

But it is time for the truth. Watching you prepare to ride away today, possibly to the quixotic fate of meeting your true father across a battlefield, I knew I had left it too late to tell you such upsetting news. Indeed, if I am to be granted the supreme gift of living to see your beloved face once more I may lose my courage yet again. So you see, I am taking the coward's way out, putting the truth in this letter.

I met your father one lovely summer day, two months before Edmund and I were to be married. Christophe Saville was a most handsome man, and I see his face each time I look at you, my darling. He was so young, we were both so young, and I was terribly frightened by the thought of marrying Edmund, a man older than myself whom I did not really know. Christophe wished for me to elope with him to France, but I was afraid. He sailed home to gain his father's permission for our marriage in Mother Church, but his ship went down and I believed him lost to me forever. I did not care if I lived or died, Lucien. But once Edmund and I were married I learned

that my husband was a most loving, honorable man. I knew then that my feelings for Christophe had been those of a very young girl, and not those of true love.

Poor, trusting Edmund. It was not until you were born that I realized that my foolishness of that summer had borne fruit. How could I tell him that the child he so loved was not his own? I could not. I could not break his heart. Moina and I decided it would be best—best for you, best for Edmund—if I lived with my lie.

Then Christophe miraculously came back to me! He did not care that I had married. He wished only for both you and me to flee with him to France, to his family. I could not hurt him either, could not tell him that I no longer loved him. But I could tell him that I had said my vows before God and could not break them. This Christophe understood. He returned to France, but he wrote often through Moina, asking after his son. You were fortunate, Lucien, for you have two fathers to love you. Christophe even made plans for your future, sending me complicated legal papers that will make you a very wealthy man. I waited years for more letters, but the Terror ruled in France and after that Christophe's letters stopped, never to come again.

Moina believes Christophe to be dead, but I cannot agree. He was so young, Lucien, so vital. Surely a spirit so strong cannot die? To me, my Christophe will always be young, and strong, and handsome. My spirit is not so strong. No matter what Moina says, I can feel my strength leaving me, slowly, every day, so that it is barely noticeable until I go into my greenhouse and sit looking at my flowers, unable to muster the energy to tend my poor roses.

That is why I have written this letter, because I believe my spirit will fail me before your return.

But what of my letter? What of Christophe's wishes for his son? They cannot die with me. I owe Christophe the right to have his wishes granted, his hopes fulfilled. I fear that once I am gone Moina, who is very old, may not

outlive me by many months. I will entrust the legal papers to Edmund's solicitor, but this letter, and the letters from your father, are too personal to have them handed to you by that cold, emotionless man. Someone you love must be my messenger.

And so, my darling, it is with a light and hopeful heart that I await your dearest Melanie's arrival at Tremaine Court. How your eyes glow when you speak of my new daughter! Your affianced bride will become my angel, the caretaker of this letter once it is sealed—and my heart can be at rest.

To the world, my darling, you will always be Edmund's son, and that is as it should be. Edmund must never know, not because he would hate us, but because the truth would hurt him. I love Edmund with all my heart, as I love you, and I ask your solemn vow that you will continue to call him your father, for he has earned that respect.

Please, Lucien, do not despise me for what I have told you. Do not hate me for burdening you with a secret I have kept from my beloved husband all these years. When this terrible war is at last over it is my hope that you will go to France and seek out the family you have there. Christophe spoke very highly of his father and his half-brother. Surely you have a host of cousins to meet! Embrace your French family, Lucien, and kiss Christophe for me. He gave me a most wonderful son.

Do not weep for me, my darling child, but only keep me alive in your heart, looking as you last saw me, waving my brave son good-bye. Put flowers on my grave, dearest Lucien, say your prayers, and remember that your mother will always love you.

Halfway through Kate's reading of the letter Lucien had turned his back, looking out over the meadow as he listened to his mother's last confession. His eyes had stung with tears as he learned that his mother had believed herself to be dying. How could she have let him leave, knowing that she

was ill? Why hadn't she stopped him? A word, a look—and he would have stayed.

Lucien wiped at his eyes, already knowing the answer. His mother would never have burdened him with her pain.

And then he had heard Melanie's name and at last, after an eternity of wondering, everything became clear to him. Stupid, besotted idiot! *He* had brought Melanie into his mother's house! *He* had been the instrument of his mother's destruction, Edmund's disillusionment—*everything* that had happened to destroy the inhabitants of Tremaine Court!

"Oh, my God," he groaned, leaning against the tree. "Katharine—it's my fault. My mother was looking for an angel—I sent her the devil incarnate."

He felt Kate's arms go around his waist as she leaned her forehead against his back. "You didn't know, Lucien. You couldn't have known. Nobody could. I've seen Melanie on her best behavior. You can't blame yourself. But Moina knew. Moina knew, and she decided to punish Melanie for what she had done, and punish Edmund as well."

"But why, Katharine? Why did she do it? Why would Melanie read the letters and then use what she had learned against my mother? She should have been delighted. Not only was Tremaine Court to be mine, but a separate fortune as well."

"Lucien, there are so many possibilities that my head has been aching for three days and nights, simply trying to sort them out. Remember, she couldn't have run straight to Edmund. She had been in residence at Tremaine Court for more than a month before Christophe's letters came to light. Moina told me Melanie was in desperate need of money, for one reason or another. She also said that Melanie had begun meeting one of the footmen in the servant's wing. Perhaps she feared discovery would cause Pamela and Edmund to banish her from the house."

Lucien laughed, the sound of his laughter hollow and mirthless, and turned to face Kate. "A month. So much for undying love. God, what a fool I was!"

Kate sighed. "According to Moina, Melanie had urges,

uncontrollable urges. Moina may not have understood Melanie until too late, but she was able to use that knowledge against her when Melanie tried to turn her off with the rest of the servants. To her mind, she had to be here when you returned—to watch you 'finish it' as she always says."

"Hence the potions," Lucien said, feeling sick. He put his arm around Kate and began walking back to the carriage.

"Unfortunately, yes. But, to my way of thinking, neither of those things prompted Melanie to betray Pamela in the first place. It was greed, Lucien. Simple greed. I sincerely believe Melanie wanted it all—the house in London, the money, Tremaine Court. Remember, you had gone off to war. If you had died, which was a real possibility, Melanie would have been left with nothing save Edmund's charity. But she had been handed a chance to discredit a dying Pamela—forgive me for saying that, but Moina did at last agree that your mother was indeed dying—and take her place as Edmund's wife."

"And Noddy?"

"I can only think that Melanie made up her plans as she went along, to suit her circumstances. Noddy's birth only further entrenched her as mistress of Tremaine Court. If you died—the disowned bastard—as Noddy's mother, she would still be in charge. If you lived, she would tell you Noddy was yours."

"Leaving Edmund. Part of what you said makes sense, but what do you propose Melanie planned to do with her suddenly inconvenient husband once I came home?"

Kate sighed, leaning her head against his shoulder. "I can't be certain, no one can, but I have had a lot of time to think about this. I think Melanie only wanted Edmund alive so that she might amuse herself by torturing him while waiting for you to come home. I believe she would have arranged a fatal accident for Edmund, after telling you he had forced her into marriage, and then she would have married you. Remember, she died still convinced that you loved her. But she made a fatal mistake. She came to you too soon, and told you too much. It was then that Moina took

full charge, refusing to give Melanie any more potions while you remained in London nursing your anger unless she obeyed her. You see, Moina promised Melanie you would be back for her. Melanie believed you still loved her, while Moina believed you would kill Melanie for her—and Edmund as well. Either way, everything hinged on your return."

Lucien looked down at Kate, his expression bleak. "Insanity. And I started it all. I brought Melanie into my mother's house. I'm surprised Moina didn't want me dead as well."

"No!" Kate took his hand and squeezed it. "I knew you'd react this way. Yes, it's true that Melanie caused everyone great pain. But the seeds for this tragedy were planted long ago. They just took a long time to bear fruit."

Lucien nodded, for he did not feel up to arguing. They had returned to the coach and now he held the door open for Kate. "Go with Hawkins now, Katharine, while this fugitive slinks off into the trees. Much as I hate to leave you, I still have a lot of thinking to do. After all, Melanie may be dead, but the remnants of her insane desires are not. She may have helped to destroy my past, my mother—but I'll be damned if I'll let her reach out from the grave to destroy our future. I promise you, one way or another, my sweet Katharine, I'm going to discover who killed her, who butchered all three of those women."

"Excuse me, sir, but if you'll be leaving now there's something I've got to give you."

Lucien looked up to see Hawkins sitting in the box, holding an envelope in his hand. "Another letter? Let me guess, dear fellow. Moina?"

Hawkins grinned. "Yes, sir. She said to give it to you once you read the first one. She said that everything must have its time, and with Mrs. Tremaine safely underground and Mister Edmund on the mend the time has come at last for you to see this. Said you could end it now, with her blessing. Strange woman, Moina, for as long as I've known her, if you don't mind me saying so, sir."

"Do I have a choice?" Lucien asked, summoning a weak smile as he took the envelope. "All right, Katharine. It's my turn to read."

He broke open the seal and extracted a single sheet of paper, frowning as he scanned the official looking script. "This is impossible, Katharine," he said when he had finished. "These are marriage lines, between Mother and Christophe Saville. You never knew Mother, knew her deep devotion to her religion. She and Edmund were married in the Church. Her father may have forced her to the altar, but she wouldn't have done such a thing unless she had absolute proof Christophe was dead."

Kate took the paper from his hand, read it, and then pushed it back at him. "Lucien," she said, looking up at him, "this marriage didn't take place in a church. Pamela and Christophe were married by a Justice of the Peace, not a priest. They must have eloped, then planned to marry again later in France after Christophe received his father's blessing. Don't you see? To your mother's mind, and in the eyes of the Church she revered, Edmund was her real husband, her only husband. But to the world, under the law of the land, you are the true son of Christophe Saville. No wonder Moina was amused to see this ring you gave me. Christophe must have given it to your mother as a wedding ring."

Lucien read the paper again, seeing the name of the justice scribbled at the bottom of the page. Kate's theory made sense. It was unbelievable, but he was not a bastard. How strange. He had lived with the notion for so long. But now he was not only a gentleman again in the eyes of the world, but he was a French gentleman.

A French gentleman? He felt a sudden shiver run down his spine as a fresh, cold dawn swept over his personal horizon.

Lucien understood at last, saw everything as clearly as if it had been written in three-foot-high letters across the rain-clouded sky. No wonder Moina had said there was new trouble brewing at Tremaine Court and she had seen it. Seen it? She had *used* it to help destroy Melanie, to help Melanie destroy herself—if what he thought was true. She had said

Edmund had seen this new trouble as well, but she may have overestimated Edmund's powers of observation. Although he had taken a turn for the worse the day—

"That's it! It fits. It all fits!" Lucien grabbed Kate's elbows, giving her a small shake. "Moina has said from the beginning that it is up to me to finish it. And now, at last, with her own game played out, she has shown me the way. Katharine—my most sweet, darling Katharine—I know who murdered those women!"

CHAPTER 27

Abash'd the Devil stood,
And felt how awful goodness is, and saw
Virtue in her shape how lovely.

John Milton, *Paradise Lost*

*D*awn of the morning after Melanie's funeral brought a reappearance of the sun, its warming light shining down benevolently on the refreshed trees and shrubs, causing the shivering droplets collected on the faces of the flowers to glisten as a soft, fragrant breeze danced over the gardens and nearby meadows. Only in the graveyard did the fresh brown scar of sodden mud amidst greenest grass and gleaming marble crosses hint that all was not well at Tremaine Court.

No more than a mile away the large rented cottage of the Comte de la Croix had likewise been washed clean by the rain, the picturesque thatched roof (a clear affectation as the cottage could be no more than five years old) a dull gold, the mullioned windows winking in the sunlight. The front door to the cottage stood open invitingly and the figure of a tallish young woman with raven-black hair stepped inside, calling for the master of the house.

"Bonjour, Monsieur," she said pleasantly enough as the man clutching a large tapestry portmanteau appeared at the head of the staircase. "Oh, dear me, have I caught you at a

bad time? *Quel dommage,* I am sure. Your door was open and no servants were about, so that I found myself forced to announce my arrival by rudely calling up the stairs."

"Miss Harvey," the comte, dressed in stylish traveling clothes, responded as he descended the staircase, gracefully bowing in her direction once he stood in the tiled foyer. "This is indeed a most unexpected, yet pleasant surprise."

Kate looked pointedly at the small mound of baggage stacked just inside the front door. "You're leaving us? And without first bidding your friends at Tremaine Court a last farewell? I should think everyone will be extremely disappointed to hear of it. Including Noddy, of course. The child was greatly entertained by your pocket watch, as I recall."

"How is he, now that this so horrible accident on the stairs has plucked our most fragrant bloom, the sweet Melanie, from our midst? The poor, dear infant." Guy shrugged eloquently, shaking his head as he set down the portmanteau, then rallied. "But, *oui,* it is just as you suppose. I leave your pleasant shores this very evening, and have already dismissed my hired servants save for the coachman. I have received a missive from my father, you see, berating me for tarrying too long among my new friends here in Sussex and quite pointedly reminding me that my duty, as well as our most fortunately restored estates, call out for my attention. I would have left earlier if not for the unfortunate Melanie's funeral and the hope I might be able to see dearest Lucien again. I cannot lie and pretend to believe this story Garth has put out about Lucien being called to London on business—not when that idiot constable has told me all. Has Lucien been located as yet, and arrested? I should hope not. Terrible. Simply terrible."

He bent down once more and retrieved his portmanteau. "But you do realize that I must be on my way now if I am to outrun the tide."

Kate nodded, but ignored his broad hint that her appearance had served to delay his departure and walked past him into the cottage's generous, low-ceilinged drawing room. "My, what a beautiful room! So very quaint, yet elegant.

You were fortunate in your landlord, sir." She stopped once she had reached the middle of the room and turned to face him as she stripped off her gloves. "I appreciate your haste, *Monsieur le Comte,* but I really must insist that you first speak with me on a most delicate matter. You will grant me this small indulgence, won't you?" she ended, her tone so purposefully devoid of expression that it held a wealth of innuendo. She dropped the gloves onto a side table, flinging down the gauntlet.

A sudden tension filled the air, an almost tangible odor of suppressed intensity, overpowering the fresh bouquet of spring flowers on the side table and smothering the sound of birdsong outside the opened doors leading onto a small enclosed garden.

Kate stood impassively, watching as Guy deposited the portmanteau just inside the drawing room and composed his features into a cunningly polite smile, two determined duelers reviewing the rules of advancing and retiring before proceeding with the contest.

"How could I refuse a lady of your beauty any indulgence, either small or large?" Guy asked, his shrug less questioning than taunting. He walked to the drinks table as if establishing the distance of their fencing *piste,* and poured himself a small glass of wine from the crystal decanter, offering her a drink as well, a move she deflected with a wave of her hand. "But before we get on with this discussion you insist upon—I have just now realized that I am remiss, aren't I? According to rumor, and as the haste of the sad ceremony yesterday and the wrath of the elements combined to make conversation of any consequence impossible, I believe I must now offer you my best wishes, Miss Harvey? You and the dear Lucien are now betrothed, *oui?"*

He took a small sip of wine, assuming the *en garde* position before slapping himself lightly on the cheek, as if belatedly remembering something else of great importance, and verbally thrusting once again. "But I am so stupid! Dame Rumor—in this case taking the form of our most noxious constable—has more than one story to tell these

past few days, *n'est-ce pas?* You are not Miss Kate Harvey at all, but the Lady Katharine d'Harnancourt. Ah, you English. So full of surprises! And so very romantic that you and Lucien have found each other."

He then frowned, his expression eloquently compassionate. "But for how long, *mademoiselle?* This obtuse fool, this uncouth constable, he has claimed to me that your dearest Lucien is a suspect in these terrible crimes that have so scandalized our little neighborhood. I objected, most vehemently I assure you, but there is no shaking the man in his belief."

Kate fought the urge to applaud Guy's splendid footwork. Clearly first blood had gone to the comte, but it had been an insufficient parry, through which she could also strike. "Lucien *is* innocent," she said shortly, staring intently into his single eye, the one that slid sideways, avoiding her scrutiny. The time had come to make a hit of her own. "But then, you already know that, don't you, *monsieur?*"

"Moi?" Guy pressed his spread fingers to his chest, his expression incredulous as he predictably returned to *en garde.* "How could you ask? But of course! I have already said it. Lucien would never do such a thing. It is impossible!"

She retired to the green-and-white flowered settee, looking up at the man. "But it is not equally impossible that Lucien will be charged with the crimes. Charged, and tried, and summarily hanged. This is also true, *n'est-ce pas?* Justice, while swift, cannot always be depended upon for its accuracy. Lucien Tremaine could hang. Unless, of course, the real murderer is exposed."

Guy finished his wine, replacing the glass on the drinks table before turning to lean against it, his hands braced against the edge. "Which he most assuredly will be, in time. I only wish I could delay my departure to aid in the search for this monster, but it is not to be. And so, Lady Katharine, if you will but get to the point of your visit, I should be most grateful, for the tide waits for no man, even one intent on returning to the bosom of his newly freed motherland."

Kate folded her hands in her lap. "Certainly, *monsieur,*" she said pleasantly, her pulses pounding, her every sense alert. Reprise. Parry. Riposte. "I have only one small request, one simple question. Why?"

The comte frowned and Kate's heart skipped a beat as she prepared for his counter-riposte. "Why? What sort of question is that, *mademoiselle?*"

"A simple one, as I said," she pressed, rising, for she could no longer sit still. She had to guide him delicately, so that he would not know he was being maneuvered. "I already know the how of it—how you murdered Melanie and the others, hoping to place the blame squarely at Lucien's feet. I am left only with the question of why. Please—won't you help me to understand?"

Ah, a direct hit! Or so she thought. Now he would trip himself up.

But he didn't.

"Melanie? But I do not understand. She perished in a fall, *oui?* Please, Miss Harvey—Lady Katharine—you should reconsider my offer of some wine. You are clearly overset."

Guy languidly pushed himself away from the table, a most fluidly orchestrated *balestra,* to stand not five feet away from her, closing the area of engagement, his smile of genuine amusement allowing her to recognize the real evil in the man for the first time. Perhaps this hadn't been such a splendid idea after all. Perhaps it would have been better if she and Garth had not overridden Lucien's protests that there had to be another way. She slipped her hands into the pockets of her pelisse, seeking the reassurance she knew she would find waiting there.

"Ah, *ma petite,* what a foolish, foolish child you are. But love has always possessed the power to rob its victims of common sense, even their sense of self-preservation, *oui?* And how very much in love you must be to come here, alone, to lay such dangerous charges against me. This is why I do not subscribe to the emotion. Only think of it. If I were guilty—which I do not say that I am—what would there be to keep me from killing you in order to protect my secret?"

"Only this, I suppose," Kate parried, withdrawing her right hand from her pocket, bringing with it the small pistol gripped tight in her fingers. A knife was a fine thing, but Lucien had already taught her that, in a woman's hands, it could not be entirely counted upon. The pistol was far less dangerous. Silently asking forgiveness from above, she launched into her litany of lies. "You see, *monsieur*, I haven't been honest with you. I was already aware of your plan to leave England, as one of your servants has a sister in service at Tremaine Court. I have sent Garth to summon Lucien from his hiding place, but I could not take the chance you would make good your escape before they arrive. Now, please," she continued, using the barrel of the pistol to motion him to a chair, "seat yourself over there, where I can keep an eye on you until the gentlemen join us. I see no reason we can't be dignified about this."

"No reason at all," Guy responded, obediently stepping in front of the chair Kate had indicated. "But we should also strive to be civilized, I think. Please, Lady Katharine, you must seat yourself first or else I, a gentleman, could not possibly do likewise. Come now, don't look so fearful. You have won the day. I won't do anything to try to escape. You have my word on it."

Kate considered this request for a few moments, then complied, taking up her place once more on the settee, the pistol still pointed in Guy's direction. She knew the day was a long way from being over but, as she felt assured of its eventual ending, she would be magnanimous and allow him to make the next move.

"There, isn't that more comfortable?" Guy asked, crossing his legs at the knee as if he were settling himself in for a comfortable coze. "What a strange scene this is, *oui*, the two of us sitting here, with that ugly little pistol pointed at my head? How incongruous it seems in your dainty hand. Lucien will be very angry with you, *ma chère*, when he learns you have made me delay my departure. But wait. You say you know I am the murderer of those two unfortunate women. Why, I believe I have latched onto the perfect way

to pass the time before Lucien and our dear friend Garth arrive. Please, *ma chère,* humor me. How do you think you know this?"

It wouldn't do to appear too secure. "Don't tease me, *monsieur,* for I know how to use this pistol," Kate warned, her hand purposefully trembling, although her heart beat at its normal rhythm. "But I will answer your question. I went to Melanie's rooms this morning, thinking there might be some clue hidden there for, as *you* well know, *monsieur,* Melanie too was one of the victims. It seemed silly at the time, but I was so nearly distracted, worrying about Lucien, that I felt I had to help in some way. I found Melanie's diary hidden in the back of her dressing table. She wrote everything down, every man she met, every lover she took to the gazebo. She wrote their names as a sort of list. Yours, *monsieur,* was the last name—the most recent."

Guy laughed out loud and Kate felt a momentary pang of fear. She hadn't considered that he might find her lie amusing. "To the gazebo? Of course, I have been there with Melanie. I do not deny it. But this makes me no more a murderer than it does Melanie a victim. And on this—this flimsy evidence of Melanie's liaisons—you dare to accuse me? You are desperate, aren't you, *ma chère?*" He stood, so that Kate also hastened to rise. "You have nothing, Lady Katharine, less than nothing. It is common knowledge that Melanie was most generous with her favors, several *cadeaux* to your betrothed included. If I am guilty of anything it is the sin of weakness for a beautiful, willing woman. Nothing more. Now, please, give me the pistol and we will laugh about this over another glass of wine."

Kate took two steps backward, ceding ground as Guy advanced on her, holding out his hand. The comte was not a tall man, and not a young man, but he was powerfully built, and she made certain she stayed out of his reach.

"Stand fast, *monsieur,*" she warned tightly, sensing that it was time for the *redoublement*—the introduction of something new and unexpected, thereby forcing his hand. From her other pocket she produced a small, marble-backed

copybook. "I said Melanie kept a diary. In it she described how you and she killed that poor woman we found on the estate. She described it in great detail, down to the last cut of the knife. It was as if Melanie had described her own murder. I think that is evidence enough, don't you?"

Guy's face turned a sickly white and he lunged at Kate, easily wresting both the pistol and the diary from her hands before pushing her unceremoniously onto the settee. *"La belle, mademoiselle!"* he proclaimed, signifying that he had made the last, deciding hit of the bout, not that he appeared well pleased with his victory.

Kate hid a triumphant smile with her hand, feigning terror—although she did not have to be a talented actress to give the impression that his violent push had all but knocked the wind out of her.

Guy stood over Kate, waving the pistol directly in front of her face. "That bitch! That stupid, ignorant bitch! I should never have become involved with her! A diary! Was there ever a more pernicious woman?" He slipped the copybook into his pocket and then pressed a hand to his mouth, looking quickly about the room as if for outside guidance.

"What—what are you going to do to me?" Kate asked, her eyes purposely wide. She cringed against the cushions as if her courage had been ripped from her along with the pistol. "Lucien and Garth will be here directly. You can't kill me, or else they'll know for sure that you are the murderer! You can't!"

"I can't? On the contrary, Lady Katharine. It would appear that I can do *anything* I want." He punctuated this appraisal by employing the barrel of the pistol to caress her cheek as she averted her head in disgust. "But, no, this is not completely true. You have robbed me of the time to do the deed at my leisure, perhaps amusing us both for an enjoyable hour, instructing you in a few of Melanie's delightful tricks. Dear, dear, it seems that I am always in a sad rush these days, with no time to savor the moment."

He frowned. "Or to make preparations for it. How I despise these last-minute plans. They smack of the slapdash,

you know. I fear, dear lady, that I shall have to dispatch you quickly, so that I may make good my escape while your beloved Lucien mourns his new loss. A pity. I should have liked to stay, to watch him suffer. As I would have so enjoyed seeing him struggle for breath at the end of a rope. Melanie robbed me of that particular pleasure in her eagerness to be rid of the woman she saw as her enemy. You were to be next, you know, if Melanie had lived. It would appear I shall be doing Melanie one last favor, which pains me deeply. Ah, well, one must do what one must. Sooner or later that clod of a constable will discover Lucien's knife hidden in the gazebo and raise a hue and cry throughout the neighborhood. I have been tempted to draw him a map, for he is so obtuse. And now, my lady, I must bid you adieu."

So saying, he leveled the pistol at Kate's chest.

"Wait! Oh, wait, please!" Kate begged, holding up her hands. He barely had need of the pistol, for the man could talk a person to death. But he had not yet said what she most needed to hear. "If I am to die, *monsieur,* can't you please tell me why? Melanie's death, all three deaths, and this hatred you carry for Lucien—none of it makes sense to me. How can I die, not knowing why?"

"Rather badly, I should say," Guy remarked, chuckling at his own wit. "And then there is this business of Lucien and Garth riding, as it were, to your rescue at any moment—if I were to believe that little fairy tale, of course. Never play at cards, *mademoiselle.* You are too nervous, you see, so that I am sure you are acting alone. Oh, very well, I suppose I owe you some explanation—but only if you stop that whimpering. I do so detest a whining female. I would have told Melanie as well, although she didn't seem to be interested in the why of it. But, like you, she did want to live, poor creature. She came to me desperately unhappy, almost suicidal, but in the end she wanted so very much to live."

Keeping the pistol trained on Kate, he pulled up a side chair and sat down, facing the settee. "It's simple, really. We shall deal with the deceased ladies first, *oui?* Melanie's enemy, a Lady Southcliff, and a most terrible woman, had

been very naughty, blackmailing dear Melanie for a past indiscretion, one involving sisterly love, if you take my meaning. *Fatherly* love as well—if I am not being too shocking? Melanie became obsessed with the woman's destruction, feeling it would help clear the path to Lucien's heart. I had no feelings either way. The murders were no more than a favor, and a prelude to Melanie's death, of course."

"You hoped Lucien would be blamed for all the murders. Why?"

"It is simple enough. Christophe Saville—my brother. My much older, most responsible half-brother, to be exact, and heir to our father's estates. Ah, you seem to recognize the name."

"Christophe Saville is Lucien's father," Kate said, shifting uncomfortably on the settee, just to be sure the door to the garden had not been blown closed by the breeze. It hadn't. Sunlight streamed through the opening, making a pattern on the carpet. "But I still don't understand. Lucien is a bastard. He cannot inherit, even if Christophe were to acknowledge him. It makes no difference that you are the product of a second marriage."

Guy smiled at this conclusion. "I see you are familiar with the cumbersome strictures of entailments, *ma chère,* but in this case they do not apply. My foolish brother had eloped with this Pamela Kingsley, this love of the moment, thereby stripping his younger brother, me, of his inheritance. Again, this complicating business of love. You can understand my dislike of the emotion."

As Kate sat quietly, hoping not to call attention to herself, Guy continued his explanation, his gaze focused on the middle distance, as if talking to himself, his torment visible. "If only I had known, but Christophe kept his secret until the end. Even rotting in that terrible cell, awaiting his engagement with *Madame Guillotine,* he kept his silence, and only instructed me to forward his last letter to England and to personally deliver his final farewell—his so touching confession of his marriage to this English nobody and the

brat he'd sired on her—to our father. To think that I, in all
innocence, followed his wishes."

He turned back to Kate, his smile chilling. "This is what
you English call irony, *oui?* Yet for some time it did not seem
to matter, as I too soon found my name on the list to be
arrested, and faced the prospect of my head parting company with my shoulders, as did nearly every Frenchman of
good blood in the land.

"You cannot know what it was like, Lady Katharine, to sit
in that stinking hole, that great cavern of a jail, waiting for
the daily roll to be called, to hear your name among those to
be kissed on the neck by *Madame Guillotine.* I was visiting,
bringing food, the day they called my brother's name, the
day he rose and walked with stiff-backed pride through the
door beyond which lay sure death. Idiot! They were all
idiots! Like sheep, they rose as their names were called. Like
sheep, they marched to their deaths, their heads held high.

"But not me, *mademoiselle. Non!* I am no sheep. Once I
was imprisoned I found myself a poor, incarcerated felon
willing to stand up when my name was called and take my
turn in the tumbril. He died in my place after I promised I
would provide for his starving family in Rouens. And I did,
even after his head had rolled into the basket, even after
Robespierre and St. Just met their fates and I was freed from
both the prison and the fear of discovery—for I am an
honorable man."

Kate bit on her knuckle to keep from gifting the comte
with her opinion of his twisted logic. Poor Lucien, to hear in
this cold-blooded way that his father truly was dead. But she
would think of all this later. She had to get Guy back to the
subject at hand. "So your father knew about Christophe's
marriage, about Lucien. But why did you feel the need to
remove Lucien? Surely your father had made provisions for
you as well, even if you could not inherit everything?"

Guy turned on her, his face nearly purple with rage.
"Another idiot! Why should I not inherit everything? Because I refused to die? Because I chose to live? I ask you,
mademoiselle what good is a dead Frenchman? But that

stupid man, that woefully obtuse old man, he could not understand, refused to see that *I* was the clever one, that *I* deserved to be his heir. Christophe had not even married in the Sacraments, and still our father favored him. My foolish, dead half-brother became a martyr to our father, a saint, while I, the product of his second marriage, was branded a coward, a failure, a disgrace."

He approached Kate, leaning down over her as he spoke, his face contorted in anger. "What can an old man safely hidden in the country know of courage as it is played out in the damp cells of Paris? Do you see this patch? There was once an eye there. My eye! A guard plucked it out one night, just for the humor of it."

He smiled, his expression losing its savagery to be replaced by something much more repellant—blood-chilling satisfaction. "I neatly plucked *both* of his, *mademoiselle*, like raisins from a tart, before I allowed him the blessed relief of death. So many years later, it was not difficult for me to use the knife again. Strange, is it not, but of them all, the maid died best. Courage. An empty word. Dead is dead, *oui?*"

"How very true, *oncle*. I call you uncle because I am sure you have not been using your real name since landing on our shores. Or is it perhaps that you are the Comte de Saville? But I digress. I believe we have heard enough now, don't you, Garth?"

Kate relaxed a fraction at the sound of Lucien's voice. Her part in this little farce was over, and none too soon, for she had never been at her best playacting. She had known all along that he was near, he and Garth and Constable Clemens, but it hadn't kept her from an almost overwhelming desire to escape the evil of the man who had spoken so congenially of death and dying.

She turned, as did Guy, to see Lucien step from behind the draperies at the opened door, moving from the shadows, and into the light. She looked deeply into his eyes, gauging his mood, and he smiled at her, wordlessly assuring her that he was all right. Guy's words, his terrible admissions, may

have shocked him, but they had not scarred his soul. Only then did she begin to tremble in earnest, knowing that, at last, Lucien's long journey back from the darkness had ended.

Garth appeared from the enclosed garden a moment later, half dragging the confused-looking Clemens into the drawing room, the constable's mouth still gagged, his hands still tied behind his back—for the man had not made up one of their party by choice. "Well done, Kate. You were marvelous, no matter that Lucien put up such a fuss about not using you in our little farce. Look at our esteemed constable, Kate. His eyes have all but bugged out of his head. You measured his intellect correctly. He would never have believed our explanation. Even having heard it himself, the poor man is still trying to understand." He untied the gag, then slit the ropes that held the man's hands. "Isn't that right, dear sir?"

The constable flexed his jaw a time or two and then scratched at his head. "Plucked out his eyes?" he questioned, as if trying to picture such a scene. "What—what did you say? Oh—oh, yes. Yes, I understand well enough, I suppose. At least, I think I do."

Kate closed her eyes, giving thanks. But it wasn't enough to absolve Lucien in the murders. They all needed to know so much more. Responding to the barely perceptible nod of Lucien's head, Kate stood and made as if to join him— moving slowly so that she could be halted by the uncharacteristically silent Guy, who suddenly took hold of her arm and pulled her in front of him to act as a shield. "You think you are so very clever, don't you, *mon importun neveu?* But as always, my opponent makes a fatal mistake."

Lucien took a step forward as Kate winced involuntarily, the pressure of the pistol against her ribs as well as Guy's tight grip on her arm, although expected, proving to be most painful.

"I would strongly suggest against any foolish moves, Lucien, if you truly value this little trollop turned lady," Guy said, pulling Kate with him as he backed toward the

foyer. He stopped near the doorway to look at the assembled company, disgust as well as satisfaction unattractively mingled in his expression. "But it has been an enjoyable interlude, has it not, this little game we have all either willingly or unwillingly played out?"

Lucien took a cigar from his pocket and placed it, unlit, in the corner of his mouth. "I was unaware, *oncle,* that the game had ended."

"Hah! My compliments on your composure. It is a family trait, *n'est-ce pas?* I cannot tell you how pleased I was that the fools I hired to dispatch you failed as I had expected and you arrived in Sussex, the picture of my dead brother come back to haunt me. Not that I had not hedged my bets, as you English say, for my little conversation with Edmund Tremaine, detailing in exquisite detail my liaison with his wife, served to severely weaken his health, assuring that, if you survived my hired killers, you would still most definitely appear in Sussex. You see, I could not take the chance of confronting you in London, in your own milieu. I needed you here, where I was accepted and you had become the interloper."

"Oh, he has been a crafty little bastard, hasn't he?" Garth remarked, availing himself of a nearby tinderbox and lighting Lucien's cigar. "Melanie must have given him an earful of your checkered history, my friend."

"As did you, my dear Garth, with that lovely story of society's belief that Lucien might be involved in devil worship," Guy said, so that Garth cursed himself for his own stupidity.

Guy ignored him, although he twisted Kate's arm more fully behind her back. She refused to react, for she could not trust Lucien to remain passive while the loquacious comte obligingly answered the last of the unspoken questions that nagged at all their brains. "How the sight of you fueled my hatred, Lucien, my resolve. Melanie, that beautifully twisted creature, had provided me with your direction, but she had not succeeded in adequately describing your strength of character, your intelligence. It became a game to

thwart you, to insinuate myself with you—then watch as you were hung for Melanie's murder. Ah, sweet Melanie, that mad, bewitching creature. From the very beginning, from the day we first met, I knew that she would make the perfect victim."

The constable spoke up, demonstrating that he had yet to fully understand. "Seems deuced complicated to me. If you hated him so, why didn't you just hide somewhere and shoot him in the back?"

"Lucien," Guy said invitingly, "with this small entertainment you have set up today you have amply proven that you are of Saville blood. That, and the reputation you so carefully built for yourself in London. Perhaps you would like to enlighten the gentleman?"

"Too simple," Lucien supplied coolly, gracefully bowing in the comte's direction, "too easy. Isn't that correct, *oncle?* Why merely kill someone when first you could pluck out his eyes? And then there is the business of my French grandfather. I don't believe he likes you above half, *oncle.* If I were to have been shot in the back, he might blame you. But if I were to be totally discredited, hanged as the violently unhinged murderer of my former *fianceé*—well, how could my grandfather believe his son had played any part in it? He would have no choice but to cling to his sole remaining heir."

"Ah, Lucien, if only Christophe had been the younger son. We might have enjoyed each other then, *oui?* But enough of this. I insist you all stay perfectly still while Lady Katharine and I take our leave. If you behave, you may find her alive somewhere along the road. If you do not behave—" he shrugged, allowing them to draw their own conclusions.

Lucien ignored this warning, tossing the cigar into the cold fireplace and advancing on his uncle. "No. The game is over for you," he said, drawing his own pistol from his waistband. "You have been very ingenious, but you are the one who has made one fatal mistake. You tarried too long, to wallow, piglike, in the sty of your own genius. It is time to

give up, for the last move of the pieces has been played out. You've lost, *oncle.*"

Guy backed up another pace, frowning, then leveled the pistol at Lucien, who only smiled quite evilly, so that for the first time Kate saw a faint family resemblance between them. The comte released Kate and lowered the pistol to his side. "I won't debase myself by pulling the trigger. It's empty, isn't it, *neveu?*"

Lucien took the pistol from Guy's unresisting fingers, then held out his arms so that Kate could run into them, pressing her head against his chest. "As empty as the pages in Melanie's diary, as you would have known if you had taken the time to look," he said, ushering Kate away and into Garth's arms.

"Melanie!" Guy exploded, his hands balling into fists. "I did not love her, you know. I love no one but myself. It is a rule I set long ago. But there was this fascination, as you surely must understand, *neveu,* this undeniable attraction of her beautiful body and her inspired perversions. Each night as I went to the gazebo I went there to kill her, to end it. But each night she showed me something new, unwittingly teaching me more and more about myself. And so I lingered too long, became too involved with her madness. I allowed myself to be distracted and, in the end, betrayed. If only she hadn't loved you so much, *neveu.* If she hadn't persisted in loving you I may have let her live. I might have settled for the shot in the back this buffoon of a constable spoke of and taken her with me to France—*ma petite araignée, ma nymphe jolie.*"

He lifted the copybook from his pocket and, not bothering to check the pages, tossed it to the floor. "I should have known she would not write anything down. Melanie did not live for the past, but for the next encounter. Always the next encounter. Except for you, *neveu.* She convinced herself that you held the answer to her torment, that you, and you alone, could give her the peace of spirit, of body, of mind, she spent every waking moment searching for. Yet it was I who gave her that peace, *n'est-ce pas?* The everlasting peace of death. I

am happy I killed her. She betrayed us all, Lucien, but she has destroyed me, even from beyond the grave, while saving you. I have become Melanie Tremaine's last victim."

Lucien cocked his pistol. "If it is mercy you're seeking with that self-serving speech, you have sadly missed your mark."

Guy looked toward the other inhabitants of the room, and then, lastly, concentrated on Lucien. "So, you think you are going to shoot me now, *neveu?* Kill me, even as the so confused constable stands watching, his finger so very delicately stuffed up his nose? I think not. I have come to know you these past weeks, Lucien Saville, *Marquis de Soissons*, legal heir to *le Duc de Compiègne*. No, I think you will let me go. I am, after all, of your true family. You could not go to France and introduce yourself to your grandfather as the man who has killed his last remaining son. You are too honorable."

Garth gave a sputtering laugh. "Oh, *darling*—and the man says he knows you?"

Kate's eyes closed for a moment as Garth used the term Lucien had once employed as a protection, as a warning—the word he had used with such obvious love only yesterday as he held her in his arms. She stood very still, praying that Lucien would not pull the trigger, sending himself back into the darkness of spirit he had fought so long to overcome. She could understand his passion, his pain, but to kill the man who had been the author of such tragedies? No. It would serve no purpose other than to damn himself.

"You're correct, *oncle,* I cannot shoot you." Lucien handed his pistol to Garth, and Kate flinched as she saw Guy's triumphant smile. Perhaps she had been wrong. Perhaps the man did deserve to die.

"I cannot kill you," Lucien continued unhurriedly, "but I can turn you over to the constable. You will hang, *oncle,* although I do not believe I shall find it necessary to my happiness to watch you dance. I do, however, find it impossible to resist this—"

With one swift move of his arm, Lucien's fist slammed

directly into Guy's smiling face, and the man crumpled to the floor, unconscious.

"Constable Clemens, I believe I should tie him up stoutly before he wakes," Lucien said, taking Kate's hand and leading her past the fallen Guy and out into the sunlight. "And one thing more, dear sir. Please accept my apology for kidnapping you from your breakfast. I am sure you will find an ample meal awaiting you if you wish to visit Tremaine Court for luncheon."

Garth stuck his head out the door, saying he would remain to help the constable escort the prisoner to his cell in the village. "And where would you two lovebirds be flying off to now that we have settled everything so right and tight?"

Kate slipped her arm through Lucien's, her smile bright even though her cheeks streamed with tears. "Lucien and I," she said evenly, looking up into his face, "are going to get on with our lives, Garth, putting all of these past years forever behind us. But first," she hesitated, hoping Lucien would understand, then concluded, "first we are going to the cemetery, to place flowers on Melanie Tremaine's grave."

EPILOGUE

Summer

1815

The world was all before them. . . .

John Milton, *Paradise Lost*

Flowers of all hue, and without thorn the rose.

John Milton, *Paradise Lost*

So, you found your grandfather to be well? That's good to
hear. Will you be staying in England long?" Edmund
Tremaine's speech was still slow and somewhat labored, but
it, like his mind, was blessedly clear.

Lucien walked slowly, measuring his gait with Edmund's
as that man leaned heavily on a sturdy cane. He and Kate
had arrived at Tremaine Court only that morning, and they
had just finished a buffet luncheon Hawkins had ordered set
up on the terrace.

"It will be several months before I can pry Katharine
away from Noddy again, Father," he said, smiling as he
looked across the well-kept garden to where his wife and
young Noddy, having run down the terrace steps ahead of
them, frolicked on the grass. Garth Stafford, his arm still in
a sling thanks to a ball he had taken at Waterloo, stood
nearby, urging the child into greater mischief.

"Noddy and I will enjoy your company, Lucien, almost as
much as we will Kate's. We men need the softening influence of a woman's hand."

"I'm glad you're agreeable, Father, for, except for Garth, who is expected at his uncle's house party, I'm afraid you shall probably have to put up with us at least until the late fall. We've promised to visit Katherine's uncle and cousin, and I've already told *Grand-père* we will return for Christmas. How convenient it is now that Napoleon is finally firmly leashed on his island. Fortunately, Katharine enjoys traveling on the *Pâquerette*," he ended, chuckling as he mentioned the endearingly ridiculous name Kate had insisted upon christening their yacht.

The men walked out of the immaculately kept rose garden, strolling past the refurbished greenhouse where Edmund, Noddy by his side, spent endless hours working with the exotic plants that had been imported from all over the world, and joined the rest of their small party.

Lucien looked across the meadow to the stone walls of the family cemetery and frowned, remembering that another grave had been dug there in his latest absence. "She didn't suffer, did she?"

Edmund lowered himself onto a stone bench beneath the cooling shade of a large beech tree, unconsciously rubbing at his weakened leg. "Moina? She died as she lived, son. Quietly, and at a time of her own choosing. Her last words were of my dearest Pamela."

Lucien nodded, still amazed at Edmund's capacity for forgiveness. Perhaps his unwillingness to forgive Pamela, and his subsequent loss, had taught him the wisdom of charity.

Kate glanced up from her seat on the grass where she had deposited herself, unmindful of her gown, to watch Noddy and Garth chase after a butterfly. Her unbound hair caught the sun, setting small fires of light in her dark curls, and Lucien smiled with real pleasure as he heard the music of her laughter.

Kate laughed often, as did he. They had spent this last

Praise for Kasey Michaels's

THE LEGACY OF THE ROSE

"A powerful and gripping story . . . Kasey Michaels handles it with aplomb."

—Barbara Hazard

"*THE LEGACY OF THE ROSE* is absolutely absorbing . . . combining Michaels's famed humor and wit with haunting romance."

—Parris Afton Bonds

"Do not pick up this book unless you are willing to forfeit slumber—with *THE LEGACY OF THE ROSE*, Kasey Michaels has crafted an engrossing, sleep-thief of a read!"

—Joan Hohl

"*THE LEGACY OF THE ROSE* is a treasure, and sure to become a classic of top-notch historical romance."

—Gail Link

year and more in a near-perpetual state of bliss, interrupted only by the dark days of Waterloo, now mercifully past. They had traveled twice to France, where the Duc had welcomed them with tears and open arms, Lucien nearly overwhelmed by the unconditional love the frail old man so generously offered.

At first Lucien had been fearful of this new contentment, this seeming perfection, worrying that perhaps it would not last. But slowly, over time, those feelings had left him. Whether their happiness extended into eternity or tragedy struck tomorrow, he and his Katharine had found each other, had loved each other, and the light of that love would guide them, together or separately, for the remainder of their lives.

Out of the corner of his eye he saw Kate's personal maid Amy appear on the terrace, cradling a small white bundle in her arms. He smiled, knowing that as she neared them the sound of Christophe's demanding wail would be clearly heard.

Excusing himself from Edmund, Lucien walked over to relieve Amy of her precious charge. Shifting Christophe entirely into his left arm with the ease of long practice, he picked a perfect, blood red rose from a nearby bush as he approached Kate, and offered it as his gift to her. "My lady," he said, bowing as best he could, for the child was in full voice now, demanding attention.

"My lord," Kate responded as she took the bloom, sniffing its heady bouquet before stripping it of its thorns and placing it in her hair.

Lucien extended his hand again and Kate availed herself of his support as she rose to her feet, then closed her fingers over the kiss he had placed in her palm.

"You're being summoned to your work, my darling wife," he said, grinning at her playfully, their world suddenly narrowing to include only the three of them. "He has been most wonderfully cooperative this past hour, but I believe our son is calling for his lunch."

Kate smiled down at Christophe, the tangible evidence of their love, and then looked into her husband's face, her beautiful gray eyes stung by happy tears. "Yes, Lucien. Our lives at Tremaine Court seem to have come full circle—and in the best of all possible ways."